The
Stones of Bau

By the same author

The
Stones of Bau

Nicholas Wollaston

Hamish Hamilton
London

First published in Great Britain 1987
by Hamish Hamilton Ltd
27 Wrights Lane London W8 5TZ

British Cataloguing in Publication Data

Wollaston, Nicholas
  The stones of Bau.
  I. Title
  823'.914[F]   PR6073.045

  ISBN 0–241–12041–1

Phototypeset by Input Typesetting Ltd, London
Printed in Great Britain by
Butler and Tanner Ltd, Frome and London

The author acknowledges his debt to
the version of *The Epic of Gilgamesh*
by N. K. Sandars in Penguin Classics.

Part One

The Forest

The plantation is called Aurora, nobody remembers why. With the help of Beaconsfield, who used to be headman and is now owner, Clive Ackerly has cleared a glade at the edge of the forest on the slopes of an old volcano above Aurora, and built himself a small native house. On a wall inside, next to a fishing-rod hanging on hooks, is pinned one of the Admiralty charts he brought to the Mendana Islands when he first came here. It is streaked yellow and pocked with mould, but still says 'densely wooded' faintly across this island, with no exaggeration. It also marks the mountain, Bau.

Clive is now about seventy: once a gunnery lieutenant on a battleship that was torpedoed, later the skipper of a trading schooner that was wrecked, before settling at Aurora half his life ago. Beaconsfield – his son, in a tribal sense, as well as heir – is fifteen or twenty years younger. Age in this country is counted by yam harvests and can be vague. Probably Beaconsfield is now the richest islander in the Mendanas: a pitch-black bush boy like a charred stick pulled from the ashes of a fire.

Below the house, over the plantation trees, Clive has a glimpse of the lagoon, the froth of surf on a coral reef, the misty tones of another island. Behind, when it isn't in cloud, he can see the top of the mountain, as high as a mountain in Scotland – the one above Strathpolly. He once climbed it with another white man and two small boys, led by Beaconsfield – cutting all day through the forest and spending the night in the crater among the Stones of Bau. Most Mendanans would have been troubled by the strange forces living up there, devil-devils and their terrible wives, but Beaconsfield was at ease: perhaps they were his friends. The other white man, clever but without vision, laughed when he was told not to. The two boys behaved better. In different senses they were both

Clive's grandsons. Now they are young men, lost and feckless among the split, uncertain population of Aurora.

Clive chose the best place for his retirement. Sometimes an extraordinary bird call, a mixture of whoop and whistle and laugh, comes out of the forest, and something purple and scarlet flits across the corner of his eye. Sometimes a great cooling rainstorm rattles on the trees, a benediction in the heat, a sacrament to save the day. Sometimes, especially after rain, a sudden whiff of spices – ginger, vanilla, turmeric – fills the air.

Cocoa is planted on the slopes below his house, coconuts on the flat coral ground near the lagoon. Every morning, though he knows it makes Beaconsfield uneasy, Clive goes stumping down the wide paths, grassy avenues through the trees, to inspect and gossip and snort and revel in Aurora: a tropical garden full of leaves and fruit, animals and people, a stretch of rich fertility between the lush forest and abundant sea. This is Eden and he created it.

He wears an old panama hat, white shirt and shorts and stockings, English leather brogues, and carries a long knobbled stick, a crook cut from a wild holly. A big man, though not tall: thick neck, large chest and shoulders, heavy legs. Ox-like, but far from bullish. A spray of sun-bleached hair froths from under the panama, like the surf on the reef. More of it rises from his open shirt-front. His face is strong, unrefined, smooth for his age, the bronze bust of an emperor, ready to scowl or smile. His bright blue eyes are sunk deep under slanting lids. A touch of effeminacy – though he would prefer some other weakness – lies in the flexible, unrigid shape of his mouth, saving it from cruelty. His voice, commanding and resonant, is spoken from the bottom of a well.

'Morning, Beaconsfield!' he shouts, approaching the plantation office and the house he used to live in by the lagoon, now the bush boy planter's home. Piccaninnies squeal, chickens scuttle, a pig waddles over for a back-scratch from the holly stick. One of its piglets is being cuddled by a black baby, sitting in a puddle. Clive looks up to watch a hornbill flying up into the forest, with a yellow beak and a whirr of feathers. In time Beaconsfield appears from his house. Clive asks, 'All well today?'

'Mr Clive, you are worrying too much. All is always well today.'

Clive grunts doubtfully, the pig with more pleasure; and stalks away on his daily tour, through colonnades of palms. Every morning the beauty astonishes him. He greets Aurora like a lover. It doesn't matter that the property is no longer his, or that Beaconsfield is making a mess of it. Nothing spoils Clive's delight.

He takes a path to the shore where a man is cutting up a turtle, hammering it on the head, opening the shell with a knife like a tin opener. Clive likes to stop and talk, but not to see the blood. High over the lagoon four frigate birds – forked tails, slender bent wings – wheel in the morning sun: four pirates, waiting lazily for another bird's catch. Four is an omen: the number of completion, as perfect as the quarters of the world. It may mean good or bad, but can't be ignored. Among bush boys a new baby is passed four times over a fire; among saltwater boys it is dipped four times into the sea. Clive enjoys these things, and feels part of their infinite pattern.

In the lagoon at this hour the fish are lively, playful, hunting or escaping, before the sun drives them down to the cool. There are long-jumpers and high-jumpers, skitterers, belly-floppers, and crazy thin fish that stand up on their tails and taxi over the water, wishing for wings. A shower of minnows leaps in silver hundreds out of the danger, into the bright morning, and back again. Sometimes a fin marks a pale quiet shark below, or a turmoil of bonitos fractures the surface. Two men come paddling home from a night's fishing on the reef, side by side in their canoes: their voices over the water, talking of women, land, magic. Magic to these people is what logic, or simply common sense, used to be for Clive: undeniable, implicit, universal. Another canoe drifts out from the village, full of piccaninnies. They are singing a hymn, but switch to 'My bonnie lies over the ocean' when they see Clive on the shore.

He waves his stick at them, then strides on into the village, calls to his people, tickles a baby, swipes at a

naked snot-nosed girl: 'There's my Elizabeth!' He knows
them all, but can't be sure whether they treat him as a
patriarch or a clown, and doesn't care. One of them came
back recently from Tulagi, capital of the Mendanas, with
a new slogan, hailing friends and holding up two fingers:
'Peace, and a one-way ticket!' It was slick and easy, and
caught on. To Clive it was awful. Peace was acceptable,
but the ticket must be made into nonsense: something
harmless, meaning nothing. 'Peace!' the children now
shout as he comes through the village. He holds up his
fingers: 'And a one-way biscuit!' So everyone is happy.

Occasionally there is a visitor to Aurora, though less
often than before. Once a year the Bishop of the Mendana
Islands, Beaconsfield's elder brother, comes to bless the
plantation, confirm the piccaninnies and drink as much
liquor as he can get. Once a month the government patrol
boat, a gift from the departing imperial power to the new
republic, now rather knocked and frayed, roars into the
lagoon, ties up for an hour or two at the wharf by the
copra shed, and sweeps away. It is the substitute for
colonial officers – agriculture, fishery, veterinary, police –
who made regular tours. Chinese or half-caste traders still
call, but the Aurora crop has been falling with world
prices, though the world is far away. Not long ago a
Japanese trawler anchored nearby. Clive caught the old
cockiness of Nippon in one of the crew rolling through
the village: a small man in shorts below his knee, with an
elongated back, immensely strong. He might have cut a
Mendanan in half with one chop.

The Mendanan people are usually not beautiful – squat
noses, thick lips, graceless bodies, square feet – but with
soft voices and gentle shoulders. They rub themselves
with coconut oil to give their skin a lustre and disguise its
natural smell. Some have a ginger sheen in their fuzzy
hair which the young ones, boys and girls, improve with
peroxide or a scarlet hibiscus flower and a brilliant smile.
A few have bruises and scratches made by their lovers
with teeth and fingernails, or with sharp pieces of shell
or bamboo: marks of success in love. Others have had
their eyelashes nibbled off at the height of passion – eyes
being objects of excitement, the first passage for desire.

Lovers also catch and eat each other's lice, which brings an exquisite intimacy. Clive knows which are bush boys like Beaconsfield, and which are saltwater boys. The difference is critical but he loves them all, especially the piccaninnies.

By mid-morning, sweating and content, he starts back up through the coconut and cocoa trees to the edge of the forest. He will stay at home till tomorrow – the house catches any breeze – and view the lagoon, the mountain, his old age. It is unlikely that anyone will come up to see him, but with books and a gramophone he has enough to think about.

The seasons aren't distinct here. There is no spring or autumn for birth and death, no winter when growth is dormant, but always summer. The trees are never bare unless they are dead, though a few leaves are always falling and new buds sprouting. Birds breed, and rain comes, according to no calendar. Months and years are lost. Only the change from day to night suggests any progress, but less through time than space. Clive inhabits a kind of eternity in this ageless place. He knows he will be remembered at Aurora and beyond: perhaps as far as the suburban apartment of a retired American diplomat's wife, in Washington DC. And he has something better than any property, even than Strathpolly.

It is Isabel who magnifies his happiness: a young woman of unusual beauty for an islander, different from her half-sisters and cousins here, faintly translucent like waxed teak. She must be about thirty now, and walks like a queen. As she cooks and washes and tends the vegetable garden, and fills her mouth with water to blow a fine spray over Clive's clothes before ironing them, and leaves dark hairs in his ivory-backed brushes – his parents' christening present to him, with his initials in gold – and draws down the mosquito net over his bed at night before slipping off to her lover, he wonders what she knows. On her finger she wears a zircon ring and possibly remembers who gave it to her, but has never asked why. She hardly speaks, except to her many-coloured brood of piccaninnies – ten or eleven of them. She doesn't know that her grandfather was only an old photograph, an army officer in khaki with a moustache, or that her grandmother was pulled into a river by a salmon and drowned. It would mean nothing if she was told.

Clive seldom asks what he himself has found out. He came here in flight from someone, in quest of someone else. He prefers to think of those piccaninnies. They play private, ancient games. They make windmills out of leaves and spinning tops from almonds, and bigger humming ones from coconuts, and cat's cradles with funny erotic functions. When a pig is killed in the village they use the bladder for a football. They also roast grasshoppers alive, or knock stag beetles off the trees and whirl them on the end of a string to make them buzz, or turn a pigeon into a kite and let it go, then pull it back, or put a collar on an iguana like a puppy and run with it down through the plantation, or torment an opossum till it bores them, when they cook and eat it. Clive hates to see it, but can't stop them. Childhood at Aurora is much like it was at Strath-polly. He and his brother once put a ferret and a rabbit together in a stable, to watch the murder.

But thoughts don't keep him awake. He sinks into the dark, to the chatter of insects and rustle of trees, the bark of flying foxes, the insistence of frogs and crickets, the sense of being at the heart of an intense life. The forest is never quiet, except in the hour before dawn. And Clive is a prodigious snorer. Almost all his life he has slept alone.

Part Two

The Battle

1

Lieutenant Clive Ackerly was glad when the Japanese planes were sighted high in the sky on the starboard bow: a trace of death in the brilliant morning, tiny bacteria in a huge and nearly spotless dish. They had been expected since dawn. Everyone knew they were on the way and would appear somewhere up there before long. The weather was ideal: no haze to hide their target, but a fleck of cotton cloud to give them cover. They couldn't have had a better day. The two big warships and their escort of destroyers, speeding back to base after a raid that had never happened, hardly rolling on the easy swell, pushed a clean white wave across the surface from each bow and left a trail of tell-tale foam astern.

This was the second day since setting out from Singapore. 'We're off to look for trouble,' the admiral had signalled. 'I expect we shall find it.' The tone of his message, clipped and wary, sounded between heroism and foolhardiness. 'We must all be on our toes.' Now his show of confidence had been worn to a nervous fatalism felt by all the crews. Yesterday a warm vapour, stirred by squalls that warned of the monsoon, had weighed on the sea. For ships hoping to be unobserved it was a comfort to be clamped below, sealed from the invisible sky, but today the mist had gone. Painted in crazy stripes to deflect attention they were exposed in dazzling clarity.

The sun was already high, pulling up the temperature. Inside the turrets and below decks, with everything closed for battle, it was reaching furnace heat. Some men had changed into clean clothes, an old sailor's trick against infected wounds; or for fear of flash had put on football jerseys and woollen stockings above the knee, ready for a game. Anti-aircraft gunners were masked in white hoods down to the shoulder, with a hole for eyes and nose and mouth that gave them a look of secrecy and ritual. All wore steel helmets, most were smoking, a few were playing cards.

'Shoot to sink!' was the admiral's order. Then the chaplain's voice came down the loudspeakers: 'O Lord, Thou that knoweth how busy we must be today – if we forget Thee do not Thou forget us, for Christ's sake. Amen.'

Men were tired and jumpy, waiting at the edge of danger, or thoughtful or frivolous. Many hadn't shaved. They were at first degree of readiness. A sailor who threw a banana skin overboard was bawled out by an officer: it might be picked up as a clue. But nobody believed the enemy would come by sea, or could keep their eyes out of the enormous sky.

The planes flew in tight formation, turning for their approach. Loudspeakers rasped again and a bugle sounded action stations. A moment followed of precious crystal peace. Unreality pierced the senses, illuminated the truth, defied the terror. This, or whatever came next, was the function of ships and planes and more than three thousand men. It was why they were here, out in the South China Sea on a hot December day of 1941.

To Clive, in command of four high-angle turrets on the starboard side of the *Prince of Wales*, it was familiar and unfrightening. He had never been bombed before, had never seen an enemy plane, but as a boy on the Strathpolly grouse moor he had felt this flutter of joy. 'Birds coming over!' the gamekeeper used to call. Here they were again, winging across in front of the guns, churning the blood into a sort of ecstasy.

The first blast of gunfire split the innocence. Muzzles flamed, and tons of explosive disappeared into the morning. Clive's guns could fire every three seconds: the next salvo was on its way before the last had burst. Shots flicked across the sky, intense black spots with a core of fire that cropped out like a disease, swelled into each other, faded harmlessly behind the enemy. When they had the range the smaller guns opened up, beating a tattoo on the metallic air. But nothing stopped the planes.

They never swerved or broke formation – a knot of courage and danger humming through the cannonade.

'The Nips can't fly,' Clive remembered Hutton, an engineer, saying over a pink gin in the wardroom. 'Their planes are copies of ours from the last war, made of rice paper and bamboo.' Clive hated Hutton, who knew everything and was usually right.

These were modern twin-engined machines, close together, two miles up, laughing at the shells. They ignored the *Prince of Wales*, keeping her for later, and dropped their bombs on the *Repulse*, one lethal turd from each plane, primed for killing. She was an old ship built when broadsides were flung from one horizon to the other and bombs were hardly thought of. They planted sudden pillars of water alongside her and a big flash amidships that threw bits of steel to the masthead, chased by smoke. Nobody had imagined such accuracy, so easily won. Men over there were already dead. The planes, their formation perfect, flew away. Hutton was wrong today.

Clive knew it wasn't over. Though the *Prince of Wales* was untouched there was worse to come. His gunners wiped the sweat, kicked away the empties, put fresh ammunition ready, lit cigarettes. And vaguely he knew that something else, not just the first round of a fight, was ended. This was the navy's newest battleship whose big guns could hurl seven tons of explosive twenty miles, twice a minute. But barely a week after her glorious arrival in the East, trumpeted round the world as the weapon to save the empire, she was struck with helplessness, as archaic as a battleaxe. Today was Wednesday. Only last Sunday in this ocean a fleet of such ships had been sunk by the same enemy at Pearl Harbor.

In fifteen minutes – time for a cigarette and a half – the next planes arrived, twice as many as before. They dodged into a cloud to tease their victim, then came out at speed in twos and threes, diving for the *Prince of Wales*.

The bugle sounded. Someone shouted, 'Stand by for barrage!' All guns exploded, a terrible punch from the turrets, a clattering roar from the rest, to rock the big ship and blow anything in the sky to pieces. It seemed impossible for a plane to get through. But they came on unruffled, lower than the first lot and more deadly, between the hard blue sea and the tropical sky. The pilots twisted and sideslipped to align their sights, then steadied on course to drop their load – a long torpedo splashing into the water, running for its target. It was beautifully done, nobody could deny.

The gunners ripped into them, knowing what was coming under water. Orange flames leapt out, tracer shells stitched the purple smoke, the solid noise was crammed with cordite fumes. Blisters rose and bubbled on the paint-work, the men's white hoods grew stained with sweat. The planes swept past, their torpedoes spent, and sprayed the ship with a parting hail of bullets. Sailors screamed, or slumped and died. One plane flowered into an instant blaze and was scattered in tiny petals, a funeral wreath for its pilot. Another, gliding alongside, a winged bird losing height, was chopped to pieces with a cheer. But any hatred was topped with astonishment at such bravery and skill. The Japanese, thought to be primitive or mad, were superb.

Driving through the sea, forty-five thousand tons of floating steel – power wagon of an empire and admiral's residence – began to turn from the torpedoes' track, swinging by degrees. Shadows edged too slowly across the deck as the white ribbons rolled towards her under the surface, coming faster than she could get away. It was cruel to watch, and hopeless.

Clive felt a double crash, as if she had bounced twice on the harbour wall. They had caught the stern, a stroke of luck or brilliant shooting. A tall fountain rose over the quarterdeck, hung for a spell of triumph – a lovely, hideous geyser full of oil and blood – and fell back, leaving a drift of smoke to mark the score. Far below in his guts Clive sensed an infinite pain, a mounting horror from vital parts which he knew at once: a propeller had been severed and without resistance the machinery was racing to destruction. Hutton and his engineers would be having a busy time.

The ship lost half her speed, listed quickly to port with the water in her, continued to turn unchecked: the rudder too was smashed. Two black balls were jerking up a signal halyard: 'I am not under control.' The defences were almost useless. 'No power on the guns, sir,' Clive's men reported from inside the darkened turrets. The hydraulic and electric arteries were cut, the result was already settled. A plane that gushed smoke as it tumbled, and smacked the water with a yellow bang, only mocked the losers.

The agony lasted an hour and a half. At noon another flight came in, swarming round the carnage in the sun. There was a smell of blood as well as cordite. First-aid teams stumbling over fire hoses and a swill of empty shells, the worthless jackpot from a fruit machine, did their best to deaden the last wrench of life. But morphia wouldn't hold back the next torpedo or bandages stop the bombs. The *Repulse* hauled herself on a zigzag to dodge what she could. The *Prince of Wales* lumbered in a circle round the sea as if marking out a ring to die in. She listed further and wallowed deeper. Only one turret was firing, with some of the smaller weapons.

'Got him!' a gunner yelled when he caught a plane in a point-blank volley and spattered it into nothing. But a moment later he was himself annihilated, dying uncared for among his friends.

Lieutenant Clive Ackerly watched the blows and said aloud to his wife, on the other side of the world, 'I'm not afraid, Jenny, I'm really not afraid.' He was surprised that it was true. But above all he was stunned by the effrontery, the utter absurdity. They had been sent out for slaughter so that other Englishmen could enjoy their sundown drinks this evening, their bridge parties and illusions of importance, their tinsel life. Clive wondered when the letter he had written to Jenny from Singapore, before sailing on this futile raid, would reach her; and told his men to flood the magazines.

The planes broke formation and came in from all directions. The sea was scribbled with torpedo trails, plugged with bombs, cut by twisting wakes. Through the smoke a shrivelling heat fell on the ships with the weight of failure. From deep inside, as bulkheads and engines broke, shocks of doom came up. Dying men lay round the guns among the dead, their heads streaked and dripping. The mystery was exposed, the ritual hadn't worked. Others were lucky, only singed or scorched. They lit cigarettes, the flick of a match against the unbelievable flash of bombs, and blew out the battle smells with tobacco. This was all a big mistake, the cost of someone's incompetence. Danger and fear were lost in the muddle. The game had turned macabre.

Three stokers came up on deck after a fire in the engine room, fury in their eyes, the skin falling off their flesh like burnt paper. 'Compliments of Mr Hutton,' one of them said to Clive, 'and he hopes you're getting a nice suntan.' They were in time to watch the *Repulse* go down. 'They're good, those Nips, aren't they?' Half a mile away the warship quietly heeled over, stopped for a minute, then finished the roll and slipped backwards under the surface. It wasn't a bad performance, seen from the *Prince of Wales*, and nobody doubted whose turn was next. Crippled, waterlogged, hobbling on a long curve, she made an easy target.

Three torpedoes hit the starboard side in one salvo. She settled deeper with the water flooding in: the pumps were broken. Another turret was got into action. Some of these sailors would go down fighting, and to show it a plane turned into a flaming ball to match the sun before splashing down, a handful of cinders. The quarterdeck was awash, the remaining propeller couldn't push the bulk much further, the bugler's lips were cracked. But some loudspeakers still worked: 'Stand by to abandon ship!' All hands were ordered up on deck to drop nets and ropes over the side, clear away the rafts, launch any boats that weren't smashed. Men came up from the dark hell below who didn't know how bad things were. Dazed and shaking and incredulous, they couldn't understand how those little planes had done this to their fortress.

The last flight was like the first, a knot of planes coming at speed from above the cotton clouds. Each dropped its bomb with the same precision, a globule of poison that fell and grew hypnotically in the sun, impossible not to watch. The air cracked with lightning, to burn the eyes

and split the ears, while desultory puffs from the battleship merely smudged the sky. Steel decks were folded
back, stanchions bent and twisted, tall superstructures
crumpled. Metal and water, bits of boats, ropes, bodies
were hurled everywhere. The admiral's barge was cata-
pulted like a toy into the sea and landed upside down. A
fire broke out on the port side, blowing foul smoke to
suffocate the ship. But her heart had been torn out and
life was draining from the wound. Each spasm might be
the last. No stretcher party with a tourniquet or chaplain
with a prayer could prevent the end. Already she lay in
a shroud of oil that wrapped round to welcome her and
soften the plunge. It was many years since big warships
had gone down in the South China Sea. This was the
second within an hour.

Men were ready to jump. One kissed the small gold
cross round his neck, another couldn't stop laughing, a
third farted. The horizon was tilting towards them, they
were being tipped into the sea. A sailor at his gun, feet
braced and earphones clamped, squinted up into the
sights for one more blast. His friends shouted, 'Come off
it, Spud! – it's time to go ashore.' But Spud took no notice,
he was dead. A young marine held up a bar of chocolate,
took a bite – 'Watch me!' – then slid overboard, but caught
on a ring bolt which tore his trousers off with a two-inch
strip of flesh.

Through the clamour, shouts, stunning bangs and thin
high wail of escaping steam, Clive heard his name being
yelled: 'Ackerly, you bastard!' It was Hutton, unmistakably, joined by a chorus from the underworld: '*Ackerly!*'

The voices came up a ventilator from the engine room.
But nobody could be heard from right down there. They
must have started climbing the shaft and found they were
trapped. Hutton would know that it led close to Clive's
action station and screamed above the rest, rising to a
terrible curse that cut the noise of fire and lapping water.
His escape was blocked unless someone did something –
went back or shouted down the ventilator or lowered a
rope.

Clive's men watched him with empty, ungiving faces.
Everyone had a life and conscience to save or lose. They

would see what he did with his, if they could spare time
from their own.

'Race you to Singapore!' a wardroom steward cried and
did a lovely swallow dive into the sea, then began to
swim. A signalman who jumped from the bridge broke
himself to pieces three decks down. Anything to float was
tossed overboard – wood, old paint drums, hammock rolls
– till the ship was ringed with debris. One propeller gave
a kick, half a turn of life, and a man already in the water
was sucked under. 'Get it over, for fuck's sake!' Nobody
knew how many minutes were left or whether panic
would shatter the orderliness or what was going to
happen next. It was beyond their strained belief. Anything
that came after this was only shipwreck – part of a sailor's
myth. They blew up lifebelts and watched each other,
hoping for a clue. For months they had been a ship's
company together, but in a moment everyone would be
alone, swimming for his life.

Clive heard the order, 'Abandon ship!' Or it may have
been a scream up the ventilator: 'Ackerly, you shit!'

Suddenly he didn't want to go. To save himself in the
muck and stink down there wasn't the only way out. Or
at least he could put it off. But the *Prince of Wales* was in
a hurry and the admiral was sending signals to his men:
'You put up a good show – thank you. Now look after
yourselves.' Clive pulled off his steel helmet, stuck to the
skin with sweat, and flipped it down the slanting deck.
'Good luck and God bless you!' the admiral called.

The bilges curled out of the sea, hung with weeds. Clive
joined the crowd shuffling over the painted camouflage
as they might go down a beach to test the water. 'Enjoy
your swim, sir,' a man in a chef's hat said. In the red
underplates among naked vents and orifices – the last
humiliation, all privacy exposed – a jagged hole came up,
bleeding oil, where a torpedo had spiked the hull. Then
Clive's feet shot sideways. He crashed down and was
swimming. 'Get away from her!' men shouted. Oil slipped
over his head, into his mouth and nose and lungs. He
coughed and spat. 'Goodbye!' came through the oil in his
ears, from the admiral on the bridge or Hutton in the

engine room. But hundreds were alive, black heads
bobbing in the filthy velvet stuff.

Clive turned to look, through stinging eyes. She was on
her back, blood-red and obscene, filling up for the drop
to the seabed. A propeller blade surfaced like a toenail.
Hutton must be dying, somewhere under those rivets
driven through the steel in thousands. The armour, for
protection against another battleship, would keep him
from the fish. Clive wanted to be sick, retching up the oil.
Now she was gone.

'Get away from her, for fuck's sake!'

'Jesus wept.'

The ship sank behind a hump of sea that rose and
advanced, a huge rainbow hill to mark the spot, while
Clive's legs were grabbed, nearly pulled off, and he was
swallowed far down into the black turbulence, deeper and
deeper in a whirl of missiles and oil and vomit where he
wondered, 'Do I gulp it all and go on down to the bottom
with Hutton?' and in a piercing instant, a jab that shot
from the darkness and stopped his fall, he remembered
how much he hated Hutton who bullied young officers
into buying him drinks and insulted those who didn't and
boasted of all the women he had poked, his favourite
word, and Clive knew in a flash that he was going to live,
that he was going back to Strathpolly one day and would
take Jenny there, even with the thought of having failed
to save Hutton which was a kind of murder though
nobody could have done it, and at the same moment the
darkness broke into green and gold with a taste of breakfast bacon-and-eggs in the oil as he rose higher and higher
through the wreckage, swiftly into brighter gold, up to
the warmth and daylight, out again into the tropical
afternoon.

'If the bastards machine-gun us, dive!'

But Clive knew they wouldn't. They had had a good
day, they would be satisfied. The last flight came wheeling
over like grouse at the end of a shoot, safe enough, and
flew off into the silent sky. It was two hours since they
had first appeared. Now futility and defeat lay over the
sea, thick with sailors lifting and falling on the swell. The
escort destroyers would pick them up in time, but it might

take till sunset. Some were frightened of sharks, jellyfish,
electric eels, and struck out for the nearest ship; or died of
swallowing oil, or slid below the surface without troubling
anyone; or clambered into rafts, slithered out and were
hauled back in – wounded, blistered, thankful, squinting
behind tender sticky eyelids, grieving, crowded with the
shocks of life and death and with each other.

'Did a good job, the Nips – they'll be wagging their little
yellow tails.'

Clive held a rope attached to a raft and let his legs float
up under it; pulled off his shoes and blew his nose. Greasy
arms offered to hoist him up: 'Come on in, sir, we'll find
a space.' But it was overloaded and he was happy in the
water. A mouth organ was produced and they sang,
'We're here because we're here,' laughing through the
blood and oil and tears. When the song was over a man
gave a gurgle, an act of scorn; and after a decent interval
for someone to say, 'Poor sod,' and someone else, 'Good
luck and God bless you,' putting on the admiral's voice,
he was tipped off the raft to make room for another.

More bodies lay face down in the scum, worn out with
the effort and freed from having to save themselves. But
most had survived and were on the rafts or clutching the
boxes, oars, canvas gun covers that drifted on the swell.
Patches of froth bubbled quietly in the sun which coaxed
fumes from the surface to mingle with the jokes and
prayers. A leg, unattached but hardly spoilt, turned over
in the stew.

'Just what I always fancied – basking in a swimming
pool in the tropics.'

'Bastard bloody oil.'

'Keeps the sharks away.'

'We must all be on our toes,' someone said, quoting the
admiral again.

A boy of sixteen said, 'Fucking arseholes.'

A man of forty said, 'I see what you mean.' It was the
chaplain.

'Jesus, sir, sorry.'

'Wish I'd had more breakfast – I could do with beans
on toast.'

'All I want is a little Chinese girl to bring a beer,' a man said, whose guts were full of shrapnel. Another toppled off the raft, well oiled for a quick descent, and went straight down.

Clive pulled his socks off too and emptied his pockets of penknife, money, wallet. His lifebelt, though soaked in oil, would keep him up for hours and luckily he was unhurt, with only the sickness in his stomach. He would try to bring it up, perhaps by swimming; he let go the rope and gave a kick, slipping away from the raft – a yard, two yards.

'Going far, sir? It's fifty miles to Malaya. You'll be better off with us.'

Just to get out of the oil was enough, and to think. It was good to be alive, still better to live at the edge of death. Danger, he had learnt today, was only terrible at a distance. When it was all round him it amplified his sensations till mere breathing was a joy. He would like to tell that to Jenny. He hadn't had any time with her since yesterday under the friendly mist, except for the brief message to say he wasn't afraid in battle. He wanted to think of her now but she wouldn't come.

She was pushed out of his mind by Hutton down there on the bottom. What were those final moments like? Or perhaps he was still alive, sealed up, waiting for the oxygen to run out. That woman in Singapore, a Eurasian whore he picked up at the racecourse and told the wardroom about, was the last. No more poking for Hutton. A hand, Clive found, was on his cock but it was his own, not Jenny's. She was too busy for that, fighting the Germans over London. Jenny was still in action. For Clive the war was finished.

He kicked again, floating on his back, the raft perched beyond his feet. It was awash, weighed down by the scrum of men – smeared faces, torn clothes, jaunty tattoos – but one of the destroyers would be here soon to rescue them. Already the news must be round the world. Two warships sunk. Many drowned. Jenny would hear it on the radio and wait for the telegram. 'We deeply regret' or 'We are glad to inform you.'

He wished she could know he was alive in the burning afternoon, not far north of the equator; he turned over and swam a few strokes to escape the oil. The sun was halfway down the sky, skimming off the surface into his eyes. It must be three o'clock – his watch was too blurred to read – which meant five o'clock this morning in London. Jenny would be asleep if she wasn't on night duty. Clive's little battle had ended in ignominy, but hers had been going on for more than a year. The exercise made him sick, the rest of the oil came up. He had to swim to be free of it.

He passed a sailor riding on a paravane like a man astride a porpoise, who saluted him smartly: 'Lovely day for it, sir!'

Clive had a sudden sense of fantasy. This was a fairy tale, something from childhood. He was sure he wasn't going to drown – less sure that he could ever return to real life. Across the water he heard the mouth organ and men singing, 'We're sure to meet again.' But it came from another direction. The oil on the sea or the hot afternoon was playing tricks. Hutton, who had all the answers, would have explained it. Below him, six feet down and spotlit against the dark, a man was rolling in a stately dance, waving goodbye with both hands, streaming blood from his head.

Clive kicked to get away. Now the mouth organ was on the other side. He turned on his back and saw the raft rise on the swell, further away than he thought, then fall out of sight. Perhaps it wasn't the same raft. A finger of smoke beyond it must be one of the destroyers. They had a good three hours to pick up everyone, but after sunset there wouldn't be a hope. Thank God the Japanese had left it to be done in peace. They could have had a blood-bath if they wanted.

The mouth organ and singing reached him in broken waves, like bagpipe music in the distance. There was a place at Strathpolly where it could be heard in the next valley if the clouds were right for a sounding-board, but on a sunny day it was lost from one side of the river to the other. Now there were angry voices rising to a splash. They were quarrelling, the fools: not to know that survival was a matter of saving energy, spending as little as possible. Clive was glad not to be on a raft, spared the trouble of being an officer. He could go on like this till nightfall, kept up by his lifebelt, sometimes taking a few strokes. But he would love to hear real bagpipes.

After an hour he found a heavy wooden platform from the quarterdeck or the bridge, hardly breaking the surface, and rolled on to it with his fingers through the crisscross slats. Though he was still in the water, it was warm and less oily here. He was content. All he wanted, more than bagpipes, was to get in touch with Jenny.

2

Awang bin Daud, a Malay fisherman, was careful to offend nobody. He sprinkled the boats with sacred rice flour before going to sea and took a piece of ambergris in his betel box as a talisman. But he dreaded the monsoon.

Two days ago he had heard the first thunder over the north-east horizon, already late. For the next two months there would be no fishing, except for mullet along the beach – only good for boys and old men. No fishing, no money. But plenty of work mending boats and nets, planting out rice seedlings, making copra, journeying on foot into the jungle for timber and bamboo and rattan.

This was the last trip to the fishing-ground till next season, perhaps the middle of February. The boats were having a rough time. They would be lucky tonight if all five got back to the beach without capsizing in the surf with half the catch lost. When they were pushing them down the sand before dawn this morning, Awang's wife Petimo had come out of the dark and hung a garland of flowers on the prow of his boat to please the fish. But by sunrise it had been torn off by the waves: it hadn't pleased the spirits of the sea.

The little sailing fleet – painted prows and taut ropes and patched canvas – danced towards the morning sun, five bright seabirds skittering before the offshore breeze with three or four men aboard each, chewing betel, washing from the planks the blood and scales of yesterday's fish to avoid frightening today's.

More than luck or skill, a fisherman needed contact with the fish. He couldn't presume that they were ignorant or unaware. They knew what he was up to. They must like him if they were to be caught, and would be saved by the spirits unless he also understood. He owed the same respect to his boat – a living object, something more than fine carpentry. A good fisherman never mentioned a pig or a dog while in his boat, or wore shoes or brought an umbrella aboard. Half a dollar and a mackerel might buy the prayers and blessings of a holy man, but were useless without proper feelings.

Awang shouted over the water to his brother Berahim in the next boat: 'The last catch before the monsoon! – it must be a good one.'

'You'll enjoy the holiday, don't pretend!' Berahim shouted back. 'Time to fly kites.'

'You're the one who flies kites all day – nothing else.'

'Time to lie with Petimo in the afternoon and listen to the rain on the thatch. Between those big fat thighs.'

'Fat!'

'Like two horse mackerel.'

'You know too much.'

'With a prawn in the middle.'

'Ai!' Awang spat a jet of betel juice overboard, like blood in the sunlight.

'Ai!' Berahim sang too and men in the other boats took it up, 'Ai! Ai!' above the splash and tremble.

Twenty miles out, long after the land had sunk behind them, they saw their bamboo marker anchored in the sea. They hadn't fished at this one for days. By now the coconut branches tied to it under water should have drawn some good shoals: fish loved to shelter and feed among the fronds. Sails were dropped, spars laid in the crutch, oars got out.

Awang dipped a hand into the sea and splashed water over his face, muttering, 'Peace be on you! I pray for Allah's favour, the bounty of the sea . . .' He took off his turban, shirt, sarong and sat naked on the gunwale, his feet over the side, the sun kindling the huge brown knob left by circumcision. Sometimes Petimo hung flowers on that too, for the bounty of love: her breasts as round as rice bowls, her eyes as hot as peppers. The thought of it passed with pleasure through his blood. He didn't mind: these men were his family and friends and in a minute he would be in the water under the boat, listening for fish.

It took long to learn – a year or two with a master fisherman and nobody was much good whose ancestors hadn't also been listeners. As they drifted quietly under oars towards their marker the listener would slip from his boat into the warm sea, hang on to the forefoot till it stopped, then take a breath, sink below the surface and listen. In a single breath, if everyone above was silent, he could tell the kind of fish and size of shoal. Mackerel made a noise like the wind, sprats sounded like dry rice being dropped, thin scabbard-fish chattered like a flock of crows, a shark thumped its tail, drumming loudly in the water. When the listener had found what he wanted and made his plan the other boats would put out the big square net, one at each corner thirty fathoms apart, and let it drift to the bottom on the current while he lured the fish to the middle with a bunch of coconut fronds.

For Awang, who was one of the best, it had brought prestige and profit. He owned these five boats, a rice field, an orchard with a monkey to climb the trees and knock down coconuts, and a share in a coffee shop. With a wife who made money of her own, cooking fish and selling it in villages at the edge of the jungle, he counted as a rich man. One day he would sail down to Singapore and take the pilgrim steamer to Mecca.

'There is no God but Allah, and Mamat is his prophet,' he prayed, and with one foot he touched the sea. The soles of a fisherman's feet were as tough and coarse as sharkskin. In the monsoon when the boats were pulled up under the palms he would spend days on his back scrubbing the bottom with his feet, with a little sand and water.

'Ai! Ai!' the young man in the bows called, with a voice like a girl's.

Awang hissed at him: 'Eunuch! Shit-eater! Crab! – be quiet!' It was Muda, son of Petimo's sister. He wouldn't be taken in the boats next season if he couldn't make less noise. He would have to sell turtle's eggs on the beach, shouting for his life.

'Ai!' Berahim called from the next boat.

Awang looked ahead, perplexed. Something was tangled with the bamboo marker. Paddling closer, they thought it was a half submerged box dropped from a ship, one of the coasters between the Gulf of Siam and Singapore. Then they saw oil on the water round it. It must be a steel drum, useful in the village, but it would have driven away the fish. Then part of it moved. An arm rose from the sea, with a hand on the end of it, and swayed for a moment before falling back.

'*Ai!*' Muda screamed.

As they came up to it they saw a creature, *orang* of a kind, lying in the water, held up by the thing beneath it and tied to their bamboo marker. With great strain it raised its arm again, less high, and bubbled to itself: a greasy dark-skinned creature, neither Malay nor Chinese nor quite *orang-outang*, wild creature.

'He is alive?' Awang wondered, putting out a foot to touch the object.

The man opened his mouth painfully, the lips puffed with salt and sunburn, but only a drop of spit came out. His eyes were gummed into slits, he wore strips of gold on the shoulders of his shirt, his trousers were foul. Round his chest was a lifebelt, also thick with oil. Slime ran down the prickles of his chin and throat, now chased with slobber, then with tears.

'Man?' Awang asked doubtfully.

The man moved his lips a little, slowly shook his head and surrendered to a flood of tears.

'Nippon! Nippon!' Muda cried, prodding him with an oar.

'Shut up!' Awang ordered. His thoughts were still on fish.

'Nippon,' Muda whispered, afraid that it might be true.

'Nippon?' Awang repeated. It was a possibility. They had promised it on the radio. They would arrive from the land of the Rising Sun, far in the north-east where the monsoon came from, and bring liberty and riches. There was a radio in the village owned by a Tamil who spoke in a gentle but disturbing way of a place where they would all live one day, without district officers in white suits and sun helmets to make them pay taxes to the English king, a place called the Greater Asia Co-prosperity Sphere – the name rippled from the Tamil's lips like pilchards falling out of a net. Awang never quite believed it, choosing to rely on his ears – the peculiar noise of pomfret under water, or moonfish – but the Tamil had worked in a tin mine owned by a Japanese company and knew more about the world than other villagers. Also he had married a Malay woman and become a Muslim, so he might be right. Awang had never seen a Japanese except in pictures. True, this man's eyes were half-closed, squinting up at the fishermen like Nippon in a cartoon, but he looked too large and hairy.

Awang was naked, aware that the big proud knob was wrong to greet a stranger with. He swung inboard, tucked it into his sarong, stuffed his turban on. Suddenly he knew for certain: 'English!' he cried. The Tamil's radio had spoken of battleships sunk off the coast two days ago and it might not have been thunder that Awang had heard.

The man nodded and the flip of a smile cracked his face, no more than the gasp of a dying sprat.

'Catch him!' Awang growled with menace, still careful not to make much noise. They mustn't waste time on the fishing-ground, they couldn't come back tomorrow. They pulled the man into the boat, dropped him on the bottom boards, put a limpet straw hat on him, offered him betel, gave him water from an earthenware jar. All day he lay there while they fished, speechless and dreaming among the herring and mackerel and jewfish scooped from the net and piled round him. In the end it was a good haul – five thousand tails, they said. Perhaps the man had lured fish to the bamboo marker, drawn by the shade under his floating platform or by sympathy.

Late in the afternoon they stowed the oars, hoisted sails and made for home, steering into the falling sun. The monsoon threatened from seaward, the swell rolled more steeply and broke into stiff blue waves under an inshore wind, stronger than this morning's. Twenty miles to go: the boats raced the weather, but sunset had drained into the palm tops when they reached the surf, a fringe of cresting breakers in the dark. Sails came down, waves washed into the laden boats. To broach sideways was to be wrecked, and there were rocks jutting in the shallows. The steersmen heaved their rudders to keep head on to the sand, men jumped into the foam. But none of the boats turned over, not a fish was lost. Half the village were on the beach to pull them up under the palms, safe for the monsoon. The other half came running when they heard what had been brought in.

'Ai! – what a lovely tuna fish!' Petimo cried when she saw him, and showed her crimson betel teeth.

Clive woke on a rush mat in the corner of the floor, with rain pelting on the thatch. There was no furniture but a smell of rotten kippers through the noise of drumming water, and the smell of oil from himself. He knew where he was, it came back vividly: being led up the beach into the village among a laughing crowd, guided to a house by the fishermen who had rescued him and up a ladder to this airy, friendly room. They had given him a tin plate of rice and fish and a prickly fruit which someone peeled for him: hands pushing things at him, faces shining with fun in the white light of a pressure lamp. But he couldn't eat, he only wanted to sleep.

It was the earlier part that wasn't clear. He tried to trap it before it fractured into nothing. The destroyers must have missed him. He floated through that afternoon, sometimes catching the sound of the mouth organ or sailors' voices, or meeting a piece of wreckage. In time, when it was nearly dark, he knew he was alone. He didn't worry, he was pleased to find that he wasn't frightened, but his mouth felt stuffed with sawdust, the oil stung in his eyes. It was a relief when the sun went down and he could roll over on the platform, as big as a bed, to watch the stars.

Next morning the sea and sky were empty. Without panic or self-pity he found himself wondering how long a man survives in the tropics, awash in salt water with nothing to eat or drink. Perhaps Hutton was lucky to have got it over quickly. Even if he had been trapped in a bubble he must be dead down there by now. But Clive didn't care to think of Hutton and switched to Jenny. He loved her then, a shipwrecked sailor on a raft in the South China Sea, with more generosity and hope and simple humour than ever in their Chelsea flat. He watched his toes beyond the filthy trouser legs; saw them wriggle in the morning sun, the fine hairs coated with grease, the nails black, but with a distinct gladness in the way they moved; and felt intensely that Jenny was with him and could see it too.

Towards midday the sun became ferocious. The sawdust swelled in his mouth to a lump that clogged his tongue, reached down his throat. He could neither spit nor swallow. Trying to soothe his flaming eyelids with seawater he only rubbed them with salt. Waves slopped over the platform, he was drenched. 'But I'm alive,' he said aloud, 'and life is all.' Lying beside him, her ambulance driver's uniform as messed up as his own, Jenny agreed with every word. But the smell, instead of the unique and provoking odour that usually embalmed her body, was of seaweed.

It must have been at the height of the unpitying sun, when Jenny too was getting less buoyant and amused, that he saw whatever it was. It couldn't be a periscope, it looked like nothing off a warship. 'But why is it coming closer?' he asked Jenny. She didn't answer. Slowly it stalked forward, nodding on the waves as it approached – a pole standing in the sea with sticks tied to the top. For a moment he was alarmed. Could it be dangerous, even Japanese? Jenny didn't know either.

It came right up to the platform, an arm's length away, stirring the water as it passed. Suddenly he saw that it was his platform that was moving, and this thing was fixed. He was drifting past it on a current. With a lunge,

nearly falling off, he reached out and pulled it in: a thicket
of green branches lashed under water to the bamboo float
– some kind of fishing gear. With bits of stringy fibre off
it he attached himself through the platform slats. At once
the sea began to flow past. 'We're anchored to the bottom!'
he shouted, choking on the ball of sawdust. 'The fishermen will come and find us.' Clive laughed, but Jenny
didn't. He rolled over on the platform to tell her the good
news. She had gone. Only the smell of seaweed remained.

He lay there for the rest of the day and the next night;
perhaps for two more days and nights, he couldn't tell.
Over the edge of the platform he saw fish among the
foliage under water – big pale ones with grey tails and a
shoal of silver pencils. They were alive like him, waving
in the gentle current below, and friendly. He spoke sometimes, to the fish or Jenny or anyone listening. Nobody
spoke back though in the night he heard a terrible sob,
the noise that Jenny had made in her dreams the first time
they slept together, two summers ago in her Chelsea flat.
He put out his hand, feeling for her over the empty crisscross slats.

The sun climbed overhead to scorch another morning
and with it came an increasing drone, the sound of aircraft
gathering for one more attack. But he knew they would
never come back, they had flown away for good. This was
a false alarm, a mockery in the burning sky. And if it was
real, if they came swooping in again with bombs and
torpedoes and machine-guns, he would slip over into the
water, sink into the leaves down there among the lovely
fish.

The noise throbbed louder, hammering at his skull, and
through it came men's voices: 'Ai! Ai!' But these weren't
shipwrecked sailors. There was no mouth organ. Knowing
it was the last thing he could do, Clive raised an arm with
difficulty and held it for a moment, and let it drop.

From the corner of the floor, on his mat, Clive watched
the rain through the doorway. Two children sat at the top
of the ladder – a boy playing with pieces of coral and a
girl plaiting strips of palm leaf. When they saw he was

awake they giggled and scuttled away. A woman in a
black skirt and a bodice that flattened her breasts, with
shiny hair drawn into a bun, brought another plate of rice
with bits of vegetable and a glass of sweet coffee. Later
Awang bin Daud arrived in a velvet cap and smart check
sarong – a fisherman ashore.

'Now you feeling good?'

'Much better.'

'One more day in sea without rescuing and monsoon
will sink you.'

'I want to thank you, I'm grateful, I don't know – '

'Ai!' Awang dismissed it with his hand: 'We catching
many fish, one more is good.' He dropped to his haun-
ches, took out betel and spices from a tin and began
chewing; then looked at Clive sharply: 'You coming from
battleship?'

'You know about that?'

'We have one Tamil with radio.'

'What did it say?'

'Many English rescuing, now in Singapore.'

'How far is that from here?'

Awang laughed: 'You will go to Singapore? Two-three
days in sailing ship, maybe four-five days, but now is
monsoon, not possible.' He tossed a gesture at the wind
and rain out there, and spat a perfect arc of betel juice
through the middle of the door. 'In monsoon no sailing,
no fishing, you staying my house, you my very good
friend.'

Clive must somehow get back to Singapore but he had
no money, nothing to sell. He must discover where he
was, then work on this man who had saved him and
seemed friendly: a seaman like himself, perhaps powerful
along the Malaya coast. He asked, 'Where did you learn
your English?'

'Ai!' Awang rolled the betel over his tongue. 'Once I
was boy, very beautiful, so living in sultan's palace, doing
all things for him because he is loving me very nicely and
I learn some English, and by-and-by I was man, so going
to rubber plantation, I am tapper first and after in the
factory, latex drier, I am assistant foreman and manager
is Englishman, very kind and big drinker and always

speaking English, good words and not good words, all same they speak in London, and when I am telling him I will come home my village he give me fifty dollars to buy old boat, is how.' Before visiting his guest this morning Awang had rubbed Petimo's coconut lotion into his hair, then a little into his face and polished it so that it shone as he told his story.

'I can go to Singapore by road,' Clive said.

Awang laughed again: 'Is no road here to Singapore.'

Clive learnt that there were paths through the jungle, but nobody from the coast dared go far inland and he wouldn't find a guide. There was no way along the coast to the south. In the dry months a Chinese bus travelled up and down the beach between the fishing villages and Kota Bharu, a town far in the north near the Thai border; in the monsoon it couldn't cross the flooded rivers. But Clive couldn't believe that if he started walking there would be no boat to take him over the floods.

'Is taking six days by foot,' Awang said. 'By bicycle three days. And already Nippon is winning. Now English soldiers running backwards.'

'Nippon?'

'Is from Tamil's radio. Sultan there is also running from palace and taking express train to Singapore.'

The Japanese had landed at Kota Bharu and captured the airfield, now they were driving across Malaya and down the coast. Clive felt a tide of exhaustion, almost indifference, wash over him. The thrashing rain, the bamboo house, this fisherman squatting beside him were new and believable, but defeat was impossible. To be sunk and rescued and now killed in an unknown country was beyond grasping. He had done nothing wrong, he had fought till his guns broke down, and nobody could have saved Hutton.

The woman came back up the ladder, her brown face streaked with rain, bringing bananas and a pair of old trousers. 'Is Petimo, my very good wife,' Awang said, and held up the trousers: 'Belong English plantation manager, very kind man, extra kind with whisky in him.'

When the rain stopped Clive went barefoot in the planter's trousers through the mud and puddles to the beach.

Villagers came down to see this white man in the surf
trying to get the oil off himself with sand, so unlike the
government officers touring in a motor launch full of
Chinese clerks and policemen. They followed him through
the village among their boats and nets and chickens,
enjoying his happiness and gratitude: he was saved from
drowning, he was a strong young man ready for anything,
expecting surprises. At Awang's house Petimo was
washing his naval shirt. Later she cut his hair short,
rubbed wood ash into it to absorb the oil and brushed it
out, finishing with her coconut lotion. Awang found him
a pair of rubber sandals.

The Tamil, thin and dried and dark as a cheroot, came
with the news. He spoke from memory in the tones of
the radio, in the language of Japanese propaganda: 'The
forces of imperialism are in flight. The sea was swept
clean of them and then the sky and now the land. Their
promises were false and their hearts were greedy.' The
Tamil's eyes turned on Clive, two black stabs from the
burnt crust round them, but passed through him to something more important, perhaps the Greater Asia Co-prosperity Sphere. 'The hero of the battle is General Yama-
shita, Lion of Manchuria. All Asia is on fire. Our enemies
are running home, taking everything they can save. But
many of them will leave their bones.'

At night, with the pressure lamp hissing in a cloud of
insects, a meeting gathered in Awang's house to collect
dues from the fish dealers and pay the fishermen. In the
middle of the floor Petimo sat on her heels, knees apart
and a pot of money between them, with other women
and their children in the shadows. Men who had bought
fish for market took money from their betel tins, fingered
it and passed it to other men. Coins were verified, notes
unfolded, before being handed to Petimo who laid little
piles round her, transferring bits from one to another and
in and out of the pot. Nothing was written down, nobody
could read. A moth circled the lamp, a brief shadow
stroking the people's faces, then sizzled for an instant on
the glass. A child picked its wings off and let the body
crawl away. On the wall a lizard made a dash to catch a
fly; stopped short for a moment before the final leap – 'to

let it say prayers to Allah,' Awang told Clive – then swooped and gobbled it. In time the dealers gave up their money and Petimo performed her sums and the fishermen were paid.

'I want to go to Singapore,' Clive told them, hoping someone would find a way, speaking his words carefully. 'I will give my watch to anyone who helps me reach Singapore.' He took it off and held it to the lamp – Jenny's wedding present.

They looked at the shining thing and muttered 'Singapore' in a troubled way among themselves, assessing the chances, but there were none. Overhead, in a bamboo cage hanging from the roof, a myna bird let out a fortissimo 'No-oo . . . !'

The Tamil's voice came from the doorway, quoting his radio: 'From Penang all white men have been safely evacuated, with no cares for the people they have abandoned there. So we see the true face of our protectors. But Nippon is the liberator of Asia, the friend of all who are trodden by the heels of imperialism.' His thin figure stood against the night, waiting for liberation, and the myna bird rustled impatiently in the dark.

Clive stayed nearly two weeks in Awang's house, a time of utter peace, before Nippon came. In the early mornings he walked on the beach between the tumultuous breakers and the coconut and banana trees. Dawn came up, an announcement of the world and life, and he felt himself at the beginning of some tremendous privilege.

He watched the children digging shellfish out of the sand with their toes or sifting it for coins. He learnt that the tides were caused by the great crab that lived in the navel of the sea: twice a day, when the crab went out to find food, the water plunged through the vast hole into the world below and the sea went down; when the crab came back it plugged the hole, for the rivers to raise the sea again. On calm days Clive joined the fishermen in shallow water, scooping up mullet, gutting and laying them out to stink and shrivel in the sun; or helped mend nets, scrape boats, patch sails, chop coconuts for copra.

He had only his hands to offer these people, but would show that he wasn't useless. In the storms he listened to them talk of next season's work, putting what they could into English for him, and explain the speech of fish. A jewfish under water made a noise like frying rice, a shoal of herring twittered like sparrows, pilchards sounded like the surf on a quiet night, sprats like the rustle of casuarina trees in the afternoon. Some fish, sadly for them, had no voice at all.

Clive wondered about the river at Strathpolly. Not much would be heard through the water tossing over rocks, but he could believe that deep in the pool where his mother hooked and played her last salmon, before being pulled in by it and drowned, there might be music.

On Friday he went with Awang to the little white mosque and listened to the prophet's words, the old message from the desert retold among these weathered fishermen and their painted boats. And every day, even through solid rain, the Tamil came with the latest bulletin: 'Before escaping to Singapore the English are setting fire to their rubber factories and flooding their mines. They built an empire for their profit and they wreck it rather than let it fall into the people's hands.'

Clive could do nothing, stranded between the sea and jungle – between now and the unknown – but make the most of what was left and sometimes guess what might follow. Days of massing clouds exploded in deluge, with a pause of livid heat before the clouds came piling back. He lay on the burning sand and saw Jenny's shadow slip across his closed eyelids; opened them and raced over the empty beach, splashing into the sea, happy to drown. On fine nights he swam naked in the surf with Awang and his friends, their bodies shot with phosphorescence, tumbling and laughing in the starlight. Kick a foot and it threw off sparks; raise an arm and a stream of diamonds fell from it. Afterwards, hearing Awang and Petimo through the palm leaf walls, the creaks and whispers of a bamboo house, Clive wrung out his mind to exclude everything but Jenny.

3

Nippon came on Christmas Day, riding down the beach on a horse. His sword lay strapped across the saddle, his feet dangled above the sand. He was a colonel, and his staff officers were also on horseback. Lesser ones rode bicycles. Ahead of them the troops stalked in a line that stretched from the water's edge to the trees. Further in, moving through the little rice fields and orchards, were hundreds more. It seemed likely that they could go trudging on for ever. They carried rifles and enormous packs, and wore split-toed boots that looked like cloven feet.

The colonel dismounted; walked stiffly down to the sea where he undid his trousers; squatted to relieve himself while his soldiers waited. He was a soft rectangular man, becoming a pyramid when squatting, with a slight polish on his translucent flesh: carved from soapstone or moulded in a substance between wax and rubber. Then he climbed on his horse and unstrapped his sword – the signal for a volley of shots to be fired into the village ahead. Screams came out and Nippon advanced.

Three people were killed in the capture of that fishing village. Two of them were children who stopped bullets in the first volley. Their heads were cut off with a sword and spiked on bayonets, then hurled like coconuts into the sea. Their livers were removed for some private purpose by Nippon's servant, leaving the rest for the villagers to bury. They might have been the only deaths if the colonel hadn't learnt that an English sailor from one of the sunk battleships was hiding in Awang bin Daud's house. Probably it was the Tamil who told him.

Clive wasn't hiding, it would have been impossible. He came down the ladder, followed by Awang, while Petimo with the children watched from the room upstairs. The two men were punched briskly with rifle butts in the chest

and stomach; winded in a moment without time to speak
or defend themselves; wired together by their wrists
behind them, back to back, and prodded with bayonets,
shuffling sideways, through the village to the colonel. He
sat under the trees in a fishing-boat, mildly eating his
lunch, surrounded by his staff.

'Nippon takes no prisoners!'

The voice was shrill and too mechanical to belong to
one human being. It wasn't the colonel's at all, or not his
alone. It may have originated in him, but came through
the interpreter beside him, a figure put together from bits
of someone else's uniform, with tapering head and comic
glasses and excessive teeth and outsize boots – the
colonel's dummy, a deadly joke.

Behind him, tied to his back, Clive felt Awang stagger
as if hit by another of Nippon's blows, though it was only
Nippon's voice, and shrink a little. He sagged on the wire
that joined them, cutting the skin, drawing blood. Clive
hated blood, especially his own. The rest of the villagers
were keeping away, holding their breath in the heat of
this unhappy day.

'Nippon takes no prisoners!' The colonel gave a grunt
that faintly disturbed his body, more visible than audible,
and another sentence was emitted by the high-pitched
interpreter: 'To be captured is the last dishonour!' The
interpreter waited for the colonel's next grunt between
mouthfuls of his lunch. He was a clever toy being
controlled by a trick, too cheap and tinny to last, but at
present working well. 'What is your name?'

'Awang bin Daud.' The Malay's voice was weak, diluted
by terror.

'And yours?'

'Lieutenant Ackerly,' Clive said loudly, to his surprise.
He had claimed an identity, the one that once was his.

'Ha! The fisherman caught an officer in his net and now
Nippon has caught them both.'

This time there was no sound but the merest finger
flick. Instantly two soldiers slapped Clive's and Awang's
faces, the dry clap of hand on cheek, while a third untied
the wire between them, leaving them each with their
wrists bound behind. They were whisked round to face

the colonel and kicked on the hamstrings to bring them
to their knees. Bruised by the first punching, stung to
tears by the slaps, now crippled by kicks, Clive tried to
kneel at attention. Beside him, Awang had lost some of
his stature and was no more the strong fisherman of ten
minutes ago, but cracked like a spar in the monsoon wind,
ready to break. He too, condemned before next season,
would be replaced by a new one. Clive heard him praying
and wondered if he should do the same.

With chopsticks the colonel drew from a tin bowl a thin
brown length of food, which he held in front of his mouth
like an asparagus: 'An eel from our beautiful island of
Formosa, one of my favourite dishes, dried and salted and
baked. . . .' He lowered it between his lips and closed
them, but in a moment opened them again without swallowing the eel, to scoop in more food from the bowl:
'Some pickled radish, some beans, some rice. . . .' He
chewed it all together, making noises for the interpreter
to put into sense.

Clive and Awang, on their knees among the soldiers,
watched him eating, prayed or listened to their own heartbeat, and wondered if they would be finished off quickly
like the two children.

'I have never met an English officer alive. I have only
seen them when it was too late to tell them what I think.
This is my opportunity. But first. . . .' The colonel dabbed
his chopsticks at the soldiers, then at Awang, lastly back
into his bowl for another eel.

Awang the fisherman – who could listen under water
and tell a snapper from a ray, who knew where the turtles
laid their biggest eggs, who had fished a white man from
the sea and sheltered him though it might offend the
spirits, who never launched his boat or slipped naked into
the water without a prayer, who had brought wealth and
honour to his family but now had lost his chance to go to
Mecca, and whose wife Petimo would lament in terrible
anguish but in time be comforted by his brother Berahim
between her generous mackerel thighs – surrendered
without resistance, with only a feeble 'Ai!', the gasp of a
doomed man, no fish's noise. He might be already dead.
They caught him by the arms and legs and in silence

carried him from the village, out of sight beyond the trees. Clive was kneeling alone.

'When Nippon landed in Malaya,' the colonel went on, his mouth full of food and his words coming from the interpreter, 'your English governor treated us like rabbits.' Another grunt. 'He signalled to his army, "I trust you will chase the little men off." ' The colonel spat something from his mouth, drew his sword from its scabbard and across his lips in one motion, a ritual kiss on the steel, and with wonderful agility for such an unlikely athlete bounced out of the fishing-boat; came rolling on his toes towards Clive, swinging the sword for balance. 'Who are the little men now?' He wasn't tall, but he rose above his kneeling prisoner. The interpreter, creeping close behind to stay within control, repeated, 'Who are the little men now?' A small light, less of triumph than of redeemed humiliation, showed in the colonel's eyes. Revenge would follow. 'Do you want a haircut to make you shorter?' With speed and strength and accuracy he swiped his sword across Clive's head, shaving the hair. A fraction lower and it would have sliced the top off like a boiled egg.

Clive felt the wind over his scalp. His knees were sore, the wire was pinching his wrists.

'We jumped from the ships and swam under your English bullets to the beach.' The colonel put the edge of his sword to Clive's throat below the chin. 'With our fingers we dug trenches in the sand and crawled up through the mines to your concrete defences.'

Clive felt the sharpness on his throat, an inch from death.

'Some of us died in the water and some on the beach, but the rest advanced over the corpses of our friends. We were like the sun rising from the sea.' The colonel allowed himself a smile and pressed the sword into Clive's throat to make a tiny dent without slitting the skin. 'You are a sailor, Ackeree, so you have seen the sun come up. Some mornings there are clouds to hide it, but they can never hold it back. Your empire is a cloud.' He looked up through the palms to the expectant monsoon clouds and said, 'When Nippon landed on the beach at Kota Bharu and I saw that you would not stop us, I made a promise.

I will take no tobacco and no alcohol and no woman till
the English are driven out of Malaya.' He nearly smiled
again. 'And Nippon never breaks a promise to the gods.
But I am a greedy man. I find pleasure in my appetite. So
I ask you, Ackeree – how long must I wait?'

Kneeling stiffly, his wrists tied back and a hole in his
stomach that was nothing to do with hunger, Clive could
only say, 'My name is Lieutenant Ackerly.'

'How long must I wait, Ackeree?'

At that moment a shriek of infinite unbelieving horror
– an '*Ai!*' to scare the giant tide-crab in the navel of the
sea and drown the fish and perhaps reach Hutton in the
carcass of the *Prince of Wales* – came from beyond the trees,
slicing the tropical noon. 'It is their bayonet practice,' the
colonel explained. 'They begin at the eyes so that he may
not see what they do to him below.' It came again, the
howl of an animal at life's final insult. It couldn't be
Awang, he would never scream. It must be his wife
Petimo or her nephew Muda or her next comforter, the
victim's brother Berahim. 'It is a kindness, Ackeree – do
you not agree?'

Clive felt pole-axed. He toppled sideways off his knees
and heard a great 'Ha!' from the colonel before passing
out. When he came to, he was propped on his knees
between two soldiers and the colonel was still in front of
him with the sword-edge at his throat: 'Ha!'

Clive blinked and swallowed. He would try not to faint
again. He knew he mustn't think of Awang, but it was
difficult.

'You have not answered me, Ackeree – how long must
I wait till the English are driven from Malaya?'

Clive remembered the rules for a prisoner-of-war: tell
them nothing but your name and rank. He said, 'My name
is. . . .' At each syllable his larynx flicked the steel.

'Can you hear me, Ackeree?'

The blade pressed into Clive's skin, deeper every
moment. He would snatch it away if his hands weren't
tied behind him.

'Ackeree-ee!'

It punctured him, he felt the pressure give and a trickle
on his neck that couldn't be sweat. It cut further in, driving

him backwards. He had tried to kneel upright, but now
sank slowly to his ankles. A pain shot through him, a
scorching whip of lightning.

'How long must I wait, Ackeree?'

Clive had never felt his bones being bent like this.

'Ackeree?' The voice had become softer in contrast with
the pain.

They had put a wooden roller, used for hauling boats
over the beach, across his legs behind the knees. As he
sank back it forced open the joints. He was trussed and
skewered. The colonel's sword pushed him down. Thigh
and shin strained under the weight, kept apart by the
wood. The sockets wouldn't hold, the hinge must snap.
And the trickle grew: his own blood.

'There are soldiers of Nippon,' the colonel said in
confidence, very close to him, 'who would hold their tins
to catch it and drink it.' But he changed his mind, or
remembered his promise to the gods and his question
to the English officer, and stepped back in a dancer's
movement, grotesquely elegant, whisking away the sword
and letting Clive rise from the piece of wood and kneel
upright. 'Nippon takes no prisoners!' The colonel pulled
the handkerchief from his neck, wiped his sword, kissed
it again and drove it into the scabbard; then, indicating
the cut on Clive's neck, tossed the handkerchief to a
soldier who cleaned away the trickle and held up the
square of silk. It had a picture of a naked woman lying
on her back, legs open, now smeared with Clive's blood.
The colonel laughed, which set off the soldiers: hoots and
giggles at what the colonel wore round his neck.

'Nippon takes no prisoners, Ackeree,' the colonel
repeated. 'For a soldier there is only victory or death. Even
to die on your knees among other soldiers, by the sword
of my ancestors, would be an honour. One stroke and
your head is on the ground – I can do it well.' He tapped
the hilt. 'But you are not worth it, it is too good for you.
Today, you will live with your dishonour. Tomorrow – I
cannot tell.'

The colonel danced back over the sand, into the boat to
finish his lunch, and waved to a servant for a bowl of
soup. He drank it noisily, threw the empty bowl at the

servant, wiped his mouth with the silk handkerchief and with a thunderous belch, untranslated by the interpreter, said, 'Now Ackeree, I tell you a secret. I would like a glass of wine and after that a cigarette and after that. . . .' He held up the naked woman, creased and soiled with blood and soup: 'But Nippon keeps his promise to the gods. How long, please tell me, Ackeree-ee?'

Clive swayed in agony on his knees. There were sharp stones or shells coming up into them. The wooden roller lay across his legs, a soldier at each end with one foot on it and a hand on his shoulder. They only had to step off the ground for the lightning to shoot again, without help from the sword. Repeating name and rank would be enough for the colonel to give the signal. Clive said, 'Sir.'

'Ha! You have a voice that says other things. I am pleased, for we have much to talk about.'

'I can only tell you,' Clive said, 'that my ship was sunk and I was picked up by Awang bin Daud.'

'He was a fool, he should have left you in the sea.'

Clive found himself saying, 'I wish he had.' Two men, a naval engineer and a Malay fisherman, had died while he survived. He swayed on his knees again in the soldiers' grip, and wildly shook his head as if it might throw out the unforgivable, impossible shame.

'You feel guilty of his death, Ackeree? But you couldn't stop it.'

'He did nothing against you, you had no reason to kill him.'

'You are wrong, Ackeree – he saved your life.'

'I'm the one you ought to kill.'

'It is too late for that.'

'He wasn't your enemy.'

The colonel spat: 'Even a fisherman is more dangerous than you. You will never fight again, Ackeree.' He belched and settled happily in the boat, legs crossed and fat hands capped over his knees. For better digestion, to help his lunch go down, he would tease this English officer a little more. With grunts and thumbs he ordered him to be hauled to his feet and the wire untied: 'You will not escape, there is nowhere for you to go.'

Clive shook himself to disperse the pain.

The colonel waited for him, then said, 'I wish you could see my soldiers going into attack. Into the gunfire, into the jungle – their courage is beautiful to watch.'

Clive didn't speak.

'They are like blind men who are not afraid of snakes.' The wind rattled the palms, the monsoon breakers rolled and crashed and sucked at the beach. It hadn't rained for two days, it couldn't fail to break today. 'It is your Christmas, I believe – a day for gifts.'

Clive nodded.

'Nippon has given you your life. Will you not give thanks?'

Clive nodded again and kept his head bowed.

'Nippon too gives thanks. The fruit is ripe for us. We need only shake the tree and it will drop.' The colonel lifted a finger to ease the silk handkerchief round his neck. 'Fifty days? A hundred? Tell me, when will Malaya fall?'

Clive looked up. 'My ship was sunk,' he said quietly, out of a kind of loyalty to someone, 'but we aren't finished.'

'You are doing what you have been taught, without believing it. Shoot and run, shoot and run – you are playing cricket. But this game is more difficult and you don't understand it, so you are losing.'

'In the end, I think, we shall win.'

'That is one of your English jokes. How can you win if you abandon airfields and leave everything ready for us? The runways are undamaged, and the stores and petrol tanks and magazines are full. Are these also your gifts, to help us take Malaya? We can drop your own bombs on you and kill you with your own shells. We drive your trucks – they are good, like the English cakes we eat. In an armoured car we found a map of your positions – it was kind of you. We can depend on you for all we want.' It was the colonel's turn to bow.

Clive said, 'You can depend on us to fight.'

'Ha! You call it fight,' the colonel laughed, 'but it is only scratch and peck. Nippon has taken a sword to kill a chicken.'

'One day you will be beaten.'

'Not while Nippon's sword is sharp. But your cigarettes

are excellent, I am told, and your whisky. It will be a pleasure when I can taste them.' Christmas Day was growing dark. The afternoon storm thickened overhead, pressing on the palm tops. At sea the horizon blurred, then vanished in the descending sky. A foolish cockerel gave a cackle of alarm, as if nobody else knew what was coming. The Japanese soldiers in their shoddy uniforms shuffled with impatience at the colonel's delay. They would advance no further down the coast today, but spread through the village to share their conqueror's right: no more killing here unless it went with rape. 'Your women also are said to be appetising,' the colonel said with a softer, darker relish, 'if they are not too young. They must be mature, I hear, and taken when the flesh is soft but before the skin is wrinkled – then they are at their best, like plums.'

Clive knew he was meant to hate this man who had spared his life out of contempt, not mercy, and knew he must get through the ignominy without showing arrogance or degradation.

'*Ackeree-ee!*' the colonel suddenly bellowed. 'You refuse to tell me how long I must wait, so I will tell you. When the monsoon is finished, Nippon will be in Singapore.'

Rain squalls were chased in from the sea by gusts of wind, overtaking each other to reach the village, dodging among the trees, tearing through fences, whipping the flimsy homes till the place was a mess of streaming leaf and tattered fibre. Puddles were dropped wholesale on the ground and blown back into the air. The colonel, with another turn of agility, passed in an instant from the boat into the nearest house. His troops bolted for cover – for plundered food and fermented palm juice and muffled, unstruggling copulation. Nobody would shout but few would sleep, and by tomorrow Nippon might be satisfied and move on.

Clive never saw the colonel again, or Petimo or any of Awang's family. Sloshing through the village he was hustled by two soldiers to a house he didn't know and up the ladder. In defiance of the storm a military march was coming from the radio.

'The prestige of the white men is exposed,' a gentle

musical voice said from the shadows, 'and their bravery is seen to be a sham. In the Singapore hotels they are dancing in paper hats among the balloons and Christmas trees. They are paper people. They pray in the cathedral for peace and good will to all men, but by peace they mean their empire and by good will they mean their profits and by all men they mean only white men. What kind of rulers are they, who fight secretly among themselves for steamer tickets to escape? Is it surprising that their empty factories and offices and shops and homes are looted by the people they leave behind?'

Hearing the Tamil speak English one of the soldiers hauled him into the middle of the room, smashed his teeth with one ferocious jab of his rifle butt and brought it up hard into his groin. The other soldier bound Clive's wrists again with wire and tied the end round his own ankle.

The wind chased the rain into the interior of Malaya, over the forest to the tangled hills, and by night it had blown itself away, leaving the dark sea beating on the beach and the Tamil whining on the floor. His radio was tuned to the news from Tokyo.

Bicycling northwards up the beach, the two Japanese soldiers took a week to get back to Kota Bharu where they had first landed in Malaya. They were out of the fighting, they needn't hurry.

All day they pedalled side by side along the white hot sand; waded through shallow creeks, commandeered boats to carry them across flooded river mouths, turned inland to avoid mangrove swamps where old fumes rose sourly from the mud and roots – no place for bicycling. For sport they stopped to shoot at coconuts, chickens, ducks. They killed a water buffalo working in a field, then killed the farmer for howling at them. They shattered a peasant's home with a version of football, forcing the family to kick a melon with them till it turned to pulp, kicking another and another and getting through the season's crop. At some villages there was an army post where they reported for the night, but often they were free to find a billet. They would have a swim, demand a meal at the most promising house; choose a woman. Each took her in turn while the other guarded their English prisoner.

Clive had no bicycle. His wrists were wired to the soldiers' saddles and he jogged close between their back wheels. If he lagged, his arms were pulled forward and the wire bit his skin. But with rifles and full equipment and cranky old machines they didn't go fast.

A puncture meant a welcome rest, though Clive had to mend it while the soldiers lay down and watched. He rather enjoyed it: levering off the tyre, listening for the hiss of air, patching the tube, stuffing it back and pumping it up. It took him back: he used to do it as a boy when he went bicycling with his brother, Victor.

Once they sheltered from the monsoon in a fish paste factory – two Japanese soldiers and their blistered sweaty prisoner helping themselves to jars of shrimp and anchovy – but the Chinese manager ignored them, too frightened to interfere. His workers, stringy dark men and women in a state of decomposition to match the stink of rotting fish, pounded the stuff in mortars with salt and spices, and sand and maggots; and stared at the white man as if at last something surprising, even funny, had happened in their lives.

In Awang's village Clive had sensed the start of some immense dispensation, to intimidate and excite him. Delays, like this pause for shelter in a fish paste factory, made him impatient to reach whatever might be ahead. He was glad when the storm blew over and he was wired to the bicycles again, to be towed on up the coast to Kota Bharu.

Part Three

The Return

1

'Clive! Clive!'

He stepped on to the platform at Waterloo station among the scuttling pigeons and London taxis – one of a hundred returning prisoners-of-war, tired and thin and unconfident, to be grabbed off the train by their families and friends. A porter took his suitcase.

'Clive! Clive!'

A sombre October afternoon in 1945, four years since he had left her. She was calling urgently through the people. He couldn't call back, his voice was locked. For one thousand three hundred days he had been a prisoner and spoken her name fifty times a day. The word filled him utterly – Jenny, Jenny. . . . But now it wouldn't come. Dreams were for dreaming, not for coming true.

'Clive!' She wore a belted coat with a cameo pinned under the collar, and no hat. Her hair was brushed away from her forehead, set in ripples down the sides. A bag swung from her shoulder, the strap denting her breast. The tears were only in her voice, not in her soft grey eyes. 'I've got something to tell you.'

Something to tell him. To tell each other. That the war was over and they had won. That they had waited four years for this, knowing it could never happen, never losing hope that it might. That life began on Waterloo station this afternoon. That they would be in love for ever.

'There's something I must tell you, Clive.'

There were things to tell her too, but they could wait. Hers were more pressing. Far up under the glass roof a gramophone was playing military music, welcoming the prisoners home.

'This way, sir,' the porter said.

Jenny took his arm, 'Listen, Clive,' and led him, not to the ticket barrier and the way out, but back towards the end of the platform, beneath the station arch and out under the pale London sky. The porter followed with the suitcase, watching them. 'I got your telegram. It was the first I knew. . . .'

Jenny, Jenny, Jenny. . . . It thumped in his head like malaria: the ringing noise mixed with a military band under the roof, and the rush of sweat and nausea.

'I was a widow.' She gripped his arm and talked. She would save him from the heroes' welcome, the cheers and clapping of the little crowd that had come to greet the party. No applause for Lieutenant Ackerly. His name and rank were stencilled on the new suitcase carried by the porter. It wasn't much, but it was all he owned. Inside, wrapped in tissue, rolled in a pair of socks, was the zircon ring he had bought in Rangoon before boarding the troop-ship. 'I was a widow,' she said again and again. She was telling him something too big to bear: a woman lurching under a load, trying to pass it to a man who wasn't ready for it or didn't want it. Her face told it all: the happiness of today, the misery on top of it. 'They told me I was a widow and I believed it.'

Those people would tell her anything. They knew nothing, they were always wrong. Half their time was spent congratulating each other on having a good job, the other half looking for somewhere better. They were the men at Rangoon, glib and evasive with cold superior smiles, who had questioned and probed and listened and taken notes: medical officers, welfare and transport and intelligence officers, the experts with labels that were said to give them value and importance. Four years ago Clive might have agreed.

'You were missing. . . .'

They reached the end of the platform and stopped. Jenny slipped her arm out of Clive's to face him. Already there was a gap between them. They should have met and stuck, but had bounced apart. He wouldn't take the thing she was trying to give him. Let her keep it, it was hers. Beyond the platform the rails went bending away into the afternoon, locked in pairs but joining and crossing and parting like skaters' blades on ice – the polished, fluent dance of steel.

Clive's eyes slid down the track, back the way he had

come. Back to the Southampton docks, the troopship
voyage from Rangoon, the rehabilitation process, the
Dakota flight from Thailand. Back to another railway in
the distance, and a prison camp among the trees and
graves.

'You were missing, believed killed.' Belief was knowledge for Jenny. 'In the end I accepted it. The letter you
wrote in Singapore – it was like getting a letter from the
bottom of the sea. There was no more news. You weren't
in the lists of prisoners. You never sent another word.
They gave me a widow's pension. Try and imagine, Clive
– a widow of twenty-two.'

He had imagined so much, but never that. As a slave in
a jockstrap on the railway, hungry and bruised, humping
baskets of mud in the rain and heat, he had never thought
of Jenny as a widow. For that, he would have to be dead,
and life was his obsession. He was alive if nothing else.

'Then I got your telegram last month.'

'You believed it?' They were the first words he had
spoken to her since 1941.

'I was stunned. But yes, I knew it was true. Though I
rang the admiralty to check. They said your name had
come through.' The glib evasive men: they would be calcu-
lating the back pay due to him, deducting her widow's
pension. 'Now it's your turn to be stunned, Clive.'

'But I'm not. I was expecting it. In your telegram back,
you warned me.'

'Warned you?'

'Told me the truth, your secret – '

'There's something else, Clive.'

'You mean. . . . ?' He knew already; had known for
years. He was beyond astonishment. A whistle blew,
doors banged, a train came fussily out of the station, steam
gushing round the wheels, smoke lifting to the glass roof
where pigeons flew and the band played.

'I've got a little girl.'

These were the last moments before Jenny disillusioned
him. But it had never been a true illusion, there was
nothing false in it. Belief was what mattered, for Clive
too. Everything was as he had believed, till this afternoon.
What he knew, was so. And it was impossible to mark

the exact destruction of belief. There was a pressure wave, a blow of air that struck before the actual detonation and shattering explosion. It hit his ear drums, burst his lungs, tripped his feet. His balance went, he rocked and stumbled. Though he had been a gunner in a battleship, he couldn't cope with this. He was still too weak. 'Give me time, Jenny. Wait for me to recover a little.' They had warned him that adjustment might take time.

'I was bombed out of the Chelsea flat.' The band was playing 'A Life on the Ocean Wave'. Along the platform the prisoners were crying and laughing, getting through their happiness. 'I was on duty and came home after the raid and found it gone. I was lucky not to be in it. But shaken badly. They wouldn't let me go on driving the ambulance. Anyway the blitz was almost over. I got a job in a club for American officers. Clive, there's so much. . . .' She took his arm again and reached for his hand. Both his hands in both hers. 'I never doubted you were dead.'

Clive had never doubted that she was alive. The certainty of Jenny, her life on the other side of the world, was the root of his survival. The departing train, rolling faster out of Waterloo, was on its way to Southampton. Clive should be travelling down the line again, starting the long journey in reverse. It had been a mistake, he shouldn't have come home, he had no place here. Nothing belonged anywhere any more, except the suitcase with his name on it and a zircon ring inside.

'Taxi, sir?' the porter asked.

Jenny went on: 'No letter, no word, nothing for four years – can you understand? Till your telegram. Since then I've been racked.'

'You've got a child?' She was a mother. What did that make him?

'I had so little warning. Everything that happened after you . . . I couldn't put it in a letter. I tried, Clive. I tried to catch up, but on a few sheets of paper, to reach you on a troopship somewhere, in a cabin with everyone celebrating, sailing home to wives and families . . .' The little crowd was emerging from handkerchiefs and kisses, moving away to find taxis. The London commuters were taking over. 'I couldn't write, I had to wait to see you.'

'A child?' It wasn't his own, he knew.

'I was alone, Clive.' She rubbed his hands. 'I. . . .' The grey eyes drifted over his face, neck, chest, down his front, up to his face again, on up to the autumn sky.

'You fell in love.'

'He's called Max. We have a daughter called Rebecca.'

It was coming back to him. This was nothing new, he had always known it. He wasn't surprised, except by the place where it was happening: the trains rolling in and out, the busy passengers and porters, the band playing under the roof. Even the people she was talking about – a widow called Jenny, an American called Max, a little girl called Rebecca – were familiar, though strangers, like characters in a modern version of an old story. He could reply with names of his own, people Jenny hadn't heard of, but suddenly he didn't want to bring them here. Doc Davis, Smithy, Weigall and Robbo, the old woman by the river, the Turd and Goldilocks and Captain Ishi – they belonged somewhere else, they lay in a forest cemetery, the dead and the living, too precious to share. And Jenny didn't give him a chance.

'Max saved me from being alone, but it was more than that. Something I'd never felt in my life. Clive, I loved you and I love you still and always shall. It's the normal thing. It fits. It's obvious and easy and straightforward. But this isn't a straightforward time. You've come back to a cock-eyed world. And Max suits it, somehow. He helped me understand it. He doesn't belong in London, he looks at it from outside. For the first time – '

'You're in love.'

'Clive, it isn't true.' There was a way she used to pull one of his thumbs, exploring the joints. She was doing it now. He had forgotten the acute pleasure of it.

'Jenny, you've done nothing wrong,' he heard himself saying. 'Nothing to what I've done.'

'I've betrayed you, Clive.'

'If anyone's betrayed anyone, it's for me to be ashamed.'

'What of? Of thinking everything would be the same? Of expecting to be met by a faithful wife?'

'I expect nothing from anybody – nothing, nothing. Except from myself. It's what I've learnt. I'm different now. Why shouldn't you be too? If I expect anything. . . .' He saw it so clearly, he couldn't believe he hadn't heard it before. This Max came to London with the American army and stayed in the officers' club where Jenny worked. She was a young widow, heroine of the blitz, who had faced the bombs and done brave warlike things. Her home was destroyed, she was alone and free and beautiful. Max was cosmopolitan, confident, clever, successful – everything that Clive wasn't. He had a wife in America who had left him, and Jenny's husband was safely drowned in the South China Sea. They fell into bed, into love, into a flat in Regent's Park where their daughter was born. When Max's divorce came through they would get married, though Jenny's pension would be stopped. To Clive it was a fairy tale, part of life, that he had known as long as he could remember. 'If I expect anything,' he said, 'it's a happy end.'

The returning heroes were thinning out, dispersing into London, to lose and find themselves. Clive felt less than heroic. This wasn't what he had lived through Kota Bharu, the camp, the railway for. There were no rules, no drill for it. But having survived imprisonment he wouldn't be broken by the first lethal breath of liberty. The atom bomb two months ago and the Japanese surrender, the weeks of recovery, the lovely autumn afternoon as a passenger riding through England again, to find Jenny at the other end – it couldn't end in defeat.

'Where will you go?' she asked. She was working on the other thumb.

Clive must make a move. Till now, the decisions had been someone else's. He said, 'I thought . . .' and forgot what it was. Everything looked different now. All he could be sure of was that he mustn't lose sight of the porter with his suitcase. More trains were sliding out of Waterloo. Crowded carriages, people standing in the corridors with evening papers: the daily ebb-tide of Londoners, brought up on the flood this morning, was being sucked back into the suburbs. 'Give me time,' he said. He was working something out.

'You must decide.' The tears had risen into her eyes now.

'Thank you.' He couldn't have kissed her if she hadn't put her lips on his. Thank you for the tears, he meant. He freed a hand from hers and touched the cameo under her collar, wondering if he had seen it before; or had given it to her. 'Where are you going now?'

Jenny looked up at the big station clock. 'It's Rebecca's birthday.'

'Rebecca?'

'She's two today, she's having a cake. But we've got time for a cup of tea. Then I must get back. Clive, darling. . . .' Under the roof the band changed to 'The British Grenadier'.

'I'll go . . .' He saw what he would do. It struck him like a light, winning flash. 'I'll go straight up to Strathpolly, I'll take the night train.'

'But Clive – '

'And stay with Victor if he's there. I needn't warn him, he'll have me for as long – '

'Clive, didn't you know?'

'Know?' This was another attack coming in.

'Strathpolly's been sold.'

'Sold?' It caught him in the guts, nearly fatal.

'The army left it in a mess. Victor was in one too. He couldn't pay his debts, he had to sell it, he's living down at Brighton.'

'Victor at Brighton?'

'With someone called Brenda.'

'Brenda?' These were direct hits, like the ones that sank the *Prince of Wales*. But Clive could take them. Already he knew he wasn't going down.

He was alone in the back of a taxi. They had had tea in the station buffet, hardly speaking, fumbling in the emptiness. All he could remember was Jenny telling him that next week Max was going back to America where he would be released from the army and join the foreign service, and he wanted her to follow with Rebecca as soon as possible. Now she stood with the porter on the kerb

outside. Through the window she looked as she had done
for the last four years – the only woman in the world.
That was what stunned Clive: the fact of Jenny, her being
Jenny, not the things she had told him. The tears had
gone, her cheeks were dry. She nearly waved, nearly
smiled, but stopped herself, turned away and vanished.
The last he saw was her hair set in ripples over her ears:
set like that, he knew, for ever.

The taxi wasn't moving. Someone should tell the driver
where to go. On the floor against the folding seat was the
suitcase with Clive's name on it: proof of who he was. In
it was the zircon ring. The Chinese jeweller in Rangoon
had made a quick bargain: it was probably a fake.

The porter opened the door and looked in: 'Everything
all right, sir?' The driver turned to see what was going
on: 'Where to?'

'Just drive.' Clive waved his hand forward.

The ported banged the door shut and spoke to the
driver. They understood that coming home was an unset-
tling thing. As the taxi swung out of the station Clive put
up a foot to stop the suitcase falling over. Inside the shoe
his toes were gnarled by the butt of Goldilocks' gun
crunching into them, and would never be straight again.
He had been going to show them to Jenny tonight after
giving her the ring, when they undressed. Instead she
had had something to tell him. Suddenly he remembered
what he should have told her in return: that she had saved
his life. He would have died on the railway if he had
known the truth.

'Will you stop?' he shouted to the driver. 'I've forgotten
something – just a moment!' He jumped out and ran back
to the station. 'Jenny!' He ran everywhere, searching the
buffet, shouting at strangers, looking into taxis: 'Jenny!'
She had gone, and the big station clock told him where:
to Rebecca's birthday party. He went back to his taxi and
waved the driver on.

'Had a spot of trouble with the Nips, did you?' the
driver asked over his shoulder, heading through the
stream of commuters, making for Westminster Bridge.
'Rather you than me.'

They crossed the Thames, grey and purposeful after the

brown river below the prison camp: stone parapets instead of mud banks, and barges of another shape. The old scenery – Big Ben, red buses, fawn overcoats, peeling copper-green plane trees – was unbelievable but comforting, smiling at Clive. Somewhere in it there must be friends.

'Will you stop?' he called again, in Hyde Park. It was a long time since he had given a man an order. Go and he went, stop and he stopped: a small victory, the first move in a game he hadn't played for years. 'Will you wait? I won't be long. . . .'

He walked under the trees on short thin grass, among chairs, bits of paper, a few lovers. Nobody noticed him, he wasn't as conspicuous as he felt. Hutton, Awang bin Daud, Smithy, Captain Ishi might never have occurred. But they would return, he knew, to haunt him in the future. Dead leaves were falling everywhere, lying deep across the ground, dropping like cholera victims. He had dreamed of them on the railway: Jenny scooping them up for him, tossing them above her head to see them fall, laughing in the autumn sun while he dreamed. And one day, in the Strathpolly woods, they would have made love on a bed of leaves. Now the place was sold and she was at her daughter's birthday party with her daughter's father: balloons and funny hats and two candles on a cake. But Clive mustn't torture himself. He had told Jenny she had done nothing wrong, he must show her it was true.

He had told her also that he expected nothing of anyone but himself: nothing of life but life itself, the only gift. He would ask a lot from Clive Ackerly. Anything from other people would be pure bonus, not taken for granted but an extra bounty for what he made of life.

A solitary man in a London park: he walked for a quarter of an hour, half an hour, perhaps an hour. Though the day would continue, time of another kind, the private rhythm of the prison years, had stopped. It couldn't be wound up, nothing could set it going again. It had passed like the hunger, pain, cruelty. Once it had been the factor that could save or crush a man. Some had been defeated by it, but Clive was lucky. More than lucky: he had got away lightly. Jenny had betrayed in ignorance, Clive in

shame. The ordeal this afternoon at Waterloo was the
price of escaping from the railway. The convulsion was
devasting, scorching, a private Hiroshima two months
after the universal one – the one that had set him free.
Yet dimly he understood, as he walked back to the taxi,
that it could make his freedom real. Liberation would
come from inside. It wasn't Jenny who had met him on
the platform, but himself.

2

At Kota Bharu, after being towed for a week up the beach
behind two bicycles, Clive was put in the old colonial
prison of the English, his own people: a courtyard
enclosed by double-storey blocks of cells, each built for
two prisoners and now holding fifteen, caged behind steel
bars. In the yard was a well with a banana tree beside
it, drooping limp finger-leaves over the cobbles; also the
whipping triangle. At the corners were the latrines, cookhouse, governor's office and a watchtower with a machine-gun. The whitewash was defaced with cracks, stains,
slogans. The surrounding wall was ridged with spikes.
The entrance arch over big wooden gates was draped with
the Rising Sun. In the road outside, six severed heads
were impaled on bamboo poles: waxy and indifferent and
quite ungruesome, often replaced by fresh ones, usually
Chinese.

One of the upper cells was for white men – soldiers,
officials, planters, mining men. Though all had stories of
escape, hilarious or brutal, lucky or tragic, they kept them
locked like themselves in an inner darkness. They spoke,
joked, laughed, but as strangers, without letting out
anything too tender. That might come later, when one
man's grasp of his predicament could illuminate
another's. Till then they would guard their privacy as a
precious chance of life.

'I'm Davis – welcome to the white man's country,' a

long thin figure said, sitting in khaki on the only furniture,
a broken car seat. He held out a hand to Clive and named
some of the others: 'Coltart, Atkins, Smithy, Weigall,
Robbo, Joker – '

'White man's grave, more like,' Joker said.

'Welcome all the same.'

'Beriberi, malaria, dengue – which d'you fancy?'

'Got any cigarettes?' Weigall and Robbo, the two
youngest in the cell, asked simultaneously.

Two men lay on each of the cement beds, the rest fitted
roughly on the floor with kitbags and suitcases, a Gladstone bag, an umbrella, a set of golf clubs. They shuffled
around, adjusted a hip, bent a leg, to make a slot for the
newcomer. Clive had no possessions and took up the
least space. He couldn't yet distinguish between these
strangers – love or hate or resent or admire them as
separate men – but only observe and wait; observe himself
too, for his unknown resources, the way he would behave.

'Two meals a day – rice and rice.'

'Shout for the guard when you want the latrine.'

'That's rationed too – one shit, three slashes.'

'Unless you've got my problem – twenty-seven times
today.'

'Got any news?' Davis asked. He was Australian, a
doctor in government service who seemed to have taken
charge. 'We've heard nothing since we got here.'

'Except tales of victory from the Nips.'

'Will Singapore hold out, you think?'

For the first time Clive felt himself a prisoner, with the
cell block across the yard for horizon and the banana tree
to give a stunted, teasing hint of liberty, but no fruit. This
was starker, more stripped of possibility, than floating in
the sea after the *Prince of Wales* was sunk, and his
companions destroyed the sense of promise he had felt as
the only white man in Awang's village. Brought out here
from home as masters, they personified what they most
scorned or pitied: the helpless beggary of Asia.

'Did a good job, the Public Works, when they put this
place up,' Smithy said. 'Solid as the Bank of England.
More than I can say of the house they gave me. Washed
away every monsoon – what was left of it when the ants

had finished.' He had been a telegraphist in the post office and was the easiest with his friendship; the easiest for Clive, and everyone, to like.

Days followed of aching boredom and a nothingness that reduced men to the next-to-nothing minimum of life, a fragile obsession with not dying. Clive saw it in himself – a trimming of ideas, memories, hopes, till there was a danger of being left a creature of instinct, efficient like an animal but empty of any human trace. It was his worst fear.

'How long will it be – another month?'

'Give yourself a year.'

'I'm counting on ten – it's the only way.'

'Piss off, Joker.'

'The US marines . . . ?' Weigall began, and Robbo finished: 'Is it true they're coming in?' The two kept together like a pair of schoolboys, allies against authority.

They wondered aloud, picking grains from each other for the unfillable vacuum; or speculated in silence, pretending it was a comfort; or slept for hours, exhausted by the loss of all that was normal and by the single thought that took its place.

Any convicts left in the prison from the English days vanished among the hundreds mopped up on suspicion by the conquerors – Malays, Chinese, Indians. Through January and February they poured in till the wooden gates, opening and shutting on them, must burst. Two more cells were emptied for another batch of white men: they alone were kept locked up. The rest camped under makeshift awnings in the yard, on the steps to the upper storey, along the verandas. By the fall of Singapore a thousand men were living, and some were dying, in a prison built for sixty.

There was no room for exercise or punishment. A week after Clive's arrival, for saying there was nothing to choose between the King of England and the Emperor of Japan and that Karl Marx was best, a Eurasian clerk was beaten to unconsciousness on the triangle, revived with a bucket from the well and beaten again. He was the last: it became impossible to wield a bamboo. The sword was used instead, on the cricket pitch of the English club at sunrise.

'They did it to a bloke on my tin mine,' Coltart said –
a huge but very quiet engineer, like a machine running
below full power. 'A Scotsman who was drumming up
resistance behind the lines after the Nips went through.'
'Betrayed?'
'He asked to be shot but they refused. Made him dig
his grave and kneel beside it.'
'Medieval, I call it.'
'They were doing him a kindness because they admired
his guts – fighting on after we'd lost.'
'They'll never win, they're just not civilised.'
'Civilisation's a washout. Look where it's got us.'
Twice a day they lined up for a pint of grey, gluey
unsalted rice which they ate with fingers or bits of wood
out of rusty tins, hub caps, banana leaves. It smelt of
soap, musty and sour. 'Boiled in a Chinese laundry,'
Smithy said, 'in the water with the clothes.' Sometimes a
piece of cucumber or a small fish or sweet potato
appeared, diminishing as it passed from hand to hand.
Less often there was soup with a rare wedge of gristle to
underline the uselessness. For fit men, for a while, it
was enough. They knew they must eat, though the rice
brought troubles which made the need to swallow another
pint of it a torture. 'Happy feet' was one: the soles were
stabbed with pain, and a man would stand all day and
night rocking from foot to foot or dancing in a circle on
his patch of floor. 'Rice balls' was another: his scrotum
turned raw with splits and sores, a dangling agony. And
nothing was more ironic for a man whose bowels were
pulled inside out every hour, who retched at the sight of
rice and vomited most of it, to force it down and try to
keep it there.
At sunset the night dropped quickly, a foreboding
falling on the prison: tomorrow might be worse. Electric
bulbs hung round the yard, each in a mantle of insects.
The odour of unwashed bodies and excrement settled over
the population. A figure scurried to the latrines, weak
with dysentery, and was screamed at by a guard. A dwindling pack of Malay rebels, chained like dogs to the whipping triangle and told that at each dawn one of them

would be taken to the cricket pitch for execution, wailed
all night, wondering which was next to go.

Clive lay at night on an old rice bag, feeling the hard
concrete under him and the weight of endless imprisonment above.

With a matchstick, in the dark but seeing every detail,
he etched a tiny map of Strathpolly on the floor – house,
river, bridge, track to the mountains, scenes of his childhood. He followed old adventures with his brother Victor,
and picked up their conversation as if the words had lain
for twenty years in the bracken, beside the pools and
waterfalls, waiting for him to come back. Before sleep he
laid his hand over the map to keep it, but in the morning
there was nothing there.

Also with a finger, more dangerously, he traced Jenny's
body: the shell-like secrets of an ear, the divide of flesh
below her spine, the smallest agitation of her nipples and
clitoris. Though it made him miserable he had to do it.

He never felt Jenny close beside him again after the first
day on the raft. The best he could do was go through old
conversations with her, as closely as he could remember,
but in time they wore thin and inaudible, like records. He
would try to start a new one, with no response. She was
in London, fighting the blitz, and couldn't get away. For
Clive she was only in the past or future, and both were
false if she wasn't there. Still, he talked to her now in a
way that he never had during their short marriage.

He was going through a vast emptiness, but also a vast
experience. He couldn't doubt that he would survive and
return to Jenny, who would absorb much of the memory
for him. But images would come flickering back for the
rest of his life, to disturb him. 'Shall I share them with
you?' he asked her. 'Or would you rather be spared?
Probably we'll find an answer.'

The bow legs, squat body and suet pudding face were
common shapes of Nippon, but this sergeant could shout
in English: 'All mens work! Damme-damme, no work, no

rice!' He had a revolver and a bamboo truncheon which twitched with menace if his temper was stirred by anyone taller than himself.

Singapore had fallen four days after the English general had called Nippon an army of clever gangsters. Malaya was conquered, and a platoon of European prisoners carrying spades was marched round Kota Bharu on their way to hard labour. A few jeers and gobs of spit reached them, but the people were afraid to show enthusiasm. Clive was one of the fittest, except for festering blisters on his feet. He still wore Awang's sandals, not the best for marching, more string than rubber after jogging for a week up the coast behind the bicycles.

'Nippon so'dier number one, English so'dier number ten!' the sergeant shouted every twenty paces. His own soldiers, though armed and bristling with power, were far from smart. The platoon marched out of the town and halted by a river where a captured staff car was waiting. A young army captain got out of it: a tall, slim, supple figure, well-tailored in olive breeches, with a moustache and a touch of imperial courtesy; the opposite of the bandy-legged short-sighted sergeant; the most unbrutal Japanese soldier Clive had seen. The sergeant saluted him: 'Captain Ishi!'

'Just the place for a cemetery,' Joker said, looking round: there had been too many stories of prisoners forced to dig their graves. 'A view of running water, a quiet spot under the trees. . . .' A leafless shell-blasted casuarina stood on the river bank with a crow watching from the top. 'Now I understand the spades.'

'Christ, Joker, shut up for God's sake! – we've done nothing wrong.'

'So why bring us here?'

'All mens dig snakes!' the sergeant shouted; and saluted the officer again: 'For Captain Ishi!' Saliva shot from his teeth.

Smithy repeated, 'Snakes?'

One of the Japanese soldiers showed them, pushing a spade into the soft wet earth, digging up a worm.

'Snakes!' The sergeant snatched it, held it close to his

eye-slits for approval, then raised it on the end of his bamboo for the prisoners to see: 'Snakes!'

'It's all right, boys, we're going fishing,' Smithy said, and corrected the sergeant: 'We call them worms.'

'Damme-damme, in English is snakes.' The bandy legs became steel coils, the squatness turned to muscle and the pudding to a hissing ball of rubber: '*Snakes!*' The word ripped and darted like a snake itself. The sergeant came at Smithy with the bamboo; pushed the worm down inside his shirt, then struck the side of his head, tearing the ear.

'In English it's a fucking worm,' Smithy said bravely, pulling it out, the other hand on his ear, blood coming through the fingers. 'And it's a long way higher up the scale than you.'

'Careful, Smithy,' Doc Davis warned, 'or he'll make you eat it.'

The sergeant raised his bamboo for another swing, but was stopped by Captain Ishi, who drew his sword like a knight taking up a challenge and with it made Smithy kneel at the toes of his jackboots, the black leather glistening with nearly divine authority. He had the face of an idol and eyes in it like small darkened windows: nothing could be seen inside and there was no telling who or what looked out. He didn't need sunglasses, his own lenses were opaque. His nose was a hawk's, his hands were a woman's. He spoke in clear English with a strong American accent, as if he had learnt it from a gramophone: 'The first lesson you must be taught is not to contradict Nippon. It is an insult to the Emperor.' He held the sword quivering above Smithy. 'I could order you to be shot like a dog. Or I could offer you compassion and use my sword.' He stretched it higher overhead: 'It would be a compliment, from the Emperor.' He lowered it and with a flick of the tip under Smithy's chin made him stand up, then returned it to its scabbard. 'Therefore, gentlemen, I ask you to agree with the sergeant. With respect I call you gentlemen, and if you behave so, you will be treated so. But you are prisoners and therefore worthless. Do you understand? You must call them snakes.'

'May we be told what they're for?' Clive asked, as calmly as he could.

'I will tell you,' Captain Ishi said, his dark eyes on Clive, drawing him into the blank behind them. 'Five years ago I left my home to fight in China.' He was a young man speaking of simple, distant things; proud to recite one of his favourite pieces, a gift for showing off his English. 'My grandmother gave me a singing bird in a cage.' Nostalgia sounded in his voice: so he was a human being with a heart as well as a sword. 'He sings in the morning and the evening, and when I hear him I am taken to the garden of my family. I know I shall not go back there before we have conquered all Asia and the war is finished. So I keep my bird. He is a little part of Japan. I promised my grandmother to take him everywhere and in the end to bring him home and set him free. But yesterday morning he did not sing and I waited all day, and in the evening it was the same. Perhaps he is sad because he has been away so long, but I think he is only hungry. Therefore, gentlemen, today you will dig snakes for my bird and tomorrow he will sing.'

Captain Ishi stepped quickly into the car and drove away, ignoring the sergeant's salute. The platoon began to dig. The soldiers took off their belts stuffed with bullets and grenades, and their helmets and cotton caps for the sun to fall on cropped scalps; opened their trousers to cool their underpants; and sat down to watch, working their rifle bolts, itching for target practice. The sergeant scampered up and down the line of prisoners, whirling the bamboo: 'Snakes! Damme-damme, more snakes!'

'He goes by clockwork and it won't run down,' Atkins said.

'No talks!' The bamboo crashed on Atkins' shoulder, tearing his shirt. 'Snakes!'

'It's a screwy war,' Coltart muttered when the sergeant wasn't looking. 'Digging up worms for a canary.'

'Damme-damme, I order Nippon so'dier shoot you, bang-bang!'

They sweltered for hours, a motley bunch – Smithy the telegraphist, Coltart from a tin mine, Joker from a trading company, Atkins a rubber planter, Weigall and Robbo a pair of junior government clerks, the Australian Doc Davis, only Clive from the navy, with thirty others from

the army and air force and civil life – under the barbaric
sergeant and his squad of soldiers. None of them, prisoners or guards, belonged in that washed-out landscape
– swamps, rice fields, orchards with the sea hidden by
sand dunes and a limp palm fringe – but were brought
there for a trivial episode, a mere detail of world war.

Clive dug next to Doc Davis, sharing a rag of cotton to
wrap their worms in. Quietly he said, 'An animal in a
cage, another in prison – what's the odds?'

'Birds of a feather.'

'You're a captive feeding a captive, Doc,' Clive said.
They came from different ends of the world, keeping
secret pictures of their own and each other's country.

'When I was a free man in Australia – '

'Free to kill.'

'I'd shoot a pigeon and take it back to camp and cook
it.'

'Taking its freedom.'

'Or a wild duck – they'd get them on a river estuary
like this. What d'you say to roast duck?'

'We'll have it tonight,' Clive agreed. He recognised
similar feelings in Doc Davis, to be released only at the
right moment, as carefully as his own.

In the afternoon they were marched back to town,
welcomed by the row of pole-top heads outside the prison,
too puppet-like to have ever been real. Inside they were
paid a few cents for their worms and could buy a coconut,
a handful of shrimps or whitebait, a tin of condensed milk
or pumpkin jam from traders in the yard, to go with the
evening pint of rice; to be shared with men too sick to
work, who got no ration.

At night Clive thought of Captain Ishi's garden in Japan:
clouds and blossom, a willow by a waterfall, a bridge with
girls looking from it at their reflection in a stream, the old
grandmother asleep – all in a birdcage.

Clive didn't need a bird to sing for him, he knew his
place by heart. Sometimes he had to drag it up through
the smell of feet and pus and latrines and fouled cement,
the sleeping noises of a thousand men, the awful close-

ness of the next man's dreams, divided from his own by
the thickness of a ragged shirt or trousers. Often it just
arrived, a truth conjured with no effort, as necessary as
food or water. He must hang on to it for life and sanity.

Jenny had never been to Strathpolly. The war had
clamped down before Clive met her and he never got a
chance to take her there. It was a treasure they would
share when he got back: more than a promise – a consummation. 'When all this is finished,' he told her, squeezing
out his consciousness of Kota Bharu prison, pressing his
fists into the floor through the old rice bag, 'we'll go and
live there – you'll love it.' He told her things he hadn't
had time for when they were together before the *Prince of
Wales* sailed to the East. Strathpolly, where he and his
brother were born, was the darkness he came out of,
brightening as he grew up; expanding round him,
releasing him but never letting go.

It also enclosed the darkness of another, earlier war.
When Clive's and Victor's father had come home after the
armistice in 1918 the house was lit with a bonfire on the
lawn and fireworks streaming from the roof. For children
of three and four the sombre man with a moustache
standing beside their mother, a stranger but said to be
important to them, was eclipsed by the dazzle. Later Clive
began to think it must have been an odd welcome for a
soldier who had just survived four years in the trenches
under mortar and howitzer fire. Perhaps that was why he
stayed in the shadows, not throwing squibs into the
bonfire with his sons or baking potatoes in the embers
like everyone else, but slipping back into the absence he
was supposed to have emerged from. Then, having
haunted the place while he was away fighting and
returned briefly to wander through it – more remote and
impalpable to the boys than when he wasn't there – he
was removed finally by Spanish flu in 1919, taken ill and
buried in a week, to haunt the place again; lingering as
an officer in khaki with a moustache, in a photo by his
widow's bedside, till she died too.

'Damme-damme, snakes no good for sing-bird,' the

sergeant told them. 'No more sing, altogether stop.
Captain Ishi too much angry. He tell me hold cage while
he chop him. Number one sharp sword.' The sergeant
swiped the air with his bamboo. 'Cage fly away, many
pieces. Sing-bird drop down, head off, finish. One chop,
very good shot.'

'All those worms for nothing,' Smithy said. 'Beauties,
some of them – they'd get music out of a rubber duck.'

'Now Captain Ishi very sad from sing-bird dead. Drink
plenty English whisky. Tell me he never go home his
family. Grandmother too much sorry. I tell him all Nippon
very soon go home, Englishmens never. Damme-damme,
Nippon so'dier number one, English so'dier number ten!
Now whisky bottle all finish, Captain Ishi plenty sleep.'

For a month the prisoners collected scrap iron – old
wheels, pumps, rusty bits from garages and factories,
bicycles, barrels, rods and sheets and cylinders, obsolete
machinery, anything – and loaded it on railway trucks to
be shipped to Japan. 'All go make guns tanks bombers
battleships, shoot Englishmens, bang-bang. Very soon
war finish, Nippon go home.' For six months they cleared
the damage done by war and repaired railway lines and
dug irrigation ditches. 'Damme-damme, no work, no rice.'
They did what they were forced to do; were beaten with
bamboos and prodded with bayonets, slapped and
punched and threatened with torture; and were amazed
how strong they were, though undernourished. They
outwitted their guards and stole from them, sometimes
from each other, and at night lay down, filthy, bruised,
bloody, weary and dreading tomorrow.

They also died faster than at first. Death was part of the
pattern, another function for men whose derelict bodies
were an outrage on themselves. The older ones were
alarmed at their speed of withering. The rest, of Clive's
age, couldn't believe this insult to their youth. But apart
from the space it left, a death – the sharp gurgle, the hiss
and silence – could benefit someone else. With Awang's
sandals in ribbons and his own feet septic with blisters,
Clive pulled off a dead man's boot which had been kept
on for fear of theft, in defiance till the end, and found

they fitted. He felt like a vulture picking at a corpse, but the man would have done the same.

In the man's kitbag Clive found a photo of a child, the soft half-smiling face of a boy stuck to a piece of card, creased and fingered. He nearly took it too: an unknown son who would otherwise be lost. The sergeant saw him with it and came hissing over his shoulder, suddenly benign and wistful, thinking it was Clive's. He pulled out a crumpled picture of his own son, a pretty Japanese boy in a sailor suit, and held the two together, then turned the faces to each other and made a long kiss with his lips: 'Damme-damme, all same brothers, love never stop.'

The contradictions were hard to live with: the way a man who was known for savagery could become sentimental in a moment; the mixture of contempt for human life and yearning for a family; the playful switch from cruelty to kindness that must come from some mysterious, ancient whimsicality.

After four years of widowhood Clive's and Victor's mother had been found one evening – a long summer evening of the north – in the Strathpolly river, at the bottom of her favourite pool.

'This afternoon I've got an appointment with a fish,' she told the boys at lunch. She had seen it in the pool that morning: a twenty-pound salmon straight up from the sea, jumping to rid itself of saltwater lice, waiting for more rain to swell the river and let it swim further up to spawn. 'I'll stay there till I get it, till dark if I have to, or by tomorrow it'll be away upstream.'

'If you miss it,' Victor said, 'it'll breed lots more for us to catch.' He was nine years old.

'Act now, your father used to say,' she told them, 'for it's later than you think.'

'Good luck, mum,' Clive said. He was eight, but as big as his brother. 'Salmon for lunch tomorrow.'

Nobody worried when she didn't come back. At supper-time the gillie was sent out to search, muttering that it would have saved trouble if she had taken him fishing with her. She was ten feet down, lying on her back. The river's movement put life into the smile on her white face, tinted by the peat-brown water. There was a gash of blood on one temple. Her hair drifted like weed over the pebbles, her hands waved dreamily up at the gillie. Round her legs the fishing-line was knotted in loops and twists, impossible to untie without a knife. One end of it led to her rod, floating near the rock which she had been standing on; the other to the hooked salmon, still floundering in the shallows of the pool. She must have lost balance while playing it, got tangled in the line, been pulled in, knocked her head, gulped fatally and gone to the bottom, her lungs and waders full of water.

The gillie ran back to the house for help, warning everyone to keep the boys out of the way. They pulled her up with a gaff tied to a pole, laid her on a ladder and carried her home. Next day the gillie went to fetch her rod and fishing-bag. The salmon had worn through the line on a rock, broken it close to the hook and swum away. The boys got chicken for lunch, and were taken to see their mother in her bedroom before the funeral. She only looked asleep.

'She's with your father now,' someone said.

But the officer with a moustache in the photo beside her had never been properly alive, so his death was also unreal. Why should hers be different? The brothers were orphans now, which sounded like a cause for pity but turned out to be more like part of growing up, almost an honour, cancelling the sorrow. To cry would have endangered the mutual courage they needed. Without making any pact they never spoke of their parents to each other, not knowing how far to trust this fragile new maturity; hoping not to give themselves away. And on the river Mum's Pool became a favourite with them too: nothing tragic about it, just a special place for games and picnics. When they started salmon fishing they always hoped to catch a big one with an old hook in its mouth: there would be justice in eating their mother's killer. But as the gillie said, it would soon have rubbed the hook out.

For ten years they were looked after by relations and family friends who took turns to bring them up the way it was thought their father and mother would wish. It wasn't difficult: they decided on their careers by instinct and Strathpolly had its own momentum. They were prisoners of the place, though masters of it. But Victor was a year older, so one day it would be his, which sharpened Clive's passion. As boys they took it as their joint property, a common world left to them equally – childhood itself. As men their feelings separated with their lives. When Victor went to university Clive joined the navy. At the start of war in 1939 he was a gunnery lieutenant of twenty-four and hadn't yet met Jenny.

'You'd never guess it, to look at Victor now,' he said to her in the nauseous cell at Kota Bharu, wondering if he had ever said it to her in London, 'but till we went opposite ways there was nothing between us, hardly a year apart and we did everything together, lessons at home, going to school, ponies and bikes, learning to swim and fish and shoot, the same for both and I thought Strathpolly was just as precious for him, we were neck and neck and the only difference was the bagpipes, I became quite good and Victor gave it up, otherwise we went through the normal things, comparing moustaches and counting pubic hairs, though he was first to wank himself, but I caught him up and soon we were having a race, seeing who came quicker, and I never suspected he didn't look on the place the way I did, except that now I see he was acting half the time, mimicking me, he never loved it, it was useful for a while, somewhere to spend his youth in, that's all, he'd hate to live there, he only goes for weekends with his dubious friends and it's falling down, but we'll get it back from him, he won't mind, he'll be thankful to be rid of it, and put it in order and go walking by the river and vanish into the woods and tear off our clothes and make love on the leaves, Jenny, Jenny, oh God, this fucking floor, no fucking good for love.'

Sometimes in the early months, through the stink of prison, he caught the sexual smell of Jenny in excitement, the strong musk of an animal, more rousing than sight or touch. And in dreams with her he had wild spells of ejaculation, waking in the morning to sticky emptiness and loss and another day of slavery in that inferno, for a few cents and a stomachful of rice.

3

The glib evasive men gave Clive six months' leave after his return to London, with four years' pay to spend.

He stayed in a hotel off Gloucester Road, a pair of big Victorian houses joined and partitioned, owned by a refugee called Heinz whose fingers tapped the desk where he sat in the hall from breakfast to midnight; whose watery eyes reflected a vague bond of shared suffering whenever he saw his guest: 'You see, Mr Ackerly, we are brother victims.'

Clive had a room on the fourth floor which had once been half the nursery, with bars across the window to stop children falling out. The other half, through a thin plaster wall, was occupied by Heinz's daughter, a singer in an opera chorus who practised scales between climaxes of abuse shouted in her loneliness to whichever prima donna had stolen the show, without deserving it, at last night's performance. Along the street the avenue of trees had almost lost its leaves when Clive moved in, in the autumn of 1945. He promised himself that before they grew next spring he would move out.

He didn't want to see Jenny again, he would divorce her. She could pack herself off with Rebecca to join Max in Washington where one day they would be married. Clive had little idea of Max: a general image of any American officer, strongly Nordic or darkly Latin, with rubbery handsomeness and too many medals. He preferred to keep Max in uniform: the picture of him naked was too painful. But he was glad to find that though he was sad, angry, perplexed, sometimes disgusted, he was totally without jealousy.

Restlessness preoccupied him. The habit of walking, adopted on the troopship deck on the voyage home, persisted. He couldn't stay in his hotel room, listening to the singer's scales and rages, waiting for meals; waiting for something to happen, someone to come – knowing he was only waiting for himself. He tramped the London pavements, kicked the soggy park leaves, wandered far into the suburbs, to districts he had never heard of, peopled by English men and women whose lives he couldn't imagine.

Sometimes he took a train into the country, walked all day in any weather through woods and fields and over hills, and took a train back to London in the evening. He sat in theatres and cinemas without much pleasure, tried reading books, drank alone in pubs, slipped into the hotel and up to his room, avoiding more than the briefest talk with Heinz. Next morning he would be out again, walking purposefully through London, unsure what the purpose was.

He went into Selfridges, Harrods, Lillywhites, all the big shops, following the crowd through the departments; and nearly bought a dog, a gold watch, a lawn mower, a double bed, but told the salesman he would think about it and come back tomorrow. He listened to the choir in St Paul's and a catholic mass and several sermons, also a debate in the House of Commons. He sat at the back of a wedding, and joined a funeral that ended in a crematorium, and attended a murder trial. He found himself in Sotheby's, caught up in an auction, and for a few seconds owned a Spode dinner service for sixty people before someone raised the bid. He considered having lessons – Russian, golf, flying, cookery, piano – and instead hired a horse in Richmond Park, and a motorbike which he drove to Canterbury one day. He was looking for something, he knew, but he had lost nothing except four years of life and couldn't think what he hoped to find: only discover the man he was, and strive to become him. But there were no clues, no threads to pick up.

Solitude became habitual but slowly, like the leaves swept into heaps and burnt by park-keepers or washed into gutters and down drains, his sadness and anger were shed, and only the perplexity was left. He was a stranger here, less of a Londoner than Heinz. 'You should buy property,' the refugee told him, 'and you will be content.'

But Clive watched the fingers tapping on the desk, and didn't take the advice.

One winter night, when he felt strong enough to bear it, he tracked down the Chelsea pub where he and Jenny used to drink. Till the last moment he wasn't sure if he dared go in. When he opened the door, crossed to the bar, took a stool and ordered a drink, he felt he was watching something from one of the comedies he had been to. The leading part was called Clive Ackerly. He was an actor playing himself, not performing very well.

'Long time no see,' the landlord said, emphasising the kind of play it was, and Clive nearly walked straight out, but decided to put on a better act.

'Come again?' he asked, catching the idiom.

'Never forget a face. Early in the war, wasn't it? You were often in. Dressed in navy blue, or I'm a Dutchman.'

'Must have been my brother. He lived round here.'

'First time I've been wrong – a near miss, you might say.'

'People couldn't tell us apart, we were mistaken all the time.'

'All right, is he? Give him my best.'

'His luck ran out, he was sent to the Far East.'

The landlord whistled breathily: 'You don't say.' He picked up a glass, began polishing it, whistled again.

'Went down in the *Prince of Wales*.'

'Now that's a. . . .' The landlord held up the glass to a light, blew on it, polished it more, then put it on a shelf. 'I can only say, please accept my sincere. . . .' He picked up another glass. 'My very sincere sympathy. And the girl he had? – a smashing looker, if ever there was. Married, weren't they? Ambulance driver, as I remember.'

This was the cue for Jenny to come in from the wings in her uniform, but she missed it. She would make her entrance somewhere else, another time. Clive said, 'Not to worry. She got over it.'

'Fixed up again, is she? Not the girl to stay a widow long, if you'll pardon me. A real smasher. Give her my very best, if you're in touch.'

Clive drank a lot. Jenny had never felt so close since the day he came back. She was behind him, beside him, all over him – an enveloping Jennyness that he was too drunk to throw off.

'One for the road – have it on me,' the landlord said when he saw Clive button up his coat to leave.

'Happy days!' Clive swallowed it, lurched through the door and was struck by the cold night, the dark vacuum of his life. He would fill it somehow, he was confident. This was the lowest he would go, since the railway, but he must get through the final scene, then start to rise. He crossed the streets, turned the corners automatically, knowing the part by heart, not thinking about it. It was nearly over. The street where they had lived had empty spaces as if pieces of scenery had been removed. Neighbouring houses had been turned inside out by bombs. Theirs was a hole in the ground, lined with weeds. It must have had a direct hit. Jenny had said she was lucky. For a moment Clive wondered about the kitchen, bathroom, bedroom, then stopped himself. The empty space, a hollow where there had once been such repletion, jerked him from the fuzz of drink and aimlessness. He felt glad, to his relief, and went back to the hotel. Heinz, tapping the desk, tried to detain him with a lament for the world's sufferers. His daughter, in the room next to Clive's, was repeating the arias that had been ruined in the opera house tonight by some upstart soprano.

Clive was overtaken by the feeling he had had in Awang's fishing village before Nippon came: of being at the start of some tremendous privilege. This time he would be in charge.

At Christmas he went down to Brighton to stay with his brother Victor in a flat with a high balcony over the seafront.

'Back from the dead!' Victor cried, pumping his hand in an excessive welcome, then pinching and squeezing his arm: 'Make sure you're not a ghost – can't be too careful.' Through the window the sea came rolling out of a mist against the promenade. 'Meet Brenda!' Victor clapped and there she was, in a puff of silver hair and mauve satin, wobbling inside her clothes, perched on high heels. She

tripped a step or two towards Clive, offered him a set of
fuchsia fingernails, opened her enormous lips and said,
'Howdy?' watching Victor for his approval. Both of them
were nervous.

The flat was furnished with things from Strathpolly –
dining chairs, carpets, ornaments, Victorian pieces that
Clive remembered. Only Brenda was new, more suitable
for a Brighton flat than a house in Scotland, unless she
was a species of salmon that Victor had caught and was
enjoying, fresh and wet and plump. She would look good
on a bed of lettuce, garnished with cucumber and
radishes, smothered in mayonnaise. With a flip and a
totter and a couple of gasps she produced a bottle of
champagne.

'Brenda's got friends in high places,' Victor said.

'Low ones, he means,' she said, 'like wine cellars.'
Under the make-up she blushed to a genuine deep pink
and picked a hair, or a fish scale, from the shining bosom.

'Quite handy, these austerity days.' Victor poured the
champagne. 'Nothing like bubbles to raise the tone.
Well. . . .' He clinked glasses: 'Here's to your resurrection
– may it last for ever!'

Clive picked up an easy relationship with his brother
and liked Brenda at once: not the silly toy she looked, but
an adoring lover who delighted in her own succulence
and the pleasure it gave Victor. Their happiness spilled
through the flat and saved Christmas from the awkwardness that Clive had feared. The champagne hardly
stopped, or the laughter.

'Pity about the old place,' Victor said that evening.
'Riddled with holes by the time the army finished. Slates
off, ceilings fallen in, doors broken up for firewood, half
the trees cut down – no way out, it had to go. If you'd
been around – '

'Didn't they pay up?'

'Compensation of a sort. Wouldn't begin to cover the
damage. Clean up the fishing, mend the fences, one thing
and another. . . . Besides, I needed the money.'

'Who bought it?'

'Shipbuilder from Glasgow. Nice enough. Made a killing

out of landing craft in the war. Said it was just the job. Promised to restore it to its former whatnot.'

'You kept some of it, anyway.' Clive looked round the room. From a velvet chair Brenda exuded contentment. In sequined shirt and iridescent trousers she was more like a lovely fish than ever, in ripe condition, asking to be filleted. All she lacked was fins.

'Fact is,' Victor said, 'it became a bit of a bad dream. You can't go snoring on for ever with a thing like that, you have to wake up one day and shake yourself into life. If you're lucky you do it with Brenda.'

She turned pink again, glistening with juice and love, and said, 'I'm lucky too.' The kiss she blew was followed by a stream of liquid laughter.

Slowly over the next two days Clive found that Victor had paid off his debts with the money he got from Strathpolly and was now a property dealer, trading in small hotels, shops, flats, doing well out of the postwar market. Servicemen were being demobilised, civilian life was starting up again, thousands of people wanted to live in Brighton. Without much skill or energy Victor could earn a stylish life with Brenda.

On Clive's last morning Victor gave him a present – his old fishing-rod: 'Saved it from the wreck, I can't think why. No use to me. Never imagined you'd be back. And there's another thing – you say you lost your bagpipes.'

'Neptune's got them,' Brenda said. 'He's playing to the mermaids.'

'You'd better have mine, you're welcome,' Victor said. 'I was never any good.' He got them out – the tartan bag, polished drones and tassels. 'Give them a blow for old time's sake.'

Clive hadn't played since the *Prince of Wales* was crossing the equator. On the deck of a battleship the noise was lost among raucous sailors, drifting into the midday heat. Here, overlooking the Brighton seafront, the flat exploded with the hum and screech and wail.

When it stopped Brenda said, 'I can't help thinking of the mermaids in kilts.' She let loose a laugh of bubbles, floating and bouncing off the walls, a happy end to Christmas, and Clive went back to his room in Heinz's hotel with a fishing-rod and bagpipes.

4

Early in 1943, a year after Clive was captured, the Europeans in Kota Bharu prison were told they were being moved to a land of abundance where they would live in rest camps up in the hills till the end of the war. The sick would go too: the climate was better there. They were given aluminium mugs and mess-tins, water bottles, spoons and knives, before being marched out of the gate, past the lollipop heads – 'one of them's winking at me,' Smithy said – and loaded into a train, thirty men in each steel wagon with their precious bags and boxes. There was room to squat cross-legged or with knees drawn up, but not to lie down. A guard with a gun sat in the half-open door, his legs hanging out.

'Tip the bastard out, easy as anything,' young Weigall said, as they lumbered northwards into Thailand.

His friend Robbo agreed: 'When it's dark.'

'Say he went to sleep and must have fallen.'

'Quickest way to the grave,' Coltart, the engineer from a tin mine, told them. 'You've got a ticket to a holiday camp – why spoil it now?'

'He doesn't like it here,' Atkins, the rubber planter, said, 'any more than we do.'

'You think he's human too?'

The railway noises, the lurch and groan and hoot, started boyish thoughts in Clive who snatched any twinge of vitality from the evidence round him of men grown thin, taut, brown, older than they were. They trailed through forests of extravagant green and flaming red, along beaches of gold, past tranquil villages. A white pagoda flashed on a hill, a swarm of children rushed out of school to wave. But the wagons were ovens with a hot breath from the door by day and ice boxes with a cold blast at night. For hours they stood in sidings, to swelter or shiver in airlessness. Skin ran with sweat or turned to gooseflesh, backs scorched or froze against the steel walls, tongues thickened. Men with bladders or bowels to empty crawled over the others, hoping to reach the door in time, and soon the outside was as foul as the inside.

Once a day they halted for a wodge of rice from a bucket with a spoon of curry soup and a cup of dirty water. Anyone who couldn't walk down the track stayed hungry. Doc Davis and Clive got the driver to draw off water from the engine, good for a wash but oily for drinking though safely boiled. When he saw it a soldier came crashing at them with his rifle – a Japanese flag tied to his bayonet, a sun hat on top of his helmet, puttees on his dwarf legs – and knocked them over in a sprawl of grease and cinders.

'We got it wrong, it's why they beat us,' Doc Davis said, limping back to the wagon. 'We mistook the joke for the real thing.'

'I'll get my hands on the throat of one of them,' Weigall muttered.

Coltart said, 'Don't be bloody silly.'

'D'you believe in these rest camps, Doc?' Robbo asked.

'I believe in a future beyond them where things like compassion and grace haven't been lost.'

'And imagination,' Clive said. It was what he fed on.

The sea receded from the railway, the forest shrank into small plantations, then endless rice fields. Buffers clanked and brakes screamed, not for a food halt but to unload the prisoners at Banpong, where they were counted three times by a corporal and a fourth by a sergeant. Nobody had died or jumped off, though they were less like men than when they started.

For a week they were held in a barbed wire compound near the station without shelter from sun or rain. Nights under the stars, with the gasp of steam engines like sleeping animals and sometimes a temple bell, were a blessing. Trains came in each day with prisoners from Singapore, Sumatra, Borneo, Java – thousands of men who had been promised something healthier than the jails and barracks and requisitioned cinemas where they had lived since capture.

The Thai people, too timid at first to take notice of this herd of Europeans, began signalling through the wire and holding up bananas, grapefruit, boiled eggs, vital food for men frightened by their diet. Fountain pens and army badges, spare shirts, old postcards of Big Ben or Sydney harbour bridge, a treasured penknife or a packet of French letters saved from a man's last leave and unlikely to be needed, even identity discs and paybooks – for name and pay had no value now – were traded for a few vitamins.

'They'll buy any sodding thing you've got,' Smithy said. 'I'd flog my crucifixion if I could get it off – what's left after the bambooings it's had.' It was tattooed in blue and pink across his back, the whole of Calvary in a frame of snakes that twined and tapered to the base of his spine where a pair of nudes, dancing on his buttocks, waved a banner with the word 'Mother'.

Clive only had his watch, Jenny's wedding present which he had offered to anyone in Awang's village who could lead him to Singapore. He shut his eyes to kiss it and passed it through the wire, telling himself she wouldn't mind. In exchange, from a shaven-headed monk who pulled a brass begging pot out of his yellow robes, he got a clutch of paper money. The monk put the watch on his thin smooth wrist, gave it another kiss and squeaked with happiness. Now Clive was stripped of everything he had had when the *Prince of Wales* was sunk: a final reduction of himself, a simple purity which he found he liked. He owned only his ragged clothes and an empty rice bag. With one of the monk's notes he bought six green oranges and a piece of mouldy Bombay duck.

In gangs they were loaded into lorries and driven in convoy through flat country laid out with rice fields, thinly spiked with trees. An armed patrol car travelled behind each lorry. Fine white dust was spun by the wheels into a cloud to blind and suffocate the men, rolling their sweat into a dirty paste. The usual rainstorm didn't come that day.

The Thai driver of Clive's gang wore a mask. He had worked for a foreign engineering company and told them, in muffled English through the gauze, that a railway was to be laid over the mountains into Burma two hundred and fifty miles away. Before the war his company had surveyed the line, finding that the six years' job would cost too many lives. Now Nippon wanted it for the Burma campaign, before an advance into India. It was to be built by European prisoners and Asian labourers from the occupied countries, and finished in a year.

'Holy Christ!' Atkins whistled. 'They can't be serious.'

Late in the day they were delivered at a camp, its huts and inmates emerging into focus as the convoy's dust drifted away.

'Holiday camp! Take a look at that!'

Clive caught an impression, before it vanished in the sudden evening gloom, of a primitive settlement of bamboo and leaf, a litter-deep farmyard neglected by everyone except the scraggy creatures, once human, probably Indian, who stood twitching and pecking in the filth like a flock of poultry. It gave off a smell of dung.

'All mens number!'

The gangs were lined up and counted, then led away from the camp to a big river. Covered barges were moored to the bank: pots cooking on wood fires, brown children waiting for food. Some prisoners waded into the water, thick as cocoa with monsoon sediment, but were driven out by screaming guards. They were ferried to the far side in crescent sampans paddled by delicate black-trousered boat-girls standing at the stern, a vision of aching impossibility to the starved men, and by the time the last of them were across it was night.

'All mens march!'

On empty stomachs, engrained with dirt, they made ten miles the first night, stumbling in a ragged column along a track that might lead in the end to Burma or Assam or China – nobody cared. They tripped and fell, swore, tried singing, even praying, and plodded on. Some were given oil lamps to carry, and after midnight a half moon came through the cloud to put faint shapes into the dark: a stream to be forded, a causeway across a patch of open country, a broken lorry with a cigarette glowing suddenly behind the windscreen to show the driver's face under a veil of mosquitoes. Guards marched at the front and rear of each gang, setting the pace and goading stragglers. Every hour a whistle was blown for a five-minute halt, a sanctuary in time till the whistle went again; then the pain of standing up, lifting a pack, pushing a foot one step further along the track, dragging up the other. By dawn they were hobbling into a village, dropping to the ground among chickens, dogs, babies under the houses – under the unfriendly village eyes. Later a lorry brought an army field kitchen with rice and onion water.

'Come and get it, for God's sake!' Doc Davis urged, stirring bodies from their exhaustion. 'Or tonight's march will be your last.'

Some had fever, others dysentery. Nippon had captured huge stocks of drugs, but released nothing for the prisoners. The weakest was Joker who would have to be carried, and a bamboo stretcher was made. Before sunset the men were allowed down to the river – pale figures splashing in the golden landscape. Barges piled with rice or straw were pulled upstream by stuttering motor tugs, and rafts of teak logs came floating down from the forests. Clive saw how beautiful the country could be, without the agony.

Two hours after dark the whistle was blown, and the men were lined up. 'All mens number! All mens march!'

They picked up Joker and stumbled into the night, up into the hills, behind the guards. The track followed the valley, the line the railway would take, cutting through forest or traversing a steep ravine with the river far below or crossing barren stretches where only clumps of bamboo grew and the moon glanced off harsh white rocks. The moon grew bigger each night and cast a magic incandescence, also a satanic curse, on the journey. In London, Clive suddenly thought, it was called a bomber's moon.

Before joining the ambulance service Jenny had had a job in the furniture department of Peter Jones, and a flat at the top of a house in Chelsea where she took Clive not long after they had met in the spring of 1940.

'Race you into bed!' She pulled off her clothes and got

there first, with fewer buttons to undo. 'Sorry about the size,' she apologised, naked on the sheets.

'What's wrong with it?' he asked, kissing one delicious breast and squeezing the other. 'They're pretty perfect, if you ask me.'

She laughed: 'Wouldn't you prefer them enormous – something to wallow in?'

He kissed the other: 'Exactly to my taste.'

'Actually,' she stretched the length of him, 'I meant the size of bed.'

He wasn't put off: 'It fits, doesn't it?'

'In the trade it's called a gentleman's occasional double.'

'Room for a close friend?'

'Sometimes.'

'At a pinch.' He had a nipple between two fingers.

'It was going at half price to the staff – an old demonstration model.'

'Demonstrate for me.'

She bounced on the mattress: 'For trying out by customers in the shop.'

'In the nude like this?' Clive pressed her to stop.

'The springing's rather dented.'

'By occasional doubling?'

'Something tells me it'll be more often now.'

'What kind of something?'

'One like this.' Her hand was on it.

He was astonished at his luck, also at his love. At moments through the night he tried to remember how it had grown: a gathering of incidents, messages, experiences – the news of Dunkirk, the fall of France, the toppling of Chamberlain by Churchill – till this became more than a need, almost a consequence of war.

'When did it all begin?' he asked.

'When's it going to end, is what I want to know,' she said, running her fingers downwards from his navel, slipping him into her again.

'Why should it ever?'

'You'll be posted to Fiji or somewhere, the China station, a gunboat up the Yangtze, you'll find a millionairess with a ranch or a diamond mine or an oil well or something, with a smell like a goat and teeth to go with it and tits out to here.' She showed him, then pulled him further in.

'And a beard and horns.'

'But you won't notice, you'll fall for her money, you'll never do anything like this with her, you'll forget you ever made love with me in a gentleman's occasional – '

'Shut up, Jenny.'

'You can't get out of it by giving commands – I'm not one of your ordinary seamen.'

'You're not ordinary at all.'

'Say when! Or you'll be drowned before – '

'Coming . . .'

Later Clive said, 'A life of surprises, it would be, with you.'

'Nice ones, I hope.'

'Lovely, so far.' She had the softest grey eyes he had seen.

Clive's blistered feet, oozing and poisoned, were rubbed to the limit by the boots he had taken from the dead man. He bandaged them with strips of sacking but each uneven footstep along the track, tilted by a stone or root, doubled the pain. He tried counting, watching the heels of the man in front, placing his feet in the same spot, wishing he could stop counting but tied by his steps to the tens and hundreds even when he didn't give them numbers, passing a thousand, approaching another thousand, losing count at last, losing sight of the other man's heels.

He drifted to the end of the gang, where the guard clouted him with his gun. Clive dodged it and fell off the track into the edge of the forest. The guard kicked and yelled, Clive retreated further, the guard lifted his gun to aim and Clive raised his hands. 'For Christ's sake!' he shouted, not wanting to give Nippon a victory though not believing in his own death. 'I'll change the bandages and catch you up, it won't take long and there'll be another gang coming behind, I can join them, you needn't worry, you needn't shoot, you godforsaken . . .' He made gestures to the squinting man, who fired once at the full moon over the trees before loping away in pursuit of the gang.

Clive hobbled to a rut just inside the forest, where a lorry must once have driven off the track. A few inches of rainwater in it caught the moon. He had seen men drink from these puddles and double up with cramp. He sat down, took off his boots and bandages, peeling away skin and pus with them, and soaked his feet in the cold dark liquor: surely no harm to the blisters which had grown like crimson socks from toe to shin.

Something fell beside him and he looked up into the trees. Monkeys were stalking along the branches, shadows across the stars. 'Hello, up there!' he called. Jenny hated monkeys but she wasn't here. A soft chattering came down with a bunch of leaves. For a tiny moment, the first in a year, Clive was free. The monkeys rescued him from captivity. He felt a link with them, and a rush of gratitude. On this appalling journey, counting footsteps from one hell to another, there was hope.

He got more sacking from his rice bag, tore it into strips, wrapped them gently round his feet; then reached for the monkeys' leaves and stuffed some for padding in his boots. He put them on and tied them and slowly stood up, testing the pain. It was eased a little by the water and fresh bandages and leaves. He looked up again.

Suddenly they weren't monkeys any more. Three men were watching him, neither prisoners nor guards but people of the forest, hunched in shawls. One of them jumped for his neck like a dog and flung him back on the ground, snarling at his throat. The others hovered over his feet. He saw a blade slip from under a shawl. They hardly spoke, they were expert at this: feeling for a watch or money belt, opening his mouth to look for gold teeth, going through his pockets and rice bag. Then two of them snatched his arms, the third his legs, and he saw the blade again, curved in a man's hand, as they dragged him further off the track.

A whistle pierced the night, sharper than a knife. The monkeys scampered away over the trees, dropping more leaves. Clive bellowed, a noise he hadn't made since he was a boy playing with his brother Victor at Strathpolly,

and the men let go and were gone. On the track he saw
the lamps of the next gang gathering for a halt. He would
go back to them and explain.

A bullet cracking in his ear, then the bang, was the
first gunfire he had heard since Nippon came to Awang's
fishing village, the day he was captured. Before the next
shot he was running the other way, to catch his own
gang. The pain in his feet was nothing to his fear and he
swore at the moon for shining on him, picking him out
in the night, but no more bullets came. At dawn he
reached his friends as they were trailing into a camp. It
was like coming home.

Everyone had been getting married that summer, three
years ago, with Hitler across the Channel and a sense of
desperation over London, poised for the blitz and then
invasion. Clive and Jenny bought a Woolworth's ring and
lined up at Chelsea registry office, asking the couple
behind them to be witnesses. Clive was twenty-five, on
leave awaiting a new ship. Jenny was twenty, having left
Peter Jones and volunteered to drive an ambulance.

'You must teach me to double-declutch,' she said that
night.

'In a gentleman's occasional double? There's nothing
you can learn from me, Mrs Ackerly.'

'The registrar called me Jennifer – did you notice? I
didn't recognise myself. But it sounds more like a wife.
I'll try to live up to it.'

'Shall I call you Jennifer?'

'I'll keep it for my second husband.'

'Over my dead body.'

'It's hardly that yet – too full of life, darling.'

'You seem to cope. But perhaps we should get a bigger
bed.'

'After the war. I like the – '

'Propinquity?'

'That sounds fun – let's try.'

After the war he would take her for a honeymoon to
Strathpolly. It was shut up now but Victor, who had found
a job in the War Office, had offered it to the army: better

to have it occupied, and if they knocked it about he would be paid for the damage. The fish anyway wouldn't be disturbed. A week after their marriage Clive was posted as gunnery officer to the *Prince of Wales*, a new battleship being built. She and her four sisters, claimed as unsinkable, were meant to reassure the English public and strike the enemy with fear. 'A slight anachronism these days,' he told Jenny, 'but rather splendid.'

'Sounds like an old prima donna hoping for a comeback.'

'I'm very proud of her.'

'Sorry, darling – are we speaking of the woman you love?'

In the winter, with a lull in the blitz and the *Prince of Wales* not ready for active service, they escaped for a few days to a lonely Welsh pub. The mountains weren't as majestic as the Strathpolly ones, but far enough from air raids and dockyards for the war to be unreal. In a blizzard the rocks grew a coat of silver feathers. On a frozen lake the birds slithered in surprise.

'One day we'll vanish off the map up there and forget everything except us,' Clive promised.

'First you've got an appointment with the *Prince of Wales* – remember? To win the war. It might be years.'

'I'll take my bagpipes and play on the quarterdeck, going into battle.'

'That'll scare the Germans.'

The ship was completed in a hurry, and without proper sea trials she was sent out with the old battlecruiser *Hood* to intercept the *Bismarck*. Through bad tactics and jammed mechanism half her big guns couldn't reach the target, but the German fire was deadly. She had to swerve to avoid the wreckage of the *Hood* which blew up and sank, and broke away under smoke after only twenty minutes' fight to bury the dead and bring home the wounded. Clive's guns had never fired.

'Don't worry, darling,' Jenny said. 'A virginity can be very troublesome – I was just lucky.'

The prisoners weren't told where they were going or how

far it was: probably the guards didn't know either. Every fourth day was a rest day with no marching. Once they stopped at a temple and were sold bottles of coloured drinks, green and red and yellow, by the monks.

'It's a seller's market,' Atkins said. 'Half a dollar to paint your guts like a rainbow.'

'It'll give the bugs inside a thrill,' Joker said, weakly from his stretcher. He was obsessed with disease, which he had transformed from a cause of death into something worth living for. He almost wanted to be very ill, to stand at the edge and not go over.

'It's holy stuff, it might turn them into good little Buddhists who wouldn't do you any harm,' Coltart said.

Usually they lay at camps built by men who had come up ahead – veterans who had cleared their adopted patch of Thailand and felt threatened by these novices passing through. 'Told you about the rest camps, did they, same as us?' a man in bits of air force uniform asked, implying that talking to them was a favour. From deep in his skull the eyes watched for signs of danger, dodging everywhere. The teeth looked huge in his shrunken face. A pale violet stain showed under his skin as if the airman's cap had been rained on and the dye had run. His voice was flattened by weariness or ill health or pessimism. 'You'll learn the score soon enough. Three weeks we've been here and already buried seventeen. But you may be lucky further up.' He lifted the sharp point of his chin towards the mountains, suggesting that things could only be worse up there, and shuffled off with his thin resentful bones.

'Shake him and he'd rattle.'

'Miserable sod.'

'You get them at home like that, if you're unlucky.'

'Only difference – they die quicker here.'

'I know when I'm not welcome.'

'Sit tight and wait for the end of the war, is the message.'

'And hold your breath at the sight of strangers, in case of germs.'

'You'd think they'd like a natter with us.'

'They're jealous because we're not as miserable as they are.'

'What gets me – they look so lonely. I'd understand if they were locked in separate cells.'

'They've lost respect.'

'They despise themselves probably.'

'Watch out, boys – three weeks and we'll be the same.'

A man with crinkled greying hair, dignified and quiet and older than the rest, sat alone on the ground against a hut. A wisp of humour flecked his face like an old joke that needn't be repeated, it was too well known. His shorts were pulled down to his ankles and between his thighs lay a testicle, swollen to a football, which he nursed gently with both hands. A tube led from it into a bowl.

'Jesus – what's that, Doc?' Smithy asked after they had passed.

'Beriberi, I'd say.'

'Any hope?'

'Drain the fluid's about all you can do, but when it reaches the balls . . .'

In a rainstorm, when the track became a channel of mud, Joker on his stretcher could be hauled along the surface, skimming like a toboggan. The men cursed him for groaning – 'You want us to leave you to the snakes and tigers?' – and Clive saw how they were losing their unselfishness. The mud pulled at their feet, the rain was soaked up by their clothes. In disgust, to ease the weight, they threw away pieces of kit they had saved till now. Spare shirts, books, photos, letters from home were dropped along the way. Clive had nothing to jettison.

They marched from one half-moon to the next. Doc Davis had no drugs for Joker, but as they climbed into the hills his groans became gentler: the fever brought its own painkiller. At night, taking turns on the stretcher, the men tried not to hate him for the extra load. At daytime stops, though he couldn't eat and hardly spoke, they saw a pale satisfaction in his eyes. 'Looks as if he's getting more fun from this than anyone.'

At dawn on the sixteenth day they reached the end.

'All mens halt!'

There was no camp for them, only a tilting shelf of trees

and boulders on the valley side, with a bluff of rock above it and the big brown river below. To the west the purple mountains rose over the forest. Nobody was sure – nobody had a map – but they must have come a hundred and fifty miles. Having marched at night they had little idea what they had been through. This exotic site, beautiful in the early morning – a silky mist clearing from the trees, a warmth already touching the air, a cackle of parrots somewhere – could only be reached by their track or by river. It was remote from any world they knew, too strange and incomparable to be convincing; too false, after years of war, for them to believe in. Though they were in Thailand, the mountains might be in Burma and the river might rise in Tibet or China. This was nowhere, a mythical country beyond reality, part of the infinite limbo they had inhabited since being captured.

'Look at the view! – you'd never guess you were in prison.'

'All mens number!'

One man couldn't. A moment of disbelief filled the silence when he should have called his number. Then the guards screamed – a danger warning to the men, a signal to show who ruled the forest. Nobody moved, but disbelief vanished and for another moment turned to anger: this was the depth of thoughtlessness – to let them carry him through the night and all the time be dead. The guards closed in on the stretcher, poked at Joker's legs with rifle butts to stir him back to life, and screamed again, first at his papery grey face, then at the men. Within an hour someone had found a glade near the site and they had dug a grave, buried the body and said a prayer. It became a pattern: the exasperation, the brief sorrow, the stark little ritual in the loveliest cemetery anyone had seen.

Lorries came up the track with tools, supplies, more guards; also the new camp commandant. It was Captain Ishi, the well-tailored young officer in olive breeches whose grandmother had once given him a singing bird in a cage; who had killed it with his sword for not singing, and then got drunk on captured whisky.

He stood that evening on the tailboard of a lorry with the men mustered in front, and made a speech:

'Gentleman, the Emperor is pleased that you have come so far to work for him.' The American accent explained his unreality and fitted the illusion: they were all taking part in a spectacular Hollywood movie, filmed on location in this outlandish place. Captain Ishi was an actor of uncanny power. 'I regret that the rice is not more plentiful, but in war we should not complain. We are sharing a task of great importance. The Emperor has called for a glorious effort. There will be much hard work, but we shall do it willingly, whatever the suffering.' He was supercilious, deferential, cruel, polite, yet he was none of them. He liked to tease, giving a hint of some human quality that another man could recognise, then quickly cancelling it. He was either mad or the one chance of sanity here. 'This morning one man died and I am confident there will be more. I regret that also, but our lives are nothing to the Emperor. His orders accord with the laws of humanity and will be obeyed. You are his prisoners and will salute his servants with a bow, and in the morning you will face the Rising Sun and bow. If you try to escape, you will be shot.' The lenses of his dark eyes, scanning the men without seeming to see them, found Clive; settled on him for an instant, absorbing him into whatever they concealed before moving on. 'Some of you are my friends already, and all of you soon will be. Gentlemen, I believe we shall understand each other. When we have finished the railway the Emperor will be proud of us. Now we have one week to build a camp.'

They slashed at matted creepers, felled the trees, rolled away the rocks. Huge poles were hacked from bamboo clumps and brought to the site on men's shoulders, springing with life and spiked with thorns. Raw timber was sawn and adzed into a double row of huts under the remaining trees, with a cookhouse, hospital, guardroom. Each hut, a bamboo frame with a low roof of palm thatch tied down with vines to make a long tent without walls, would hold a hundred and fifty men. None of them had built anything like it – none of them had been prisoners before – but somehow it was done.

The thatch came by river on barges, to be carried up a steep path that turned to a mud-chute, another torture in

the trembling heat. Sacks of rice were also manhandled
from the river; and drums of water, before a channel of
hollow bamboos could be piped from a forest stream. Pits
for latrines were sunk through roots and stones deep into
the red earth. A network of drains was dug to remove
stagnant water. Wasps' nests were destroyed, anthills
chopped down, snakes and scorpions hunted, baboons
abused with the loathing that nobody dared hurl at the
guards. Bonfires consumed the rubbish, their smoke
smudging the yellow lace of the forest and drifting to
the purple mountains. Inside the huts, on a platform of
bamboo slats raised above the earth, each man had a strip
as narrow as a coffin – his cell, the limit of his privacy.

Fresh parties arrived till there were three thousand in
the camp. And an endless column of humanity, a frieze
of sorrow, slogged past on the way to camps further up
the line. Most were Asians, hobbling towards the mountains with their abject women and children. Many were
prisoners of war. Clive searched them as they trailed in
line through the forest: there might be a friend, another
survivor from the *Prince of Wales* who had been captured
later. But there never was.

'Being married, I feel so innocent,' Jenny had once said,
though Clive wasn't sure where. In his memory, in his
prison hut in Thailand, they had hardly talked except in
bed. 'Before, I was old and wise and cynical. It takes a
husband to wipe it all away.'

'I didn't mean to,' Clive said. 'I like your past – what I
know of it. It's more surprising than mine.'

'Now I'm a girl again, all fragile. You could crumple me
like a leaf. Stamp on me. Blow me away. Do you feel it
too?'

'The opposite.'

'You were pure before you married me? And now you're
contaminated?'

'Don't get me wrong,' he said. 'I'm more complete than
I was. And solid. But I feel a danger somewhere. Of the
unknown, mostly. Like a child, yes – frightened of the
dark. Though with you I'm safe.'

'You're an explorer? Discovering yourself? Or me?'
'Both. It'll be fun together. We might find anything.'
'Not much, darling. We're very ordinary. A married couple like the others.'
'But bewildered. It's happened so quickly.'
'The best way. No time for questions.'
'I still ask them.'
'Such as?'
'What do we hope for?'
'Can't we be idealistic without ideals? They're so grey.'
'The colour of your eyes. Grey as a donkey. I love them.'
'A donkey? Thanks.'
'It's a pleasure.'
'Making love? My favourite.'
'Or a pleasure dome – an edifice we build together.'
'It needs a man and woman, that's all.'
He kissed her eyelids: 'Grey pebbles on the beach, polished in the surf.'
'The tide goes down and they're stranded like a million others, dry and dull.'
He kissed her eyelids, trying to make them real; pressed his mouth into his own bruised knuckles, crying for her tears which never came, licking the salt of his own sweat. The bamboo slats under him cracked and squeaked, a whisper lost in the song of tropical insects and the intermittent noises of men's sleep.

5

With the fishing-rod and bagpipes, a few months after Victor had given them to him at Brighton, Clive landed as an immigrant in Sydney. It was 1946, and he had very little else.

At the end of his leave he had been interviewed at the admiralty by an officer who had become a captain during the war in a job ashore. 'Well, Ackerly,' the captain said, straightening his papers, looking at his watch. 'Been

shaking down, have you? We don't want to waste more
time.' He had a long list of appointments before lunch.

'I'd like to get back to sea,' Clive said. 'After nearly five
years – '

'Back to sea,' the captain repeated, trying to think when
he had last been there. 'They say it's still all round us and
I'll take their word. Myself, I trust never to put a toe in it
again. What I can tell you is, the ships in it aren't the
same. A battleship's a dinosaur nowadays, er – let me
see . . .' He looked at his papers to check Clive's name.
'We'd be putting them in museums if we didn't need the
scrap, Ackerly.'

'I'd be happy in a small ship, sir – frigate, destroyer,
almost anything, anywhere.' Clive knew instantly that he
must get away. A steward brought in a cup of tea for the
captain.

'You'd have to go on a course. Be retrained. To put it
bluntly – getting sunk, you missed more than just
promotion.' The captain reached for the sugar spoon as if
the gold rings on his sleeve, twice as many as Clive's,
were heavy to lift. 'You know what I'm talking about?' he
asked doubtfully. 'You think you could catch up?'

'Radar, you mean, sir?' It was a new invention when
Clive was in the *Prince of Wales*, though it hadn't saved
her.

'More than that, I'm happy to say.' The happiness
didn't show. 'The navy's not the one you were in. It took
a war to drag us up to date. Cut off our pigtails, abolish
sails . . .' The captain gave a pale smile: he would make
the same joke many times today. 'There'd be a lot to learn.
The future's in electronics, that kind of thing – we've got
some clever stuff to play with.' But he found the subject
as distasteful as the sea; stirred his tea and wiped his
fingers on a handkerchief. 'Knots and splices aren't
enough these days, er – Ackerly.' He tested the name
carefully, like his tea, to make sure it was right.

'I'm not too old.' Clive looked round the office: he could
never work in a place like this. And suddenly he had a
vision of himself on his knees after being captured in
Awang's fishing village, a sword at his throat. At least the
Japanese colonel hadn't forgotten his name.

'It's not for me to put the blame – '

'Thirty-one next month.'

'But some men find it all too much after going through what you . . .' Stopping in mid-sentence, the captain left a hint that Clive had been careless to be taken prisoner.

'I could cope, sir, I think, I'm sure – '

'I don't say they're incompetent, but often they find it easier to start from scratch in something new. They ask their friends – you have the odd one or two? Or they shop around. Or buy an atlas and turn the pages to see what's what and where and . . . I don't suggest the navy doesn't care. In fact we have a scheme.' He sipped his tea, picked up a paper, handed it to Clive. 'There's no compulsion, I needn't tell you, but it's worth a thought. You might care to read it through. Sleep on it. Consult the little wife. You have . . . ?' The captain raised one eyebrow over the teacup, keeping the other on his watch. 'Let me know in a day or two. No sense in drifting. We don't want to hang around.'

Clive was in the street, disgusted for having wilted so fast. Ten minutes ago he had wanted to go back to sea, now he wanted to leave the navy. He would jump ashore before they threw him, rather than get swept with the bureaucratic tide and watch Clive Ackerly make a fool of himself on other men's terms – men like that captain. 'Knots and splices aren't enough' rang through the London traffic. They were telling him what to do, controlling his life, offering him a lump sum for retirement without a pension.

'Take the money,' Heinz advised, tapping the desk in his hotel, gratified that Clive hadn't gone straight up to his room. 'Or the socialists will take it for you.'

'Socialists?'

'Your government. They take it, they throw it away. It's funny. Last year they took power. Now look – they throw away your famous British Empire. They say India must be given to the Indians. Soon it will be Africa. They say it's modern. I say it's rotten. So I tell you, take the money and buy property. Always it's best.'

Up in his room, with the singer's scales through the wall and London through the window, reminding him too sharply of Jenny and the life he had dreamed of, Clive saw no choice. Everything was alien and uncomfortable. He should have stayed on the railway. 'Knots and splices aren't enough, Ackerly.' If he needed retraining he would have it somewhere else. Australia was the best place. Doc Davis may have planted the idea, but Clive didn't hope for help there, only the emptiness ahead and his ability to fill it. Australia was asking for British immigrants to balance the refugees from the rest of Europe. He could get an assisted passage and sail back the way he had come, with nobody to meet him at the other end: no danger of another Waterloo. In London the leaves were returning to the trees. He would put the world between him and Jenny again.

'I've seen them bring in fishing-rods before,' the customs man at Sydney said, 'but never bagpipes.'

'Bagpipes!' someone shouted. 'Let's have a tune!'

It was different from the platform at Waterloo: this bright morning on the Sydney quayside with the ship unloading passengers and cargo. People stumbled down the gangway and into the customs shed, to wait for their baggage from the hold. Clive strolled up and down among cranes and bollards, boxes, trolleys, patient nervous immigrants – piping for the future, for hope and sunshine and for himself: the triumphant peace that came from surviving the railway and the great sadness of his return to Jenny.

'I thought I was going crazy,' a man called Frazer said later, in a harbour pub. He had approached Clive on the quayside and held out a sinewy freckled hand: freckles on his cheerful face too, under a wide felt hat. Clive saw that this was what he had crossed the world for: a straight welcome, fresh and appreciative. The bagpipes had served well. 'I had the office window open,' Frazer said. 'I could smell the haggis, never mind the heather. It's not every day in Sydney . . .' He whistled one of Clive's tunes, badly, and they both laughed. 'You'd better come and have an Australian beer – you've got to start somewhere.' He ran a small shipping line from a building on the waterfront. 'In fact you'd better come and work for me, Mr Ackerly – caught and bowled first ball.'

'I'll look around,' Clive told him cautiously, though he liked the cricket metaphor.

'Pardon the blunt approach – it's the local habit.'

'Take my time.'

'Got something fixed? I'm not surprised, a man like you – just what this country wants, not these Poles, Balts, Wops. You'd never catch a Wop with bagpipes.'

'Give myself a month or two.'

'Forget it,' Frazer said. 'You're in luck, I don't mind telling you.'

'Get back to sea, perhaps. I'd sink behind a desk.'

'All the sea you want in Frazer's. Half the Pacific Ocean pinned up on the office wall. Put your finger on Fiji, Samoa, the New Hebs, the Solomons, anywhere you fancy and shut your eyes . . .' Frazer's little fleet of cargo boats had most of the island trade. 'Or look out of the window and you've got the finest bloody harbour in the world.'

'I'm just passing through, really.'

'Passing through?'

'I'll move on somewhere, probably.'

'Have another beer.'

'I only landed this morning.'

'Landed on your feet, I'd say.'

'I can afford . . .' But Clive knew he was surrendering to this amiable persuasion.

'Look at the alternatives,' Frazer said. 'You've got sheep and sheep, and sheep and wool, and sheep and . . . You've got nothing to lose, only sheep.'

'When do you want an answer?' It would do for a time, before moving on, and Clive admired Frazer's direct manner.

'Before you get to the bottom of that beer.'

'I could always . . .' He thought of the captain who had interviewed him at the admiralty, and his opinion of Frazer went higher.

'Give it a go, Clive – I'll call you Clive. Get yourself a bed tonight and start at eight o'clock in the morning. Now drink it down and have another.'

Clive felt touched by the benevolence of Australia. He

couldn't share it yet, he was too busy salvaging his life to
give much time to the city he had arrived in, he could
only let it treat him to its gifts. But generosity was infec-
tious, and in time he would bestow his own. And the
novelty, the stranger's wariness, the sense of merely
passing through, helped him to stay apart. Unlike
London, Sydney contained nothing to forget or cherish;
no old contacts to pick up or avoid. He found a flat in
Manly, across the harbour, and watched himself – as
he watched the people on the ferry every day, going to
work and back – with curiosity and even optimism.
There were possibilities here: of work, of friends, perhaps
of love.

'The silent service never had a better man,' Frazer said,
with mild irritation but approval, when Clive had been in
the office for several months.

'It's the way I like it,' Clive told him, giving away more
than usual. Modesty wrapped a mist round his past.
Everyone in Sydney was noisy but he preferred to keep
quiet, though it meant being aloof and unsociable. He
didn't deny he had been in the navy, sunk in the *Prince
of Wales*, taken prisoner by the Japanese. Captivity, the
ordeal he must have been through, was an excuse for
reticence. Nobody could complain that he left gaps,
seeming happy to let people fill them for themselves.

He was very happy. The office was friendly, the job
interesting enough. Flags on the wall chart showed the
position of Frazer's ships across the Pacific. At first Clive
thought of studying for a master mariner's ticket: he knew
the work already, he would soon get command of his own
ship. Later he found he liked being Frazer's assistant, part
of another man's livelihood till he saw where to make his
own. If this was retraining, it was less painful than the
captain at the admiralty had suggested. And knots
and splices weren't needed. Frazer liked it too: having
a British naval officer who knew what the captains
were talking about and talked back in a perfect English
accent.

Usually there were one or two ships in harbour and
Clive would go aboard for a drink, to listen to problems,
requests, stories. It was a one-way dialogue. When busi-

ness was over he took the ferry home; cooked supper, read a book, slept alone. He didn't care for the raucous city, he had no objection to his own company after the dense humanity of the railway. It had taught him all about close living, the ceaseless exposure of men together, and he didn't want to try again. When he spent an evening in Frazer's home, or someone else's from the office, he showed delight in other people's successes – marriage, children, sport, hobbies – without envying them. Sometimes he asked them back for huge feasts of sausages and baked potatoes, pineapples and beer, always ending with the bagpipes. Though he ate and drank and laughed as much as anyone, he kept his faultless status: splendidly hospitable during the party, mysteriously single at the end.

Three or four times a year he wrote to Victor, and got letters back from Brighton that read like pages from the local paper, full of property prices, the weather, the iniquities of the socialist government, the trial run of a play before opening in London. There was always a message from Brenda in coloured ink, sending love and kisses in curious globular handwriting that conveyed her satisfaction and repleteness. Clive could see the bursting happiness she shared with his brother, and hear the champagne froth.

In his second summer in Australia he bought a small boat which he sailed at weekends into the remote harbours of New South Wales: camping in lonely places, cooking and lying awake in the warm nights, sometimes joined by ghosts from the railway that often, too crudely jogged his memory. He was building a kind of life again, he thought at first he could escape. Later, when he found it was impossible, he wasn't sorry. These were his friends: not just the men he had known, but bright visions of an occasion, sharp recurrences of a thought or feeling that had once been important. He couldn't lose or banish them. The past was in the present – as inextractable as the salt in the sea, the wind in the dark gum trees, the spit and crackle in the camp fire – and would be repeated in the future, to nudge him intermittently all his life.

*

'Dearest Clive . . .'

This wasn't Brenda's handwriting. He looked down the page, feeling gratitude, then greed, then anger. It was the letter from Jenny that had never reached him on the railway. It had caught up too late. Since the war they had communicated only through solicitors. This was a violation, an insult. The thing that he had longed for, that would have lit the darkness, was now unnecessary. He didn't want it.

Then he looked at the date at the top: 1949, written last month in Washington DC. His eye slipped over the pages. Names of unknown people, someone else's news, irrelevant facts made familiar and agonising by Jenny's handwriting . . . Waterloo four years ago . . . horrendous last meeting . . . in such a muddle at the time . . . the American foreign service . . . now promoted to consul . . . Rebecca growing up . . . school . . . forgiveness . . . next three years . . . love as always . . . in haste – the words came like shrapnel out of an envelope, too scattered to defend himself against. He hated the effect it had on him, the old sores it rubbed, the lust it stirred. He started reading slowly from the beginning: 'Dearest Clive . . .'

Max had been appointed to the American consulate in Sydney, the family would live there for at least three years. They would arrive in time for Christmas: 'Fancy! – roast turkey at midsummer.' Rebecca was now six, looking forward to meeting her mother's first husband. She had been told all about him. 'We're older, Clive. Can't we try to look at our lives from a distance? Perhaps forgiveness is a lot to ask, but we could show understanding. Living in the same city, we might find the friendship we never had before. Let's face it, it was never a marriage, was it? Just a lovely honeymoon.'

She might be saying more than lay in the words, more than a warning that they were sure to meet, but Clive couldn't see what it was. He took it as a threat. Australia wasn't big enough for them all. He asked Frazer to be transferred.

'Too crowded in Sydney?' Frazer teased him, annoyed

at losing his English assistant. 'Too many Australians – is
that it? You can't take the accent? Or the beer?'

'I've been here long enough, I'd like a change. One of
the branch offices . . .' Clive looked at the chart on the
office wall. Any of the islands would do.

A week later Frazer told him he could be manager at
Tulagi, capital of the Mendana Islands: 'Outpost of the
empire, arsehole of the Pacific – call it what you like. On
the way to nowhere. Three ships a month. You won't be
overworked. Or troubled by the crowds. A few of your
own kind, that's all. Nobody'll catch up with you at
Tulagi.'

It sounded promising. Clive would feel safe there and
could breathe again, without risk of shocks like this. Four
years ago an electric cable had been cut, but the raw end
was still alive.

Part Four

The Islands

1

Tulagi was stranded between sea and mountain, pressed in by forest like another of the war relics littering the Mendana coasts, a formless mix of shabby Nissen huts and rusting metal and unfinished concrete, holed, cracked, aged by the climate. It marked two desperate years of battle that had turned back the Japanese; marked them with a hint of fatigue and boredom.

In the little port the hot blast of copra scent, spiced with diesel oil and cement, was only drowned after a rainstorm by drifting forest vapours. Behind the warehouses, beyond the market and haphazard Chinese stores, an avenue of flame trees – King George Avenue, or simply KG – led half a mile to the government secretariat, a group of huts trimmed by paths of dead white coral and brilliant flower beds. There a messenger dozed, a typist dabbed talcum on her prickly heat, a colonial officer initialled a memorandum for the London mail and wished he could go with it.

Along KG, between gaps that had been robbed from nature but never gathered into the imperial scene, were the post office, bank, hospital, court house, police station and the Tulagi hotel. Each lay among gaudy shrubs, striving for dignity in these awful tropics, achieving only vanity, harmless but too fragile to be convincing. The smallest building was the museum, a reconstruction of a chief's house with a war canoe and a display of head-dresses, scalps and beautifully woven penis sheaths to show the darkness from which the islands had been saved. Next to it was St George's Cathedral, a big open-sided thatched barn, full of hymns on Sunday, with a mission school and the bishop's house behind. To the Mendanan islanders the George of the cathedral and the George of the avenue, saint and king, were the same man.

The Mendanans lived in shacks on the empty lots, or

in a shanty settlement beyond the port, or in villages at the edge of the forest. The Chinese lived close to their shops and warehouses. The British had cleared a ridge of the foothills for an estate of bungalows, in three sizes according to rank and salary, that breathed complacency with a whiff of racialism. At the foot of the ridge was the club with swimming pool, tennis court and golf course, closed to anyone who wasn't white. At the top was Government House, the home of power but less temple than suburban villa, in an English garden planted by a previous governor's wife.

Along the coast, past a huge copra plantation where coconut trees marched in line for miles – so much soap and margarine – was the prison, a small version of the one at Kota Bharu. In a future revolution Clive could see the row of poles outside, with the morning's crop of British heads. Beyond it was the little airport, scene of the bitterest fighting. It had been built by the Japanese invaders, captured and lost and recaptured by the Americans, and given after the war to the British. The runway, the islanders believed, was laid on a bed of bones.

Clive's office near the port was rented from a Chinese. There was little work unless a Frazer ship was in. Weighing and costing and storing cargo, drawing up bills of lading, writing to shippers, telegraphing to Sydney, visiting the bank – the routine started at eight in the morning and was often finished by midday. Clive also ran a small import business and opened an insurance agency. But he hardly needed the two Chinese clerks or the English secretary, wife of the government fishery officer, or the half-caste driver, son of a New Zealand nurse and her mission boy lover. With a few Mendanan porters in the warehouse he could have handled it all himself.

For two years he lived in the Tulagi hotel. He could have joined his countrymen on the ridge, as a resident in the club or lodger of one of the British wives who offered him a guest-room, but he liked the unrefined air down on KG and cared for none of the wives. The hotel was dilapidated, the staff dishonest but cheerful, the bar haunted by the more raffish colonials and sometimes a stranger, a passenger off a cargo ship, a banana tourist washed ashore who talked of escaping or writing or beach-combing, and lost coherence as the drink went down.

Clive didn't want to escape or write or beachcomb. He took to reading. Having got through the club library he sent to Frazer for books from Sydney, and between ship-ments he borrowed from the mission behind St George's Cathedral. He read the early navigators who discovered these islands – whose full-rigged ships, the Mendanans said, could still be seen in the billowing clouds that sailed from one horizon to the other – and the traders who came for sandalwood or slaves, and the missionaries and rulers who followed, and the ethnologists who picked apart the islanders' secrets, and the novelists who wove them back into their fantasy. Slowly he saw that he would spend his life here.

Two years after Clive came to the Mendanas – soon after he had opened up his office one morning – Jimmy Dundas was hauled out of Tulagi harbour in his blood-stained pyjamas.

Clive heard shrieks and a peculiar howl, scarcely human, and sent one of the Chinese clerks to find out what was going on. Jimmy was a weathered old pirate who wore pyjamas at all times, though he put a monkey jacket on top when he went ashore. He had left Edinburgh as a boy and never gone back in fifty years. For the last thirty he had sailed his schooner *Catriona* through the islands, trading and drinking, earning everyone's impatience with his unreliability, also their helpless affec-tion. Nobody knew if he acted the caricature, or was truly what he looked. They were only certain that he had no enemies, and the *Catriona* was welcome in any harbour.

Alongside the Tulagi quay to unload a cargo of copra from another island, having breakfast in his cabin – two poached eggs and a glass of gin – Jimmy was told that a rope had been caught round the propeller when they berthed last night. Any of the crew could have freed it, but sometimes the old Scot liked to show he was still a seaman, as good as the rest of them. He swallowed one of the eggs and all the gin, went on deck in pyjamas and his famous straw hat – bristling with porpoise teeth, a present from a missionary who had saved it from being given to his wife, knowing the erotic meaning of a porpoise – and lowered himself over the stern. Slipping into the water he passed the straw hat up to the coxswain, Laki, who put it on his own head. The crew laughed and took the end of the fouled rope, ready to pull when it was free.

'When I wave,' Jimmy said before swimming down to the propeller, 'tell the engineer to run the engine slow ahead.'

They peered through the surface which glinted with the morning sun, shaken by his movements, and saw him wave. 'Slow ahead!' Laki shouted, and the big diesel throbbed.

Suddenly there was a shriek from the crew. The rope tore from their hands, ripped over the side, into the water. In three seconds it was over. The engineer had gone astern. When the propeller stopped, a cloud of blood floated up. Laki and others dived straight in, and swam down to their skipper. His head was nearly severed by the propeller. They got him up, along to the end of the quay, out on to the beach. He was lying there in his pyjamas when Clive was told about it by his clerk and ran from the office. Laki, in Jimmy's straw hat, was howling with grief. Jimmy's second poached egg was still warm on the cabin table.

A week after the funeral the *Catriona* was put up for sale by the creditors. Eighty feet long and as old as Jimmy Dundas, she had been built as a North Pacific halibut schooner, later converted from fishing to island trading: a raised deck forward over the fo'c'sle, a long well over the hold, another raised deck at the stern for the wheelhouse, galley and cabin. Both masts were rigged with cargo booms. Two plywood hutches by the foremast were for the coxswain and supercargo. The crew lived down in the fo'c'sle, dark and stuffy, smelling of Mendanan bodies. The hottest place was the engine room, aft of the hold. The cabin was as airy as possible for the tropics. But the copper sheathing had been torn from the hull on reefs, the timbers were worm-eaten, the deck leaked where the caulking had been neglected, the booms and gaffs hung from rotten rigging, the masts needed scraping and varnishing, the sails repairing, the engine overhauling, the whole ship painting. The hold was dirty and damp. Rats lived in the bilges, cockroaches ran everywhere.

By now Clive knew he wasn't merely passing through the Mendanas, as he had been in Australia. But if he was to spend his life here he would make it nobody else's. At the auction for the *Catriona* in the hotel bar he was the only bidder, remembering the time he nearly bought a Spode dinner service at Sotheby's, and got her for eight hundred dollars, good will included, no liabilities accepted. Jimmy Dundas's popularity was worth more than his creditors believed, and the auctioneer – son of a drunken half-caste whore and some unknown sailor, who had rejected both alcohol and the sea for a steady job ashore – suggested that Jimmy's kindly ghost would never leave the ship. Through the hotel window Laki, the coxswain, raised the old skipper's straw hat and cheered. Clive was pleased too. He gave the repair job to a Chinese boatyard, resigned his job with Frazer's, and a month later flew to England. It was seven years since he had left.

'Churchill's back in the saddle,' Victor said when he went down to Brighton. 'Things are looking up, just see.' Brenda was a little plumper than before. She dabbed at Clive with soft fingers and kissed him, leaving a cool wet patch on his cheek. He thought she was nicer than his brother. 'Why've you come?' Victor asked.

Clive wondered: not to hear about property prices, anyway. 'I don't want to lose touch. Go native, file my teeth, put a stick through my nose, that sort of thing – it's not for me.'

'Do they wear grass skirts?' Brenda asked. Her own was sea-green with a metallic shine, as if threaded with wire to hold in the flesh. The champagne bottle looked unsafe in those flipperish hands. 'Or nothing at all?'

'Sea captains aren't supposed to know,' Clive said. 'It's bad for the crew.'

'Will you grow a beard? And be tattooed with sea horses? – they're very sexy.'

'Slave trade – is that it?' Victor asked. 'Blackbirding? Fancy! – my own brother.'

'Shark's fins! For Chinese soup – I love it.' Brenda smoothed her stomach with her free hand.

'Copra, mostly,' Clive told them, 'from small plantations that the regular coasters don't visit. And mother-of-pearl, maybe. The odd crocodile skin.'

'I can't believe it – it's so romantic . . .' Brenda's voice dissolved in moisture.

'And general trading – tobacco, medicine, anything that's wanted.'

'You'll keep the native crew?' Victor asked. 'Be careful they don't eat you. I can see it in the Brighton paper – "Local man's brother cooked for supper." '

'It'll make a change,' Brenda said. 'The recipes they give! – you want to *puke*.' The word came out between a squeak and a gasp.

In London for a fortnight, sitting in theatres, visiting galleries, feeling thankful for his own anachronism, with a twitch of sadness, Clive wondered why he was here. Perhaps to reassure himself that he was right to settle in the Mendanas; to go back without regret; to take with him, not anything of this unfamiliar London but some samples of what had once seemed valuable, knowing they were absurd and liking them for it. He opened an account at Fortnum and Mason for a supply of marmalade and English biscuits to be sent out, and at Gieves the naval tailors in Bond Street, and Aspreys the jewellers next door, and Heywood Hill the bookshop in Curzon Street. He ordered a monthly shipment from a St James's wine merchant. He was fitted for shoes in Jermyn Street – nothing ready-made had been comfortable since Goldilocks smashed his toes – and arranged for a new pair once a year. Finally he bought all the admiralty charts of the Mendana Islands and a stock of white shorts for the *Catriona*'s crew, and flew back to Tulagi.

Laki and his boys were waiting. The schooner was repaired, bright with paint and polish. Clive would keep a room at the hotel as base for his trading business, but live on board.

*

Laki was father or uncle of most of the crew, and vener-
ated by them all. They were saltwater boys from villages
along the coastal fringes of the Mendanas, hardly out of
canoes since they were born, having suckled and played
and fished and voyaged in them and often made love.
Laki was a big brown giant like a sea god, in Jimmy
Dundas's straw hat and new white shorts strapped round
his enormous waist with the belt and brass buckle, bought
in a Chinese store, of the City of Glasgow fire brigade.
The tip of his nose had once been pierced for a shell
ornament, but he liked to keep a spare fish hook in the
hole, reminding Clive of the Strathpolly gillie who stuck
salmon flies in his tweed cap. Laki had been on the
Catriona for years, a priceless coxswain who knew every
island passage and channel without need of charts, who
had a way with rope and canvas that Clive envied, who
could keep an old diesel going after an orthodox mechanic
would have given up and condemned it. He swam underwater longer than anyone; caught fish when nobody else
could find them; thought nothing of paddling a canoe a
hundred miles across the sea in any weather to visit his
wife.

One man on board wasn't a saltwater boy. The supercargo was a small, nimble, pitch-black bush boy called
Beaconsfield: not his tribal name but one he had taken
from a brand of cigarettes with a picture of Disraeli on
the packet which he admired. The bush boys considered
themselves an ancient aristocracy, descended from chiefs
who had fled from the coast when white men first arrived
in the Mendanas and led their people into the forest to
preserve the purity of their blood from corruption, while
the saltwater boys had become tainted. The feud between
them would have rumbled more dangerously on the
Catriona if Beaconsfield hadn't been the only bush boy.
But he was shrewd, he knew his weapons, he was in no
hurry.

With or without old Jimmy Dundas's good will, or his
ghost on board, the *Catriona*'s return was hailed by
isolated planters – European and Mendanan and every
mixture – also by missions and villages off the track of
bigger ships. And this was a new *Catriona*, turning up

when she promised, bringing the goods that were wanted,
not waiting a week in harbour while the copra rotted on
the jetty because the skipper was too drunk to load up
and sail away. Clive's style was different, and soon his
schooner was seen in every anchorage of the archipelago,
trim and pretty, the hatch battened down and at sunset
the skipper playing his bagpipes up and down the deck
– 'Westering home' or 'The Lament for Maclean of
Ardgoar' – to the joy of his crew and the islanders ashore,
knowing that at first light she would weigh anchor and
be off.

She picked up what cargo she could find: copra in the
hold, teak logs on deck, or a bag of areca nuts or trochus
shells or *bêche-de-mer*, the green sea slug relished by
Chinese, or a passenger – a government officer,
missionary or gang of plantation workers returning to
their home island. One end of the hold became a shop
where Beaconsfield sold axes and crockery and frying pans
and calico, hurricane lamps and tinned meat, aspirin,
soap, fishing lines and mouth organs, peroxide for
bleaching black hair, Tiger Balm for impotence. It was
known that on the *Catriona* a good price would be paid
for woven mats or model canoes, and malaria or tubercu-
losis or whooping cough would be dosed, and the skipper
could be persuaded to bring coloured beads or Jew's harps
next time. With regular sailings and honest trade Clive
became rich, revelling in life and the beauty round him.

Some islands were bigger than Corsica or Long Island,
sweltering under a coat of vegetation, lifting it in ancient
humps and untrodden ridges – untrodden because there
were no paths and nobody to tread them anyway. Thick
mangroves lined the shores, standing on their infinite
stalks – nature's special torture, a device for shipwrecked
sailors. Behind grew trees: no land visible, only trees,
though there must be something solid for them to put their
roots in. Blanketed with trees, the big volcanic mountains
lifted the forest to the clouds. Clive could see them at the
beginning of the world when they were all exploding.

Other islands were a mere clump of trees growing on
the water, a patch of greenery afloat in a ring of bright
surf. There were even submarine islands, Laki said, that

had never emerged: not yet fished out of the sea, but sometimes seen swimming down there in the translucent water, waiting to be caught. Any day one of them might come boiling and steaming up into the sun, breaking surface like a hooked shark – a new island already planted with trees and inhabited by its own spirits; a new roosting-place for the terrible flying witches.

Unless the colours were cracked by waves or dazzle Clive could tell shallow water by the change from blue to green, but he knew the dangers and left the ship to his coxswain, freeing himself to watch and wonder. In a narrow channel Laki would stand up on the fo'c'sle – the whole voyage borne on his huge brown shoulders, the sun flashing in his Glasgow fireman's buckle, a fish hook in his nose – and signal to the boy at the wheel: a whisper or flick of a wrist, no more. In the open sea he sailed by wind and smell and a sense of rightness, the gift of an old pilot, when the *Catriona* was on course. Even on a thick night he could do without stars to navigate, though he knew Orion's belt, which he called the war canoe, and the Southern Cross, four men letting down a net for fish, and the Pleiades, the tangle of girls, and Mars, the red pig. Sometimes, when sea and sky were stirred into a wild stew of elements, the crew stripped naked on deck to soap and rinse themselves in the downpour, and Clive joined them. Sometimes, after a windless day, the sun dropped into a sea so smooth and metallic that he felt it should clang like a gong as it hit the rim.

This wasn't revenge on Jenny: revenge, like jealousy, was no sentiment for a man who was never mean. Yet often, sailing among those astonishing islands, he did feel a kind of sublime victory.

Beaconsfield, the small bush boy, supercargo of the schooner, dark as a half-burnt stick and no use as a seaman, kept apart from the saltwater crew who laughed at his clumsiness in a canoe. He worked close to Clive, happy to be trusted with the cargo and trading, and with the white man's friendship. Clive gave it easily: his evaluation of human life had grown and modified as he got older, as if symptoms of the bitter railway years, like malaria, were returning more benignly. They sat at the cabin table with a bottle from the St James's wine merchant, going over the books, working out prices, discovering each other's past.

Beaconsfield's ancestors had been cannibals. After work one day, rummaging in his childhood for something to please Clive, he said, 'Once when I am piccaninny they give me little-little bits cooked on hot stones by the fire,' and shyly watched for the effect.

Clive asked, 'Bits of what?'

'Is covered with leaves and sweet like pig, but I don't eat much of it because I am too full.' Beaconsfield's English was precise and usually correct, though always in the present tense: for him the past and future, when put into words, were occurring now.

Another time, sharing a precious but shameful memory, he spoke of the gongs that were banged and the bullroarers that were whirled to drown the screams when it was his turn, with other boys who were ready, for initiation: 'My father is planting a new garden of yams in the forest and when they are ripe they are made into puddings with bananas and cooked all night, and a house for boys is built by the village dance ground where we are living alone with our husbands.'

'Husbands!'

'You can say uncles, because every boy is having an uncle to show us things we don't know.'

'To make love with you?'

'Mr Clive, we are nothing before that, nothing-nothing, because we are like a woman and we must be given power of a man to make our prick grow strong, which comes down from our ancestors, by stroking and rubbing.'

'Did you like it?'

'Is the way they do it, to pass the power into us.'

'How old were you, Beaconsfield?'

'Just a boy, and in early morning they are taking us to the river and covering our eyes and filling mouths with leaves to chew . . .' Beaconsfield hesitated.

'To stop the pain?'

'They tell us not to shake and cry while they are cutting

us with a sharp bamboo, and after it we can see what it is, and they wash it for us in the river and squeeze some juice on it from a tree and tie it in a leaf, and we go back to the village with the gongs and bullroarers, and they are killing a pig and dancing, but I don't dance because I am too sore.'

'And now you were a man?'

'We are living thirty days in house for boys, and they are teaching us to play the magic flutes which women must not look at, and beating us with branches and playing jokes on us.'

'Jokes?' Clive filled their glasses from the bottle.

'They tell us that the ghost of a great-great warrior is coming back, and one night we hear him whistling in the roof but we don't see him, and they bring a lamp and we see him sliding down the pole, and he stamps and kicks and tries to catch us and rushes out of the house into the dark, but we know it is man with banana leaves all over him and red flowers and wild ginger.'

'Funny joke.'

'And one night they call us out of house when there is no moon and no stars, and we know they are dancing because we hear them singing and stamping on the ground but we don't see them, and suddenly we see them shining in the dark, but is only their pricks which are grown so big and nothing else, and they disappear again, but still we hear them dancing towards us, and we see them again, only the big-big pricks waving like giants in the night, and they disappear again, each time dancing closer and appearing and disappearing to frighten us, and they are singing louder and coming closer and bigger, and they are on us and beating us and shouting and stinging us with their big-big – '

'How did they do it?'

'They are rolling some long leaves together which are used for puddings and tying them on like pricks for a giant, and rubbing it with mushroom juice from the forest.'

'Which shines in the dark?'

'Yes, Mr Clive, and they come dancing backwards to us so we don't see the front, and twisting round so we see it, and twisting again so we don't, and they say the ghosts of our ancestors are bringing it to us and we must touch it and pull it to make it lift and wobble, and if I scream too much my father must pay one pig.'

'And after that?'

Beaconsfield laughed: 'I am free for women, any I want.'

His father had sent him out of the forest to join his elder brother at a mission school. They were a clever pair. The brother had gone on to the high school in Tulagi, then to college in Australia and had been ordained a priest, one of the first bush boys in cassock and surplice: the starched collar gripping his black neck and the light of astonishment in his bulging eyes. But Beaconsfield's schooldays had been stopped by the war. In his second year the Japanese reached the Mendanas, coming down the islands in landing craft, their bayonets hailing the Rising Sun. The British government escaped without a battle, but a few men – officials, planters, traders, missionaries – stayed behind in hiding to report on the enemy by radio: the coastwatchers, who knew that to be caught was to be beheaded.

From the mission school Beaconsfield watched a dogfight between Japanese and American fighters, diving like eagles among the towering clouds: it looked such fun up there. Next day Japanese soldiers pitched tents on the football ground, machine-gunned the church, plundered the garden, raped the nuns and shot the pigs. Before he could be forced to work for them, without going home to tell his father, Beaconsfield slipped into the forest and after three days' travel he found an Englishman in a leaf hut with a supply of food and whisky, also a kerosene refrigerator and a Shakespeare.

His first job, while the white man practised pistol-shooting at cockatoos, was to hide the radio mast with vines. The rest of his childhood, till the end of the war, was spent carrying messages, learning forest tracks, avoiding Japanese patrols, spying. For six months he lived up a banyan tree, off wild fruit and sometimes a bird, with a pair of old binoculars and a conch shell to blow if he saw the enemy. At Christmas, when the Englishman thought it safe to have a party with another coastwatcher

from the far side of the mountain, Beaconsfield led them
and their teams of forest runners to a waterfall where they
all bathed and feasted on bush turkey, and afterwards
played cricket.

The little bush boy liked these curious white men who
valued his skill without asking too much about his beliefs.
He told them that the bush turkey's scarlet feathers were
the best for head-dresses; that its enormous claws were
for digging long tunnels where it laid its eggs, which were
delicious scrambled; that one village would present a bush
turkey to another village as a token of perpetual friendship
and there would never be war between them, but it didn't
happen often because nobody wanted peace for ever; and
that a bush turkey skulked through the forest and barked
like a dog. He didn't tell them that at night it cried with
a human voice; or that it tunnelled underground, down
towards the heat of the earth which caused volcanoes,
because it was the guardian ghost – nobody knew whether
man or woman – who barred the way into the land of the
dead; or that there was a secret society who could turn
themselves into bush turkeys for evil purposes, and a
favourite trick was to copulate with a victim's wife, who
couldn't resist the scarlet feathers, so her husband quickly
died of jealousy; or that a bush turkey, if you saw one
watching you in the act of adultery, was the woman's
husband in disguise and you could expect death within a
week, or that a baby bush boy had once been hatched
from a bush turkey's egg, and he had seduced a saltwater
woman whose husband had sworn vengeance on all bush
boys; or that bush turkeys generally were birds of ill omen,
spirits of the newly dead, and to eat one, even at Christmas, was more dangerous than to eat your brother, even
if he was a Christian priest.

The Americans drove the Japanese out of the Mendanas,
the British came back to rule their colony. To many islanders it was no good. The Americans had paid better
wages, had been generous with their canteen food, had
shown that a white soldier could be ordered by a black
sergeant. On one island a prophet announced that the
British wouldn't last much longer and soon a fleet of
Liberty ships would sail over the horizon carrying the

ghosts of the ancestors, who would now be white, with
a cargo of guns, ice cream, tinned peaches, chewing gum,
jeeps – all the goods that everyone desired: goods, the
prophet said, manufactured by the ancestors as gifts for
their descendants, but always snatched by white men for
themselves. He set up a rival government, drilled his
police with dummy rifles, occupied a hut full of old newspapers in imitation of a white man's office, and sat with
his friends in their best clothes at a dinner table laid out
with flowers in Coca-Cola bottles, waiting to entertain the
returning ancestors who were coming with the food.

The cult caught on. Jetties for the ships and storehouses
for the cargo were built. All would be provided, but only
to people who showed faith by doing nothing for themselves. Gardens must be abandoned, pigs killed for feasts
of welcome, stocks of food eaten up, money thrown away.
The fleet was on its way, some said from America, others
from Jerusalem. Fires were lit along the coast to guide it,
and the singing and dancing went on. Ships' engines were
heard one night, and the rattle of anchor chains. Next
morning nobody minded when the sea was empty: the
British were up to their old tricks. But the ancestors would
conquer them in the end. Though there might be earth-
quakes and floods, and the islands might be turned upside
down in the sea, a reign of eternal bliss was at hand,
when nobody need ever work again and everyone would
shed their black skins for white ones.

Beaconsfield was doubtful. Perhaps he had other
beliefs, older and darker than the prophet's. His brother,
the priest, said he should either follow him into the Christian church or go home to their village in the forest.
Instead he found a job with a Chinese trader dealing in
scrap metal and army surplus. 'I am staying to watch what
happens,' he told Clive eight years later in the *Catriona*'s
cabin, with a glass of whisky in his hand.

'And the Liberty ships never came,' Clive said, 'and the
jetties and storehouses fell down, and you've still got the
British Empire.'

Beaconsfield laughed: 'And prophet is still in prison.'
The Chinese trader had made a fortune from old trucks
and guns, huts, wire and equipment left by the war. Later,

when he started a restaurant, Beaconsfield worked as assistant cook. One night after a fight the police found opium hidden in a mahjong set, and the Chinese hanged himself. Beaconsfield was scavenging in the port, picking over empty tins and bottles under the wharf, when the manager of the Tulagi hotel heard of it and gave him a job, first in the kitchen, then in the office, lastly in the bar where Jimmy Dundas saw him. On his schooner Jimmy had had many supercargoes, all half-castes who had cheated him. A single bush boy might stay honest from fear of the saltwater boys, hoping for the skipper's protection. This one looked clever, tidy, not too civilised. Before getting drunk, buttoning up the monkey jacket over his pyjamas for the ceremony, Jimmy signed him on at his barman's wages with commission on trading.

Beaconsfield was as frightened of the sea as of the saltwater boys; frightened too of going back to his father one day. He had left home as a child, he could put off returning till it was time to get a wife. As supercargo of the *Catriona* he made money and a name, after one disastrous voyage, for saving Jimmy Dundas from worse losses. Laki was suspicious of his wily bush boy's ways, but saw that without him the schooner would never go to sea, and reassured the crew. Beaconsfield, though staying silent, was glad that the saltwater boys and not himself were involved in Jimmy's death. And Clive, when he bought the *Catriona*, was glad to keep him.

2

At the end of a week – with the forest noises and aromas banished by the muttering of three thousand prisoners' labour and the stink of their excrement, with bugs and lice established in the huts, with maggots turning into blowflies everywhere, with Doc's hospital filling up and two more deaths from malaria and the cemetery growing among the trees – work began on the railway. The camp had a section to build to link with its neighbours up and down the line; to level the track, slice cuttings through the hills, raise embankments over the valleys, put bridges across ravines. It would be hell in dry weather, and worse when the rains began.

'Unless you work,' Captain Ishi told the men, 'you're no use to the Emperor and you won't be fed.'

They were paid ten cents a day for a quota of work marked out by the guards each morning. Fail to finish it, and they weren't paid; finish early, and next day the quota was bigger. A third of their pay went to a fund for the sick who earned nothing, and the rest to the barge people trading on the river. An onion or a bit of dried pork made a heap of rice acceptable. One duck's egg a day might save a man's life. But often the egg had been in the sun for weeks, in the rice field where it was laid and on the barge journey up river. It was black inside or exploded in a burst of gas, driving men out of a hut till it was buried, safe from vermin. Even a fresh egg, fried in coconut oil in a mess-tin, was a risk. Unless the yolk was broken it would be kicked by Nippon into the forest, its owner too, for insulting the flag – a blasphemy on the Rising Sun.

Clothes soon rotted or were torn to pieces. The last rags were stitched into a pair of shorts or whittled down to a jockstrap through the crutch, tied with string. Boots fell apart, straw hats were bought from traders, turning the prisoners into authentic coolies. Their skin became brown, dry, grained, stretched over the bones. In a few weeks they had the ageless look of a lifetime toiling in the sun.

The guards of Clive's gang were led by two corporals, the Turd and Goldilocks. The Turd was dark, pock-marked, very strong, with a hint of some ancient sadness in his massive drooping shoulders. He prowled, his arms hanging in front, or sat nearly motionless, flicking his trigger, sometimes turning slowly to fix a different prisoner in his narrow eyes. 'I can tell when the Turd's looking at me,' Smithy said, 'by the two wires that bore into my back and come out through my chest.'

'It's your crucifixion that fascinates him, it's a torture he hasn't tried.'

Goldilocks was smaller and as yellow as possible, an

ugly sulphur. To make up for his size his eyeballs were enlarged behind thick glasses and his scream was the loudest of all. At first he was taken as a joke. 'He's a reject from a puppet factory,' Smithy said, 'who got thrown out when they found he was alive.' By the end of a week on the railway they saw that he was as dangerous as the Turd. In the midday break he fired at a monkey, wounding it, then bayoneted it to death, skinned and cooked it, and shared it with the other guards. Next day he poured paraffin on a dog that came into the camp, and set it alight.

Some prisoners' feet hardened well and they could work barefoot. Clive's were blistered, cracked, swollen and septic from thorns, with running sores that climbed his legs and grew a crust of flies. The bandages he made with leaves were torn off by undergrowth. 'The Emperor understands,' Captain Ishi announced, 'that his servants must have healthy feet.' A bale of rubber-soled canvas boots was released from the store – all one size, a dollar a pair. They fitted Clive and his feet improved. Lieutenant Ackerly of the *Prince of Wales* was now a slave in nothing but a straw hat, a jockstrap made from his naval shirt and a pair of Japanese canvas boots.

Captain Ishi remained the perfect film star commandant, always in clean uniform with the same impenetrable air. He never inspected the work on the railway, though he appeared at morning and evening parades to harangue the prisoners on their duty to the Emperor. His cabin, between the guardroom and the cookhouse, acquired a sanctity – the temple of imperial power in which he rang a melodious priestly bell at any time of day or night, to call a messenger from the guardroom. Sometimes he sat in a wicker chair on the little veranda, among potted flowers, and twitched his beautiful moustache or stabbed at insects with the point of a cane. After dark, with his radio turned up for everyone to hear, he listened to propaganda in English from Tokyo or occasionally a Wagner opera: the music of the Rhine beside this mysterious Asian river; of Teuton gods in a tropical forest. It was his only music since killing his singing bird, the gift of his grandmother.

*

'I still don't know much about you,' Clive had said to Jenny on their first wedding anniversary in the summer of 1941. They went to one of the night clubs that had opened again after the worst of the blitz, and came back to bed in the Chelsea flat.

'After a year,' Jenny said, 'wouldn't it be awful to know each other inside out? Those couples who have nothing more to find out except what it's like when one of them dies and the other's left.'

'You'll be the one who's left. And I shan't be around to watch you. I'll never know what you're like without me.'

'Who was I before you met me?'

'Who are you when I'm not there?'

'Perhaps you don't care to find out too much. It's too complicated. You stick to the simple thing, like this,' she took his cock, 'but it's as far as you want to get inside.'

'Can't you take me beyond? Show me the mysteries?'

'You're suspicious. Perhaps because your mother died – the woman who created you and let you down. You don't want to be caught again.'

'I'm fascinated. Go on.'

'Fascinated but uneasy.'

'And a little envious.' Clive hadn't put it into words before. 'You're five years younger but cleverer.'

'Balls.' She rolled them carefully.

'You're achieving more. Driving the ambulance. Fighting the war.'

'But you love the navy – the manly world of a ship. Nothing devious, that can't be explained to a sailor.'

'Don't underestimate them, they're full of good things.'

'I know, darling, I'm married to one.'

'I just get impatient, cooped up in dockyards.'

'Your time will come, don't worry.'

In August 1941 the *Prince of Wales* carried Churchill and his staff across the Atlantic to meet Roosevelt. They anchored in a bay in Newfoundland where the larch woods caught the copper sunset as they did at Strathpolly, and Clive got out his bagpipes. ' "Speed Bonnie Boat" was all I could think of,' he told Jenny, back in the flat, 'but Churchill and Roosevelt were very polite about it.'

In the morning, getting breakfast in the tiny kitchen,

she put on his shirt, 'to warm it for you, darling' and to bewitch him. A small dark fringe of hair showed below it when she stretched for something on the shelf. Soon she took it off again.

Two months later the *Prince of Wales* left England on a voyage round Africa to the East, and the world was told about it. Britain's most modern battleship would stop Japan coming into the war. It was a grand gesture of power, a flourish of vainglory by romantic admirals, a death sentence for hundreds of sailors who were unfamiliar with their ship and hadn't been trained to fight her. Crossing the equator they put up a canvas tank on deck for ducking everyone who hadn't crossed before, as if horseplay and superstition could save them, with the engineer Hutton dressed as Neptune in artificial seaweed and Lieutenant Ackerly playing a highland lament in nothing but a wig of blonde pigtails and a sporran made from a mop: 'A crab would look better,' Hutton said in his nasty way. In Colombo they were joined by the old battlecruiser *Repulse*, a minor version of the *Hood*, and in Singapore they were fêted as heroes of the empire. Hutton went to the races where he picked up a Eurasian whore whose beauty, as he boasted in the wardroom, was surpassed by his performance. Clive wrote to Jenny about the voyage and his love, and played cricket for the *Prince of Wales* against the *Repulse*.

Eight days after reaching Singapore – eight months after the *Prince of Wales* was completed – both ships were on the bottom of the South China Sea.

Sleep was the most precious thing, where prisoners could dream. Too soon they were blown out of it by the guards, kicked into the dark, to stumble to the cookhouse for a mug of rice porridge without salt or sugar or any taste but its own sourness, close to fermentation, and the smoke from crackling bamboos that burnt under the huge iron pans. It was a mercy, before dawn, that the stuff couldn't be seen. At first light, when the river below the camp was sheeted under layers of mist, the men slithered down the path to wash among the reeds, and climbed back to line up by the guardroom for morning parade.

'All mens number!'

They bowed to the Rising Sun, collected tools and another mugful of rice, the midday ration, and filled their water bottles; then marched off under guard to the railway where work began at once. They scraped the soil into baskets, hundreds of men elbow to elbow; made skips of bamboo and sacking, two men to each; plied back and forth, filling, spilling, carrying, tipping – so quietly that it was a shock when anyone sneezed or spoke or fainted with a groan. Basket by basket, skip by skip, they took a slice out of a hill and put it in a valley. For themselves, threading an impossible line through a nightmare, the object was to get to the end of the day without annoying the guards too much. For Nippon their only use was the work to be extracted from them; the daily quota of soil to be shifted by each man, however sick, shovelling and dumping and trimming towards Burma.

By ten o'clock the sweat ran grubbily from armpits, the sores tingled and oozed in jockstraps. A break was allowed for tea, brewed with dubious leaves in dirty water, stale and bitter. At midday the men flopped into any shade with their precious food. Though it was hung in branches to be safe, the ants had found it and the morning's heat had turned the rice to rancid lumps. On such refreshment the men faced the afternoon, slowed down by the fatigue and the malignant sun. In a trance they rocked from foot to foot, ponderously swung a pick or pushed a shovel, blundered through the hours till dusk. Water bottles were drained, a mouthful at a time, rolled round the tongue, gargled and swallowed, never enough for such thirst.

It was a scene dragged from a murky time in history, performed for some mystic reason unintelligible to the men. Copper-coloured by sunburn and dust, speckled with bush bees which drank their sweat, bitten by lice and mosquitoes, gaunt and hollow-eyed, their skin tight over jaws and cheekbones, their rib cages exposed like laths, their stomachs bloated out of shape by rice, their hair cropped or matted, their jockstraps mildewed and shredded and slipping off their hips, their minds clouded by submission, as weak and wasted as their bodies – they might have been labouring for any tyrant of the past. Or if this was the present, they were the chorus in some epic spectacle: young men disguised as old, the flesh stripped from skeletons, the life washed from faces, the light snuffed out of eyes by what they had seen. They scraped and shuffled, sometimes muttered, never moved fast, hardly wondered at the monotony and humiliation, too taken up with a red-raw blister, an aching muscle, a skull banging with fever.

The near-silence was sharpened by the scream of a guard, the whack of bamboo or slap of a fat hand on someone's parchment skin, the cry of pain as a boot struck a bandaged ulcer to see if it was genuine. Men unable to stay upright sat on the ground and shovelled earth till they collapsed, then were carried into the shade. Occasionally, in a coma, a man dropped his tools and slouched into the forest, heading for Burma or Piccadilly Circus or New South Wales, and had to be brought back and watched till he recovered, but remembered nothing. About twice a week there was a crunch like a cabbage being cut in half and a man fell dead, his heart ruptured.

Dimly Clive saw that work, even this murderous kind, was good. It was one of life's needs, the feeling of mastery. Without it there would be no purpose, thus no sense in hoping, and he almost got satisfaction from driving his body against the task. Within touch of the next man, he lived in a space of his own. The sun burnt into his brain with individual intensity, a private assault. Sweat dripping in his eyes, he watched the others as they must be watching him – a crazy pack, comic in torn hats that served as pillows or even rice bowls, a ludicrous sight – but nobody laughed. Once, unmistakably through the blur, he saw the awful engineer Hutton: nearly naked, smeared and glistening, a bunch of leaves tied on his head for shade, a primitive implement in his hand – dressed as Neptune again for crossing the equator. Clive knew there were other survivors from the *Prince of Wales*; knew too that Hutton had been drowned.

There were things to enhance the sense of theatre. The

backcloth of mountains drifted in and out of focus through different purples, moods, shapes, as the lighting changed. A rainstorm would burst across the scenery, too dramatic to be accidental. And one afternoon for special effect a swarm of butterflies, emerald and black with forked tails, came fluttering to settle on the prisoners and sip their sweat. At first the men swiped and squashed them – this gaudy insult to their troubles – but the butterflies came in thousands, bringing magic with them, and were allowed to stay. Even the guards were softened by the spell before remembering their duty.

'More three baskets!' they screamed, measuring the earth with bamboos, flailing at the prisoners. 'More two baskets!' They measured and flailed for a miserable last squeeze of work – 'More one baskets!' – till, with nothing to be got from kicks and screams: 'All mens finish, tomorrow come back!' In camp the men paraded to return their tools, to be counted several times and dismissed. The sun was down and usually there were graves to be dug, but there was time for a bathe, for dirt and anguish to be dissolved in the placid, brown but cleansing river.

For three months they laboured on the embankment, scratching earth from the forest to be spread and stamped and planted with strips of grass to hold it in the rains. Shovel and throw, shovel and throw, pick up and carry, climb the bank, dump and go back for more: as the earth was used up the journeys grew longer, but the daily quota stayed the same. When timber was wanted for a bridge they were sent into the forest for big straight trees and on an escarpment, rooted among rocks and twined with creepers, they found teak and mahogany. Tools were primitive, muscles feeble. Falling trees caught on others, bringing tops and branches down, or were hung by vines in mid-air and had to be cut free by climbing through a mesh of foliage and hidden insects; then crashed down the escarpment and after rough trimming were dragged, in the old slaves' way, to the site. For another two months the up-ended trunks were driven into the ground: a hundred men straining on each rope, pacing to a chant, hauling an iron weight up a scaffold with a guard directing from his bamboo perch; letting go the ropes for the weight to thump on the timber head, hammering it a finger's breadth further in. Plod, release, walk back, pick up the ropes, plod again, through the tropical day. Some men had no strength to haul and were carried by the others, or dropped the rope too late and were flung to the ground with burning hands. When the piles were in, beams were lashed to them with vines and a few iron spikes.

'It's a pack of cards,' Coltart said. 'The first train over and it'll collapse.'

There might be flowers and birds to marvel at, and the young stalks of the hated bamboo could be candied with yellow and blue and green stripes, but the prisoners' eyes were dimmed by sweat, their consciousness numb and weary and kept carefully dormant for tonight's dreams. The last meal was rice like the next one, and tomorrow would be the same as today. Was it Wednesday or Sunday, April or June, morning or afternoon? The calendar was blank, but every tenth day was a rest day, a haven of daylight hours free of punitive labour in the grilling sun, when a man could find humanity in himself.

Clive had run out of old conversations with Jenny, but still spoke to her in the twilight minutes before sleep. It had been like that in bed: he went on talking, a hand on her hip or breast, and found she was asleep. But his words weren't lost, they reached the Jenny who slept only when he did.

'I catch my breath sometimes,' he told her. 'Usually it's down by the river.' There was a heron standing in the water, rigid, not a quiver till suddenly it spiked a fish and swallowed it, then picked its way to another place, treading carefully as if not wanting to spoil its own reflection, and stood again. 'I'll teach you to fish – soon you'll be catching more than me.' Or a flight of geese came over, caring nothing for the men slaving on the railway, oblivious of the war. Or the mist broke and showed a vision of the mountains through the gap, quite close or they might be a thousand miles away, they might be anywhere, phantoms in the sky. 'Things like that are too much for me, they catch me in the tenderest spot. But I need them, I grab them and hang on for all I'm worth. All those years leading up to this – I clutch them as the only truth, something alive in the face of this stupefying death. That's what it is – death. There's no escape from it. But I can't accept it, I defy it with all I've got.'

The permanence was frightening. The days, months, years would never change till he was free.

In straw hat and canvas boots and a rag tied through his crutch, Clive balanced on two stones, swung a sledge hammer round his shoulders and smashed it down on the steel drill which Smithy, sitting with a pair of blacksmith's pincers between his legs, held in a hole in the solid rock. The rhythm was easy to catch, but fatal to lose through fatigue or dreaming. If Clive didn't strike the drill squarely, it jarred with shock through both men's arms or shot a splinter into one of them. If he hit the pincers, they flew from Smithy's hands and snapped at their bare shins. The least scratch could become an ulcer. Clive had to keep his eyes and mind on the top of that bruised steel shaft.

His mother, twenty years ago, had balanced on a rock like this above her favourite pool, casting with her rod for the fish that killed her.

The cutting, a furrow gouged out of the hill, rang with the dry infernal clink of a hundred hammers. From the rocks, studded with blinding crystal, the sun bounced back and struck like God's own hammer, a knock-out punch to finish off any men not laid low by sickness. And from the top, the guards pelted them with stones.

After each stoke of Clive's hammer Smithy lifted the drill and twisted it a little. Strike, lift, twist. White rock dust puffed from the hole and powdered their bodies, streaked with sweat and itching. Strike, lift, twist. Every ten strokes Smithy pulled the drill out and poured water into the hole from a tin. Soon it turned to milk, then paste, before drying into dust again. Strike, lift, twist. As the hole deepened, Smithy scooped out the dust with a piece of wire; then the gurgle of more water, the wobble of the drill dropping back into the hole, the plop when it hit the bottom. Strike, lift twist – hour after hour for a month, two months, six months.

In the blistering afternoon, when the drillers had gone deep enough, the holes were filled with gelignite. The guards liked to explode it before the prisoners were out of range, for the fun of showering them with stones. Falsetto hoots and the cackle of startled birds followed the blast. The men were driven back to clear the ground with picks, crowbars and their rickety two-man skips. After the enfeebling life they were pleased what weights they could lift, prising out and splitting rocks; and how far, barefoot and naked, they could carry them. The rubble was tipped into a ravine, crashing to the bottom to frighten the monkeys and start a new embankment. Already bamboo poles had been planted to mark its height. The railway must go forward, edging towards Burma.

An electric bell rang in Clive's skull, growing louder till the wire fused with a bang and a jab of heat, a rush of sweat, nausea, silence, before the ringing began again. It drove out other noises and left him isolated, delirious with malaria.

He was swimming through the wreck of the *Prince of Wales*, calling to the engineer who went down in her, 'Hutton! Hutton!' and listening for an answer: you could always tell a shoal of British sailors under water, Awang bin Daud had said, by the sound of bagpipes. But he wasn't swimming, he was tied to a tree, having his eyes gouged out, then his stomach: it was a kindness, the colonel told him. Now he was running along a beach behind two bicycles, one ridden by his brother Victor, the other by Jenny. They laughed and held hands, pedalling side by side up the sand but never looking back at Clive. He couldn't catch up, he had no breath to shout. The ringing faded: it was their bicycle bells disappearing in the distance. They had forgotten he was there.

Forgotten: the horror of slipping from Jenny's memory was worse than fever. He woke slowly, trying to remember who and where he was; looked down on himself from under the roof of the hospital hut where lizards lived and men's voices – his own among them – came through the odour of carbolic acid and urine.

'Tell me, Doc – what's the record for craps? I've had fifty-one today.'

'One more and you've got a pack of cards.'

'Drugs, bandages, everything I need – the Nips have got it by the ton.'

'And keep it for themselves.'

'Dead prisoners mean fewer mouths to feed. Work or die.'

'You're a coolie or a corpse – there's nothing in between.'

'I bought a load of pills from a Thai down on the barges. He charged me fifty dollars.'

'Don't tell me, Doc – they were peppermints.'

'I reckon I'm down to seven stone and once I was thirteen.'

'Dysentery's a capital offence.'

'A crime against the Mikado.'

'I saw it once in Bournemouth.'

'What does he know about it? – the shame of not reaching the pits in time.'

'And blowflies buzzing round while you squat.'

'They gave me eight bandages and a bottle of spirit for three hundred tropical ulcers.'

'You'll work the miracle, Doc – you're a bloody marvel. After the war, if they don't make you a saint – '

'Married men are the ones who survive best – don't ask me why.'

'More to live for, maybe.'

As the fever fell away Clive caught images of the scene, sketches of a tropical prison hospital. Atkins, lying beside him, had an ulcer the size of a pineapple on his shin. The next man's toes and ankles had sunk out of sight in a huge meaty swelling at the end of his leg. Beyond, a figure like a grasshopper, with double-jointed limbs and glassy eyes in its enormous head, quivered slightly all day as if ready to take flight.

'My lovely body – now it's all gone rotten, I hate it, hate it.'

'Take it off below the knee, Doc – I don't want the bastard any more.'

'I'm filling up with water like a tank, I can hear it sloshing inside, I'm up to my neck, I'm going under.'

Some of them died among their companions. Usually they were removed to the nameless section behind a screen: limp, empty bundles, soon to be corpses. One man, a few hours after being carried out, walked back: 'Bloody murder in there. I saw them coming at me with a rice bag to put over my head. Next thing, I'd be buried. No thanks – it's safer on the railway. With the Turd and Goldilocks you know what to expect.'

When Clive's fever cooled he began helping with the endless emptying of bamboo bedpans. And every morning he cleaned Atkins' ulcer; washed a spoon in hot salt water, dug it into the crater, scooped out the pus, wiped it on a wad of wild cotton, dug and scooped again, up one side and down the other, round the dark skewer of Atkins' legbone till he reached firm flesh; then poured in carbolic acid with a fountain pen filler, bound it with banana leaves and a strip of shirt taken from a dead man.

'See you again tomorrow,' Clive said, feeling some of the pain he gave Atkins with his spoon, hating the smell of pus and the crowding flies.

'I'm lucky,' Atkins said. 'Some blokes' ulcers are twice as big.'

'Some blokes let the maggots breed in them, to eat the bad stuff.'

'Or lie in the river for the fish to nibble it away.'

'Give me a good clean amputation any day.'

'With a woodsaw and no anaesthetic? – we've gone back two hundred years.'

'I'll never be able to scoop out a melon with a spoon.'

One man could only sleep with his feet in a bucket of cold water. Another, with sores all over, fluttered naked through the hospital, flicking away the blowflies with a palm leaf. A pair of friends lay side by side: one with arms and legs as thin as stalks, flowering into abscesses; the other with soft flesh, purple from heat and blown into a pudding from which two small eyes, oozing tears, looked out. A man who collapsed after reaching the pits fell in and was drowned before anyone noticed. A few stopped eating, knowing it meant death. A hundred yards away – tomorrow, next week, inescapable for many of them – the cemetery was spreading further into the forest: trees cut down, bamboo crosses planted.

3

When Laki saw the shooting star he knew they were in trouble. The *Catriona* was on a long passage between islands, far from reefs, and the weather was fine: sails and ropes and spars creaking quietly in a warm wind, the sea slopping and gurgling along the hull. But a shooting star falling through the rigging of the foremast transformed the night: it was a flying witch careering down the sky. Up in the forest of her distant island, knowing that a ship was in danger, she had climbed a tree, tied on a creeper and with a cry of magic had launched herself along it, out into the dark. The creeper had snapped at the moment Laki saw the shooting star. Now the witch was on her way, hungering for the eyes and tongue and lungs and guts of a drowned sailor. Laki should have woken Mr Clive, but was too proud to give away his terror and knew it would make no difference.

The old saltwater coxswain, as a child, had heard about the fleet of canoes driven on to a coast where the crew were all killed and eaten. And the island inhabited only by beautiful, strong, naked women who never shaved their pubic hair but grew it long like skirts and whose lust was more than any man had survived. And the octopus with arms as thick as coconut trees that grabbed a canoe and wouldn't let go till a small boy, adorned with shells and rubbed with oil, was thrown overboard to satisfy it. And the living rocks that chased ships through the sea, jumped up and smashed them. These had faded in Laki's belief. But the flying witches were real, more

deadly than storms or waterspouts or sharks, and couldn't
be ignored.

They led a double life in the village, keeping their craft
secret, passing it from mother to daughter. A woman
would throw her baby girl from one side of the hut across
the roof, then move with the speed only possible for a
witch to catch her on the other side, teaching her to fly.
At night, leaving her skirt beside her sleeping husband,
she would whip her buttocks with a palm leaf to drive
herself into the sky, for a lone flight or a gathering of her
sisters. Witches would swarm over the forest like flying
foxes, making for the swamps by the lagoon. Or perch on
tall trees at the water's edge, on the lookout for victims.
Or turn themselves into fireflies, flashing in the dark. Or
roam over the sea to their meeting-places on the reef
where they munched bits of coral, giving them an appetite
for men's flesh.

Laki might have recited magic over some shredded
ginger root, wrapped it in a banana leaf and tied it to his
arm, to protect him from the witches; but it should be
done by daylight when they couldn't see him. He might
have conjured up a mist to hide the *Catriona* and sailed
safely through the shrieks of witches who had lost the
trail; but if the magic carried salt spray from his lips, the
witches would be drawn by the smell instead of being
repelled.

Anyway, he didn't know the magic. There was no
escape. The night was clear, a shooting star meant shipwreck. Without doubt the little bush boy supercargo,
Beaconsfield, had had a hand in it.

In his dream Clive knew the *Catriona* was wrecked. The
final crack of life, the crunch of wood or bone, a prisoner
falling dead, his heart ruptured. The Turd and Goldilocks
grinning in the railway cutting. Jenny in the background
somewhere. Another grave in the forest cemetery
tonight. . . .

He was on deck before the dream was finished. The
stern was lifting into the darkness, the ship heeling with
all sails set. She would go down quickly unless they could

spill the wind. Clive heard the shouts, from himself and
Laki. The boys off watch came rubbing and pushing from
the fo'c'sle, up from their sleep. Let go the ropes! Put up
the helm! Cut free the surf boat! The sea was empty: no
lights, no rocks, nothing they could have collided with.

'Beaconsfield!' Laki's huge voice split the night,
bellowing for his terror and shame and for the sinking
schooner.

The bush boy, blacker than the moment, ran from his
plywood hutch up the length of the tilting ship to the
cabin; seized the things he wanted, knowing where they
were as if he had thought this out and could do it blind;
and ran back to the surf boat. It was being lowered into
the sea, floating clear of the *Catriona*. Nobody was
drowned. But Beaconsfield, as the saltwater boys knew,
was the only one who couldn't swim.

Twenty minutes later they were all in the surf boat, a
wide double-ended clinker boat that could take a ton of
copra through rough breakers to the *Catriona* anchored
offshore. Now the old halibut schooner was head down
in the sea, filling up. The cargo was shifting forward to
help her go. The foremast was awash, the rudder was out
of water. She would sink before dawn. The big propeller
that had killed Jimmy Dundas in Tulagi harbour, chopping
his neck and dyeing his pyjamas with blood, caught a
gleam from the eastern sky.

'What happened?' Clive asked the shivering, speechless
boys. 'What did we hit?'

Laki began, 'Mr Clive . . .' But his voice hadn't recovered from the great bellow he had given Beaconsfield. He
looked into the stars and listened for a moment, perhaps
expecting to catch a parting cackle from the flying witch.
By morning she would be back in her hut, putting on her
skirt and lying down beside her husband, a village woman
once more.

'It's deep water, isn't it?' Clive asked. 'No coral heads,
are there? No freaks out here? Miles from any land – '

'Deep water, Mr Clive.' The schooner was settling
slowly, in no hurry yet.

'It was solid enough, whatever we hit. It wasn't a tree
trunk.'

'Wasn't a tree trunk, Mr Clive.'

'Something underwater. Something from the war, perhaps. An old pontoon broken adrift, still floating under the surface with jagged iron spikes – crack into one of those at six knots in the middle of the night and you haven't a hope.'

'Something from the war – '

'Something that was never here before, anyway. We've done this trip often enough without colliding. Or do you think . . . ?' Clive looked at Laki. The sky was growing lighter, he could see the old coxswain's fright: a sullen, diminished figure. 'Was it one of your submarine islands, waiting to emerge?'

'No, Mr Clive, please – '

'I'm serious, I wouldn't be surprised,' Clive said. 'I'm not a geologist. But it's a strange part of the world. An eruption under the sea, the top of a new volcano – why not?'

'You'd hear the waves against it, Mr Clive.'

'I suppose so. And the fire coming through the water, hissing. . . .' They were silent. The only noise was from the slap of water on their surf boat and the schooner. She was now half under. And she alone, Clive felt, could tell them why she was sinking. After ten minutes he said, 'Get the oars out and we'll paddle round.' Slowly they circled the wreck, keeping clear.

'Mr Clive . . .'Laki began again, and stopped.

'Don't worry, Laki. It wasn't your fault.'

'You know?'

'Don't blame yourself.'

'So blame who?'

'God knows.' They paddled round her again. The stars were dissolving, but she would be gone before them: staying upright, sailing down into the sea, not rolling over like the *Prince of Wales* twelve years ago. And this time there was nobody trapped on board.

'Are you angry, Mr Clive?' Laki asked.

'Not angry.'

'Are you sad?'

'Well, not quite sad. I've known worse things. And we're all alive.'

Suddenly, tossing her stern up, diving without fuss, the *Catriona* vanished. Then briefly, just below the surface, she must have righted herself. The two mastheads broke out again, quivered for an instant and were gone. From the crew in the surf boat a soft groan followed her, with the drip of their oars. Nobody spoke till the sun came up an hour later, glancing across the empty sea. The boys blinked and shifted on the seats. Laki rubbed his shoulders for warmth and strength, a return of stature. His seamanship would be needed today, his sons and nephews shouldn't see him shrunk with fear. It was thirty miles to the nearest island where they could send a message to Tulagi, but they carried no sails, they would have to row.

'Give it twelve hours,' Clive said. 'Watch-and-watch, an hour at the oars, an hour off. We'll be ashore by sunset.' He kept a sealed tin of biscuits in the surf boat, with a jerrycan of fresh water, and gave the crew their first ration before they began rowing. The wind dropped as the sun rose.

Beaconsfield had said nothing since the shipwreck, but crouched on the bottom boards with whatever he had salvaged under a sack. Now he brought out a bunch of green bananas and some bread in a cotton bag. Then, with a dark smile of triumph, he held up Clive's bagpipes.

'Beaconsfield, you devil!'

They rowed all day, changing watches every hour. Up in the bows Laki stared ahead and sometimes gave a nod to Clive at the tiller. The sun crept up into the breathless morning, filtered by a white gauze of moisture, a tissue that diffused the sparkle, increased the glare. A long swell came rolling over the sea from Australia – or America, Hawaii, Japan – with a valley of immense width between each approaching hump, but not a ripple. The surf boat climbed a slope for half a minute, then slid down the other side. All round it the world rose and fell in a vast rocking seesaw. A leaping school of porpoises swam over to laugh, and the saltwater boys laughed back. A seagull was sitting on a floating coconut, for a rest. A man alone in a canoe, far from anywhere, paddling to somewhere, waved and was lost in the swell.

'Where's he going?' Clive asked, and knew there was no answer: a man, simply, alone in a canoe.

When Clive saw the boys lagging at the oars he handed the tiller to Beaconsfield and got out his bagpipes to stir them up. It was hot work, but he enjoyed the improbability of the scene: an open boat full of black men far out in the Pacific with a white man standing in the stern, playing battle music from tribal Scotland. He watched it as he had watched plays and films in London, but with much more pleasure; and noticed that he wasn't altogether sorry to have nobody to share it with. Nobody, he now believed, was better than the wrong person. He was used to the feeling of happiness alone.

A sudden storm attacked them, a blizzard of rain shutting out the day, hissing on the sea and filling the bottom of the surf boat. When it cleared, they were in sight of land. Far ahead – or were they clouds? – the mountains of a big island faintly steamed. In time, through the afternoon, the shapes hardened into the outline of a grey-green forest, the dotted landmarks round a lagoon, the flash of breakers on a reef. Laki knew the way, though he had never been here before. His broad strong back showed how he had shed the terror of last night's shooting star. Like a giant figurehead under Jimmy Dundas's straw hat he sniffed the landfall, adjusted the course a fraction and sniffed again. The fish hook twitched in his nose, as if being tugged on the end of a line by an invisible fisherman.

Late in the day they entered the lagoon by a cut in the reef where the current ran fast, taking them at speed between strips of brilliant white sand painted on the water. Soon the sea bed rose below them, patches of sand and weed and coral, and Laki stopped the oars. With a pole he stood up on the prow, one bare foot on each gunwale, toes gripping the edge, and punted them along. When it was shallow enough for him to wade, he dropped over the side and strode through the water, a sea god straining on a rope. The saltwater boys dived in and swam alongside, and Clive and Beaconsfield were towed across the reef, into calm water defended from the heaving swell outside. The crew climbed back aboard and for the rest of

daylight they rowed across a lovely inland sea, among a
hundred islands, twisting through the evening. Now the
channel narrowed to a track between the trees, now it
opened to wide horizons. On one island a man had cleared
the bush for a leaf house, ridiculously pretty, and planted
coconuts: a feather of smoke waved over the palms from
his copra drier. On another island, round a thickly
wooded promontory, they reached a village.

Someone laughed, someone shouted, and they stepped
on to the beach as the sun went down.

Clive was thirty-eight. He had traded for two years in his
schooner and made a good profit, but he wouldn't mourn
for her. He wanted something more rooted, to cultivate
and watch grow; and remembered the happiness in his
garden by the river below the prison camp. In these
islands he could find a place as beautiful, and would
never have to wait for rescue. Freedom was now, here, or
wherever he chose to be.

There were old plantations in the Mendanas, abandoned when the Japanese came in the war and never
reclaimed: derelict and overgrown after long neglect. They
were marked on charts – 'pier', 'flagstaff', 'conspicuous
house', 'water tower' – where there was nothing visible
from the *Catriona* as she sailed past. Clive felt an almost
physical desire for a piece of one of those islands, closer
to lust than anything for years. When the schooner's
insurance money had been paid he spent a morning in
the Tulagi secretariat, going through records and title
deeds with the government surveyor. A month later he
bought the freehold of Aurora, a copra plantation on a
lagoon at the far end of the archipelago, four hundred
miles from the capital. The chart said 'densely wooded'
vaguely across the island and showed a mountain in the
middle, probably an old volcano, called Bau.

Aurora had once been known for good management
and an excellent crop, but nobody had seen it lately. A
sea battle had been fought near it, a Japanese kamikaze
plane was lying on the bottom of the lagoon after missing
an American aircraft carrier anchored there. Bomb craters,

bits of rusty iron, slabs of concrete would still be in the undergrowth, to be cleared before any coconuts could be harvested. The old planter had died, the workers had drifted to other plantations or home to their own islands, the buildings must have collapsed. Clive was eager to reach his property and start working on it. The nearest neighbour was half a day's journey away, which suited him. Loneliness would be a defiant joy – the loneliness of a king.

'Better have your appendix out before you go,' they told him in the Tulagi hotel bar.

'Why pick on Aurora? The back of beyond.'

'That's why,' Clive said.

'You must be bonkers. Or soon you will be.'

'You'll be marooned out there, I don't mind telling you. A trader passing by when it suits him. A district officer once in six months if you're lucky. Half a missionary every other year.'

'I'm not worried, I don't need much.'

'A man of simple tastes – is that it? So what's this about caviare from Fortnum's every month?'

'First I'll get the copra going again.'

'Take you half a lifetime, at the local speed. In my experience – '

'Then I thought I'd plant cocoa.'

'Hell of a gamble, if you ask me. Or someone would have done it before.'

'I talked to the agriculture officer,' Clive told them. 'It should do well.'

'Stick to copra, old man.'

'I'll get a grant from the development board.'

'They'll have you on a string. A government puppet.'

'And I might try cattle one day. All this imported meat in tins or frozen – it can't be good.'

'You'll be growing strawberries next.'

'I thought of that. Why not?'

They laughed, not unkindly; ordered more drinks and poured out their advice: 'You'll have to go recruiting. Once a year. Tour the islands for your workers. Sit down in the village and talk. It needs patience. Persuade the men to sign on and be taken away with you. Promise to bring them back next year. They don't like it – away from their families.'

'I don't like it either,' Clive said. 'Having to hire new men every year and train them – it's no way to run a ship. Why try it on a plantation?'

'It's the way it's done.'

'The way they understand.'

'Standard practice. Always has been.'

'A twelve-month contract.'

'I'd rather have something permanent,' Clive said.

'Such as?'

'Something humane and personal. I'm not sure – '

'The best of British luck, old man – you'll need it.'

'I don't want just a labour force. It sounds like a penal colony.'

'It'll never pay to treat them otherwise, you'll find.'

'I want women laughing, kids playing – '

'You're one of those! Visions of your dream island. Golden sands and waving palms and big brown tits.'

'Aurora was a goddess,' Clive said. 'Mother of the wind and stars. I want families living there.'

'You'll never get the men out of their huts in the morning, you won't get the work done.'

'You'll come back to the twelve-month contract in the end, I don't mind betting.'

'I hope not,' Clive said.

He sent Laki ahead, in old Jimmy Dundas's straw hat, with the saltwater boys to clear the foreshore at Aurora and repair the jetty. With tools and fishing gear they packed into a vast canoe, a scooped-out tree that had stood in the forest for two or three centuries. Laki was just as fine, a trunk of human mahogany that could have picked up Beaconsfield, standing on the Tulagi wharf with Clive to see them off, and snapped him like a fishbone. But he had inserted a five-cent piece in place of the hook in his nose: more suitable for his new joy, an outboard engine. Even his crew were subdued by the effect and sat where they were told, waiting for him to pull the cord.

'Thirty horses!' he roared above the engine.

Thirty warriors paddling into battle would have looked better, and Clive was sorry the engine had to be Japanese.

The big canoe sprang from the wharf and ripped away, unfolding two wings of spray and dividing the sea with a smooth white furrow. In ten minutes they had disappeared. Tomorrow they would reach Aurora.

With the saltwater boys out of the way – with Laki and his endless family establishing themselves at Aurora – Beaconsfield saw his chance. Clive had made him headman of the plantation and told him he wanted workers to settle on it with their families. Beaconsfield said they should be bush boys from his own tribe. Together they would go on a journey, black man and white master, to find them. In a mission launch lent by Beaconsfield's brother, now a canon of St George's Cathedral, they travelled to Beaconsfield's island and started up into the forest, by shadowy tangled paths for a week, to his village.

The track was as slight and insubstantial as Beaconsfield, but like him it found a way through the twilight: slipping in and out of sight, never quite vanishing. In forest villages, fortified against neighbours by ditches and stockades of tree trunks, where a white man was cause for alarm and then laughter, the travellers were given roast yams or breadfruit or taro pudding with nuts. But Beaconsfield didn't want to stay among strangers. They slept in a rock cave or the hollow of a giant tree or a shelter of leaves and canes made with a few swipes of a bush knife; were lulled by the presence of infinite life, the breath and murmur of unknown beings, the multitude that peopled the dark.

'Like camping with my brother when we were boys,' Clive said, glad to have a bottle of whisky. Lying in the forest, listening to the night, he talked of the Strathpolly woods and the dim memory of his father, a photo of an officer in uniform. 'Is a warrior,' Beaconsfield said. Clive described the big silver fish with red flesh that came up the river from the sea to lay their eggs; and in return was told a story of a fish that jumped out of the sea, up into the forest where it raped a woman in her garden, which she liked so much that her husband went down to the coast and drowned himself, hoping to become a fish. Beaconsfield wasn't surprised to hear how Clive's mother had been pulled by a fish to her death in a pool: 'Is her husband dragging her down to join him.'

Clive talked of the navy, a tribe of saltwater boys, and the sinking of the *Prince of Wales*, and his time as a prisoner in another forest: 'So now you are bush boy,' Beaconsfield told him. He described his wife, her brown hair and soft grey eyes and wonderful ways of making love, and then his return to London – like Beaconsfield going back home – to find that she had deserted him for an American, and they had a daughter and were now married, living in Australia. Beaconsfield said that a snake must have dropped through her navel when she was asleep under a tree and made her hungry for a new lover. In his father's time a pebble of lava would have been made red hot in the fire and pushed into her womb. Now she would be thrashed by Clive, who could claim back the pigs he had paid to her family as bride price. The American, who would once have been made to swim across a river full of crocodiles, would have to give Clive at least one pig with a good pair of tusks.

'What about their child?' Clive asked. He had never seen Rebecca, who must now be about ten years old.

'The bastard,' Beaconsfield said. 'Is hatching from egg laid by a bush turkey in open ground and not in tunnel, so it doesn't live in the nest. But you can have it.'

'I'm not the father.'

'You are husband of the mother so it belongs to you, but is a pity because – '

'Because what?'

'Because a girl.'

Another night Beaconsfield said, 'Is chief in my village once with old wife who is ugly and young wife who is beautiful, and when he is away hunting in the forest the old wife is suspicious and follows young wife and sees her naked in the yam garden with another man, also naked, and when chief comes back is telling him. Chief is angry and shouting at young wife in public and saying she is scandal to his family because is too much in love with naked man, so she is doing what she must do and climbing highest tree in village, and when she sees her baby crying at the foot of tree she is giving it to care of ugly old wife, and jumping off so killing herself.'

They reached Beaconsfield's village one evening, twelve years after he had left it as a boy going off to the mission school. From something in the air – a simplicity of domestic effort, a natural slowness – Clive too, after twelve years, might be coming back to Awang bin Daud's village, though not as a shipwrecked sailor in the bottom of a fishing boat. People were returning from the day's work in their gardens. Wood smoke and the sweet smell of boiled taro drifted in the dying light.

Beaconsfield's old father, a loose skinful of knee and elbow joints but not so dark as his son – the blackness had been rubbed away like the teeth and hair – was sitting among children and pigs with a big ball of twine made from forest creepers at his feet. The end was in his hand, being twisted and spliced in thin craftsman's fingers. Every evening since watching Beaconsfield depart he had spun a length of twine and tied it with a knot: one knot for each day of his son's absence.

When Beaconsfield and Clive stood in front of him he was dumb with disbelief, tears, old age; empty of words to tell them what he thought of this. Only a high croak, an ancient forest noise, came from inside him while the fingers went on spinning. Beaconsfield said the inadequate things – he had been away, he had helped win the war against the Japanese, it was over now and he had come home with a white man – but his father, seeing nothing, heard nothing either. It was the fingers that first showed recognition: tying the daily knot, suddenly stopping as if the nerves were severed. The twine dropped to the ground. In a moment the old man dropped too, to Clive's feet, and let loose a stream of hoots and wails, probably of joy.

'Is saying,' Beaconsfield explained to Clive, 'that you bring back his son, and now I am not his son any more, because I am your son.'

Slowly the old man rose like a wisp of smoke at the kindling of a fire, liable to be blown out by the least evening breeze, and with the end of the twine in his fingers, with solemn words in a toothless chant, he tied Clive's and Beaconsfield's wrists together – sunburnt white man to thin black bush boy, father and son. Clive remembered once being tied like this to a Malay fisherman, who a few minutes later had had his eyes gouged out with bayonets to save him from the sight of being disembowelled.

Roped into the tribe, bound to one of the elders' families, Clive spent his days in the village talking about his hopes for Aurora: for people to go to his island, make their homes with him, start a colony of their own, share his life in it. They discussed it at night instead of telling stories, went to see cousins in other villages, muttered auspicious things over a stew of flying foxes' wings and the powdered bark of a kwako tree. After a week six families agreed to settle at Aurora, without saying why they were persuaded: perhaps because this wasn't the usual white planter on a recruiting trip who took young men away for a year's labour; or because his headman, one of themselves and now his son, told them that in the forest above the plantation there was a mountain, an old volcano called Bau.

Then Beaconsfield got married. He was back among his own people, the time was good for it. The yams had been harvested in the gardens and stored in racks to keep them from pigs, there was a full moon in two days – enough to find a bride, fix a price, arrange a party. A conch was blown on the dance ground, and like sudden blossom in the forest the news grew that there was to be a wedding. Squatting on the earth in houses dense with smoke and human odours, Clive watched the excitement and was given guidance by the bridegroom, proud bush boy son of a white man.

'Is at beginning of the world,' Beaconsfield told him, 'when a fruit is falling from big-big tree and splitting on a branch, so half is landing on one side of tree and becoming boy and half on other side and becoming girl. They live on different sides and eat the fruit falling down and know nothing-nothing about each other, till one day a fruit is landing far away and both are running to pick it up. ''Where you come from?'' they both are asking, and telling same-same story. Then they see their different bodies and they laugh, because are liking it but not knowing why. They grow big together, till at last they guess why they are liking different bodies and try to see if is true. Boy is telling girl, ''If I hurt you, you shout for peace.'' But is hurting her very-very badly so she shouts for war, and since that time is always war between them.'

Man and woman, Clive understood, were in opposition, hostile partners in a ritual that pervaded the house, gardens, forest, everything in life. Man was superior, though woman had a sinister prestige. Man was pure and sacred, woman necessary but contaminated. Man was at the mercy of woman's power and must defend himself, never so carefully as at a wedding. It was a simple matter which Clive appreciated.

On the wedding morning poles tied with bunches of yams, wild flowers, coloured leaves, were propped against a tree. More yams were laid at the foot, parcelled in banana leaves. All day the village filled up with people. Climbing over the forest the sun brightened their dog's tooth necklaces, pig's tusk bangles and bone ear-rings, feathers and strips of calico and vivid ferns tucked in waists. Faces were whitened with wood ash, striped with red and blue paint. Hair was dyed orange or planted with scarlet flowers. Ten pigs, the bride price, were dragged squealing across the dance ground and tethered by a foreleg in the shade. The crowd grew, the huge trees looked down.

A rumble, the softest hint of tonight's music, came from the gongs – three upright tree trunks, treble and tenor and bass, twice Clive's height, slit and hollowed and each carved with a face, standing in an orchestra of smaller gongs. The chief player listened like a cock bird, head on one shoulder, as his men polished their rhythms, prac- tised the wedding tunes, tried out new gong-sticks. Suddenly, with a two-handed truncheon, he showed what could be done: a booming waterfall of notes and echoes, the wonderful tumble of a man's lifelong talent. He was the best gong player on the island, famous for his all-night stamina, but quite blind. In his dark face a milk-blue film shuttered his eyes, leaving him to work by touch and the plangent sound of wood on wood. He had never seen these towering instruments, village demi-gods, phalluses with eyes and nose and mouth and a voice that spoke of the past and future, the time for planting and digging and feasting and copulating – the voice of the ancestors. And Clive had never imagined such melody from three logs; or believed, since the infernal ringing of hammers on the railway, that he could ever be so stirred by percussion in the forest.

By mid-afternoon, with excitement simmering and the gongs still rolling out an overture, the dance ground was packed. Beaconsfield was relaxed and indifferent, though hero of the event, and happy to show it off to Clive. 'Now bride is coming,' he said, speaking of his imminent wife.

The crowd stepped back to make way for her. She was startling, dazzling, a face and nothing else – but a face of bright vermilion, the supreme colour of all, the pigment of utmost beauty. For a moment this painted face eclipsed the rest. After the shock of it Clive saw how young she was: a child of the forest, ready to be taken from it by the headman of Aurora. Under precious shells and strings of porpoise teeth, the treasure of her mother and grand-mother and great grandmother – daughter after daughter back into the darkness – her body shone with oil.

'You see, Mr Clive, they are finding a tree with big-big pods, and boiling them to get the oil, and rubbing her with it, and giving some to me, to save me.' He laughed.

'Save you?'

'Because between her legs is hot and doing damage to me, so first I must pour oil on it.'

'Quite right,' Clive said. He was the bridegroom's adopted father and should sympathise.

From her vermilion face the bride passed a girlish smile towards the tethered pigs and quantity of yams, pleased to see how highly she had been valued. Then modestly she walked with her family to the middle of the dance ground.

'You're a lucky man,' Clive said. 'She's lovely.'

Beaconsfield was cautious: 'I think is good.'

'Haven't you seen her before?'

'I forget – she is just piccaninny when I leave the village. But my father is paying ten pigs and four hundred yams. Is a lot.' She sat on the ground and her family sat round her in a ring, guarding her till the end, eyeing the pigs and yams. Her father placed a single big yam between her thighs, for fertility. She looked so proud, she might have given birth to it – this holy vegetable, ripe from the earth, grown from seed passed down for generations. Above her head she held a bunch of breadfruit leaves.

'When's it your turn, Beaconsfield?' Clive asked. He couldn't forget his own marriage long ago at Chelsea registry office: the sense of urgency in the first summer of the war; the Woolworth's ring and quick request for two witnesses among the other couples.

'Is no hurry. Is going on till night.'

Taking their time, reluctant to give up such riches, Beaconsfield's family untied the pigs, counted the yams and walked with them twice round the bride's family before handing them over. The bride's family counted the yams again, the pigs squealed. Nobody looked satisfied. The afternoon passed, the gongs warbled, the sun sank towards the trees.

Then Beaconsfield stepped forward, carrying a bow and arrows decorated with feathers; stepped through the ring of people, who turned their backs on him, and with his bow touched the breadfruit leaves above the bride's head. Her father took the leaves from her, gave them to Beaconsfield, took them back, returned them to the bride and made a speech. Two girls from the bride's family hauled her by the wrists out of the ring, following Beaconsfield. Her father shouted and some of the women cried at losing her. The girls were met by two from Beaconsfield's family who led the bride away. She had dropped her breadfruit leaves and the big yam. The gongs rumbled louder, the shadows reached over the dance floor. The wedding was over.

The pigs' squeals, tearing through the gongs, were suddenly stifled. Their snouts and feet were bound, they were lifted wriggling on poles over a fire to singe their hair – to cries from women who had loved them as their

sons, who probably had suckled them – then were stran-
gled and cut up, to be wrapped in leaves and baked on
hot stones. At dusk they were eaten with taro puddings,
men and women sitting apart. Beaconsfield, next to Clive,
watched his wife, at ease among his sisters, aunts, female
cousins. Their marriage bed would be under the falling
moon tonight, shared by the whole village. In the short
twilight the feasters gorged quickly, then chewed areca
nuts. Flaming bamboos were brought out and stuck into
the ground.

'The ancestors are very-very pleased, I think,' Beacons-
field said. 'We are doing it right.' He gave some areca to
Clive: 'Is making you happy for me.' The juice dried
Clive's mouth, the pulp clogged his teeth.

Under the torches, under the full moon, Beaconsfield's
old father stalked into the middle of the dance ground,
trailing a fine red woven mat. Round his neck he wore
his dead wife's jawbone. His ear lobes were plugged with
his best pair of wooden discs, his mouth was stuffed with
areca nuts, mint leaves, ginger root. Through the mixture
he chanted a spell of vowels and gulps; spread the mat at
his feet and spat the holy medicine into it, then crammed
his mouth with more. 'Oh areca!' he sang, and Beaconsfield passed it on to Clive. 'I kick the mountain and see
the mountain moving, the mountain falling down, the
mountain lying flat. . . . Oh areca and mint and ginger! I
come out through the mouth of the man and go in through
the mouth of the woman, and out through the woman and
in through the man . . . Oh areca!' The crowd hummed a
requiem for this wedding night, as the old man chewed
and chanted and spat. Clive felt the areca working in him:
a light-headedness, an emptying of all troubles from his
mind to leave it bright and clean and quick.

Like a wind starting in the trees – in two squads, men
and women – the people took up the old man's chorus;
stamped with the gong-beat, slapped their thighs, surrendered to the rhythm, a compulsion that drove them across
the dance ground and sucked them back. They gathered
at one end to sing a verse, or take a breath or watch the
blind man or listen to the stars or catch a signal from the
moon, then shuffled – as a forest fire, with a hiss and

crackle – to the other end; swayed, tossed, sang, filled
the night with music, danced through the vibrant hours,
forwards, and backwards, stamp and turn, whoop and
twist and yell. Nothing could stop them, they couldn't
stop themselves while the heart-boom of the gongs
pumped a wild pattern in their blood. In the torches their
bodies gleamed with oil and sweat, their heads grew crests
of sizzling woolly hair, their huge mad shadows leapt into
the dancing trees.

Beaconsfield's father was overtaken and consumed by
the nightlong blaze. Beaconsfield caught Clive's wrist and
pulled him in. A shrill soprano took flight over the forest,
a helpless bid to get away, ending in a scream. Arms
whirled, hips brushed, ankles rattled with bangles of
empty nuts above the thudding ground. The air was
choked with an intense and guileless clarity, inescapable
for anyone with the energy to live. Hands met stealthily
in clutches round Clive's waist.

In a wave of feathers the women swooped among the
men for a moment of froth and gentleness, a touch of the
probable dawn, before tearing away. The three big gongs,
tall cylinders topped with demon faces, quivered under
the sticks, the pulse of human need. A wail came from
an aching womb, a shout from a man's impatience. Each
change of rhythm pulled excitement from the darkness,
put force into the dancers. Flutes trilled above the gongs,
a noise of wind and reed that Clive's bagpipes could never
have smothered. The areca enhanced the harmony, the
one-ness of the foot-stamping thigh-slapping night, the
village's total ecstasy rising to the apex moon. This was
the world, there was nothing else.

People might drop out for a slice of pork, a mouthful
of pudding or sit talking in the firelight, but the dance
throbbed tirelessly past midnight, unwinding into the
morning and a last display of love. Limbs recovered their
weight, heads reeled with fatigue and a single thought.
Each surge of women into men stayed longer, with
groping fingers, thrusting lips and breasts. The torches
were burning out, the ground was ploughed with the
grooves of stamping feet, littered with trampled flowers
and fallen skirts. Only the blind player kept at the gongs,

to coax a diminishing melody from his gods. The rest sank and shivered their sweat-limp bodies into the dark, falling in soft haphazard couples.

Lying naked after the moon had gone down, the one white man in the blackness before daylight suffused the forest, Clive felt no hangover: only stiff with cold, goose-pimpled, hungry for breakfast and happy never to know whose nutcracker legs had held him in the night.

Part Five

The Lagoon

1

Aurora was transformed. The forgotten corner of an empty island became a prosperous settlement, as bustling as anything could be in that lethargic climate. A year after Clive took it there were sixty men on his payroll, and with families and friends and visitors the population was nearly three hundred. They lived in new houses on either side of a school and church – saltwater boys by the lagoon, bush boys further inland. In a clearing below the forest each family worked its vegetable garden.

Across a bay from his people's village, on a tongue of sand jutting between mangroves into the lagoon, Clive found a place where he could see the top of the volcano Bau: a sharp lopsided crater pushing the forest up from below but not quite piercing it, with the lordly profile of the mountain above Strathpolly. There he built himself a spacious bungalow. Two black figures – a young man with his ring-shaped pig's tusk of bride money facing the sharp-breasted girl he wanted to buy – were carved on the big wooden posts that held up the corrugated iron roof. Woven palm leaves made a ceiling and the partitions of two bedrooms. On one wall Clive pinned the admiralty chart showing Aurora and the rest of the island, 'densely wooded', with the peak of Bau in the centre. On another he hung an old shotgun and his fishing-rod. Between the sitting and the dining part he filled a long bookcase with Kipling and Conrad, Stevenson and Tolkien, the Waverley novels, the literature of an empire, the stories of his heroes – a library ranging from Pacific history and race relations to tropical agriculture and naval fiction, all rather spoilt by damp and insects. On the top shelf he kept the bagpipes, still in working order and liable to be played. The front of the house was open: nothing stopped any breeze that cooled it. A veranda dropped into the lagoon where fish leapt and turtles lounged and sometimes a dugong swam; a rare crocodile too, the saltwater boys said, with four eyes – the ominous number – two for clear water, two for the mud among the mangroves.

Each morning he was up before dawn to set the clock. There was a marvellous suspended moment when the night was over but the day hadn't quite begun. The sun was rising fast and in a minute would light the world. Till then, Aurora held its breath. Clive loved that moment and often thought how Jenny would love it too – the young wartime Jenny, not the present wife of an American diplomat. He had no radio, he went by the sun. When it came over the top of the trees it was six o'clock. Work began and Jenny was dismissed. From then till one-thirty he hardly paused, touring his tropical kingdom at a pace that would knock out a lesser man. With several thousand acres he might have had a jeep and did once consider a horse, but preferred to go on foot. 'There's no manure,' he told Beaconsfield, 'like the farmer's boots.' Sometimes he got a ride on Beaconsfield's motorbike.

Planter and headman, white father and black son, each believed that he understood the other, while each kept a private side which he wouldn't share. Beaconsfield paid the wages with a calculator, and as well as the motorbike he owned a radio and a camera and a plastic cuckoo clock, all Japanese, yet he still inhabited – or was inhabited by – the dark forest surrounding the plantation. He led the hymns in church but when his brother, now the first black Bishop of Tulagi in robes and purple stock with a bamboo crozier in his hand, came every year to confirm the Aurora piccaninnies, Beaconsfield thought it was a poor exchange for the ordeal he had been through at that age. He could brew medicine from the bark of a kwako tree and arrange for a man to be cursed, with good effect.

Laki remained coxswain, in charge of canoes and a weekly trip fifty miles beyond the lagoon to the nearest township for mail and stores. His saltwater boys went fishing, looked after any machinery and worked the copra drier, leaving cultivation to the bush boys. In numbers they were equal, and generally under Clive's discipline the village was peaceful.

For his servant Clive picked Loloa, a gentle smiling bush

boy with big eyes, strong thighs straining under a tight
sarong, who slipped in and out through the kitchen
curtain, washed his clothes and laid them out, polished
his shoes, tidied his rooms, shared his bathroom and
happened to be beautiful. Clive loved Loloa for his velvet
youth and soft footsteps and shadowy obliging presence,
never far away: the perfect servant, but not yet much of
a cook.

Work stopped in the afternoon, unless a trading ship
came into the lagoon to load copra. A solid, nearly opaque
torpor settled on Aurora, trapping all but the smallest
movement. Chickens and pigs and children rootled quietly
through the village. Some boys kicked a football across a
patch of powdered coral, but gave up and vanished into
the shade. Clive sat reading on his veranda. A lizard
plopped from the roof and landed in astonishment
between his feet. A brief explosion of laughter reached
him. Or was it a scream and a girl was being raped behind
the copra shed? Half a verse of a hymn, 'Jesus loves me,
that I know,' drifted out of nowhere, then was stifled by
the heat. Sometimes a canoe sliced across the indigo
lagoon, gently flickering the water. Otherwise it was an
unshattered sheet of glass, the details of every palm and
islet doubled in its surface. When a fish jumped it was a
surprise that it didn't tinkle among broken pieces as it fell
back, and leave a hole.

The evenings, after the opacity dissolved, were as transparent as the early mornings. The summit of Bau grew
more scowling, seeming closer and higher. Towards
sunset Clive went to his office for a little desultory paper-
work, alert for the moment when the coconut trees were
struck with a magic glow of pink, available for anyone
who wanted to see him. Beaconsfield came in and they
discussed today's and tomorrow's work – father and son
in a real sense. Laki paddled over with a canoe full of his
family to show off the newest baby and ask Clive once
more to be godfather. Others turned up with complaints
and requests or just to talk. When the sun dropped it was
quickly dark. The hymns of evensong came rolling over
the lagoon from the village church, and Loloa appeared
through the kitchen curtains with peanuts and whisky.

The years would pass like this: Clive's happiness – the child of his benevolence, his private kind of love – maturing with the trees; and reminders of his prison life dropping into view from time to time, like the unexpected leaves that were always falling in this climate without seasons.

'Mr Clive,' Beaconsfield said one evening in their second year at Aurora, 'I am asking something very-very private.'

'I know.' Clive had been expecting it without knowing what he would do, only guessing that there might be a way to suit everyone. 'Go on.'

Beaconsfield laughed: 'There are white men bringing white women to live in Mendanas.'

'I told you, I divorced my wife and she's married to an American.'

'Also are white men taking our Mendana girls.'

'I don't want to be married again. Last time was perfect.'

'I mean not for marrying properly in church, with everything like that and my brother bishop also. Only for having babies perhaps.'

'Babies!' Clive saw Laki's infinite descendants and his own forsaken godchildren.

'Your wife is doing it when you are in prison. Is having baby for the American man. But only daughter. Perhaps you can have son.'

'You're my son, Beaconsfield. Your father said so.'

'I mean blood son. We have many-many in Mendanas, in Tulagi mostly. Are not bush boys and not saltwater boys, they are nothing-nothing, so going where it doesn't matter. But are good people, Mr Clive, the half-in-half ones.'

'Good? How?'

'With some of our skin and some of your brain.'

'I thought you valued your purity – you don't want it to be mixed.'

Beaconsfield shifted his angle: 'You are man, not missionary, and boys are saying is not right for you because is not healthy, so they are sorry for this question and puzzling how to answer it.' Beaconsfield shot a black glance at Clive: 'Mr Clive, we have a story.'

'Yes?'

'Two men are friends, called Happy and Sorry, and living in next villages with stream between. And Sorry is one day coming to Happy and saying, "You have plenty pigs and plenty piccaninnies, but I have plenty wives with no piccaninnies. So I buy one more wife, beautiful young one, and please you go with her and make piccaninny for me." And Happy says, "Yes, I like, because you my friend." They fix a day and Sorry says, "You come to stream and I bring my wife and then you manage it." So Sorry takes her to stream and leaves her there and says, "You wait and man is coming for you, so you make piccaninny with him." But she can't see, because Happy is hiding in black-black cave which is door to country of the dead, to make her think he is spirit, not real man, so no matter if she is making piccaninny with him and Sorry not jealous. She is waiting-waiting-waiting too much, and beginning to go home. But Happy is making whistle and sucking lips and breaking stick and throwing stone, and she sees him and together they manage it. When is born, is son, and Sorry says, "Now I buy a pig for my piccaninny, because I very-very happy also." Pig he buys is mother, already pregnant, and she runs away to Happy's village and has five more piccaninny pigs there. Everywhere Sorry looks for pig and can't find, but sees footmarks in wet ground, because is raining yesterday, and follows to Happy's village. Sorry takes mother pig and family back home and next day picks ten good yams and says to wife, "Go and give these to Happy, because he is making one piccaninny for me and five for pigs." So she brings yams and Happy says, "Now I know is way for making piccaninnies and pigs and yams also, and Sorry is big-big fool to send you here, because I like it and is good idea you live with me and we manage plenty more." ' Beaconsfield shot the black glance at Clive again: 'Mr Clive, do you know Loloa's sister?'

'Are you tempting me, Beaconsfield?'

'Is pleasing us, too.'

'Would it make you happy?'

'Happy for you, because all girls are loving you very-very much and she is best.'

A week later Loloa opened a tin of Fortnum and Mason's cockaleekie soup for Clive's dinner and grilled two pork chops, his most skilful dish, with a sauce of mustard and tomato ketchup but too much wild ginger tonight, the bush boys' favourite aphrodisiac. After coffee and brandy and a cigar on the veranda, after calling good-night to a canoe paddling home to the village and listening to the opossum that lived above the palm leaf ceiling depart on its nightly hunt – stalk over the rafters, climb out on to the iron roof, pull down a branch, creep away into the trees to munch leaves till dawn – after waiting for the stars of the Southern Cross to dip their first pointer into the top of the water tank and letting out the pressure lamp, Clive took a candle into his bedroom and found what he knew was there: Loloa's sister under the mosquito net, glowing with coconut oil.

She stayed a year, from one yam harvest to the next. For Clive she was another luxury, as soothing and extravagant as the food and wine and books that came from London, making his solitude easier: a gift from the people of Aurora. She asked for nothing, she hardly spoke, but knew how she could give delight. Certainly she was beautiful, an uncanny version of her brother, with Loloa's gentleness and her own agility, though Clive marvelled that the warm colour of her skin should be so cool to stroke and her full dark eyes so empty of anything he understood. Like the opossum in the roof – a rare unblinking gaze from a pair of tiny jet buttons in a crack of the ceiling – she was almost unimaginable by day, caught only in glimpses in the kitchen while snatching a potato or a piece of English cheese. If by chance Clive saw her working in the gardens or washing in a forest stream or cheering the bush boys' football team, she waved to him no differently from the other girls: nothing to show she was the one who enclosed him at night in a black vortex of generosity and ultimate sleep. When he woke before dawn she had always gone, creeping out through his waking dream as the opossum came back, leaving coconut oil and a trace of frangipani in the bed.

Clive couldn't explain his pleasure. It was more than the fun of making love again, an end to celibacy – the simple welcome when he lifted the mosquito net, her pliant body, their melting happiness together. Bigger than the joyful nights, nearer the puzzle that had troubled Beaconsfield, it touched the whole place like a consummation. The overgrown plantation had been cleaned, the copra had recovered, a reputation had begun. On high ground towards the foothills of Bau the forest had been cut back and cocoa trees planted. A pedigree bull and six cows, the start of a herd, grazed under the coconut palms. There was a sparkle of adventure and well-being. This extra joy illuminated the purpose of Aurora, filling it with light and music. Bush boys chopped the copra with special vigour, saltwater boys explored the furthest reefs for fish. Beaconsfield said, 'Everyone is glad for you,' and gave a sideways smile. Loloa's cooking improved, and his sister got pregnant.

Clive had never felt a woman's tautened rounding stomach and later, when she put his hand there, the knock of his child inside. It was her own first baby too, a magic as new as the morning. Then without a word she told him what he couldn't say: this was the way for it to end. At seven months, a bursting mother, she stopped coming to his house. Perhaps Aurora had decided.

Beaconsfield tried to explain: 'We have big-big problem because for white people is your shame and for black people is our pride. And the child isn't yours, is only hers, because you not married. So we are waiting to see if boy or girl.'

'What difference does that make?'

'You see we have other story,' Beaconsfield said, clarifying nothing. 'There is boy who asks his mother to give him taro pudding. "Why give you taro?" mother says. "You are not working in taro garden," and gives him a basket of stones. So boy says, "All right, I am running away and you looking for me and never finding." And father cries, "My son is running away!" And boy climbs up a breadfruit tree and sits on top like bird. And father tries to catch him. Boy climbs on other branch and father also, and boy flies to an almond tree, to eat almonds, and father climbs up, but boy flies away for ever, because now is proper bird. Is a hornbill.'

Clive understood that his child, implanted in Aurora, was seen as his gift in return, to be fostered by people who had let him lure them from their origins to share his fantasy. All he could do was show how passionately his life was grafted here.

'We have one more story,' Beaconsfield said. 'Is man and woman working in garden at night. Man is in the dark, but woman is hiding the moon in roots of big-big tree, and taking it out each night and hanging it in tree for light to work. Man asks, "How does she find light?" and looking everywhere and then seeing moon. So woman's secret is no more, and she says, "Now this thing must go up on top," and she sends man to hold it in the sky for everybody.'

There was jubilation at the birth. It was a girl and over the years, from a distance, Clive would watch Isabel, his dark brown daughter, with feelings close to fear and far beyond adoration. She was his own Rebecca.

'You're quite a legend,' they told him in the Tulagi bar, four hundred miles away.

'What's the secret, old man? Won their hearts, have you?'

'Or lost your own?'

Tulagi twice a year, for business and the dentist, was enough for Clive. But he was pleased when a taxi driver, seeing him come off the trading schooner that had brought him from Aurora, shouted, 'Mr Ackerly, here!' and got out to open the door. Clive asked how he recognised him. 'The famous Mr Ackerly! Everyone in Mendanas knows you.' Immodestly, surprising himself, Clive asked if he knew the governor. 'Well, that's different. . . .' The taxi driver didn't know the present governor, only the one before last, whose wife got drunk at a dance for the Queen's coronation and boasted of having screwed the prison commissioner, the fishery officer and the first black magistrate. The publicity made her husband famous.

'It's not just that you've put Aurora back on the map,'

they said in the hotel. 'It's the bloody success you've made of it. Held up before us – the perfect plantation, a model labour force – '

'We can't keep up, old man.'

'Quite a martinet, by all accounts. Run it on naval lines, is that it? Defaulters lay aft on the quarterdeck, an efficient ship's a happy ship – all that stuff, eh?'

'I don't see much use in doing things wrong,' Clive said, catching himself on the brink of more conceit. But it was better to play along with them than argue. He had learnt it on the railway: the futility of not giving what was asked for, if he was to keep the rest.

'Come off it, Clive! You're human, aren't you? All the old weaknesses of man, same as the rest of us. What do you do with yourself? Can't spend your time knocking down coconuts – don't tell me. Tropical afternoons, long hot nights on your own.'

'I play the bagpipes sometimes.'

'Bagpipes! – I've heard it called some funny things.'

'I find there's plenty. The accounts and wages and a stack of books to read.'

'Not enough to make up a four at bridge, are there, out at Aurora?'

'Clive, don't take it to heart, old man, but there's another name you've got – for being different, not one of us.'

'One of you?' Clive looked along the bar: those washed-out white men, fingering their frosted beer glasses and shrivelled superiority.

'You'll stand by us, won't you – at the end?'

'The end?'

One of them began to sing the evening hymn, 'The day thou gavest, Lord, is ended,' but forgot the words: 'Something about earth's proud empires pass away – remember?'

'Just because you've got a freehold doesn't mean you're safe.'

'It's your affair if you don't want to be sociable, but when the crunch comes it'll be nasty if we don't stick together.'

'I trust my people,' Clive said. 'Otherwise I'd feel a fraud.'

'You can't pretend you're the same as the Mendanans, let's face it.'

'I don't pretend anything. Nor do they. They just agree with me – it's the best way to run the place.'

'Treat them like human beings, you mean? – and they'll let you get away with murder.'

'I don't have theories. I just do it the way that looks right.' Clive knew he sounded smug, but didn't mind. These men drew the caricature out of him for their amusement and comfort, and he was happy to keep the truth to himself. Happy too, in his way, to know that they were helping the legend spread through the Mendanas and seep out into the Pacific.

Clive had another reason for keeping out of Tulagi. He was hardly aware of it, he had been protecting himself till one day he went to the secretariat for an appointment with the agriculture officer. In the entrance he collided face to face, to the astonishment of both, with Captain Ishi. The tall well-tailored figure in a dark suit instead of imperial uniform, the blank little eyes and cinema moustache, the idol's face without a trace of ageing, the familiar deference, not quite concealing scorn, as he stepped back and bowed: in twelve years the camp commandant hadn't changed.

Clive couldn't escape. More and more, his life was penetrated and scarred. He took it as a private visitation, a reminder to haunt him, impossible to shake off. Beaten back from the islands in the war, Nippon had returned, faceless and persistent. In the Tulagi stores the goods that used to be British – copra knives and fish hooks, cement, paint, pencils and malaria pills – were made in Japan. But one man's boycott would be useless, and Aurora's isolation couldn't save him. At dark moments, though more rarely each year, he still heard Hutton shouting from the *Prince of Wales*'s engine room, and Awang being blinded by the colonel's men, and Smithy's last laugh before the Turd swiped his face away with a hammer, but they were nothing to the most repulsive memory of all. Even the toes crumpled for ever by Goldilocks were less mutilating to Clive's life – perhaps for being his own since birth, just rather spoilt – than the hideous flashing visions of the man who had picked on him for special treatment.

It wasn't really Captain Ishi coming out of the secretariat, as Clive saw in an instant, but it left him shaking. The agriculture officer said it was the agent of a company that was building a fish cannery, the first factory in the Mendanas: 'Industry at last! – it's what this place needs. And not a penny of our own. All paid out of war reparations by the Nips.' To Clive it was a cynical gesture of remorse. Within a year there were trawlers sailing past Aurora and he didn't need binoculars to see the Turd and Goldilocks on board, screaming at the crew, scooping up tuna and skipjack from his beloved lagoon for the world's supermarkets and a Japanese tycoon's profit.

The best the British could do was build a road from Aurora, the only harbour on the island, twenty miles to a corner of the forest where a timber company – from London or Edinburgh or Sydney or even Tokyo, nobody knew where – might take a concession for cutting teak. An engineer from the public works department, in disgrace for his debts at the Tulagi club bar, was put in charge. To encourage local enterprise an ambitious Mendanan called Dikea was given the contract. Dikea raised money from a Chinese trader and did a correspondence course in business, and cracked his finger joints – a sign of triumph.

Aluminium huts were set up, an unearthly shimmering camp reflected in the lagoon, occupied by motley workers from other islands. An old landing craft brought tractors, bulldozers, graders, yellow monsters that tore into trees, munched the branches, spat out the roots and left a bare red wound on the island, growing bigger. For months the roar of diesels and crash of timber came out of the forest, receding as the road advanced.

Sometimes Clive walked along it to watch the work and be struck by echoes of a railway being built through another tropical forest. This was a softer job, irregular and haphazard: one man assaulting the world alone with his machine, two others arguing over a broken cement mixer, a gang idly dragging rubbish to a bonfire, while in a hut the engineer drank warm beer over his diagrams and Dikea thought of reasons for another trip to Tulagi. There were no rocks to be drilled for blasting, no guards to beat the men with bamboos. The earth was spooned away without resistance, the streams were simply pushed through pipes under the road. There was nothing to obstruct or deflect or stop the work; nothing, either, to ensure that it was done.

All went easily till they reached a river five miles from Aurora and a bridge was needed. The engineer squinted at his red and white poles, finished his beer and went away to Tulagi with Dikea, to consult the public works department. They never came back, but there were rumours. The engineer had had a breakdown and left the Mendanas. Dikea had bought a house on the exclusive ridge, the first Mendanan among the British, and was building himself a swimming pool – cracking his fingers with pleasure. The government couldn't find a timber company for the concession, the quantity of teak was too uncertain. The road would be abandoned.

The aluminium camp lost its shimmer, the machines their yellow paint, and sank into the undergrowth – relics of another war. The workers drifted away. No vehicle ever drove down the road. It was quickly choked with vegetation, the surface broken by the climate. The Japanese at least had got their railway finished, and built their fish cannery.

'That Dikea is no good,' Beaconsfield said. 'Is saltwater boy – how can he understand the forest?'

'But you'll use the road, won't you, as far as it goes?' Clive asked. 'For hunting trips.'

Beaconsfield said nothing at first; then began to speak, and stopped, and began again: 'Bush boys don't like this road. Is very-very hard. Bush boys keep to our old tracks, because are softer on our feet, and very-very friendlier. Are tracks of our ancestors, Mr Clive. The spirits are our black ones, not white man's ones.'

2

'I have received your letters with thanks. My health is excellent/normal/poor. I am/am not working for pay. I am in hospital. My best regards to. . . .' The prisoners crossed out and filled in and signed the printed cards which would be taken down to Banpong and sent home by the Red Cross within a month.

'How can you believe anything they tell you?'

'Like the bags of mail for us down there, waiting for the first train to bring them up.'

'And four tons of Red Cross parcels.'

'Say one thing and do another. I'll never understand. They're on my nerves.'

'Don't let them under your skin, that's all. Keep them on the surface. You can't help the bumps and bruises on the outside. But once they get inside and start tampering –'

'Let them burn their own guts out.'

'Look after yourself or there'll be nothing to take home.'

Three times, in two and a half years on the railway, letters reached the camp, but nothing for Clive. Smithy had a long letter from home which he gave to Clive: 'It's a year old, it means nothing to me, it's all untrue, it could have been sent to anyone – you're welcome.' It was about Smithy's family, people Clive didn't know, people in a story, but as he read it he could see Jenny in the familiar places, the flat, the pub, the bed, not these strangers wherever they were. Jenny was in his hands, on thin blue airmail paper under someone else's handwriting. He got more from it than Smithy did, but couldn't tell him. He couldn't speak.

Three times he sent one of the cards addressed to Mrs Ackerly at the Chelsea flat: 'My best regards to Jenny! Will you ever get them? And will I get one single small regard from you? Received with thanks. Yours faithfully. . . .'

The malaria kept coming back. No work, no pay: Clive marched out to the railway in a stupor of oblivion, weak and blind, shivering with waves of heat and cold. The dazzle of rocks, the din of drilling, punched like a demon industry – the force of blast furnaces, liquid white hot metal, heavy machinery – through his head. Strike, lift, twist. He thought of the rivets of a battleship, the armoured plates of steel that curled out of the sea before the *Prince of Wales* went down. Strike, lift, twist. . . .

The hammer wouldn't swing straight. Anywhere but on the knob of Smithy's drill. One blow hit the rock and the handle jumped from Clive's hands. The next struck the drill sideways and tore it from the hole, out of Smithy's pincers, into Clive's leg. Blood gushed in the morning sun, falling on his canvas boot, mixing with the white rock dust.

The Turd, hunched and brooding like a flat-faced vulture, shuffled nearer. 'Bang-bang!' he yelled when Clive missed again, and unhitched his gun as if to shoot.

'He's ill, you fucking cannibal!' Smithy shouted.

Goldilocks sniffed a victory, his huge glasses flashing from his sulphur face, and scuttled to the scene. The other men stopped work, snatching a rest. An airless silence hung in the cutting.

The Turd yelled again, 'Bang-bang!'

Clive swung the hammer; swung it over his shoulder and let go; fell on the ground, dazed with fever. The hammer landed halfway to the Turd.

'*Bang-bang!*' The Turd dropped his gun and grabbed the hammer; came loping to the drill, still in Smithy's pincers; swung a mighty blow and missed.

Smithy laughed. Nobody else dared. Goldilocks unhitched his own gun.

The Turd swung again and missed.

Smithy laughed again – the last noise he ever made.

The Turd swung once more and deflected it from the drill to Smithy's head; missed the top of the skull but caught the forehead, drove the sledge-hammer through nose, cheekbone, jaw, through a ruined man to mock the laughing face, the blazing heat, the outraged silent prisoners, the useless drill and pincers, the fever-broken and half-conscious but bereaving Clive, who tottered to his feet with one piercing thought among the fuddled others: to get the Turd.

The men shifted, growled, jeered like a chorus. They were more than angry or frightened, they felt violated on behalf of Smithy: anything to avenge him, even from an unarmed naked prisoner with malaria. But the quickest to move was Goldilocks. He didn't have the Turd's strength, he couldn't do such damage with a hammer. Instead he raised his gun and aimed at Clive. Then something held him: the men crowding closer, perhaps, or the blood and dust mixture on Clive's boot. And the Turd yelled, 'All mens work!'

Goldilocks didn't shoot but lowered his gun, flew at Clive with a scream, and smashed the butt into the blood-wet canvas; smashed it again and again, grinding it into the rock, screaming and smashing Clive's foot inside.

They lifted Smithy into the shade where he lived for the rest of the day. It wasn't enough to die for Nippon on the railway: his face must be demolished first. Clive lay with him, his foot swollen and the malaria thumping in his head with the metallic din of hammers. He passed into a coma, numbed by pain, and wasn't aware when Smithy died: alone, lying on his tattooed crucifixion with flies feeding on his wounds. The body had to be carried back to camp for the evening parade and numbered with the rest: only burial could make Smithy truly dead. But despite the damage he looked more real, more living, than the others. In a way, he had been born again and become a man.

Next day, without an anaesthetic, Doc Davis tried to straighten Clive's toes. Three were broken, crumpled out of recognition, crooked for life: 'Something to remind you of Goldilocks. Better than a bullet.'

'Or a hammer.'

The rainstorms were friendly, a cool wash for sweaty dirty bodies, till the days became solid water. The weight of rain, the load that dropped week after week, seemed more than the world could bear. There was a danger of the entire place, with hills and trees and rocks, being launched over a cosmic waterfall and lost. The men wouldn't be surprised: anything could happen here, there was no ordeal too unlikely. They might escape or drown, it was beyond control.

They lived under water, holding their breath and groping like divers on the sea bed. The river swelled and covered the banks, a chocolate tide too fast for barges, tearing through a swamp. Paths were washed away, drains overflowed, the sewage rose in the pits and poison flowed through the camp. Mud got into the rice, into jockstraps, into dreams. For a month the huts were awash, filled with spray, and nothing in them was dry.

On the railway it was impossible to get a bonfire going and burn the trash. The thud of axes, even the guards' screams, were muted by the rain. Red earth dissolved into bottomless mud, stinking toffee which stuck to picks and shovels and had to be scraped off into baskets. Lorries were bogged down to the axle and raised like shipwrecks by teams of slippery naked prisoners, or left there to rust. Feet shot sideways, bringing a man down with a filthy smack. Flesh was torn by hidden stones and bamboo splinters. Massive growths of mud developed round men's ankles – another tropical disease that climbed their legs, circled their waists, rose to their necks. They sank helplessly, sucked down by an enemy below, more subtle than Nippon. They had no weapon against it.

The Turd performed a dashing slither, landing on his back, and Weigall and Robbo cheered: two cheeky boys, caught being disrespectful to the Emperor. The Turd called up more guards who made them kneel and press their faces in the mud, with bamboo blows falling as thickly as the rain and bayonets hovering above. The mud was warm, and smelt of rot and gas.

'I keep such vivid pictures,' Clive said to Jenny. 'It's like having an album of photos from the other side of the world.' He flipped through the pages for diversion or dreaming or just for sanity. Some were from the past, some from the future. Some had Jenny in them, others had only a hole where she ought to be. None of them was complete: just bits – a partial view or a portrait with a blurred shadow across it. He tried to fit them together, but by the time he had found new bits the old ones were lost. 'You need two people to make a whole, you can't sustain it alone, or not if you're half a person like me, a skeleton with no strength left, no power to concentrate, only an instinct deep in the bag of bones that somehow I must keep control of everything, every chance to cheat the enemy, every little daily tactic – everything except hope.' He could never control hope. If he tried – if he gave the least encouragement to despair as some men did – the last two years would have been wasted. 'Jenny, Jenny, I must hope without limit. Do you understand? Smile and kiss me and say you do.'

Slowly his crooked toes mended, though it was months before he could walk without a limp.

Cholera sounded like a biblical plague, a scourge without remedy that swept through distant countries and left nobody alive, but now obsolete: nothing to be frightened of.

The first whisper of it, a rustle in the air, came after the rains when the river was still in flood. It had broken out in camps up towards the soft purple mountains, safely far away. Then bodies came floating down the river with lips curled back from their teeth in agony. It had reached a camp of Asians, the next one upstream, and they were getting rid of the dead the easiest way. The good old river, a friend for battered men, had turned traitor. Everyone was terrified.

Doc Davis had no experience of it, but the men looked to him to save them and he gave orders: bathing prohibited, water to be boiled and cooking things steril- ized and food thrown away if a fly had settled on it. Nobody disobeyed, least of all the guards whose panic upset the strongest nerves. They built a fence round their huts, wore gauze masks and screamed through them with extra venom. Captain Ishi summoned Doc to his cabin as if it was the prisoners' fault, then sent urgently for materials to build a saline condenser. Soon it was steaming on the river bank, stoked day and night with bamboo fuel.

The fear of cholera – the hot days waiting at the edge of danger, the jumpiness and false bravado, the suspense and ignorance – reminded Clive of the morning the *Prince of Wales* was sunk two years ago. And with a triumphant roar of laughter, like one more bomber diving out of the sky, it fell on them.

The laugh came from a hefty Australian sheep farmer on the path back to camp from the railway, a laugh that cracked the twilight and marked the opening shot. He clutched his naked stomach; doubled up with a look of recognition; laughed again. Goldilocks flew at him for being frivolous, before he saw the green vomit that came out with the laugh, and slunk away. Somehow the man got himself to his hut and lay twisting and shrivelling all night, as if being roasted. The juices were escaping from him, blood and mucus and bowel liquids retched or squirted in helpless pain, till next morning the flesh was drained. His body looked punctured, his arms were hooked round his legs for some trace of comfort. Yesterday this man had laughed. Doc Davis pushed a saline injection into a vein to restore the fluid but at midday, half waking from a coma, the man pulled it out: 'What's the fucking use? I'm never going home.' He was angry more than sad and died in the evening, twenty-four hours after that laugh.

Burial was dangerous, he must be cremated. A farmer who used to wade among sheep in the pens and toss them to the shearers was reduced to almost nothing, dry and rigid, each end tied into a rice bag, lifted by two friends on to a bonfire near the cemetery and quickly burnt up. Captain Ishi came to watch, keeping at a distance. Someone uttered the holy words, someone choked on a gulp of wood smoke. Standing back from the heat and crackle everyone asked, 'Who's next? How can I escape?' Afterwards the man's bed was scrubbed and dusted with quicklime.

Eleven died in the first week, twenty-six in the second. This new killer, so fast and random, was worse than anything before: picking the best and most loved,

finishing off the toughest in a few hours. At any moment,
on the railway or in a hut, it would spring the next attack
– a ripper with a mad system of its own. The signs were
griping pain, sudden vomiting, pale watery excrement,
which were common anyway. Now, among men seldom
free of stomach troubles, the least upset was proof of
cholera and a speedy end. Each trip to the pits became a
life-or-death inspection. Anything looked fatal down
there, especially at night if there was a moon. Annihilation
lay under the stink and flies, due tomorrow.

More bodies came down river, also the stench of human
matter putrefying in the heat, and prisoners were sent up
to destroy the Asian camp. Half its inhabitants had died,
the rest had fled into the forest or were too weak to get
away. Before starting to tip victims in the river they had
scratched graves among the huts, but cattle had trampled
through and broken out the corpses – an invitation to the
rats. They were dug up and pulled into the huts for
burning. Any who had fled but not got far, festering in
the undergrowth or picked clean by ants, were brought
in. Under a shroud of maggots an entire family lay in a
swamp of its own filth.

'Thank God,' Coltart said, sicking up a stomachful of
rice, 'I left my wife and kids behind.'

An empty skin, a shred of leather that had been an
Indian – just possibly, Clive thought, the Tamil who had
betrayed him – was propped against a tree. Flies encrusted
his face like the scabs of a secondary disease. But he was
alive if life was still the alternative to death, though eyes
and mouth were obliterated beyond any sign of it. Two
sticks rose from his lap and pleaded for water. Weigall
filled a piece of bamboo from the river and trickled it
between the infested lips, and Robbo stuck a cigarette
there: avoiding contact, holding his breath against the
smell. The Turd was more practical; snatched a spade,
staying clear of the dying man, and ordered them to bash
the last flicker out of him. When they refused he cocked
his gun and fired a round of bullets at the bundle,
disturbing the flies, and kept his muzzle on the prisoners
while they dragged it into a hut.

When the dead were cleared away and any survivors

packed off by barge to some dubious fate down river, the Asian camp was set on fire – a scorching inferno in the forest, cracking tree trunks and lifting a monument of smoke into the sky that hung till sunset and turned gold, then black, and left nothing but the charred earth to mark the lives of thousands who died for the Greater Asia Co-prosperity Sphere.

Injections of saline gave a chance of survival but the guards kept most of it for themselves, leaving Doc Davis enough for one case in ten. His needles were blunt or splintered, the pain killers he bought from Thai traders were often fake, his hospital was full. He took over another hut for a cholera ward and asked for volunteers to tend the men – a dangerous, reverential task.

Clive offered himself, and felt like the priest of some un-earthly rite alone with his secret, not quite in touch with the living or the dead. He lost fear and had no pity at the time: empty of emotions except a vague hunger of the spirit that kept him going, perhaps a kind of transfigured lust, but nothing so definite as love. At moments he knew he would die of cholera, at others he knew he wouldn't – there seemed no difference. He didn't care; didn't stop to think or pray or even hope, while the epidemic lasted, believing that if he attempted any of them he would go mad.

Along both sides of the hut the men were packed on bamboo racks, head to foot in filthy rotting rows. A man's last isolation was spent in contact with the next man's. Move a hand and it touched someone else; lose control and the squalor reached him; die, and he saw what it was like. But they died differently, as they had lived.

Clive hardly knew what he was doing. He might try to guess at a man's terror; enter his mind, share his vision, accompany him to oblivion; or mumble comfort and lies at him; or hold him down and stifle his screams, wondering about the silent screams inside; or cradle his head and forget the railway, camp, cholera hut, and – to a young stranger whose grey face and blue lips and thin stubbled throat doubled his age, whose flesh had been melted down and squeezed away, whose foul jockstrap hung loose on a frame of bones round his genitals – he might speak in a soft bewildered voice about an unknown woman somewhere else, called Jenny.

But he wasn't God, he had no authority or knowledge, he simply performed; worked at whatever was the thing to do, unaware of what it was or how he did it; and told himself in flashes of consciousness that it was worth doing.

He wiped and washed and boiled for them. He brushed flies off them, and gave a hand if they tried to rise or when they fell back. He let them shoot vomit over him and apologise for being a nuisance. He marvelled at their courage and dignity and humour, or their fear and collapse. He took their grubby photos and feeble messages for wives and mothers, and thought he couldn't bear to listen again for the awful wheeze and gargle and last rush of liquid through the slats to show they were beyond pain. But he knew he would have to. He made them more decent than before, straightening stiff dead legs, folding hands, plugging nostrils and mouths and anuses, closing eyes with a dab of cold water if they were stuck. He removed identity discs and wrote down names, saw them carried out with their paltry belongings, cleared up the black pools under the slats, sprinkled quicklime over the spaces they had left, and watched the next ones being carried in. He lived, and they died, in suffocating heat and the sweet odour of decay.

Weigall was one of the first to die in Clive's care, looking over his shoulder to see if Robbo was far behind. The haphazard ways of cholera would have left the two young men apart, but friendship had a stronger pattern. Their short careers as government clerks in Malaya, their capture and imprisonment, the sweltering months on the railway when Weigall held the drill and Robbo swung the hammer, their terror of being separated, their concern for each other, comparing weevils in the rice, sharing stories of home – they had to die together. The only hitch was that Robbo was delayed and went to the bonfire when Weigall's ashes were already in a cigarette tin. Robbo's were put in another and they were buried side by side.

Work on the railway almost ceased. Nippon, with everyone else, was demoralised by the bonfire burning day and night. There was a cry for fuel and prisoners were sent into the forest to cut it. After dark they were guided back to camp by the smoke over the trees, glowing orange from below. They added their bundles to the woodpile and stopped to see who had gone today. A row of bodies with the few scraps they owned lay waiting in their jockstraps – all the rice bags had been used. Any flesh left by undernourishment, further shrunk by dehydration, had lost elasticity and was dented with the fingermarks of men who lifted it. Like bits of fuel the dead were laid lightly on the fire. Sometimes strange things happened in the flames. Muscles contracted, sinews snapped. Slowly a corpse would sit up, turn to stare at his friends through the smoke, raise an arm as if waving, then with a moan lie back on the blaze and be consumed. Next morning some chips were spooned from the ashes into tins or bottles, labelled and buried in the cemetery. Clean, straight young pieces of bamboo were saved for crosses.

The ripper lost its stealth and ran amok, striking everyone in reach, slashing at nerves when it failed to kill. The cookhouse was thought to be a dangerous place, but not eating might be worse than the risk of infected food. Nothing was certain except that soon another man would be jack-knifed by excruciating cramp and in a few hours be dead.

In a single day there were thirty funerals. Then with no warning, with another more cautious laugh from the whole camp, the epidemic ended. There were three deaths one week, none the next. Doc Davis said there could be a second wave, but like the bombers over the South China Sea it had done its work and gone away. The cholera hut was burnt down, the bonfire was let out, the grove of new crosses in the cemetery gave the score. Bathing was allowed again, but the big brown river had lost its innocence and would never be trusted now.

Nippon screamed with relief and impatience, and drove the prisoners back to the railway.

Clive was now his own keeper, cut off from the other

men, relying on himself alone. The only privacy, the last remnant of his life outside the camp, was in his thoughts. He had come to expect nothing, to believe in nobody. Help would come from nowhere but his self-devotion. Its symbols were a spoon and mess-tin, a pair of Japanese boots, a cotton jockstrap, which he adored as a hermit in the wilderness would adore his crucifix or string of beads.

'I wish I had my bagpipes,' he said to Jenny. They were on the sea bed, collecting barnacles. 'Can you imagine – cheering up the men on the railway with "Speed Bonnie Boat"?' He had played it for Churchill and Roosevelt, and the Japanese would like it too. But it would have to wait with all the rest.

Wait, wait, wait – it was the eternal theme. But nothing else waited. 'My twenty-sixth birthday was the last with you. Soon I'll be twenty-nine. So Victor is thirty. At least he's being useful instead of languishing in futility. How can I ever catch up? Will you let me? And what will all this be like to look back on?' Though he would never forget the railway, he wouldn't remember it in any coherent way. It was too indistinct to grasp, too numbing for clear thoughts, like an anaesthetic. 'I'm beginning to see that it's nature's way of getting through the long agony.'

Selfishness was primed by fear. The weak were trampled on, the sick resented, the dying ignored. Degradation meant nothing at this level, where life lay at the bottom of a refuse heap, indistinguishable from death. Clive caught himself out in a moment of abasement outside the guards' cookhouse. After supper, full of complacence, Captain Ishi came from his cabin to watch the swill being put out for the prisoners: a ragged little pack of them, hanging on the hope of something tasty, perhaps nourishing, from the enemy. A black cauldron was put on the ground and they shoved, grappled, scraped with desperate fingers for Nippon's leavings. Clive got a handful of cold burnt stew and broke away in triumph with it dripping down his wrist, to swallow it before someone else could. This was the depth he had reached: the behaviour of an animal, licking his thin claws for the last trace of gravy. But the winner was Captain Ishi, arms folded, a figure of satisfaction in a wretched scene.

Nippon otherwise wasn't pleased. The railway wasn't being built fast enough. Officers from Tokyo, strutting through their imperial operetta, bowing and hissing and tripping over their swords, stirred the camp into a lethal fury. Rest days were abolished, the midday break was cut to half an hour, quotas were increased and sixteen working hours were demanded, starting and finishing in the dark. Time became a wild treadmill from one night to the next, divided by days of blind toil and raging violence. Bodies were battered, limbs broken as the guards screamed 'Speedo!', lashing out with fists and boots and bamboos. The railway must be finished, however many prisoners died.

Clive never saw his hut by daylight. Caught by dysentery on the railway, slipping into the forest with a handful of soft leaves and a swarm of blowflies following him, he was given one minute before being clouted back to work, to foul himself among the men.

3

The nineteen-fifties passed in the Mendana Islands without Clive's energy or enthusiasm diminishing, though the sheepskin bag of his bagpipes rotted with mildew and he never replaced it.

Every two years or so he went to England for a holiday – a week at the Ritz to eat Scotch salmon and grouse and for some elegant shopping, and a week in Brighton with Victor, his brother, and Brenda. He didn't care to see more of the country, he knew it would sadden him: the decadence and lassitude and purposelessness he had read about.

'Only the very best for the very best, Mr Ackerly,' the manager at the Ritz said – it seemed a useful rule – and each time Clive was given the same room overlooking

Green Park. His London suit was hanging in the ward-
robe, pressed and aired to clear away the mothballs, sent
round by Gieves of Bond Street who had made it for him
and looked after it between visits. Putting it on, slipping
into the ways of a colonial on home leave and looking out
of the window, he remembered again why he always
chose to come in autumn. Partly it was for the natural
melancholy, the falling leaves in Green Park and the need
they stressed in him on his first day in this disordered
city – to get back quickly to Aurora where there was no
winter. Also, it was the time of year when he had stepped
off the train at Waterloo to be met by Jenny: he must
honour the season with a sort of tribute, no longer painful
but evocative of something he didn't want to lose.

At Aurora the tailored suit would rot of mildew like the
bagpipes, but he could buy shirts and a new panama hat,
books, groceries, wine. He called at Asprey's to pay for
the pigskin diary they sent him every year and choose a
present for himself, a gold pencil or crystal ashtray or
the latest cunning corkscrew to bemuse Loloa, also a silk
handkerchief each for Beaconsfield and Laki. Going into
the shop, he was flattered but not convinced that they
knew who he was and had been expecting him at that
moment. When they ushered him out he said, 'Such good
people,' half aloud, half to himself in the part of middle-
aged man about town, acting as he thought they wished.
At least he was sure they had no other customer with an
opossum in his roof and a hut standing in the mangroves,
among flashing kingfishers, for a toilet.

'Return of the native!' Victor cried, welcoming him at
the Brighton flat. 'Let me take your spear.' Clive gave up
his umbrella. 'Brenda! – we'll crack open a coconut for our
guest.' At first sight Clive for a moment saw in his brother
another stranger's familiar face: their father's in the photo
by their mother's bed, without the officer's moustache.
He hadn't noticed it before.

Brenda came quivering into the room, plumper and
juicier, oozing with pleasure, unable to hurry, and hugged
him with fluent embracing arms while Victor poured the
drinks. She was less of a fish now than some lush
specimen of deep sea life, half sponge, half anemone,

soaked in contentment. 'I always expect there'll be a brown beauty in tow when you come to see us,' she bubbled, 'with a string of shells across her fanny and nothing else. But I'm glad there isn't – I'd be so jealous.' She released him slowly and Clive felt the liquid being drawn off, drop by drop.

He slid easily into their company. They revelled in each other, and had enough champagne to drown him too. Moving without haste, gliding through the day, Brenda kept up a flow of luscious meals that never ended. Even at night she was often in the kitchen, boiling a kettle, cutting a cake, peeling a fruit. Victor went only once to his office while Clive was with them. The property boom was dying, he could safely leave his partner and take a week off.

'Running away from it, aren't you?' Victor said one day on the balcony over the seafront, after giving Clive a survey of life in Britain now. 'Can't take it.'

'Running away from nothing.'

'Sorry, I know you're not a funk, but – ducking something, aren't you? Dodging – '

'Dodging nothing.'

'All the same, you settled for the easy way out.'

'Easy! Try dressing in the dark tomorrow morning because the matches are too damp to light the candle, and finding your clothes are full of ants. Arguing with the headman because he tells you there's a devil-devil in the copra drier and nobody will work. Wrestling with government officers who ask you silly questions but never come near you, they say it's too far and they haven't time, so you go four hundred miles to Tulagi and find they've been carted to the cemetery or transferred to Africa or retired to Devon and nobody will replace them till next year. Do you think it's easier than sitting in Brighton, waiting for property prices to go up? That's the trouble here – everyone wants a quiet life and to be paid for it. There's nothing I've seen in modern Britain to tell me I was wrong to leave.'

'It's not what you fought for? Slaved on the railway for? Perhaps that country never existed. A place of dreams.

Like Strathpolly. It was only in the mind. A figment. And now it's vanished.'

'I saved a corner of it for myself, thank God,' Clive said, 'while there was any left – while I still remembered what it was like.'

'Anyway, what's wrong with dreams?' Brenda asked.

'You can't live in one,' Victor said. 'You wake up one day when the alarm goes off, or the doorbell rings, or the telephone, and you've got the tax man down your neck, or the bank manager, the rate collector, the meter reader, every man jack who wants your money, and in the end it'll be the undertaker.'

'Aurora isn't a dream,' Clive said.

'A place of escape, then.'

'More a place of commitment.' Clive had long ago stopped being surprised how two brothers could be so unlike.

'You're mad about it, aren't you?' Brenda understood him better. 'I think that's lovely – to be devoted. Like me and Victor.'

'More like us and Brighton,' Victor said.

Clive looked out over the seafront: 'You can't imagine – it's where I follow my instincts with nothing to get in the way. Nobody to obey but myself. No limit but my own ability. I've got a chunk of tropical forest that's all my own and a million coconut trees, a thousand cocoa trees, a pedigree herd of cattle, three hundred illiterate black happy foolish people who. . . .' The brown high tide flopped on the Brighton shore, rolled back, flopped again. 'Funny we should both end up by the sea, Victor. One on a balcony by the English Channel, one on a veranda by a lagoon.'

'And neither of you would swap,' Brenda said. 'But go on about the people.'

'They're not like sailors in a ship. I'm not their captain. It's better than anything I could have got in the navy if I'd stayed – unbelievably better. Though I've been very lucky.'

'You're king, aren't you? Or God, or something?'

'Something.'

'Master – that's it. So where's your mistress? – the

brown beauty with a string of shells. Beechnut nipples and treachery between her thighs.'

Clive nearly told them about his daughter Isabel. But she was too delicate and precious and elusive, ten thousand miles from here, a shadow at the edge of the forest. He couldn't inflict her on Victor and Brenda as a piece of scandal: they would destroy her. He couldn't be certain she was real till he saw her again, playing with other children by the school or singing hymns in church. Isabel! – niece of a gentle smiling bush boy called Loloa and of a Brighton property agent; granddaughter of that dim officer in a photo and of a woman killed by a salmon.

In London before flying back to Aurora he went to the theatre. It became habitual, a last treat to take away, one he couldn't have again till his next visit. He didn't care what the play was, he only enjoyed the occasion: Clive Ackerly, coconut planter from the Mendanas, sitting in the audience while actors came in and out and mouthed their words. Perhaps he wanted to be convinced of the falsity of London life, the perfunctory gestures and plywood scenery. In the interval, in the bar, he watched and listened, thankful not to know any of these people, impatient for a drink brought to him by Loloa. The curtain at the end and the clapping were his release. Now he could go.

A few nights later he was settled by the lagoon. Beaconsfield asked about his trip; showed him the office books; left him alone on the veranda. Something flew low over the house, something splashed in the dark. Clive blessed Jenny for having sent him here.

'I have a story too,' he told Beaconsfield one evening in the office, 'about a king called Gilgamesh.'

'He is ancestor of King George?' his bush boy son asked.

'Long long ago – king of a great city with high walls round it and temples for worshipping the gods. Wise and brave and as strong as a wild bull.'

'King Gilgamesh – I never hear before.'

'But he was restless and lonely, and longed to have a friend. He dreamt of finding a man as strong as himself

– someone he could love as much as a woman, who'd never leave him. But it was only a dream, and he amused himself among his people. No man's wife or daughter was safe from him. Every virgin had to sleep with him first, before her lover. The people were terrified of him. So the gods made another man, the king's equal, his second self, for the two to compete and leave the people in peace. They created Enkidu.'

'Enkidu? – also I never hear.'

'Enkidu had hair all over him, and lived in the forest with the wild animals and swam with them in the streams and sucked their milk and ate grass, but he knew nothing about other men in the world and had never seen a field of crops or a garden with vegetables.'

'Is like proper bush boy.'

'He smashed the hunters' traps and set the animals free, and the people told the king about this wild man – how strong he was.'

'I think Gilgamesh is happy to have friend now.'

'He told them to take a beautiful woman into the forest, a whore from the temple of love, and wait by the water hole where the animals came to drink, and let the woman conquer the wild man. Perhaps her power – '

'Is like poison on him, Mr Clive.'

'For two days they sat watching, and on the third day the animals came, with Enkidu among them. The woman stripped off her clothes and beckoned to him.'

'Is never seeing it before, so beautiful, I think.'

'She pulled him close and showed him what to do.'

'Is nice for him.'

'She taught him everything a woman knows. And they made love for a week, till Enkidu had had enough.'

'Till is tired too much.'

'Then he went back to his life with the animals. But when they saw him, they ran away.'

'Is true – they can smell the woman on him, I think.'

'He wanted to run after them but his legs gave way, his body felt bound with ropes.'

'Is weak from too much woman, you see.'

'He was like an ordinary man now.'

'Is woman's magic on him.'

'She said, "Why d'you want to run wild? You've learnt wisdom now. Come to the city and I'll show you the temple of love and the temple of heaven. Every day is a holiday, and the people wear such clothes – they're wonderful to see, they smell so sweet! I'll take you to King Gilgamesh, who rules all men and is stronger even than you." Enkidu was excited, because he too wanted a friend. "Take me there", he said, "and I'll challenge King Gilgamesh". So she led him out of the forest – this wild man like an animal. He'd never eaten bread before and only stared at it, but the woman showed him, and he ate till he was full and drank wine till he was happy, and brushed his long hair and rubbed his body with oil till he looked like a bridegroom in new clothes.'

'Like me on wedding day – remember, Mr Clive?'

'Then he strode through the streets into the market place to challenge Gilgamesh, and the people crowded round and said, "He's like a god – the king has met his match!" And when the two men met they fought like bulls, locked together, snorting and grappling till the walls shook.'

'Enkidu is winner, I think,' Beaconsfield said.

'I'm afraid not. King Gilgamesh bent on one knee with his foot planted on the ground and in a single toss he threw Enkidu over. Then Enkidu cried, "You are truly the strongest man of all!" and they hugged each other and became friends for ever.'

'I like that English story,' Beaconsfield said.

Clive went on: 'But Enkidu became unhappy.'

'Because he is not living in the forest now.'

'His strength had gone, he was sick of his idle city life. So Gilgamesh decided they must go on a journey. The world was full of evil and the cause was the giant Humbaba, who lived far away in the great cedar forest. They must go there and kill him. But Enkidu had roamed with wild animals and knew how big the forest was, and that Humbaba never slept, guarding his cedar trees by day and night, and roared like a cyclone and breathed fire, and his jaws were death. "Who would dare go into that country?" Enkidu asked.'

'Because Enkidu is knowing the forest too well,'
Beaconsfield said, defending the wild man.

' "Already you're afraid!" Gilgamesh shouted. "Only
the gods can live for ever." The king looked over the city
wall and saw the bodies of dead men in the river, and
knew that one day he would die like that, with despair in
his heart. But if he died in the forest, he'd be famous. He
prayed for protection, and called the people to the market
place: "I'm going to conquer that monster, whose terror
fills the world, and my name will live for ever." They tried
to put him off and said that nobody could stand up to
Humbaba, but he laughed and turned to Enkidu: "Shall I
say I'm afraid of Humbaba? Shall I sit at home for the
rest of my life?" And Enkidu shouted, "Forward! There's
nothing to fear!" So the two set off, and after a long
journey they came to the gate of the cedar forest. Enkidu
tried to open it, but suddenly his hands trembled with
fear. Gilgamesh told him not to be a coward: "Have we
come so far, through such danger, to turn back now?
Would you rather stay behind? Keep close, and we'll
defend each other. Forget death, and follow me!" They
went on into the heart of the forest, where they came to
the first of the great cedar trees, and Gilgamesh took his
axe and cut it down. When Humbaba heard it he was
furious: "Who has violated my forest and cut down my
tree?" Gilgamesh put on his armour and clenched his
teeth and stamped the ground, but Enkidu was terrified:
"My lord, you don't know Humbaba! His teeth are
dragon's fangs, his face is a lion's, he charges like the
rushing of a flood, he crushes the trees with a look. You
can go on if you want, but I'm going back to the city."
Gilgamesh urged him on: "This isn't the time for death!
All men must die one day, but today we'll go and meet
this monster. Throw away your fear, and attack! Whoever
leaves the fight unfinished is never at peace." Humbaba
came out of his house, and tossed his head and fixed his
eye on Gilgamesh – the eye of death. But Gilgamesh called
to the gods, and they sent the winds – the freezing north
wind, the scorching south wind, the whirlwind and the
tempest, all eight winds that gripped and lashed
Humbaba like snakes, till he couldn't go back or forward.

Gilgamesh and Enkidu cut down the next cedar tree, and
the next, and each time Humbaba blazed fire at them, but
each time he lost a little power.'

'Is right,' Beaconsfield agreed. 'His magic is in trees.'

'At last they reached the giant's house, and he was
beaten. "Let me go free, King Gilgamesh," he cried, "and
be my master! The trees that I guarded will be yours – I'll
cut them down and build a palace for you." The king felt
pity and said to Enkidu, "Shouldn't we set our prisoner
free?" But Enkidu replied, "He'll block the forest paths
and you'll never return to the city." Humbaba shouted at
Enkidu, "You – a servant! Dependent on the king! And
now you're jealous, you're frightened of a rival!" But
Enkidu said, "Don't listen to him, my lord. He must die."
So Gilgamesh struck his sword into the giant's neck, and
Enkidu struck, and Humbaba fell. They chopped off his
head, and cut down the rest of the trees and cleared the
forest. But the gods were angry with them, and took
Humbaba's power and gave it to the lions and the floods
and the mountains, and to death.'

'So I think, is still some evil in the forest.'

'Or there's something of the forest in every man.'

'So one day every man is dying. Also King Gilgamesh
and Enkidu, I think.'

'In the city, when Gilgamesh put on his robes and
crown, the goddess of love saw how beautiful he was.
"Come to me," she said, and promised him riches and
power if she could be his bride. "But what can I give you
in return?" he asked. "And what would happen to me?
Which of your lovers did you love for ever?" One man
she had turned into a bird with a broken wing, another
into a wolf chased by the dogs, a third into a blind mole
deep in the earth, whose desire was always out of reach.
"If you and I are lovers," Gilgamesh said, "wouldn't I be
the same as the others you once loved?" In a rage she
flew up to heaven to tell her father, the king of gods:
"Gilgamesh has insulted me!" She asked for the bull of
heaven, to destroy him: "If you refuse, I'll break open the
doors of hell and bring up the dead to outnumber the
living and eat their food." So she got the bull and led it
to the city gates. It snorted once, and cracks opened in

the earth and a hundred men fell to their death. It snorted again and more cracks opened, and two hundred fell in. It snorted a third time and Enkidu fell, but saved himself. He dodged the cracks and jumped on the bull and seized it by the horns.'

Beaconsfield cheered: 'Because Enkidu is very-very strong.'

'The bull fumed and lashed him with its tail, and Enkidu shouted to Gilgamesh, "My friend, thrust in your sword behind the horns!" So Gilgamesh chased the bull and caught it by the tail and killed it, and they cut out the heart and gave it to the gods. But the goddess of love climbed up on the city wall and cursed them for killing the bull of heaven. Then Enkidu tore off one of the bull's legs and threw it in her face, shouting, "If I could catch you I'd do the same to you, and twist your stomach round your waist." '

Beaconsfield approved: 'I like Enkidu – is good bush boy.'

'The goddess collected her whores from the temple of love, and her dancing and singing girls, and they set up a great howling and wailing over the bull's leg. But Gilgamesh hung the horns on his palace wall, and the two friends hugged each other and drove through the crowded streets. "Who is the bravest here?" Gilgamesh called to the girls. "Who is the most famous of men?" And they shouted, "Gilgamesh! Gilgamesh!" So there was a great feast in the palace that night.'

'Like the night when I married, Mr Clive.'

'But Enkidu fell ill. The gods were angry with the two men for killing the giant Humbaba and the bull of heaven, so one of them must die.'

'Why not King Gilgamesh?'

'Because Enkidu had shown no mercy to the giant and had thrown the bull's leg at the goddess. He lay on his bed in misery while the sickness destroyed him, and wished he'd never left the forest. "See what has become of me!" he said to the friend who had brought him to the city.'

'Is wanting to be free again, like bush boy.'

' "Happy to fall in battle!" he cried. "But I must die in

shame." Gilgamesh wept for him as he died, and laid a
veil over him like a bride, and stamped and fumed round
his friend's bed, and tore his hair out and pulled off his
royal robes. He wept for a week, hoping it might bring
back his friend, and wouldn't let the body be buried till it
had begun to rot and he knew there was no hope.'

'I think Enkidu is like piece of forest in the city, very-
very important for Gilgamesh, and now is gone.'

'Gilgamesh had a statue made of him, of gold and
jewels, and then went wandering into the forest, dressed
in wild animals' skins and eating raw flesh, letting his
hair grow long, crying for Enkidu: "How can I rest? How
can I be at peace when the friend I loved is dead and one
day I shall also die? My life is nothing." He was afraid of
death now, and travelled on another journey alone, in
search of everlasting life.'

'Also I think is trying to find other wild man in the
forest, to be his friend. Is not happy in the city, because
is needing Enkidu.'

'He was hungry, he was burnt by the sun or frozen
with cold, he climbed mountains and crossed rivers and
went deep into the underworld. "Show me the way!" he
cried to the gods, but they answered, "You'll never find
what you're looking for. There's no permanence in the
world. Nothing lives for ever." They told him to bathe
and put on his robes again, to fill his stomach with good
food, to dance and be merry, to make love with his wife
and rejoice with his children, for those too were the lot of
mortal men, as well as death.'

'So King Gilgamesh is going back to the city and dying
like Enkidu?'

'The gods gave him one secret. They said that at the
bottom of the sea there was a flower growing like a rose,
with thorns. It would prick him, but if he could pick it
and eat the fruit he'd become young again. So he swam
down with heavy stones tied to his feet, to drag him to
the bottom, and found the flower. It pricked him, but he
picked it and swam up again, and landed on the shore.
He'd take it to the city and give its fruit to the old men,
to make them young, and one day he'd eat it himself and
have back all his youth. But on the way he stopped to

bathe in a stream and a snake stole the flower, and shed its skin and became young, and vanished. Gilgamesh sat down and cried: "Was it for this that I toiled and bled? I found a secret, but lost it to the animals. I've gained nothing." So he went back and ruled his people till he grew old and died, knowing that no man could escape his fate. He lay on his bed like a hooked fish, or a wild animal caught in a trap, and they mourned him and praised him and buried him in the richest tomb, because nobody was the equal of King Gilgamesh.'

'Except Enkidu, I think,' Beaconsfield said.

There were many things to delight Clive in those middle years, but nothing so much as his morning walk round Aurora. First it took him through the tall coconut palms where his shiny brown cattle grazed in the dappled light. Panama hat on his head, a long stick cut from a wild holly in his hand, he would stop to talk to the cow boy and admire his herd; then march away down the path to the big tin shed where the copra was dried in an arrangement of old oil drums and wire mesh over a furnace of logs.

He climbed into the hills where the cocoa grew, sweating heavily but alert for anything. A forgotten cocoa pod on the ground, a knife left against a tree, a sucker that needed cutting, a patch of fungus, a nest of the red ants that ate the pestilential flies that ate the cocoa – nothing escaped him. Suddenly he stopped, uttered a gruff bark into the trees and listened for an answering bark from the cocoa boys, who somewhere were picking or pruning or brushing through the groves in a ragged laughing line. He dived off the path to join them for a joke or a rebuke, the latest gossip, news of the football team or another story from the dark Mendanan imagination.

He loved it, it gave him daily pleasure to walk among his trees and people; to stand in the lofty architecture of coconut palms, the thin pillars of an impossible cathedral rising to a vault of fronds; to thread his way under the twilit crypt of a cocoa grove, shot with stabs of light; to stride along the avenues he had once cut through the forest between huge trees, where an absurdly gaudy butterfly flopped in and out of the sunshine, or a pair of white cockatoos cackled from the treetops, or a mob of green parrots came scooting out of nowhere.

He liked the picture of himself, a defiant figure in this overwhelming landscape: eccentric perhaps, but beyond caring about anyone's opinion, out of reach of the glib evasive men who couldn't touch him now. He was aware that he was as improbable and anomalous as his pedigree cows under the palms, as he stalked across this Pacific island or knelt to drink from one of the rivers that tumbled through his land, overhung with multi-coloured foliage, cascading over rocks, slipping through deep clear pools.

'If only,' he sometimes wished, 'there was a trout under that bank.'

The memory of Strathpolly receded but never vanished, and could still disturb the incomparable power and vividness of Aurora.

4

Crouched in a rainstorm in the prison camp at night, wrenched with dysentery, gripping his bunch of soft leaves – the nearest trees had been stripped, each visit meant further to go for them – Clive drank the water streaming down his face and wished it was the generous sweet Strathpolly rain. 'It falls straight from heaven,' he said to Jenny, 'and we'll go out on the mountains and get wetter than you've ever been, and washed and purified and restored. . . .'

Splashing back to his hut, he was shouted at for not saluting the guardroom. He stopped dead, bowed stiffly into the dark and waited for the next attack, his bowels turning over again: soon he would have to go back to the pits. Only a laugh came from one of the guards. Then

Captain Ishi's voice from the commandant's cabin: 'Come here.' And again, 'Come here, my friend.'

Clive approached the cabin: the nearest he had been to it.

'Come inside, my friend – do not be frightened.' The fastidious English, the American accent, were ominous.

Clive stepped on to the veranda. A screen was drawn back, he passed through into the yellow lamplight.

'I want you to pull off my breeches. It is easier for another man.'

The oil lamp stood on a shelf with a mirror behind it. At first its doubled flame was too bright for Clive.

'Hold the end and pull.'

After a moment Clive could see a low table with a brass bell on it, stools, rush mats, a black metal trunk, a radio. On the wall between a coloured picture of Fujiyama and a scroll painting of blossom, a sword hung in its scabbard. There was a smell of unknown fruit. Stripped to his olive breeches Captain Ishi was sitting on a stool, his tunic and shirt off, his jackboots on the floor. He lifted a leg towards Clive.

'Pull harder, it is tight – do not worry, my friend, there is no danger. Now the other.' He stood up in his cotton loincloth – a smoother, less blemished figure than any of his prisoners, marked only by two brown discs on the polished ochre of his chest, large and hairless and not quite like any other man's nipples that Clive had seen. Between them a small ivory ornament hung on a silk cord from his neck: a carved fish, perhaps, or a pistol. His shoulders had an almost holy symmetry, his back was balanced like a law of mathematics, his muscles lifted the skin without spoiling the perfection: an ideal model, Clive thought, repeated by the lamp in silhouette on the cabin wall, twice the size. He put on a black silk gown, tied it with a white belt and went to the mirror. 'It is a pleasure,' he said, looking at his reflection, 'to have a civilised friend to talk to.' He might have meant the figure in the mirror. 'Do you understand that?'

'I have nothing to talk about,' Clive said. The commandant's body, though such a feature of the cabin, wasn't a topic he would choose.

'Pardon me, that is not true.'

'And after three years as your prisoner I don't feel civilised.' Five minutes ago Clive had been squatting in the rain, and would be back there before long.

Captain Ishi raised both arms above his head, picked his right foot off the floor, tucked it under the gown, then sank very slowly on his left leg, speaking to Clive and himself in the mirror. 'I am a prisoner too. We are locked together in this hole.' He unfolded his right leg from the gown and bent back from his hips to touch the floor, cantilevered by the outstretched foot: the calf and thigh barely quivering, the fingers playing with their own shadows. 'It is a disgrace for me to be here, as it is for you. We should be in battle, fighting each other, not trapped in this jungle cesspool.' He formed a horizontal span, pivoted on one foot, draped in black silk. With the same precision he drew in his leg, hinged his body upright, rose to his feet, lowered his arms. The moves were exactly calculated, the timing was spun out to the limit – a marvellous feat of slowness. 'I want one friend, that is all. Someone to watch me. You were passing tonight, so I have chosen you. It is your luck, and also mine.' He performed again with the opposite limbs – tucking, sinking, unfolding, recoiling, rising. 'My control is good, do you not think? It means I have been practising. I wonder if you could do so well.'

'On the food you give us. . . .' Whatever Clive's condition, he could never have done those exercises. He envied Captain Ishi, not for his physique so much as the expert, elegant use of his body; and was surprised at his envy.

Captain Ishi stood up: 'Now we shall have a drink.' He brought out a bottle of Thai whisky and glasses from the metal trunk. 'It tastes terrible, but the result is good.' He turned his glass to Clive's with the delicacy of another exercise: 'Your health, my friend!'

'My health has never been worse, but thank God it's not as bad as some – '

'Drink your whisky, please. It may do your stomach good. But we must not talk of ugly things – they are so common here. Do you like Wagner, my friend?' He turned

the radio knob but found nothing he wanted. 'Another
time, perhaps.' He emptied his glass, gulping fast, and
poured himself more. 'Drink, my friend, or I shall be
drunk before you.'

'I'm not used to it, it's the first in years.'

'We shall practise together, and hope one day for the
Twilight of the Gods.' As he leant forward to pour whisky
for Clive, the ivory ornament slipped out of his black
gown and swung on its cord from his neck. It was neither
fish nor pistol, but a phallus.

At night the guards lit fires round the camp to keep tigers
out. The prisoners lit fires too, for cooking the extra bits
that saved them from the eternal rice. Someone had
bought a duckling on the river barges, or trapped a giant
lizard, or stolen a few sweet potatoes from the store. Bony
scavengers, pagan worshippers of some crude morsel
simmering in a tin, they stirred and prodded and tasted
and chewed. Beyond the firelight the click and buzz and
jingle of forest life reached out of the dark.

'Have you noticed how your nails have stopped
growing?'

'That's not the only thing to stop. If you brought in the
Queen of Sheba and she undressed and lay on top – '

'It's the rice. Soon as you're out of this and get a steak
inside you – '

'Same with me. I used to dream of nudes, but not any
more. It's chocolate éclairs now.'

'Potato chips and walnut cake and giant sausages.'

'Haven't had a nude for months.'

'I get that cake dream too. Plates of them laid out on a
table. Cherry cake, coffee cake, cream sponge – '

'With lemon icing.'

'Marzipan.'

'Meringues – a dish of them with steak and mushrooms
on top, and a fried egg, covered in custard.'

'For Christ's sake!'

'Funny thing is, I never eat it. It's just for looking at.'

'I go into a sweetshop, the one where I was a kid before
the war, but I don't know which way to look, I can't

decide, and in the end I buy a bag of treacle toffees, a bag
of gobstoppers, a bag of bullseyes, a strip of liquorice – '
     'And find you can't pay.'
     'I haven't got a penny on me.'
     'It always happens. Someone's cooking dinner. Frying
in the kitchen. I can smell it. Just when it's ready I wake
up.'
     'I go home every night.'
     'Tea with the family.'
     'I kept a piece of wedding cake in a box. All through
the fighting. Still had it when I was taken. Last thing I
did when they made me turn my stuff out – opened the
box and it was solid cobwebs. I ate it all the same.'
     'Brought back your wife, did it?'
     'Tasted of armpits.'
     'That's what I mean.'
     'I got a kick out of looking at my wedding photo till
the Nips took it. Dirty bastards, fuckee-fuckee-all-nightee
gabble with their fingers groping my wife, rubbing her
across their trousers – I tore it up and threw the bits at
them. Now I think about it, it doesn't matter. It was just
a picture. Probably false anyway. For all I know she's
having it off with my best man.'
     Clive was thankful he had no photo of Jenny. He would
stand close in front of her, his hands under her arms,
thumbs in her ribs, then run them down to her hips, slide
them back and pull her towards him. Sometimes he made
love with her more truly than they ever had.

The gang lined up for punishment in their ragged bits of
straw and cotton, in the stunning heat. Clive couldn't
remember what it was for: losing a shovel, failing to salute
the guardroom, not bowing deeply enough to the Rising
Sun, lagging on the railway, singing something offensive
to the Emperor – it didn't matter. The Turd drew a circle
on the ground with a bamboo, stood on a rock for a better
swing, ran his narrow eyes along the line of men, then
delivered an unearthly spitting shouting noise that came
from behind the buckle of his belt, as if something in his

stomach had burst. Simultaneously Goldilocks screamed for the first man to step into the circle.

One of them was felled by the first blow, to be kicked to his feet by Goldilocks and propped up for more. One fainted. One who staggered and put a foot outside the circle had it smashed, like Clive's once, by the butt of Goldilocks' gun. One had his jockstrap whipped off, to hoots from other guards who came to watch. One was cracked across the neck with a sickening crunch – the Turd's aim was wild: shoulders, ribs, kidneys, thighs, anything would do. One yelled, one sobbed, one managed to laugh. Each time they were sent back to the end of the line for another round.

Clive was all of them, or none of them, or someone else. When his turn came he walked forward to stand in the circle, feeling it wasn't himself who was waiting there for the Turd's bamboo, but only the astonishing flesh that contained him: a body which had shown such loyalty, a kind of doggy faith in him, though at times he had had revulsion for it. It wouldn't let him down if he trusted it in return, controlled his anger. He mustn't give in. His fear must be for what sort of man he was, not for what the Turd would do. This scene, as he watched it, was nothing new. He had been through it before. It was a detail from a painting he had once seen, a passage from a poem, a horror raised to a celebration by someone who understood what men had faced since the beginning of the world. If it was happening at all, and wasn't a timeless universal allegory, there would be a happy end.

He saw the Turd's huge knuckles, the muscles in his pock-marked face, the way he swung upwards from his feet rooted in the rock. He heard the whistling bamboo and felt the sting, the pain that twisted his guts and drove his lungs into his throat. He marvelled at how much he could take. But it was more than endurance, more even than mastery of himself: it was a fragment of something infinitely wonderful and terrible, which would last for ever. But this wouldn't. And one day the war would end.

An hour later they were slipping into the river, their toes in the gentle mud.

*

'I don't hate them, Jenny. I don't hate anyone now. I used to hate an engineer on the *Prince of Wales* called Hutton. Not any more. What's the good of hating? At first I thought I hated the other prisoners, but it isn't true. To hate them I would have to hate myself. That would kill me. Hatred is death, don't you agree? One day I shall love everyone, not only you. Not yet. I must get through this, then I shall be ready. It will be wonderful. And the joke is, it could never happen without this first.'

Clive stared at the thin, hard man in Captain Ishi's mirror: a mere sketch, a travesty of himself. Anatomy had been falsified, angles sharpened, roundness flattened. Under the parched skin the flesh had contracted, exaggerating the bones. The skull looked too big for the stringy neck to support. The eyes, hollow-ringed and without a glint of moisture, were impotent of tears. Their vision was faintly blurred, as if dryness had spoilt the polish. The hair was chopped short, the chin was slashed by a blunt old blade, the lips were raw, the teeth jutted from the softened gums, the throat was scrag and bristle. The shoulders were bruised, cut, squared off to points held out by collarbones like a coat-hanger. Below, the ribs rattled downwards to a deflated waist. Somehow all the organs must be still inside, but there seemed no room for them. The navel was stuck on the front, a buckle on the creased and threadbare stomach. Hips stood out like handles, something to grip, but that jockstrap, a grubby pouch of cotton between the wishbone thighs, contained nothing useful or valuable or funny, just some extra bits left from a forgotten function. Arms dropped in sections, tied to each other with a device of knobs. Hands were too big, fingers too long, drawn on a larger scale to show each bone. The legs were also elongated, their sinews defined, with kneecaps fixed on like the last pieces of a suit of armour. In places the skin was flaking off to leave paler, smoother patches, or was scarred by thorns, stings, blows. Near the ground it was scaled with mud.

The figure was absurd, Clive saw: a scarecrow with a dim resemblance to a man he once knew and loved, lucky to be alive.

*

Sleepers were sawn from tree trunks as the track was levelled. Then one day a steam whistle cut the hot afternoon and a train came snaking up from the plains with a load of rails to be laid ahead of it – pegged into the sleepers and checked as the wheels rolled on into the hills. To test the bridge the open wagons were loaded with prisoners piled everywhere, and Coltart was forced to drive the engine. It held up, and the men cheered. The guards fired volleys close above their heads.

A year after work began, the railway was finished. A general was brought up on a special wagon with a thatched roof, to drive a gold peg into the last sleeper. He gave the prisoners a holiday and a tin of tuna fish each. 'The imperial army,' he told them from his wagon, 'has treated you justly and fairly. Your duty now is to improve your health for any further task ordered by the Emperor.' Nobody clapped or cheered but Captain Ishi blew through his teeth, the peculiar salute of Nippon, and it was taken up by the men – a quiet hissing that grew to the strength of tropical rain, quickly torrential. At any moment the deluge would be on them, the trees would be bent and battered, the puddles would appear. The general looked frightened, the engine whistled, the train rolled away in a flurry of swords and jackboots. Without a word the men filed into the cemetery and sang a hymn. By evening the bamboo crosses were strung with wild orchids.

'You feel ashamed,' Clive suggested, feeling more than shame himself.

'I don't know,' Coltart answered. 'They said it was impossible and we built it. You should be proud.'

'I'd drive that gold peg into the Emperor's heart.'

'But the tuna fish is nice, you must admit.'

Over the next month, camp life changed. The only urgency was to keep trains rolling up to Burma with troops for the front: wagons crammed with young soldiers, horses, artillery, to fight the British. Gangs were kept to cut wood for the engines and maintain the track – ballasting, mending bridges, patching up embankments after rain – but the old pressure was gone. Doc Davis with his hospital and patients, hobbling or on stretchers, were sent down by train to the plains. Later hundreds of prisoners, with Coltart and Atkins among them, were shipped to Japan to work in coalmines. There was more space now. Only Clive, of the men from Kota Bharu, was left.

Captain Ishi freed him from the railway and let him make a garden by the river, under a cliff where monkeys whistled at him from ledges in the rock or dived carelessly from crag to treetop. He cleared the plot and turned the soft rich soil and planted lettuces, cabbages, tomatoes, and dug water channels between the beds; and found a deep happiness in it. To dribble seeds along a furrow and cover them, to push a bean into the soil and wait for the green shoot, to hoe and weed, to dam the eager water or release it among the seedlings, to reap his vegetables so soon – this was good and joyful, something to nourish the frail roots of his own life. Every day after morning parade, with a new relish for the day, he slipped down the path to his garden.

In the early morning, boiling from the river surface, tufts of vapour rose into the cold mist that hid the valley. The dew smelt of sweetness, the night's gift, a blessing that couldn't last. An egret stepped along the bank, whiter than the mist. Dawn hung a mother-of-pearl lining under the sky, filtering the day, till suddenly it dissolved to leave the brassy sun, the swirling river, the soft but deadly forest, the purple mountains. Kingfishers shot over the water and the monkeys caterwauled.

A barge came swiftly down river with boatmen working long oars to keep it in midstream, clear of mudbanks. Another came up against the current, hugging the shore, the men leaning on their poles as they walked from bow to stern. In dry weather when the sun scorched the forest, brittle leaves as big as plates rattled to the ground. The soil shrank from the stalks of Clive's plants and they needed daily watering. In the rains they were nearly washed out. He enjoyed the rhythm, the little victories, the evidence of fertility. After some months he made a bamboo shelter where he lay in the hot hours and watched the river.

On the other side a Thai family had built a house on

high tree stumps, with a ladder and a palm-leaf roof and
a farmyard mess underneath – an echo of Awang's house
two years ago. It was shaded by mango trees and a row
of tall kapoks, reflected deep in the river. A fishtrap, a
flimsy scaffold of bamboos, stuck out from the bank.
Beyond was a small banana plantation and a rice field. A
water buffalo pulled a wooden-wheeled cart, and
ploughed the rice and irrigated it, lumbering round a
pump.

A man waved across the river, and Clive waved back:
they were in the same struggle, part of a human pattern.
The man's young wife, naked above her skirt, threshed
rice in a basket tray, tossing it over and over in the sun
for the breeze to blow away the chaff. Chickens pecked
round her feet, and her children played. Her breasts, the
colour of autumn bracken, were rounder and more taut
than Jenny's, but Clive felt no lust for her, only a throb
of wonder: the simple fact of such generosity. A much
older woman, hooped over her own toes, shuffled and
nodded and worried under the trees. In the afternoon
the man hitched up his sarong and waded like another
waterbird into the shallows; slung a net that dropped in
a circle on the surface; waited for it to sink, then pulled
it back to unpick stones and bits of weed from the mesh,
and perhaps a minnow.

In time the old woman crossed over in a boat, slanting
into the current, standing half-naked behind a single oar,
her knobbled back arching to the job. She tied up to the
bank and walked through Clive's garden with a peasant's
scrutiny, as if it was hers. At the corner of the lettuces
she stopped, hoisted her skirt a little and with legs apart
like a horse unplugged a stream of urine, golden in the
sun, splashing warmly at her feet; then added a dry fart
and came to squat at a distance from Clive's shelter, close
enough for conversation without being familiar.

'Good afternoon,' he said politely.

She said nothing, but rocked slightly on her hairpin
legs: thin brown elbows on thin brown knees, skirt stretched tight over hips and thighs. Her scalp was wrinkled
under her white hair, her feet were still wet.

Clive said, 'It's a beautiful place,' and waved a hand

round the view to scoop up the river, forest, cliff, mountains, and offer it to her: it was all he could give.

She seemed to look at it for the first time, with the freshness of very old intimacy. From here, the house across the river where she lived was new to her, and the man and woman and children in it were strangers.

'Are you the man's mother?' Clive asked.

She gave a rusty, nasal squawk.

'Or the woman's mother?'

She gave it again.

'Probably you'd be my mother's age,' he said, 'though it's hard to tell. She'd be about fifty-five now. How old are you?'

She turned her walnut face on him, but didn't speak or smile.

'You might be anything up to a hundred, though I doubt if you're over fifty. People age quicker here. I've put on twenty years since I came. D'you think my wife will recognise me? But she'll have changed too.'

The old claws slipped under the withered, black-tipped breasts as if searching for their vanished shape; dug into the top of her skirt, and found a box of matches and a small cheroot. She fitted it among the few stained teeth and lit it: a strong aroma in a puff of smoke, an old woman's friendship blown at Clive.

'You're lucky to live in a place like this,' he said. 'Most people would call it paradise. You've no idea how ugly the world is.'

She pulled deeply on her cheroot and shot a gob of spittle into his cabbages.

'But it's tough, I expect. You're as thin as I am. Hours of labour for a bowl of rice and an onion and a bit of old fish. It's the same for us in the camp and we hate it, we live for the day when we can escape. But you've got it for life. Seven days a week, no holidays, no pension at the end – you should complain.'

She gave the squawk.

'The scenery makes up for the starvation, doesn't it?'

Silence.

'It does me good,' he said, looking at the river. 'Till I

came down here I never knew how beauty can be so full of vitamins.'

Still silence.

'I wonder – have I grown up as well as older? Or have I just grown away from myself? And who is myself? My past seems part of someone else's life. The man I used to be isn't me at all. At first I clung to him, but bit by bit he dropped away. Or I discarded him, to survive, and turned into a different man. Not such a nice one, I'm afraid. And I have a feeling that what I've become is what I'll always be.' Clive waited for the old woman to say something, then went on: 'That's all I can see of the future – myself in it, as the man I am now. The future already exists and I know I shall reach it, but it's out of sight. Like the river round the next bend – the water hasn't got there yet.'

Suddenly, the way she had emptied her bladder, the old woman let out a stream of words, a burst of liquid vowels and hisses under pressure from inside. When it stopped, a gleam of satisfaction crossed her face: it was her full, honest opinion, and good for the garden too. She squeezed out a few more words and then was dry.

'I'm sure you're right,' Clive said. 'I just wish I understood.'

She sat and smoked, hardly making a noise, and later rowed back over the river, the cheroot pinched between her lips.

After work, prisoners came down to bathe – hundreds of skinny pilgrims to a river that had once brought corpses. They threw off their hats, unslung their jock-straps, walked into the water, sank quickly to the chin; rinsing tired flesh, kicking to save their wounds and scars from fish. Afterwards they tried to catch them with lumps of rice on a wire hook, or groped in the mud for clams.

The sun sank over the mountains, edging the trees with flame. The river melted into gold, the monkeys shouted from their red-hot cliff. Long-beaked toucans, foolish and intent, came whirling overhead. The cicadas were already singing. Clive watched the Thai family prepare for night: dousing water over the buffalo, hauling up their fishtrap net, stirring smoke from a fire to cook on. A million frogs

began their clatter and had reached full force before he
went up to the camp for evening parade.

After dark he returned to his garden and stayed till he
couldn't bear the mosquitoes. On fine nights the mountains showed as a blank in the sky, without stars, or
flickered and rumbled before a storm. He could hear the
quiet sigh of the river flowing past, coming from somewhere, going somewhere else, and at one end or the other
he felt that Jenny might be there. The water carried the
strength he didn't have, which he could breathe in with
the warm moist air lying over it. Often he caught the
sharp whiff of a cheroot and knew that the old woman
was hidden in the dark. She never came close. Even by
day she sat at a distance while he talked, sometimes
answering with a squawk or a torrent of words he couldn't
understand. Once, on the way back to her boat, she pulled
off some of his tomatoes and tied them in her skirt. Clive
didn't mind. Next time, she brought him a bunch of
bananas.

'Shall I tell you about my wife?' he asked her one day.
'I don't suppose you've seen a white woman, with skin
like mine before it was sunburnt.' He pinched a piece of
his leg to show her. 'She has eyes the colour of a rain
cloud, and hair the colour of rice stalks before you harvest
them – can you imagine?'

Clive had a feeling that the old woman was taking it in
and, like a medium, was somehow passing it on to Jenny.

'I think about her when I'm working in my garden – I
wish she could see me. There's something in the soil.
Contact with the earth. I can almost touch her here, which
I never could when I was on the railway. There's a
message for Jenny every time I plant a seed. And an
answer from her when I pick a vegetable. D'you think
that's love? Or nonsense?'

They sat apart for hours, linked by the old woman's
cheroot smoke stretching over and wrapping them, and
their one-sided conversation.

'I talk more to you,' Clive told her, 'than to the men I
live with. We're too close up there in the camp. I know
the most intimate things about other men's bodies, and
I've come to love them and they love me, but we're not

friends. We're terribly separate. We're desperate to hang on to our identity, or what we can remember of it, in case we get boiled down into the same mush. With you, I can say anything and stay intact. I like you. I've learnt from you. You understand hunger and disaster better. I watch you and your family across the river, living on so little and never expecting more. That's what you've taught me. You make the best of what you get, thankful it isn't even less.'

The young woman on the other side of the river came down to wash herself, waist-deep in the water, sluicing her lovely breasts and throat, ducking her head in a girlish swoop, reaching down to the parts under the surface, the sun dripping on her shoulders; then stood on the bank and slipped a clean dry skirt over her head, wriggled it down and dropped the wet one from underneath on to her feet; combed and tossed her hair, a fresh young woman who never waved across the river, but went back through the shimmer to her house under the mango trees, her husband and children and lifelong toil.

'Do you not hate me?' Captain Ishi asked.

'Hate you?' Clive considered. 'For taking so much of my life?'

'For taking revenge. You invaded our ancient world. You paraded your arrogance and superiority. You stopped us being ourselves in our own land. It was not very clever of you.'

'It's you who hates,' Clive said. 'You hate me for the past.'

'You thought it would last for ever. But we broke the spell.'

'I'm a symbol of all you detest in it. You can't see me as a man. Because . . .' Clive paused: 'You can't understand how I'm still the man you brought here. Or forgive me for it.'

'Do you not hate me for this?' Impatiently Captain Ishi swept his arm to embrace everything outside the cabin: the screaming guards, the cemetery, the smell that never blew away, the imprisoning forest.

'I have nothing against you, except the waste. I'm surprised you didn't go further. You could have killed me, the way you killed your singing bird. Chopped me in my cage. But I'm alive. And I hope to get out one day.'

'You feel no pity for yourself?'

'Pity for you, that's all,' Clive said. 'You don't know what you're doing.'

Captain Ishi laughed: 'The prisoner is sorry for the jailer.'

'You're locked into something you can't escape from. Stronger than a birdcage. You've been there so long, you can't remember what it's like outside. You've forgotten you were ever human. You don't think for yourself. You're controlled by forces – '

'Laws of God.'

'Call them what you like. I'm thankful to be free.'

'You are in my power.'

'Only what you see of me. The rest is mine.'

'I can do anything.'

'Ring the bell. Snap your fingers. Draw your sword.'

'Are you not frightened?'

'I am. But not of starvation any more. Or cholera. Or Goldilocks.'

'Of me?'

'Of the darkness.' Clive had said the same to Jenny once. Now he meant something different. 'The darkness in your mind. It possesses you. It's inhuman, destructive – I think you call it honour.'

'Are you not frightened of the end of the war?'

'The darkness is the only danger. I try to see what'll happen. You'll lose, I know. But you might be driven to more revenge.'

'And drag you down too?'

'To the last minute it'll still be life or death.'

'The choice is not important,' Captain Ishi said.

'Unlike you, I want to live. You must keep your darkness – it's the best chance for everyone.'

'Perhaps I can show you that I am human too.'

5

'You're running away from something, Mr Clive Ackerly, my man.'

Victor had said the same in Brighton. Now it was Odette, on her first evening in Aurora.

'Whatever it is, it stinks.'

Clive was forty-five, appalled but amused by what he had done: to exorcise something, or reassure himself, or test a faint belief that life was missing a dimension, the one to match his brother's happiness with Brenda; the chance, just possible, that there was a woman he could share Aurora with. Also, though he loved Beaconsfield as his adopted son and Isabel as his precious tantalising daughter, he could imagine a family of children who would listen to his past and invent a new one of their own, far in the future, out of their childhood here. It would be a fine place for them, a home for the dynasty to grow up in, watched by an old man – their father and grandfather. Sceptical but curious to see what happened, he applied to a marriage bureau in Australia. In time they sent Odette, a widow ten years younger.

It turned out to be the joke he half-guessed, half-hoped it would be. Letters had passed between them, they knew each other's facts and dates and measurements, the surface bits that added up to nothing with any human truth in it. Odette bought a one-month ticket from Sydney to Tulagi, and Clive arranged for a trader to bring her to Aurora. He had seen photos of her – thoughtful with a finger on her cheek in a studio pose, cheerful with an egg whisk in her kitchen, voluptuous in a swimming costume on the beach – but they all looked different. Now here she was, unlike any of them: a lusty raucous woman with yellow hair and a brassy laugh, blinding confidence and insoluble ideas of being Mrs Ackerly; taunting Clive, as a sample of how she would perform, for being a fugitive.

Among her baggage was a portable gramophone with
some records.

'What the bloody hell's a healthy normal man,' she
asked at dinner, cooked and served by Loloa with his
gentlest bush boy's tact, 'doing in a hole like this?' She
had put on a flowery blouse and orange trousers, clashing
with her hair, and an emerald green sash tied in a big
bow over her hip. The effect was of some lavish gift, a
box of chocolates or a silly bathroom toy, to be unwrapped
in private. 'That is, if you are a healthy normal man.'

'I'll show you tomorrow,' Clive said, catching the ambi-
guity. 'Give you a tour of the plantation. Introduce you
to the people. Go for a fishing trip in a canoe if you like,
out to the reef or to one of the beaches – they're not bad,
not a soul in sight.'

'There's something in the past you didn't tell me about.'

'I had a wife, I gave you details. Now she's in Sydney,
married to the American consul.'

'They left Australia years ago – I checked.'

'I didn't know.'

'What are you hiding, Clive?'

'Nothing that I know of. Ask me what you like.'

Odette pushed her plate away unfinished and lit a cigarette: 'I'll have to take that young cook of yours into a
corner and show him a thing or two. How can you eat it?
What's he put in it? Ginger, if you ask me. You want to
be careful – it'll burn your balls off.' Afterwards, with Clive
on the veranda, she played *Swan Lake* on her gramophone,
singing the tune, and threw her cigarette ends in the
magical lagoon. A canoe passed in the dark, close to the
house, full of people. 'Friendly neighbours you've got,'
Odette said.

'They've come to see how we're getting on,' Clive told
her.

'Snooping! So let's give them something to goggle at.'
She hauled him into a waltz, round and round on the
veranda, crooning with the music: 'This is my piece – the
Duck Pond. I was conceived after my parents got home
from the ballet. It was their favourite. Hence my name.
But you don't get swans here, I suppose.' She laughed,
and an answering laugh came over the water.

'I haven't danced for years, I'm out of practice,' Clive said, out of breath too. Last time was at Beaconsfield's wedding in the forest. This was likely to end the same way, without the random choice.

'You've got some catching up to do,' Odette said, pulling his trousers closer to her own. 'I'll do my best to help.'

Clive couldn't remember what he had been expecting. He tried to think of the women he had known before Jenny, but they had sunk as fatally as the sailors in the *Prince of Wales*. Even the ones in Australia, before he came to the Mendanas, had faded beyond recovery. Dimly he saw Brenda's warmth and generosity mixed with the mystery and strangeness of Loloa's sister. He had never hoped for love, he knew it wouldn't come again. But he didn't dislike Odette, she was too wilful and straightforward for that. And a month wasn't long. He would get what he could from it, as he did from the theatre in London. This was another play, to be enjoyed if possible, and Aurora made a wonderful setting. They were halfway into the first act. He would reach the end with a few drinks in the interval.

'One more brandy?' He poured it for her.

'This little girl never said no.'

He had given her the spare bedroom where she unpacked her things: 'I hope you'll be all right in there.'

'I won't be in there long,' she said. 'Time to get your clothes off. I'll be with you.' Two minutes later she came into Clive's room, naked except for the emerald sash round her waist, and joined him under the mosquito net: 'Like lying in a meat safe. Well, what are we here for,' she took off the sash, 'if it's not for poking?' It was the word used by Hutton the engineer.

They did it hard all night for a week, each as vigorous as the other, and pleased with themselves. 'The best I've had,' she gasped, giving little explosions as if each thrust was another puncture, letting out more healthy Australian air. 'So big and greedy. Saving up for me, were you?' He rolled his fingers over a breast, thumb on the nipple, stroking delicately, coaxing more lust. In the dark, when she was asleep, he saw this splendid body beside him, her full moon breasts, an invisible woman from another life, briefly allying it with his. She would go back there without a suspicion of the new vitality she had brought him, better than any amount of poking. But their strenuous nights, which drove Clive to extra energy by day, left Odette worn out.

'It's very pleasant, don't you think?' he suggested cautiously on her second day, stopping for a moment in some of the most seductive landscape in the world.

'Pleasant, my God!' she cried, hobbling along behind, blistered and thirsty.

He strode ahead among the coconut palms, waited for her to catch up, then climbed through the cocoa groves towards the forest. At the sight of a flowering tree he had once planted in a glade, lowering his defences as far as they would go, he admitted, 'There's a certain satisfaction.'

'You think so?'

'In doing just what I meant to do. Live the life I wanted.'

'Your private paradise? So where does the marriage bureau fit in?'

Clive was no longer uneasy at having to share Aurora, he knew there was no danger: 'It's up to you. All I can do is show you round.'

'I said before, you're running away.'

'Just the opposite, Odette.'

She lay in bed half the morning, then sauntered in and out of the house, calling to Loloa for coffee, playing the gramophone, sunbathing a little, waiting for what came next – a rainstorm or a pineapple juice or another record. Bored after a few days, she asked Laki for a boy in a canoe to take her over to the village. She sat in the school, listened to the children chant their lessons, watched a football match, tried to get bits of Clive's past out of Beaconsfield, who told her nothing and drove away on his motorbike to the far end of the plantation. She wouldn't go to church with Clive on Sunday. Instead she took over the kitchen from Loloa and cooked a curry lunch. She said, 'If I had to live here – '

'You'd go mad.'

She laughed: 'I'd plant a garden. Make patchwork quilts. Learn Chinese. Anything.'

By the second week Clive was wondering how he could endure the rest. He flung himself into plantation work, stirred up the copra cutters, drove on the cocoa boys. They responded, joining a conspiracy with him, proving what they could do for Aurora. But in small ways – a secret joke that nobody would explain, a feast they didn't invite him to, a different laugh across the lagoon at night – they showed that their own uneasiness hadn't passed like his. With nothing Clive could point to or ask about, he was being warned of something unclear. An indefinable tension stretched between the village and his house. Laki and the saltwater boys stopped paddling over to the office in the evening. The bush boys vanished into the forest after work. Beaconsfield stayed in the shadows, keeping his thoughts dark. Clive was deserted by his people. They were watching from a distance. Only Loloa was happy, his big eyes bigger, his face alight with smiles. He padded quietly through the house, ground coffee beans and squeezed oranges as he never had before, and brought Odette her sunglasses without being asked, before she knew she wanted them.

'I saw one of the kids today,' she said at dinner, 'who wasn't as black as the rest of them. A little girl of three or four with a touch of the white man in her, I'd say. Very pretty, actually.'

'Isabel, she's called.'

'A randy missionary, was it? Or someone in the war?'

'She's Loloa's niece.'

'Well! – you'd never know. Though Loloa's no monster like some of them.' He was bringing in the pudding, a chocolate jelly, and she looked him up and down. 'But he's so black,' she said when he had gone, 'and that child's a lovely colour, mahogany. . . .'

One night when they were asleep the house was shaken by something crashing on the iron roof. Then another and another, drumming and rolling down, thudding to the ground. Odette jumped up, frightened in the dark: 'Your friends! – they're throwing coconuts at us.' She pulled Clive on to her, they made love and fell asleep, and were woken by more clatters on the roof and rolling, bumping objects. In the morning they found unripe oranges, hard and dry, lying round the house.

'I think I get the message,' Odette said, and Clive told Beaconsfield to stop it. But he had become sickened by the nights of rutting, sweating, gasping. He would turn his back or lie awake or sit out on the veranda, longing for an empty bed again, waiting for Odette's departure or at least the dawn.

'Well,' she said after another week, 'it's no good, is it? I haven't improved your life, if I was meant to – if any woman could.'

'Odette, you have, though it's difficult to tell you how.'

'I brought you *Swan Lake*?'

'You brought a lot of fun too and showed me things – '

'About yourself, maybe.'

'And you? – you haven't got much out of it.'

'Don't worry, I'll look after myself. And it won't be for ever. Some day my prince will come. What was he called, that one in *Swan Lake* – Alberic? Florestan? And it's funny, you know, my parents got it wrong. Odette was the nasty one, Odile was the good one. Or maybe they got it right. Because my God, I'm not cut out to be a widow – who is?'

A widow! Jenny once believed she was: infinitely remote from this real one, now ogling Loloa, trimming her ideas.

'And you're not rid of me yet,' she went on. 'I came on trial, a one-month ticket.' She would have to wait for the trader to pick her up for the return flight from Tulagi. 'I'll stay in the other bedroom till then, unless you shout. Just friends. . . .' She laughed, more tenderly than usual.

She laughed often in her last week, behind the kitchen curtain where she was teaching Loloa to make an omelette or a French dressing or a proper curry. Clive was confident that in return Loloa was showing her the best use for wild ginger, and relieved that her visit had brought consolation in the end. Alone at night, remembering Loloa's sister, he saw Odette sink her enthusiastic body into the velvet of a bush boy's limbs. He couldn't say if he was envious, and if so, of which of them. He only knew he was in danger of forgetting, after nearly twenty years, what love was like. There were no more oranges on the roof but before dawn, when the opossum was due home, Clive sensed a tiny softening in the air as Odette's lover passed through the house to the kitchen, to put the kettle on for tea.

The trader came for her and she sailed out of the lagoon, yellow hair blowing, confidence unscratched. She left her gramophone for Clive. Loloa got the emerald sash. Beaconsfield came out of the shadows and sang with special force in church next Sunday, 'Now thank we all our God.' And suddenly, in the tropical way, it was night.

And suddenly a great forest tree would fall down dead from no visible cause. A shoal of tiny fish would break out of the lagoon and fly on a brilliant zigzag through the sun – sent by the sea spirits, Laki said, to look for victims. A woman would cry out on a hot night. Suddenly the ordinary turned odd.

One morning of the nineteen-sixties was no different from the others. It began normally and passed without much happening till about ten o'clock. Clive marched out on his daily tour of the plantation. Loloa sat on an empty whisky case outside the kitchen door, polishing a pair of Clive's shoes. Beaconsfield's motorbike puttered somewhere along a path. Laki watched his boys hollowing out the trunk of an arakoko tree, the best wood for a new canoe with fine straight grain, slightly greasy to the fingers, releasing a distinct fresh smell under the axe. Isabel was at school now, learning English nursery rhymes – a bright child with her mother's instincts and father's logic and her own precocious wits. Nobody ever spoke of Odette, or not in Clive's hearing. Nobody saw anything unusual going on.

Then in the middle of the morning, between polishing one shoe and the other, Loloa sneezed with great violence: a paroxysm that screwed up his face, squeezed his eyes, kicked his feet off the ground, nearly threw him off the whisky case. He knew what it meant: at that moment someone had snatched away his soul – it didn't matter

who or why or where – and returned it to him with a
curse. A mutilated soul was intolerable. There was a single
cure for it.

He put down the shoes, specially made in London;
put down the brush and polish; left the house, walking
through quiet rows of coconut palms, treading bits of dry
frond and husk, to the place where copra was being cut
today. Bush boys helped each other: one of them would
happily stop work and give up his knife for the five
minutes Loloa needed it. He swung it in his hand, tried
it on the hairs of his leg, swung it again and walked
towards the village. Any of the saltwater girls would do.

There was a suitable one on the shore alone, collecting
jellyfish in the sand. She saw Loloa, he thought, but he
couldn't have looked a danger to her. She made no noise
or movement when his arm went up. He wasn't going to
rape her, he was one of the least ferocious bush boys. He
had never even killed a pig, though he had seen it done.
Since being sharpened this morning the knife hadn't cut
much copra. It went through the bone down to an ear,
dividing her head a little crookedly but more easily than
a coconut. Under the gentleness Loloa was very strong:
he could break a banana stalk in his hands and lift
Beaconsfield's motorbike higher than anyone. The girl
died quickly on the sand with a jellyfish in her fingers.

There were no witnesses, but Loloa wouldn't deny the
murder: he couldn't help it. He washed the knife in the
lagoon; walked back to the copra cutters to return it;
walked on calmly, with no guilt, to Clive's house where
he picked up the shoes and went on polishing. His soul
was mended, he would try not to sneeze again.

He was surprised that they made such a noise in the
village. For the rest of the morning the shouting went on.
Clive came back for lunch and asked what it was about.
Loloa said that a girl had been attacked, he didn't know
why: it was the truth. After lunch Clive sent him to find
out. Loloa didn't return, he lost his nerve. All afternoon
in his sister's house he listened to the saltwater boys' fury.
The girl must have been killed by a bush boy – chopped
with a copra knife, not stabbed with a fishing knife. They
would soon find him. He saw that his sister knew what

he had done. Probably Isabel, her daughter, knew too but she might not understand: there was half a white man in her. To the bush boys Loloa had murdered because he must. But they couldn't save him from revenge. Now he was frightened. At sunset he slipped away through the plantation and into the forest. The darkness would save him.

'Loloa is not cooking for you now,' Beaconsfield said to Clive that evening. 'Is big-big trouble, I think.'

'Why did he do it?'

'Because . . .' Beaconsfield began; then waited, sorting his thoughts, making them fit for a white man. 'I think you must ask the woman.'

'What woman?'

'I don't know exactly, but I think. . . .' Beaconsfield waited again. 'Is having baby, I think.'

'Loloa's baby?'

'And I think baby is dead.'

'I don't understand.'

'No, Mr Clive, you don't understand. But I think Loloa must pay her.'

'You mean Odette?' Clive had heard nothing from her since she went back to Australia. 'Pay Odette?'

'He must pay her with blood.'

'It's absurd.' But Clive didn't laugh.

'Because she is putting magic on him.'

'You believe that, Beaconsfield?'

'Is what I think.'

'But the girl hadn't done anything wrong – so why kill her?'

'Doesn't matter about the girl – the blood must be paid.'

Clive had whisky and peanuts for supper. He had never cooked for himself, he wouldn't start now. The night passed quietly. At dawn the shouting began again and for the first time nobody turned up for work. Clive ate a banana for breakfast on the veranda, watching a turtle. It put its head out of the water, stared back at him, then rolled its long shell through the morning sun and sank again. The noise from the village blew more strongly over the lagoon as the sun rose above the trees.

Beaconsfield arrived in a hurry on his motorbike: 'Loloa is coming back last night.'

'To your house?'

'Is very-very frightened. The spirits in the forest are no good for him, because he is not understanding them.'

'He should come to me. Tell him – '

'You also don't understand, Mr Clive – you don't know. . . .' Beaconsfield stopped. 'Loloa is asking me to get the power and use it for him.'

'Power?'

'It means I must go in the forest and find a tree and boil the bark from it with areca and ginger, and is taking long-long time. Or if I don't find the tree I must cook a black opossum and speak some magic on it. But is no time for these things, because saltwater boys are very-very angry and sharpening their knives to kill Loloa.'

'What will he do?' The shouting threatened the morning – the growl of vengeance, of men wronged by something inexplicable: the noise made by the prisoners on the railway after the Turd had driven a hammer through Smithy's face.

'Already is doing it, before they catch him. Is escaping in my canoe. I tell him he must go to the township.'

'Alone? – it's fifty miles.'

'Is very-very strong and frightened also, so is reaching quickly and must go to the police station and tell everything he did and give himself to them.'

'Good – that's the right thing.'

'Now saltwater boys are angry because they want to catch him and is too late, because Loloa is going in the night and safe in the police station.'

'Safe! He'll be arrested for murder.'

'But saltwater boys are not catching him there, and now are angry with me because I am helping him escape.'

The growl had risen to a chant, mounting like the heat, a throb of violence too urgent to be quite human. Across the lagoon the village too seemed to be growing bigger, swelling from the shore, as a fleet of canoes with fifty men launched into the water. They hungered for a victim, but had been robbed of Loloa and turned on Beaconsfield, pursuing him to Clive's house.

'What the hell are your bush boys doing?' Clive looked for fear in his headman's face, but there was only the fright of a hunter caught in his own trap, knowing how he must fight to get out.

'They are going into the forest, because saltwater boys want blood today.'

'Why didn't you go too?'

'Because. . . .' Beaconsfield grabbed Clive's old shotgun off the wall.

Now Clive knew that Beaconsfield had come to warn him, and probably would save his life. 'Don't you shoot – '

'Not to shoot.' The gun was unloaded anyway, with no cartridges in reach.

They stood together on the veranda, waiting for the canoes. Paddles dipped with the chanting. Ripples scattered over the bright lagoon. The splash and surge of boats sounded under the war cries, like buoyancy to support them, approaching fast. They were deep in the water, full of men. Clive remembered the splendour of battleships and felt the old impatience; also relief to have Beaconsfield with him. But a fight would be hopeless for them.

'Laki!' Clive shouted to the canoes. 'I'll talk to Laki – nobody else. Laki!' No answer came. Laki wasn't there. The fleet was led by nobody.

The paddles stopped, the chanting drifted away, the canoes nudged the veranda. Someone gave a yell, someone leapt out, they all followed. Fifty men landed, with slogans on their teeshirts and flowers in their fuzzy hair and fishing knives in their hands, shouting for blood. They were famous for their savagery – the coastal natives of the Mendana Islands who had terrorised the first explorers.

Beaconsfield, the cornered hunter, snarled and twitched the empty gun; showed his teeth and hissed. His craftiness, the nimble forest art of cut and dodge and jump, would hold off the knives for precious moments – perhaps for a minute.

Clive stood still, took one step back, then stood again. It was as far as he would retreat. If they wanted the bush boy, they must have the white man first. They crowded forward, pressed from behind by more coming up from the canoes. It looked nasty. Clive began to talk quietly, a stream of words in a pigeon's cooing tone, to soothe such fury. At Strathpolly as a boy he had once spoken to a pack of dogs like this. Another canoe was racing to join them, paddles beating the lagoon, waves rolling from the tree trunk hull.

'You're decadent – that's your problem,' Clive said, hardly realising that he was talking. 'You're not the men you used to be.' Their chanting had dwindled to an eerie mumble, the sound of the surf on coral pebbles. 'You should smear yourselves with lime and wear the teeth of dead warriors round your neck, wrapped in palm leaves, and come at me with spears bristling with human bones stuck in the end like barbs on a fish hook – you see, I know more about it than you do, I can teach you to be real fighters.' They began to hum and slowly prance forward, spring backward like toys, prance forward again, each time coming nearer while Clive stood defiantly and talked. 'You should have kept away from women for thirty days to give you strength for battle, but none of you could do it now, you're weak, you haven't got the will, you can't control yourselves.' Beaconsfield cowered behind him with the shotgun, tense and agile, lifting each foot in turn as if stepping on thorns of fire, ready to dart into the house, into the lagoon, on to the roof. 'The first of you who hits me with his spear should drink the blood off it.' Clive didn't raise his voice but kept this hypnotic tone, speaking through his teeth, appalled at the picture he was drawing. Gradually they swayed, back and forth, watching him, edging closer. 'When you've killed me you should take me to your village and cover me with flowers and paint, and comb my hair and hang me in a tree and leave me there for four days, then take me down when I'm rotten and stinking, and slit my stomach and pull my guts out, and singe my skin and scrape it like a pig's, and cut pieces off my arms and legs and shoulders, the meaty parts, and cook them in an oven, not because you're hungry or because you like the taste, though they say it's nice – ask Beaconsfield, he's tried it – but because I'm the

enemy you killed and you can get some of my power by
eating me.' They were very near him, almost in a trance,
their knives ready. 'But you won't do any of these things,
you've lost the old vitality, no better than anyone else,
you'll just stay there on my veranda, hopping about like
sparrows while I – '

'Beaconsfield!'

They had heard this huge voice before, more than ten
years ago, bellowing in the night when the *Catriona* was
wrecked.

'*Beaconsfield!*'

The giant Laki, an ancient grizzled sea god, came up
out of the lagoon. He had chased the saltwater boys from
the village in his canoe; came pushing through them to
the front and stood facing Clive. Nobody spoke or moved.
Beaconsfield stopped twitching the shotgun and shrank a
little more.

'Mr Clive – '

'Thank you, Laki – I think you're just in time.'

'Mr Clive. . . .' The great coxswain shook like a ship in
stays, caught between shame and anger. The straw hat,
relic of old skipper Jimmy Dundas, had long ago been
blown away. The white shorts were frayed and patched
and flecked with mildew. The brass buckle of the Glasgow
fire brigade had been used to weight a fishing line, and
lost. The hole pierced in his nose, for an ornament or a
fish hook or a coin, held nothing now. Age was stripping
Laki of all but his towering seaman's scorn.

'I think your boys,' Clive said, 'came to tell me something.' Their knives were being put away, they shuffled
back to the end of the veranda, towards their canoes.

Laki turned and glared at them – his sons and nephews,
the endless offspring of his family: 'Have you forgotten?'
Nobody answered. 'How have you forgotten what this
man did for you?' Laki was a master mariner, a master
speaker too. He paused, for their memories to catch up.
'When the schooner sank, this man brought you back from
the middle of the sea. He played music on his bagpipes for
you. Have you forgotten that? He brought you here to
make a home with him. He took your lives and put them
in Aurora.' Laki paused again. In the lagoon the turtle

rolled over, looked out from the surface at the crowded veranda, then rolled back into the cool. 'He took your lives, and now you want to take his. Where will you put it? In the lagoon, you fools?' Laki's great voice broke, 'Ah!' in a mighty sob of anguish. Then he saw Beaconsfield, a shrimp of insignificance in the corner, with a shotgun. '*Ah!*' Laki cried again with twice the force, and strode to him; tore the gun from the bush boy's hands – would have torn the hands off too, if Beaconsfield hadn't let go – strode to the veranda edge and with a last contemptuous 'Ah!' hurled it far out into the lagoon.

The ripples dissolved in the hot morning, with the danger and fury. Clive told Beaconsfield to get the bush boys back to work. Laki drove his saltwater boys into their canoes. Somebody began to grumble, 'Loloa . . .' and others took it up, 'Loloa, Loloa. . . .' Laki silenced them with a roar, then looked at Clive. Yesterday morning Loloa had cleaved a girl's skull in half, and fled. How could they be sure he had given himself up and wasn't hiding in the forest? They had only Beaconsfield's word for it. Nobody would be happy in Aurora without a kind of vengeance, even the white man's.

Clive understood. In the big canoe with an outboard engine Laki could take six men, some from the dead girl's family, to the township with a letter. Clive would ask the police officer to let them into the cells, to see Loloa locked up.

At the trial in Tulagi a month later, after the murder verdict, Clive gave evidence of his servant's character. He suggested that a visitor from Australia might throw better light on it, but she had gone away without leaving an address. 'I believe,' he said in the witness box, 'that only as the tool of forces beyond his control could such a gentle young man commit a crime like that.' The judge, who was on his last tour of duty in the Mendanas before retirement and was planning a book of reminiscences, asked Clive to repeat it slowly while he wrote it down; and passing sentence he reduced the usual fifteen years to twelve.

Afterwards, whenever Clive was in Tulagi, he visited Loloa in prison, where in time the murderer became the governor's servant and polished his boots.

'You ought to try some of the modern gadgets,' they told him in the Tulagi hotel bar. 'Electricity, that sort of thing – why not?'

'Get yourself a generator and some wire and fittings. You'll never look back.'

Clive nearly said he liked looking back, but instead, 'I hate machines. They break down. I prefer to be free.'

'Pretty reliable these days. They've got it worked out.'

'They?'

'Well, it's the Nips mostly.'

'What about radio, old man? A shortwave set – wouldn't that be useful out there?'

'Other plantations have got it, and some of the missions in the islands.'

'Once a day, stand by for a two-way call – no trouble and might come in handy, you never know.'

'Keep in touch with us, Clive old man, or we'll forget you're there.'

'Sorry, I can't see myself cranking an engine. Or talking down a microphone. But thanks, all the same.' He never bothered. It wasn't laziness. He preferred not to be dependent on something he couldn't master. The generator would have to be looked after; a radio call would demand an answer. He never needed to send an urgent message, and didn't want to be accessible at any time to someone else. Laki's weekly trip to the township for mail was enough.

So Victor had been dead for several days before Clive got the cable. For a moment, for an hour or two, for the rest of the day till sunset, the news meant nothing. It was printed on a form, an official signal from the glib evasive men who weren't to be trusted. They would say anything. They once told Jenny that Clive was dead. They had got it wrong again.

On the veranda after dark – after dinner cooked by the bush boy who had taken Loloa's place, without the skill or beauty or shadowy footsteps in and out of the kitchen – Clive tried to remember his brother in the Brighton flat, and could only see him at Strathpolly. The property agent mixing drinks and market prices and little jokes with Brenda wouldn't come. But the boy chasing through the

woods, playing by the river, growing always just ahead of
Clive, was vivid. Childhood, already haunted by a bedside
photo of an unknown army officer with a moustache and
then by a murderous salmon in a pool, was now the scene
of another death. Victor hiding in a cupboard was found
to be a corpse. Victor exploring an old silver mine on the
moors was buried alive. Victor on a mountain was hit by
a falling rock or bitten by an adder or swallowed by a bog.
It was as if only the Strathpolly boy was mortal, and the
Brighton man a dummy. Clive had to wait another week
for Brenda's letter. Victor had died on the seafront, having
fallen off the balcony.

'I'll tell you all I know,' Brenda said when Clive arrived
in Brighton two months later. She was fatter and slower:
she had needed Victor to stir her into motion. Now she
lay on the sitting-room sofa, wrapped in folds of heavy
wool, gasping faintly. The silver hair was tarnished, the
bubbles had turned to breathlessness, the juice to jelly.
'I'd gone to bed, I was practically asleep and they rang
the doorbell, I couldn't think why Victor didn't answer it,
he was still up – '

'In here?'

'Last I saw, he was getting another drink and I said
he'd had plenty and so had I, I went to bed and he never
came, he stayed on drinking, an hour at least, and they
rang the bell, and rang and rang, but he didn't go to the
door, so I struggled up and it was two policemen.' Brenda
might be still asleep, speaking with no emotion, in no
hurry to reach the point. Either she was dazed by the
memory or had lost interest. 'The ambulance was there,
and quite a crowd though it was the middle of the night,
but he was stone dead, not a flicker left, just a holy bloody
mess – Clive, I can't tell you.' For the first time her voice
was checked. 'They gave me a load of pills to knock me
out, I wonder now why I didn't swallow the lot with a
bottle of gin to finish me, but I didn't think of it then, I
didn't think of anything, just the mess down there and
how he'd done it, and I had to go to the morgue next day,
but they'd wiped him down, he was looking the way he
did when he came to bed drunk, pretty glad to be there,

horizontal at last, feeling sexy but really beyond it and I wouldn't have been surprised to hear him snore.'

'Was he drunk?'

'You know, Clive – they went through it at the inquest, they tore him apart like dogs, the pathologist and coroner and police between them, weighing his liver and his heart, asking if he'd left a note behind, probing every murky little episode.'

'But it was an accident?' To Clive now, Victor was Brenda's property, no longer his brother.

'An accident.' She got up slowly from the sofa, wobbling more painfully, less succulently than when she was young, to get drinks. 'The verdict was an accident, but Clive. . . .' She swallowed her gin. 'Just a holy bloody mess.'

'What?'

'Everything – there's nothing left. I hate to tell you. The business came crashing, the partner bolted with the police on his heels, last heard of in Spain, and Victor was landed with debts from here to Brighton pier and nothing to pay with, except an office block he couldn't sell. There's nothing now – only what you see.'

'The flat?'

'It's mine, it always was – since the beginning of the war, before I met him. Before he picked me for his crazy night club.'

'Night club?'

'Underneath the Albert Hall, safe from bombs. His little dream.'

'He never told me.'

'He didn't want you to know, Clive – you were too good, he said. It was a disaster, it never opened. Luckily I had the flat. And I suppose I'll hang on here, I'd never leave.'

Clive stayed a few days with her, going over the old Strathpolly things – bits of furniture, some books and pictures, spoons, crockery. He dreaded finding the photo of his father, and found he was sorry it wasn't there. Brenda said he could take what he liked, but there was nothing he cared to have at Aurora. Then from the bottom of a drawer, wrapped in tissue, he pulled out a tartan sash, not as bright as Odette's emerald one but made of silk. He thought it must have been his mother's. One day he might give it to her granddaughter, Isabel.

'Keep in touch, won't you?' Brenda said before he left.

'Don't worry – I'll be back,' he told her, knowing it wasn't true. The English Channel out there was a foreign sea.

'If ever you feel like coming home – '

'Thanks.' Home from the sea, home to retire to, home to die in – the word meant nothing. But Clive could see Brenda's old age in this Brighton flat more clearly than his own at Aurora.

'You can always stay here – I'd be happy. . . .' She put on a huge fur coat and tottered with him to the station, a fluffy pale grey ball on high heels, holding his arm for balance. On the platform she said, 'Victor loved you, Clive – he said the only reason he'd like a son of his own was to have you for an uncle, but we never. . . .' Her scarlet lips trembled a little, she dabbed her eyes and drew him into the fur for a soft warm kiss. From the train he waved and watched her diminishing in the distance, a puff of grey froth, losing substance, dissolving as she blew kisses back.

He would stop in London for a day or two, before returning to the Mendanas; visit the old shops, walk the streets, watch the people, go to a theatre on his last night, with an affection he knew was too close to habit.

6

The prisoners on the railway ate the weevils in the rice: there might be vitamins in them. They butchered a stray cow and stewed it, not caring if it was someone's entire property. They brewed coffee from burnt rice in a jerrycan, and sweet brown milk from the sap of a palm. They discovered that dog could taste like beef, cat like chicken, iguana like a blend of tripe and shellfish. They made kittens into dumplings, and skinned a cobra, chopped and dried it and called it haddock. They trapped forest birds and collected fungus, and caught frogs which they fed on beetles and raced for bets, then fried in coconut oil with green chillies. They held prize fights between stick insects and praying mantises. They boiled up old mango skins, soaked a bit of cotton in the liquid and used it for bait, to trap blowflies. They cleaned their teeth with charcoal and a finger, and found that their sweat was tasteless from lack of salt. They made banjos and flutes from almost nothing, astonishing themselves; or crooned all day into a microphone – a cigarette tin on a bamboo.

When a man went mad, thinking he was Lord Mountbatten, the others pretended to think it too, and soon didn't have to pretend. They still died from sickness or despair, from bacteria or the loss of will, or any interest in living. Afterwards the survivors felt a brief anger that someone who had suffered the same hope should have been cheated; then bartered his wedding ring and bits of clothing. They stole and lied and betrayed each other, and learnt to tolerate their own intolerance. There were no saints, and not many of them believed in God: they weren't such fools.

For a year and a half Clive cultivated his garden. The Thai man and his wife and children never came across to see him, though there was an affinity spanning the river: obedience to the seasons, delight in small triumphs, sorrow at catastrophe. Only the old woman rowed over, sometimes every day for a week, often letting a month pass without a visit. If she saw work to be done among the vegetables she would straddle the rows, a bent figure with the sun on her polished back and life in her deep calm eyes, and prick and scratch and mutter like a devotee, praying for growth and fruitfulness. Usually she sat with her cheroot, spitting tobacco juice and interjections into the conversation.

Once a passenger train full of whores, lacquered and high-heeled, came up the new railway and was parked for three days near the camp, for the guards to spend a night in it. They washed their uniforms, polished their

boots, trimmed the wisps round their lips and came back
singing.

Before the train continued up the line to other camps
Captain Ishi – still the model film star though the make-
up was cracking, the olive breeches were less well pressed
– called Clive into his cabin and told him, 'You also may
have a turn, if you. . .' The ivory phallus swung on its
silk cord from his neck.

'If I what?'

'In Wagner there is always a price for love.'

'You call that love?'

'For most men it is enough. For some, of course, like
me or you – '

'I'd rather – '

'But you asked the price, my friend. It is not high. You
would need to broadcast only once on behalf of Nippon.'

Clive replied with silence; and tried to pierce those dark
lenses, to find the man behind. Next day the train rolled
away into the hills, to the prisoners' jeers and catcalls:
they would rather see a load of whores go up the railway
they had built than troops.

Down in his garden by the river Clive said to the old
woman, 'I told you about the beauty here and what it
does for me – the nourishment I get. But sometimes I'm
angry with it for being beautiful. It's too much for me, I'm
tender and can't take it. Like overeating when you've been
starved – it makes me feel worse, a glutton, disgusted
with my own greed. Lonely too. I want to destroy it if I
can't share it with Jenny. I'm glad to have you to talk to,
though we're so different, but it's her I love and ache for
and get frantic about, because she'd see the beauty and
she's missing it.' He stopped while the old fingers dipped
for another cheroot into the folds of cotton skirt and shrivelled flesh: spent breasts, not sad but fulfilled and now
content. 'I'll tell you this – Jenny would complete the
beauty, but it's for her as well as me that I want her here,
so that she can have it too.'

Far away a storm wiped out the landscape, roaring
closer, beating in the trees; then crossed the river, giant
raindrops scattering the surface with perfect little silver
crowns. Streams appeared where there had been cracks.

Afterwards the air was loaded with the smell of wet earth and vegetation, spiced with wild ginger. In a few days the trees sprang into fresh leaf, red and yellow, or blossomed. Vines leapt for the branches and everything in Clive's garden grew.

He loved a storm – a reminder of bigger forces, a power behind the river and mountains, beyond defiance. It sang with the harmony of truth, a rhythm of the universe far stronger than the dead monotony of prison life; and showed the futility of Nippon, the puniness of the Turd and Goldilocks, and Clive's own colossal insignificance. Big trees could be snapped as easily as beanstalks, and clumps of bamboo plucked from the ground like lettuces. The river rose and swirled at the garden brink, ready to flick it into the stream and dissolve it in a moment.

The precariousness – the dangerous knife-edge between love and whatever was the alternative – was part of the beauty.

'Why did I let him do it, Jenny? – why? why? It was another dream. It wasn't happening, but I knew it was. Like everything else here. They fill you up with water and jump on you. They make you stand in the sun all day with a rock at arm's length above your head, ready to beat you if you drop it. They line you up in pairs and you slap each other's faces for their amusement. It's unbelievable, isn't it? It can't be true, you tell yourself. You'll wake up in a minute. And yet you're caught. There's forest round you for hundreds of miles. To escape is to die alone, instead of within inches of another man. You haven't a hope. That's why I did it – I lost hope. Not for ever, but long enough. We heard them shooting. It was morning parade. We were numbering. Bowing to the sunrise. Being slapped for not being Japanese. Then the shots. It's the time for an execution. Four men who tried to get away. They were brought back by the forest people. A captured prisoner is worth a bag of rice. Poor sods. Made to dig their graves. We were given a holiday. Jenny, please understand. I can't explain it otherwise.'

*

'I'm going to tell you something,' Clive announced one evening to the old woman, and to the river and the monkeys on the cliff and the fading purple mountains, 'but I don't know how to say it. It's so simple, it's incomprehensible. I was going to keep it for Jenny, but it would grow inside like poison, unbearable to live with. I must tell someone and there's nobody else I trust. I think you'll understand, though the words mean nothing. And if you do, and can absorb some of the poison, it'll be easier to tell Jenny and for her also to understand. I'm practising it on you. It's about a weakness. Or softness. Or tenderness. That's it – a tenderness for another human being. There was nothing strong in it. Only an urge to be of use to someone. To serve him. To soothe him. To make the moment a little better. To spread the pain. To offer companionship, and to take it. To *share* – what? A tiny warmth. One small act together. The lightest, gentlest touch, fingertip to fingertip. The contact of two people in hell.'

It didn't look like hell: the flamingo evening sky, the chuckle of water running through Clive's bed of beans. He talked slowly, translating his thoughts, waiting for them to reach the old woman.

'I recognised a man's need. It doesn't matter whether it was his need or mine. Or that he was strange and odious and powerful. Or that I was frightened of what he'd do if I didn't consent. Nothing matters. I see no evil in it.'

The old woman stood up and went to divert the channel from the beans, damming in one place and cutting through the bank in another: now it watered the tomatoes. Clive watched her in his garden. The sunset pink was streaked with green. When she came back to squat nearby he went on.

'I wouldn't have done it anywhere but here. It took a war to bring me to it. War and capture and slavery on the railway and three years with no news from Jenny.' Clive considered for a while, letting the old woman shift her bones and examine the cheroot: it would last till nightfall. 'More than anything it was the sight of so much death. Perhaps I was adding to the horrors. Piling on another torture. But flesh and blood aren't dead if they can do that. It was alive, though grotesque. A debased kind of life. A bad joke.'

The old woman released one of her happiest noises, a mixture of quack and giggle to show how funny she thought it was. It encouraged him.

'And different from anything I've felt for Jenny. If there was any desire, it was very dim. A wish for something outside ourselves. To replace the loss of hope. That's it – a gesture of despair. And reassurance. I wonder if you know what I mean, I expect you do. Sometimes it strikes a man. All his creativity is wrapped up in two balls. What's going on down there? It's the waste, the terrible pity of it. Years go by. And then this happens.'

The sky was losing colour, darkening to charcoal. Smoke from the house across the river formed a canopy above the mango trees. A weird black bird flew towards the forest, whistling and clumsily towing two white-eyed streamers at the end of long thin quills: there was nothing like that at Strathpolly.

'I've thought about it ever since. Was it disloyalty? To Jenny? To myself? To England? I don't think so. I don't believe in that kind of loyalty any more. So why did I do it with *him*? Why not one of the prisoners, with the same feelings and need, and the same voice and shape? Because I love them, I couldn't. Perhaps I had to love him too, another way. Something I'd never done before. In the navy they said it was no longer a crime after ninety days at sea. It's quite common in prisons. It's become symbolic – I'm not sure what of. The last degradation. Total shame. It's what I shall take home.'

In the dusk, as he spoke, Clive watched a boat being rowed over the river, a thin figure stooping at the oar. The old woman had slipped away without him seeing.

Aloud he said, 'I've betrayed you, Jenny!' He stood up and spoke to the advancing night. 'Did you hear that? Or did you know already? *Betrayed*. It sounds old-fashioned and quaint. I made a promise and broke it. It's such a cliché, I never thought I'd do it. But I did. Here in Thailand, as a prisoner-of-war. I was going to keep it for you, I truly meant to. And I thought of you all the time. I even told her about you. She's half a witch and half a grandmother – how could I resist? As old as you and me together. I love her, I couldn't have done it otherwise. You'd love her too – a gentle, wise old woman. She understood, I'm sure. I won't do it again, I'll wait till I get home. Trust me, Jenny, please.'

News from outside came sometimes through Thai traders but mostly on the Canary, a home-made radio hidden in a thick bamboo that was moved from hut to hut. The guards, hating to know less about the war than their prisoners, swore to execute anyone found with it.

Battle names were exchanged like smuggled goods – Stalingrad, Tobruk, Monte Cassino, Guadalcanal, Normandy – but with a sense of helplessness. Though the railway was dangerous it wasn't war. Ignorance increased the isolation. Any scrap of news was sucked into the camp and spread through thousands of men in an hour or so. The Italians had dropped out, the Germans were on the run in Europe, the Japanese were being driven back through the Pacific islands. A new American fleet was avenging Pearl Harbor and everyone knew that one day Japan would be beaten.

'How much longer can you wait?' the men asked each other. 'As if three years aren't enough.'

'And what'll happen at the end – d'you ever wonder?'

Bombers came over, Flying Fortresses at thirty thousand feet, and a black-out was ordered. Even the tiger fires round the camp, which comforted the guards, were forbidden. In the dark, rumours fed on themselves.

'You'll be slaughtered as the food runs out.'

'Or sent to Japan and used as hostages.'

'Forced to carry ammunition for them till the final hand-to-hand fighting, then shot.'

'Try to escape and you'll be caught in the crossfire of the last battle.'

'You'll be down a saltmine by then – they'll leave you there and nobody will ever know.'

'A raving lunatic.'

'Which would you rather be – mad or impotent?'

'You've got a long time to think about it – another ten years.'

'Six months, I give it.'

'I'll feel cheated if I'm cremated here. My wife was going to put my ashes in an egg-timer so I'd go on being useful to her – she loves boiled eggs.' A wife was a possibility again, more tantalising for being almost within reach.

The war was closing in, bringing an intensity of peril. The Turd and Goldilocks grew morose, their tempers took longer to erupt. Captain Ishi didn't appear at parades or on his veranda. His bell and radio were never heard. It was said that he was either drunk or had been recalled to Japan: back to his grandmother in her garden, without his singing bird. Stories of kamikaze pilots who crashed their planes on American warships increased the unreality: Nippon would sustain his curious and dangerous ideals, his romance with death, to the bitter end.

In August 1945 the news went round that something enormous, extraordinary, unknown to the world, had happened at a place called Hiroshima. It was Nippon's most tremendous surprise. Men spoke of a great light or a great darkness, but nobody could say if it was good or bad. It wasn't an earthquake or tidal wave or volcano or typhoon, or even a battle, and revolution was impossible. It must be an epidemic like cholera – a new, terrible act of war. Or God had breathed, though it wasn't certain in whose favour. Three days later it happened again at Nagasaki.

In the camp the usual gangs went into the forest to cut fuel for trains. From his garden shelter Clive watched the landscape and felt he had never seen such wonder – the hourly changes, the life-giving river, the extravagance of the world. He picked his beans and sold a bag of them to the guards' cookhouse.

In the following days the guards became nervous and sullen, keeping clear of the prisoners, not bothering to drive them out to work. One morning planes came over and dropped leaflets. Nippon had surrendered, the war was won. It was too big to take in. Victory and liberty, after such years, fluttering down on bits of paper: this wasn't how it was supposed to happen. The planes flew

away, leaving everything different though it was hard to
see what had altered. The guards were still there, the rice
was the same, the flies hadn't vanished from the pits. For
a week nothing changed, except in the smallest way: a
tiny adjustment of behaviour, a shade of variation in the
old monotony. The prisoners had grown a fraction in size,
and taken it from the Japanese. Clive walked with a spring
in his step that he had forgotten he possessed, and caught
himself saluting the guardroom when there was no need.

Then the Emperor's voice was heard from Tokyo, the
lord of heaven broadcasting across Asia, coming up the
railway. His people must obey his wishes and enhance
the glory of the empire, cultivate the ways of rectitude
and a noble spirit, construct the future. They hadn't been
defeated, the war wasn't lost or won but merely stopped.
The dynasty was preserved.

Young men came down on parachutes beside the river
– white leaves in the sun, falling against the purple mountains – and walked up stiffly into the camp in twos and
threes, awkward in their British uniform and wartime
health, more alien to the prisoners than the familiar
guards. They handed out cigarettes and pills, and said
that Churchill wasn't prime minister any more: he had
done worse than the Emperor of Japan. But they spoke
keenly about the atom bomb and made notes with
ballpoint pens, another new invention; then talked into
their radios, calling up planes which dropped tinned
peaches, spam, pea soup, lime juice, sweets, beer and
newspapers, also a supply of contraceptives.

Suddenly there was a surfeit. Thais brought victory
presents of chickens and bananas and fish, the food that
used to cost so much. The guards smiled and bowed, and
unlocked a store of Red Cross parcels that had come three
years ago: the flour now rotten, the tins blown, the drugs
removed. It was Nippon's private joke, a triumph at a
time of surprises: 'Look what has been kept for this
occasion, and none of it is any use!' A sack was opened
and letters to prisoners, many of them dead, were shaken
out and blown across the ground. They were torn apart
and bits of home news put together – births and deaths,
bombs, the weather, adultery – in a pattern that mocked

a man's four years of dreams. Another sack was full of cards, written but never sent: 'My health is excellent,' from men on the point of dying, who now lay in the cemetery. Clive picked up his three messages to Jenny. He was beyond anger, he only felt exasperation: they didn't matter now, he was no longer the man who wrote them.

Pigs were driven into the camp with fireworks tied to their tails, and roasted in the tropical night. Whisky was produced, bottle after bottle, nobody knew where from. Overfed and drunk, the prisoners sang 'God Save the King', trying to focus on something that was further away than ever, and throwing wood on the fire as they had done during the cholera. The guards may have thought they were also to be killed and cooked, but an irresistible benevolence, free like the pork and whisky, came out of the dark. Nippon was still contemptible, and now pathetic too. While the men were feasting, the Turd and Goldilocks poured drums of hoarded disinfectant into the pits: it could have saved lives once.

Though the guardroom was empty nobody went out of the camp at first: it might be a trap, they had been caught too often. Then a few men walked along the river, through rice fields into a village. Everywhere they were watched: 'For Christ's sake! – we're expected to rape them.' They were uneasy. Prison had protected them from the empty world outside. They needed its confinement to support them: 'All this space and nothing to hold on to!' They had lost balance. Their eyes couldn't reach such distances, having focussed so long on the nearest tree, the hut roof, the next man's loathsome body. They hankered to be back. But even in the camp, freedom wasn't easy to take. They had to pick up an identity again, find out who they were. They complained or boasted or shouted, after years of humility, or quarrelled over cigarettes when last week they had happily smoked wild tobacco leaves. They ate too much, making up for past hunger, also eating for the men who hadn't survived: 'Poor buggers, they won't miss it, they've got no appetite.'

Having lived together, each with the thought of dying alone, they started living for themselves: life had a proper chance now. And death became an anachronism. One man died in the night: 'Didn't he hear the news? Couldn't he hang on a few days and save us trouble?' They buried him impatiently: something left over from the bad times, a reminder they didn't need.

Time, stopped in captivity by a man's refusal to watch it pass, began to race. The years in camp crashed into perspective. The loss, the nightmare's worst element, spoilt the return of consciousness.

Early in September they were taken by train down to Banpong – eight hours on the track they had once slogged up for two weeks. Before leaving, split by joy and guilt, they went to the cemetery; walked along the rows and wondered at those severed lives, and their own luck. The morning sun had never felt so good or cruel. Too stricken to sing, they stood in the heat for ten minutes, or twenty or half an hour, and quietly wept.

'Poor buggers.'

'The fucking uselessness.'

'The forest'll be back soon and they'll be smothered.'

'Orchids, butterflies – what more d' you want?'

'Better than we'll ever get in a suburban cemetery – a marble tombstone, artificial flowers if we're lucky.'

'We ought to clear the weeds.'

'The train's going.'

'Why us, not them?'

'You feel bad, not to be dead?'

'For Christ's sake.'

'There were some good blokes there.'

'Some bastards too. One or two of them, to be honest, I'm glad are staying.'

'Jenny, Jenny,' Clive said in silence, tightening his lips. 'I'm coming back, I know it now. It's this that makes it believable – the men we're leaving here. They were too young. Death is for the old – do you agree? I plan to be an old man one day, but I want the same for them. I want them to push through the weeds and sit up and laugh at us crying in the sun. Perhaps they are laughing, if we could hear. That's another of my plans – to laugh. Will you show me how? In bed, inside you – to laugh and laugh. I'll be lost for words, just Jenny, Jenny. . . .'

Still in jockstraps and a few precious rags, squatting on open wagons, running down from the hills, rolling out of the forest, they began the journey home. At first it felt like another ghastly joke: they had been deceived enough times. But they had built this railway, a corridor through the trees – surely it was real: rattling over bridges, whistling round corners to convince them. And the pure thankfulness of today, rehearsed so often but never seen like this: it was too vivid to be another dream. And the thought of those men still up at the camp under their bamboo crosses: it was so repulsive, so typical of war and youth and Nippon, it must be true.

They spent two days in a hangar at Banpong aerodrome, treated alternately as heroes and outcasts. Everyone cheered them, nobody wanted to touch them. Their possessions were burnt or fumigated, their bodies examined like medical freaks. Numbers were written in violet ink on their arms. 'We're going home,' they told each other between injections and vitamin pills, trying to understand. They stayed close together for safety, dreading being separated. At night they lay on wooden pallets, harder than the bamboo slats they were used to, and were kept awake by the quiet. They needed the forest noises, the tireless rattle of insects, the crack and whisper of trees. They should have stayed with the men lying up there for ever.

In jungle green shirts and trousers, suffering from indigestion or airsickness or cholera vaccine – the last irony – they were flown to Rangoon. Nakedness had given them an alliance with the elements: their skin had breathed the sun, drunk the rain, felt the wind. Now, in clothes, sensations could touch them only through thicknesses of cotton. Nothing was direct, but must be reached by undoing a button or a belt or a zip. In the aeroplane a glass window kept out the feel of what they saw down there, and made it false.

Clive had never flown before and watched the forest, under the Dakota's drab wing, slip back into the haze. He looked for the river, railway, camp, but couldn't find them. Even the purple mountains towards Burma, the silhouette for a thousand sunsets, were flattened into the trees. Everything was gone, as he used to hope it would, though he never knew he would mind so much about the loss.

At Rangoon they were taken to another camp, put in huts – the first bed since being captured, with soap and towel at the foot and a detective story on the pillow – and allowed to send one telegram of thirty words.

'JENNY JENNY. . . .' Her name looked so good, Clive couldn't stop writing it on the form: 'COMING JENNY HOME JENNY NEXT MONTH JENNY LOVE KISSES JENNY FOR EVER CLIVE JENNY JENNY,' and he filled up the spaces, 'JENNY JENNY JENNY. . . .'

Suddenly he felt more alone than ever. The fabric of the prisoners' lives together, patched up for so long, was falling to bits, rotten and snapping with the stress. Sheets to sleep in, toothpaste out of a tube, chairs and electric lights, prunes under thick custard – the shocks were too bitter to be shared. Catching his breath with disbelief, Clive couldn't trust such delicate happiness unless he kept it to himself. There were things he had longed for, like showers with taps and the smell of a clean shirt before he put it on, and things he had forgotten about, like salt and pepper on the canteen tables, and things he had dreaded, like the cheery pink women in tropical dresses who served tea and meat paste sandwiches. Everyone, men and women, looked so innocent and uncorrupted, exuberant, large, successful. Perhaps it was what Clive had once been and might become again, though he wasn't sure. 'Jenny, Jenny. . . .' He would wait for her to show him what he was.

Till then, people wanted to tell him about the world he had come back to, and ask him for evidence of atrocities, and photograph the toes that had been smashed by Goldilocks, and weigh and measure and inoculate him, and sing him the new songs, and fit him out with a uniform and a bank account and a partner for a dance. Rehabilitation was the incessant word, threatening to stifle the beat of Jenny, Jenny. . . . She sent him a telegram of welcome, delight, love – the expected, unsurprising, fatal things. Already he knew what it meant: the secret truth behind the words.

Something had stopped, but it wasn't the war. For Clive, the fighting had lasted half a morning in the South China Sea nearly four years ago. This was the end of another battle, against despair, and he had lost. But he was alive, unwounded, growing daily stronger, and restless, energetic, impatient. On the month-long voyage from the bright Orient to the grey autumn of postwar Britain, pacing the troopship deck and putting on weight, he was blown by thoughts that altered with the weather, tropical breeze to Altantic gale. He walked all day, hurrying over meals, and drank in the bar all evening till it closed, then walked half the night and was up again at dawn: walking home along the deck, hastening the ship along. Sometimes, sweltering in the Red Sea or cruising through the Mediterranean or rolling up the Channel to Southampton, he stood at the rail and gave way to tears, pretending it was the wind: 'Jenny, Jenny. . . .'

7

Jenny was standing beside him. She was among the bottles in the big mirror behind the bar. Clive wasn't surprised, it wasn't such a coincidence. He had been expecting it for years, hoping it would never happen. Hoping it would. They had an appointment – no date or place fixed, but Jenny would be there.

He was in London after visiting Brenda, the frothy gasping widow in Brighton, before returning to the Mendanas. Staying as usual at the Ritz. Walking in Green Park by day. Watching the people. Calling at the familiar shops. This time he had bought new records for the gramophone Odette had left at Aurora – *Swan Lake* and the rest of her stock were wearing out – and opened an account for more to be sent. He was flying back tomorrow. Now on his last evening, for the habitual treat to take away, he had come to the theatre. The play was recommended by the hotel manager: indecent and offensive and very popular – 'only the very best for the very best, Mr Ackerly.' That suited Clive. He could disdain it, and the audience, which was the point of coming.

In the interval, standing at the bar, he caught himself in a mirror. A man of fifty. A sunburnt expatriate. Tall, healthy, not bad looking, he thought. Without wrinkles or much grey hair yet. Only a little bald. Quietly waiting for a drink among these noisy Londoners. Probably there was something out of fashion in his suit: too narrow in the lapels, too wide in the leg, or with the wrong number of buttons and pockets – he didn't know. There were men here in corduroy jackets and denim trousers, even sandals, with no ties and too much hair. Clive didn't object to them, he simply chose to be better dressed. But he couldn't be taken for a city man, he supposed. More like a rich farmer up from the country. A successful race-horse trainer. Possibly an airline pilot or, as he once had been, a naval officer in civilian clothes. Nobody would guess, and he didn't mind that nobody would care. They were bright, modern, uninhibited. He was pleased to be different.

'Yes, sir?' the barman said.

Clive leant forward to order his drink; stood up and looked in the mirror again. Next to him at the bar were two young men and a girl. Americans. Foreigners like himself. He felt oddly drawn to them. In the mirror they looked somehow pleasanter, less unorthodox and loud and sloppy than the English. They weren't enjoying the play, it seemed. Clive liked them. The girl was right beside him. She was Jenny.

He might have been on a raft in the South China Sea again, and found her lying with him. Or it was part of the play – indecent and offensive, just what he wanted. He finished his drink and asked for another, without taking his eyes out of the mirror. He was afraid that if he turned she wouldn't be there. He would kill her looking at her directly. The raft would be empty, he would be left to drift for years more and go on hoping.

'Becky!' one of the young men beyond her called.

'You're in a dream – come out of it. What are you drinking?'

She opened wide the big grey eyes, the way she always did, and shook her lovely head and said, 'Sorry – a tomato juice.' She was working at Peter Jones still, in the furniture department, or had just joined the ambulance service – Clive couldn't pinpoint the date exactly. She was unbelievably the same, or too believably. This was the woman who had saved his life on the railway; who would be waiting for him on his return, standing on the platform at Waterloo. He would show her his broken toes and give her the zircon ring. Here she was, as she always had been – meeting him in London. She had something to tell him, but this time she didn't know what it was. In the mirror she smiled at him. Taking the risk, he turned.

'What do you make of it?' he asked impulsively. He was no longer the man in the mirror, he hardly recognised himself.

'Oh, I think it's interesting, it's like nothing I've seen before.' Strangely the accent was quite natural. Otherwise she hadn't changed. A little taller perhaps, with a longer neck, thinner face. It was twenty years since he last saw her. After that nightmare tea in the station buffet, after seeing him off in a taxi, she had gone to Rebecca's birthday party: 'She's two today, she's having a cake.' Now she was twenty-two, an American girl with the same grey eyes.

'It's rather beyond me,' Clive said. 'Perhaps I'm too old.'

She smiled again: 'Beyond me too. Perhaps I'm not English enough.'

'This might be another scene – we've brought it from the stage into the bar.'

'Pardon me?' She was as puzzled as he was.

'Becky! – your tomato juice.' Her friends passed it to her and politely nodded to the stranger with her. He looked safe, no threat to anyone. They didn't mind losing their girl for five minutes, they were in an argument.

'Have you been to England before?' Clive asked. Better to be banal than cryptic.

'This is the first time back.'

'Back? You were born here?' As if he didn't know.

'I was one of your famous war babies.'

'And your mother one of our famous GI brides?' Teasing himself as much as her.

'English enough, but I can't see Mum ever as a bride.'

'Perhaps none of us can see our mother.'

'If you knew mine. . . .' She gave that marvellous laugh, on the point of mockery. Nobody else could do it.

'Your father's American?'

'Sent here after Pearl Harbor, when America came in – to win the war for you.'

'I remember.' In her last letter, the one that drove Clive to the Mendana Islands, Jenny had said that Rebecca knew all about him.

'But I can't see Dad as a soldier either. He'd stop to ask the enemy questions – how much salary he got, who he voted for – instead of shooting him.'

'He sounds nice.'

'He was never let loose near any fighting, he just had a lovely time in London.'

'It's happened all through history, I'm sure.'

'Having war babies? Fathered on the women while their husbands were away in battle?'

'I was a war baby too.'

'You were?' She looked doubtful.

'The first war.' An idea reached him, too dangerous to think about now. Instead he said, 'So you don't remember England much?'

'They carried me away to the New World, screaming in my cot.' She laughed again, then asked, 'You live here?'

'No – on the other side of the world somewhere.' He couldn't imagine Aurora at that moment. There was nothing else but this.

'Anywhere near Australia? We had a posting there – one of the best.'

'Posting?'

'Dad's in the foreign service. I was three years at school in Sydney. Mum said it was like England in the sun. Maybe just to annoy Dad – he's jealous of her Englishness. That's why he never let me come here before this trip.'

'Many other postings?'

'Madagascar, Jamaica, the Philippines – too many. We seem to get the islands. I tell Dad he'll finish up on St Helena.'

'Where are they now?'

'In Washington for a year. And there I'll stay. Unless they're sent to London – I'd follow like a shot.'

'You like it here?'

'Love it.'

'Why?'

'It's. . . .' She looked at him askew. 'It's where young people are important. It's for my generation. But America's for grandfathers and grandmothers.'

'My generation.' Clive laughed this time.

'I ought to like it, anyway – I'm half English.'

'Top half, I'd say.'

'Well, not entirely. American teeth, English legs – '

'English eyes, English laugh.'

'OK, my first breath was a gulp of London air. Where was yours?'

'Mine? – oh, a long way from here.'

'On the other side of the world somewhere,' she said, putting on his accent, sounding like her mother.

'On the other side of the border, to be exact.'

'Scotland? You look utterly English. Just what I imagine when Mum describes an Englishman. She has this romantic picture – tradition and good manners and inscrutability.'

'Has she ever been back?' There was so much to ask, quickly.

The girl shook her head: 'She longs to. She gets all soppy and girlish at the thought. But maybe she thinks Dad would be too upset.'

'Maybe she'd find it isn't what she hoped.'

'She'd hate that. She's got this wonderful belief in things.'

'Becky!' her friends called. 'You want another drink?' But they didn't insist or interrupt, they were still arguing.

'Hey!' she said to Clive. 'Why am I telling you all this?'

'I started it.'

'You did – so where's your famous English – '

'Reserve? Or was it phlegm?'

'We haven't even been introduced.'

'Is that what your mother told you? We're suspicious of foreigners, we're unfriendly, we're stand-offish.'

'Stuck up and superior and – '

'All those things – I know, I know. Is your mother any of them?'

'Superior – I guess she's that.'

'And what about the play tonight? Is that so inhibited?'

'Maybe you can let go on the stage.'

'But not in the bar?'

'Maybe bed's the place,' she said simply, with the smallest wishful laugh – for Clive alone, he thought – and a glance at her two friends. Perhaps it was her American ease, or she had been released by the outrageous play. 'But even there, Mum says. . . .' The theatre bell rang for the second act.

Suddenly Clive didn't want to hear what her mother said. 'Are you staying long?' he asked.

'Flying back tomorrow.'

'So am I. The opposite way.'

'Did you come on business?'

'Not really.' He thought of the wine merchant and shoemaker and Asprey's. He never wanted to see them again. 'My brother died. I had to tidy up.'

'I'm sorry.'

'We weren't very close. Not since we were boys.'

'On opposite sides of the world – '

'Do you have a brother, sister?'

She shook her head again: 'I'm a one-off.'

He wondered if Isabel could be called a step-sister, or if this girl would like to know about her. Probably she would. He said, 'I don't think I'll come again.'

'Never?'

'I couldn't bear it.' It was true, he saw.

'You mean, like you said about Mum – finding out it's not what you hoped? Afraid of being let down?'

'Something like that.'

'Have you been to America?'

'Once, for a weekend. To Newfoundland, if that counts.'

'It's Canada, but it'll pass. What did you do there?'

'Played the bagpipes.'

'Like hell.' She didn't believe him any more than she knew who he was.

' "Speed Bonnie Boat" was all I could think of.' He had said it long ago in a Chelsea flat.

'All to yourself? Nobody heard?'

'Just Churchill and President Roosevelt – they loved it.'

'I bet.'

The bell went again, the bar was emptying. 'Becky!' her friends called.

She put down her glass; held out her hand to Clive: 'It's been nice.'

'Give my love to Jenny,' he said, taking her hand.

'Who?'

'Your mother.'

'Jesus.'

'Becky, let's go – it's starting!'

'Christ. . . .' Wonder and misery and joy flashed in the huge grey eyes, the total helplessness of luck.

'Have a good flight.' He let her hand go.

'Becky, come on! You want to miss the rest?' They nodded at Clive again and took her away. She couldn't stop them, she was lost for words. She had something to tell Clive, but it was impossible to say.

He did want to miss the rest. He couldn't face being in there, a few seats away, hugging his astonishment, guessing at hers. He had another drink, then two or three more. He went through their dialogue again, adding lines that had been left out before, more oblique but truthful than anything happening on the stage. Out in the London night he walked for hours. Breakfast at the Ritz would be the last. He wouldn't risk another trip to England.

Part Six

The Volcano

1

Tropical storms flickered and rumbled round the islands, glancing from the mountains, sweeping the forest. A black veil rose over the horizon, so tightly stretched that it tore on the peak of Bau and broke over Aurora. Rain landed like an occupying force; crushed the village, subdued the noisy cockatoos and skittering fish, effaced the universe beyond a space of streaming water. Coconut trees rattled in the wind, bits of tin banged among the houses, the lagoon hissed and jumped. When the veil lifted, an angry sun glared through flying clouds on the wet rich earth. The plantation was left to shake off the drips and wait for the puddles to steam away, feeling washed, sweetened, briefly sanctified.

News struck Aurora more obliquely: the loom of lightning playing on dark clouds, keeping its distance. Beaconsfield's radio, when it had batteries, was tuned to Australian pop music. Clive subscribed to two papers sent from London, like his marmalade and Worcester sauce: the *Economist* for politics and copra prices, *Country Life* for shooting and fishing, though he hadn't killed a grouse or salmon since he was a boy. They came many weeks late but between them, out of date or out of season, he believed he got a fair report. The news was improved by being irrelevant and absurd. The chess problem and crossword were never stale.

Towards the end of the nineteen-sixties he found his life more and more disturbed from outside. It began some time after his last visit to London when he might have expected to enjoy his peace, safe from intrusion. At first the threat was slight. A letter came from Washington DC.

'Dear Clive. I'll call you Clive because you're not a stranger any more. We met that funny time in the theatre – remember?'

Rebecca too, during the rest of the play, had gone

through their conversation again, snatching pieces of it, inventing others to fit the gaps. 'My head was boiling, the show was ruined. It was unreal, wasn't it, in that bar? I had to say it happened, it happened, over and over, to make sure. But I kept asking why the hell didn't he tell me who he was, instead of making a fool of me. And it was tantalizing. I hated to let it drop.'

She had driven her friends crazy afterwards, tearing through the audience to find her mother's first husband, watching the exits, staying till there was nobody left in the theatre, then trying the pubs. 'You vanished, but I got a feeling you wouldn't mind if I gave chase. I clung to your "Give my love to Jenny" as a clue that you didn't want to cut me out totally. Or you'd have kept your secret. Maybe I'm wrong and it's only my self-interest. I told Mum and Dad when I came home. Mum wanted details. How was life going for you? Did you look happy? Were you alone? Had you gone grey or bald or fat? – which I never looked for because I didn't know who you were, till it was too late. "Bastard!" I called you. She said it was the word for me, not you. As for her feelings, well – she can be very cool. That English overdrive takes over like an automatic gear. She sends her love back, of course. And Dad took it better than I thought. The old jealousy hardly stirred. He even helped me track you down. It took some doing, you can imagine. Your defences are pretty good. Mum wasn't surprised. She said you were always the hiding type. Through the foreign service, somehow, Dad found the crack. Please don't mind. I'll promise not to write again if it's unwelcome.'

Clive had never read anything like this and felt a stab of danger, which he enjoyed. Rebecca asked for a letter from him, and an exchange once or twice a year. 'Not just a pen friend,' she wrote, making him wince, 'but there's so much you can tell me. Mum keeps that side of her covered up and only lets the diplomat's wife show small bits of it sometimes, like showing too much leg at a party and Dad whispers, "Pull your skirt down, sweetheart." But it's a big part of her, so it's part of me too. What I mean is, you can tell me about you and I'll find out about me. But it's sad there's nothing I can give you in return.'

There was something she could give, Clive saw, if he would allow her. Something too tender to mention yet. Something of himself. He was fifty and she was twenty-two but across the generations, halfway round the world, they would share a private comedy, a sort of innocence. And Jenny of all people would see the irony: her daughter, child of adultery, corresponding with the abandoned husband. 'You must tell me about your life,' he wrote back to Rebecca, 'if you want to hear about mine.'

He couldn't ignore the menace in the distance, the thuds and echoes of a falling empire. In the Tulagi hotel bar, with heavy laughter, they spoke of a fool's paradise and warded off the gloom with gin. The evening hymn, 'The day thou gavest, Lord, is ended,' was too painful to sing, or everyone too drunk. To Clive now, Tulagi was as pointless as London or Brighton, and he stopped going there. Aurora was enough: a world of his creation where news came in hints rather than hard facts. Someone appeared in a teeshirt stamped with 'Independence Now!'. Children picked up new words to the old national anthem, that kept God but dropped the Queen. On his annual visit Beaconsfield's brother, the Bishop of Tulagi, drank half a bottle of Clive's whisky and confessed that the mission schools were the refuge of the freedom movement. 'Like the monasteries in your Dark Ages,' he said, chuckling over something he remembered from his theology college, 'they're keeping the light burning.'

'Light!' Clive protested. 'The sort that shone in the Mendanas a hundred years ago.'

'In darkest Africa . . .' the bishop began, pleased with the phrase.

'Look how it's gone back! Tribal war again, with rockets instead of poisoned arrows.'

'Lighten our darkness, is what the white man taught us.' The bishop helped himself and his brother to more whisky.

'Darken our lightness a bit, is what I'd like,' Clive said, and surprised himself. Twice before, in a Chelsea flat and in a prison camp, he had said he was frightened of the darkness. Now he was older and more tolerant; aware how his imagination fed on obscurity, like roots in the

ground. 'There's too much light on us. Nothing can be
hidden. Everywhere the analysts and investigators are at
work. Cameras are turned on all our secrets.' He saw
the bishop giggling at this white man's secrets, and was
encouraged: 'They want the answers, they strip us bare
to get them. Everyone is being exposed so that everyone
else can be plugged with facts. We're stuffed with information but we know nothing. We want more mystery,
not less. Long live the weeds and the wilderness! Give us
back our magic.'

'Very-very . . .' Beaconsfield hiccupped and said, 'Ah!'
and again, 'Ah!' But nothing else. Shrinking into middle
age, the little bush boy got drunk easily.

'You can't have it both ways,' the bishop said,
recovering himself. 'You want your empire where the sun
never sets and you want your darkness too.'

'Not both ways – just my own will do. A small private
empire where not everything has been explained away.
Where there are still some shadows – '

'I hope you will be allowed to keep it.' The bishop,
especially full of whisky, was a compassionate man.

Clive wrote to Rebecca about him. She wrote back about
Washington: her parents' social life, her job in the library
of an ethnic museum, her friends and holidays. 'America's
so greedy,' she told him. 'It swallows you whole. I hang
on to the thought of that man down there on an island,
doing his own thing, refusing to get sucked into the
universal maw. Silly of me, maybe – all on the strength
of a few minutes in a London bar. I go to the theatre with
some idiotic nobody who'd jump out of his pants if an
original idea struck him, and hope I'll be picked up by a
stranger twice his age, who doesn't know the smart jokes
and latest ways to get a girl to bed.' These were the letters
that Jenny had never sent when he was a prisoner, but
now turned inside out: Rebecca was clutching his isolation
to relieve her predictable, unchanging days at home.

For Clive she was a better guide to a world beyond
Aurora than the visitors who occasionally, but more often
now, arrived in his lagoon. 'I'm a kind of oracle,' he wrote.
'They come for advice and wisdom. I'm totally impartial,
they believe. My integrity is famous. My knowledge

reaches wider things, outside the local scene, even into the future. I'm respected most of all when I quote my friend in Washington. So you must tell me what to say.'

Officers from each government department came once a year, followed by any commissioner or councillor or mere expert who found a reason to call on Clive. Usually they wanted comfort, to soothe the prospect of Independence and their empty lives beyond. Nobody knew when it would happen. 'Give it a good ten years,' one of them said hopefully in 1970. 'The question is, who'll take over when we go? There's nobody in sight.' To them, Aurora was a legacy to be proud of. To Clive, they were a nuisance to be kept at the brink of politeness. 'I'm considered a justification for the British Empire,' he wrote to Rebecca. 'They come with a faint odour of desperation, and preen themselves here as if it was all their doing, and go away with a faint odour of envy.'

They travelled in motor cruisers, no longer in trading schooners or mission boats, and spoke of bigger offices being built in Tulagi, and new appointments being invented and filled as the empire shrank. This was one of the few corners left, never important and usually ignored. But now Her Majesty's servants were crowding in while there was somewhere for them to go. The pantomime – a repertory company still playing in the distant provinces, reduced to second-rate actors glad of a job – was nearly over. They would show that in their last hour the British would keep faith.

'Faith with what?' Clive asked a politician from London on a Pacific tour, sweating on his boat and annoyed at not being invited ashore.

'Well,' the man blathered, waving a damp handkerchief at the model plantation, 'this sort of thing, I suppose.'

Clive kept his own faith to himself, or to his letters to Rebecca.

His household never recovered from Loloa's crime. Though other bush boys were sent by Beaconsfield to be his servant, none had the murderer's style. But to spare the saltwater boys when Loloa came out of prison, Clive wouldn't take him back. The gentle, beautiful polisher of hand-made shoes, concoctor of aphrodisiac sauces, bedfellow of the ardent widow Odette, was put to work in the cocoa groves – one of the gang moving slowly in line, snicking yellow pods off the trees with a chisel blade on the end of a pole.

'I'd like to have Isabel in my house,' Clive suggested to Beaconsfield when his daughter was fifteen. She was Loloa's niece and might have some of his skill. She was also irresistible, unique among the Aurora girls in more than colour – the glow of rare wood, paler than anything from this tropical forest, with a walnut gleam. Her mother was married now, and had younger children. Isabel was her own destiny, separate but never alone, less nymph than nubile village beauty, dangerously earthy and unreluctant.

Beaconsfield agreed, the people approved, Isabel didn't mind. She learnt the duties, even invented some dishes, and filled the kitchen with friends, songs, laughter. Clive would make no father's claims or hope to save her from herself, but could watch his child become a woman and take some of the pain which clearly didn't bother her. She called him 'Mr Clive' with no hint that she knew she was his daughter.

'When moon is full,' Beaconsfield told Clive, 'you see a black thing in the middle.'

'The man in the moon, we call it.'

'Is holding it up in the sky for his wife, but she isn't there, so is cold and lonely up there. But is loving all women, to give them piccaninnies. And so is bringing sticks to light a fire.'

'To make the moon shine.'

'And when he feels warm by the fire, is making babies for us.'

'You believe that, Beaconsfield?'

The old bush boy smiled: 'They are falling down from the moon and into mother's womb, so they find a door to come out into the sun.'

Perhaps Isabel was a moon child, unaware of her father, content to be the most desired and yielding girl in Aurora: the local whore, Clive would have said, if she hadn't been

so treasured by him, though enjoyed as infinitely by her
lovers. Soon there was a baby, fathered at night by the
man in the moon, dropped to earth and born into daylight
between her willing legs. Soon there was another. And
soon Clive's daughter, who cooked his food and cleaned
his house and washed his clothes and worked his garden
and taunted him with images of his mother and wife, had
a clutch of piccaninnies in several moon-dark shades – his
sunlit grandchildren.

'A woman in the Mendanas,' he wrote to Rebecca, 'is
called a Mary, and a pregnant one is a bubbly Mary, which
is what Isabel often is.'

He told Rebecca merely that Isabel was the cheerful
promiscuous servant who ran his domestic life, helped by
the people she drew to the house and the children they
gave her. 'Luckily she's back in the kitchen two days after
a baby. If I was pushed I might scramble an egg, but I've
never tried. It's something I've escaped.' It pleased him
to stand between two women, a young American and a
much younger half-Mendanan, though it troubled him,
trying to imagine Rebecca in Washington, that he saw
only Jenny in Chelsea thirty years ago. But Isabel was
proxy for nobody: real and fallible, cooking or laughing
or scolding behind the kitchen curtain, quickening her
father's heart whenever he saw her.

'It sounds like a nice scene down there,' Rebecca wrote.
'In the museum library where I work I found a book from
the last century, by a missionary who lived in your islands.
So my picture is strictly in black and white woodcuts.
There's one of a man who looks ready to eat his neigh-
bour, all teeth and hatchet and not an inch of clothes, just
a tassel on the end of his cock. D'you go around like that?
Please say yes. I remember the Englishman I met in a
London theatre once, and I take his suit off and give him
a hatchet and a tassel, but it won't work.'

Rebecca too had lovers, shadowy men without names
or faces who lay casually in her letters. 'I'm dined and
screwed like any other girl who's not a nun or a giraffe,
but there's something missing – love, Mum says, and she
could be right.'

Now that he never left Aurora, holding visitors off but

not relaxing work for the plantation and its people, Clive had only Rebecca's letters to take him beyond the furthest visible islands or over the forest and the peak of Bau. Probably, he thought, he should be glad not to see her distinctly: no woodcuts, no naked portrait to sharpen the figure. Better to keep the illusion than lose everything outside the view from the lagoon. And in his letters back, colouring the black and white sketches, clothing the cannibal for her, he defined himself. He wasn't modest, he knew his strength, he liked to show his points in exchange for hers. With luck she might grasp that his love for her mother had swelled and overflowed into something more wonderful, a rejoicing in life itself, and it could only have happened at Aurora. But in time he would be cut off here, and then decline into a cartoon of himself, not funny enough for a laugh except in his own privacy.

'I wonder if I convey the *power* of this place,' he wrote. 'Can you smell coconuts when you open the envelope? Or feel coral on the paper? Yet it's the power of fiction, it has no existence. I only have to post the letter and shut my eyes and I'm in a dugout canoe, paddling up the Potomac to take you out to dinner, absurdly happy, though I've never been to Washington.'

Slowly, with two or three letters a year between them, the comedy became a need. And one day, as Clive expected, Rebecca wrote that she was married. To a lawyer: 'You've seen him, he was one of the men in London – remember?' But Clive hadn't looked at them, being intent on Jenny's daughter. 'For God's sake don't stop writing,' she said. 'It makes no difference – I'm not even in love with him. Mum said I was crazy. Any port in a storm, I told her. It was just I couldn't stand the pressure. I wanted a refuge and he was the best in sight. Now I'm on my lonely island, you on yours. So please, Clive – let's reach out. . . .'

At the end she mentioned an English graduate who had been working in her museum: 'An Englishman! How could I resist? He's writing a thesis on the impact of whites on black culture, or vice versa, in the twilight of your empire. The Mendanas are about all that's left, so he's going your way. He's so boring, he's almost fascinating.

I did all the wrong things, just to get him out of my hair.
The wrong things – I mean nothing at all, except I gave
him your name. His is Godfrey. One day he'll land in
your lagoon. Sorry. You'll hate him.'

On Clive's sixtieth birthday they killed the best bullock in
the herd and roasted it by the lagoon. Clive had spent
twenty-five years in the Mendanas, twenty-one at Aurora.
Most of his people had lived with him since the beginning,
some had never been away. There was enough to
celebrate.

Bush boys collected wood, saltwater boys dug the pit.
Loloa, who had once cleft a girl's skull in half with a copra
knife, did the same for the bullock. Beaconsfield chewed
a mixture of herbs which he spat on the raw carcass. Laki,
grey-haired among his descendants and creased with age,
folded his limbs under a blanket and watched the fire.
Clive remembered the bonfire when his father came home
from the trenches, with fireworks and baked potatoes.
Isabel picked her lover for the night, while her children
sang English nursery rhymes – 'Where are you going to,
my pretty maid?' and 'Pop goes the weasel', in brilliant
half-tuned voices. Gongs and flutes and a guitar started
up. When the bullock was cooked Beaconsfield stepped
into the pit and carved lumps to be eaten off a banana
leaf with yams. It was less wild, more drunken, than his
wedding in the forest. Cases of Australian beer, imported
for tonight, were opened. The dancers stamped patterns
in the shore, the lovers made beds in the crackling fronds
under the coconut trees.

After midnight, in the first hours of his seventh decade,
Clive left the feast and went to his house; slipped under
the mosquito net and listened to the gongs. He had lived
longer than his father, mother, brother, and felt a strong
momentum bearing him through the years. He hadn't
been ill since he was a child, except with malaria on the
railway. The gongs were like the throb of fever, the day
Smithy died. He was still listening to them when the
opossum crept back into the roof from its hunting.

*

Next morning a number of Mendanans, in shirts and trousers and shoes, came to Aurora by motorboat. They spent the day in the village – a quiet holiday after the party. Across the lagoon Clive thought he heard clapping, and three cheers. There was no pork left, but a tuft of smoke rose from the roasting pit where children were grilling fish in the embers. One of Isabel's sons brought Clive's lunch – she was tired, she wanted to sleep. In the hot afternoon Clive sat with a book on his veranda. At sunset Beaconsfield arrived with the visitors.

'Mr Clive,' he said, introducing the leader, 'you remember Dikea. . . .' It was the contractor who had started to build a forest road across the island, and then defaulted. Clive hadn't heard of him for fifteen years. He wore a gold watch and a great smile, with no sign of friendliness behind it.

'You've come back to finish the road?' Clive waved him courteously to a chair. They all sat down, side by side along the veranda. Dikea's watch was the biggest, and the others had no smiles. None of them were bush boys. Beaconsfield kept apart, scornful of these men from Tulagi but uneasy. He wouldn't sit too close to Clive, it might show he was on the white man's side. He knew that Clive would understand.

Dikea laughed and cracked his finger joints: 'Mr Ackerly, I am no longer a contractor – I have no time for it.' His voice, a cultured baritone, spoke of success and confidence and a wide acquaintance with the world.

'You built a new house in Tulagi, I heard. On the ridge, with a swimming pool.'

Dikea dismissed it with another laugh: 'A small house – I will give it to my son and build a better one.'

Clive showed mock surprise: 'I've always found one house is enough.' He called to Isabel to bring whisky and glasses. 'So what is your job, that takes your time and makes you rich?'

'I am a politician,' Dikea said.

Elaborately, solemnly, Clive stood up, walked to Dikea's chair, shook his hand with exaggerated ceremony: 'Yesterday I was sixty and you are the first politician I've ever seen.' He kept Dikea's hand in his, bowing his head in deference; then remembered it wasn't true: 'Or rather, I did meet Churchill and Roosevelt once.' There was a stir among the visitors, a shuffle of feet as they kicked off their shoes. Night had dropped, the moon was late, the lagoon lay nudging the veranda in the dark. The men's cigarettes flared in a last puff and fizzed as they hit the water. Through its veil of insects the pressure lamp caught most of their watches and a few gold teeth. Clive went on: 'But neither of them honoured me with a visit to my house. I'm overcome, speechless – I hardly know . . .' Isabel came with the whisky. Clive released Dikea's hand and returned to his chair; lifted his glass to them each in turn. 'We shall drink to the occasion! My birthday is complete!' Eyeing each other, they sipped as if it might be poisoned. 'Now tell me, gentlemen, how do I deserve your presence here?'

'Mr Ackerly,' Dikea said, 'I am secretary of the Congress.'

'Congress?'

'The Mendanan People's Congress – I am sure you have heard – '

'We're out of touch here. I can't pretend I mind. Aurora is beyond politics.'

'No, Mr Ackerly – not beyond.'

'Till today it was.'

'Politics are worldwide.'

'You've travelled a lot?'

Dikea drank his whisky: 'You can say. . . .' He shut his eyes, counting the countries he had been to, cracking a finger for each one.

Clive interrupted: 'You must be paid well, as secretary. Does it come from the members?'

'Not so much the members, because the Mendanan people are poor and backward still. So we have investment companies and we have international agencies and we have – '

'They give you money?'

'They want to see democracy in our country.'

'I'm afraid you'll find it doesn't mean much at Aurora. My headman, for example. . . .' Clive turned to Beaconsfield in the shadows behind him: once a runner for the

coastwatchers, later the supercargo of a schooner, now
the ritual son of a white man. Nervously Beaconsfield
swallowed his whisky. 'I think,' Clive said, 'you'll have a
hard job explaining democracy to my people.'

'Today,' Dikea waved his glass towards his friends, 'we
went into all the houses and gave them our pamphlet and
then we had a meeting in the school, and my speech was
received – '

'You're working fast.'

'We are in a hurry. It is a big country and we must
cover it in five years.'

'Five years?'

'We expect our independence then – it will be
announced quite soon,' Dikea said. His friends shuffled
again, becoming less inhibited: their leader was doing
well.

'I can't see it making much difference to most
Mendanans,' Clive said. 'To you, perhaps – '

'To you also, Mr Ackerly.'

'In five years? I shall have a lot of life in me, I hope. I'll
be doing what I've done since I came here. Working for
Aurora, my people.' He poured more whisky for them all.
Suddenly he felt very sad. He couldn't speak about the
fun, the rewards of his years here that were bigger than
any profit. 'You'll never turn me out.'

'What I can tell you,' Dikea began slowly, as if he
wanted to sound like an official letter, typed words over
an unreadable signature, 'is that no foreigner will be
allowed to own land in the Mendanas.'

'You mean, don't you, that a white man's success is too
good for you?'

'I don't understand.'

'You know that none of you could have created Aurora
and it's an embarrassment to you, you'll feel uncomfortable with me here.'

'No, Mr Ackerly, it isn't that. But in a democracy like
ours – '

'Democracy like yours! With men like you in power!
The whole Mendanas in your hands! And people like
mine getting a worse deal than they do with me.' Then
sadness turned to anger. Clive shouted, 'You've no idea

what I've put into Aurora. It's beyond you. Not one of you is capable. There's no Mendanan who'd have done it, who'd begin to see. . . .' He stopped. It was ridiculous to shout at these dark figures on his veranda: the glow of a cigarette and glint of a whisky glass or gold watch – otherwise no light, nothing to show the warmth or spark of a man's feelings. 'But you'll never turn me out.'

'Mr Ackerly, the plantation will not belong to you.'

'I have a freehold.'

'There will be a law – nobody but a Mendanan may own land.'

'You can't take my freehold, you can't break the rules.'

'That will be changed.'

'If that's your democracy . . .' Suddenly Clive saw just what he would do: 'Then it's simple.' It was like that moment thirty years ago at Waterloo station, when he knew in a flash that he would take the night train up to Strathpolly and stay with his brother Victor: 'I'll become a Mendanan. I've been one for years. Now I'll do it legally.'

'Mr Ackerly, to be a Mendanan you must have two grandparents who were Mendanans.'

'So you want everything.' Jenny had told him that Strathpolly was sold. This was another blow but he could take it, like last time: 'Well, you won't get it – I'll defy you.'

'Mr Ackerly, your ancestors – ?'

'Thank God, of course they weren't Mendanan.'

'Then your land will be taken.'

'Then I'll sell up and go. It's very valuable.'

'You will be allowed to sell only to a Mendanan.' Dikea's voice came through the smile, warm and toxic. 'With at least two grandparents – '

'That's absurd – you know it. There's no Mendanan who could afford to buy Aurora. It's worth half a million dollars, a million, I don't know – more than any of you could pay.' They sat in silence: not even the crack of a finger joint. 'You think you've caught me, don't you? You think I'm in a trap.'

'Mr Ackerly, we have investment companies, banks – '

'You're mistaken.' Clive stood up with the whisky bottle; poured the rest into their glasses. The last was

Beaconsfield's. Then he turned to Dikea: 'Nobody but a Mendanan may own land, you say. Well, I shall do the same as you with your new house. On Independence Day I shall give Aurora to my son.'

2

One day, as Rebecca had warned, Godfrey landed at Aurora: an Englishman of thirty with sprouts of red beard round his face and, through glasses, the eyes of a perpetual feeder on information. Most of it he swallowed but some, like a predator giving half-digested morsels to its young, he passed to anyone in reach. Its taste or value didn't matter: it was his life, he would expire if he couldn't get enough.

'Didn't Becky write that I was on my way? She promised – '

'She mentioned something.' Clive would hate him, she had said, but she was wrong: he had been cured of hatred on the railway. So far he couldn't tell his opinion of Godfrey, who had been ashore five minutes.

'You won't mind if I fill you in?' Godfrey suggested, speaking down his nose more than through his lips. 'Rebecca's not a girl for wasting time, she probably didn't tell you much about me.'

'Or tell you much about me.'

Godfrey gave a thin snigger: 'Not a lot – only that you'd write my thesis better than I could and turn me upside down in the process.'

'I'd hardly know a thesis if I met one.' Clive looked along his shelves: nothing academic, simply the books he liked.

'It's for my doctorate – a hundred thousand words to glorify the library of London University.'

'I thought it was Washington.'

'I did three months there last summer – didn't Becky

explain? Researching in her museum. We had a lot of fun.
She's a great girl, you'll agree.'

'She's – well, I only met her once.'

'The way she put it,' Godfrey took off his glasses, blew
on the lenses, polished them on his shirt front, then produced a pencil as if he was going to take notes, 'she's
known you all her life.'

'We write letters on and off. But it's rather faded since
she got married.'

'Husband comes first?' Godfrey squinted through the
shiny lenses.

'Before an old man on the other side of the world.'

'Then I'll put you in the picture. Plug the gaps.' Godfrey
was settling easily into Clive's house. 'Three months in a
museum last year, three months fieldwork this year – and
from what I've seen,' he waved his hand over the scene,
'it's a dream. But before we start, could I have a drink –
a beer or fruit juice? I'll pay my way, don't worry. Or the
department will. And Clive, I've brought you. . . .' He
went to his baggage – rucksack, typewriter, tape-recorder,
cameras – and unpacked a bottle of brandy, a box of cigars,
a Stilton cheese. 'From what Becky said, they'll hit the
right note. The cheese ought to go in the refrigerator.'

Isabel came in with a jug of pineapple juice and peanuts.
Godfrey stopped talking and put away his pencil to watch:
the quiet tread, her almost translucent brown and slender
figure despite so many babies, her large ungiving eyes.
He lifted his own eyes when she had gone and closed
them in a mock prayer for help.

Clive saw it and quickly said, 'You can have the spare
bedroom – I'll tell Isabel.' He had once said the same,
more or less, to Odette.

'Isabel?'

'It's a local name – she was Queen of Spain when the
Mendanas were discovered.'

'They don't come like that any more,' Godfrey said, 'or
not in the standard texts. We're losing touch. Which is
where this trip comes in – there's nothing like material
collected in the field.'

'I've never heard Aurora called a field,' Clive said, half
sadly, testing his ability for sarcasm with politeness.

'Because nobody has come here before. Which makes it exciting – virgin ground, the classic conditions, and not another thesis in sight. You know what I mean?'

Clive didn't know but guessed, and felt threatened by his uninvited visitor, more worried than he had been with Odette. Though Godfrey wasn't aggressive or dangerous Clive was put on the defence, uncomfortable and furtive in his own house.

'All I want,' Godfrey said that night over brandy on the veranda, with fireflies signalling through the cigar smoke, 'is to dig myself in for three months. Watch and listen, eyes skinned, ear to the ground – the old routine. I've landed on my feet, wouldn't you say? I bless my luck.'

'Shouldn't you bless Rebecca?'

'Becky? I'd hug her, kiss her all over, practically rape her if she was here – if she'd let me.' Godfrey pulled on his cigar, blew the smoke over the dark lagoon with a sigh of disappointment: 'The bitch.'

Clive kept quiet. At first he would show Godfrey enough for his work, no more. Somehow he must endure three months of his company, and would prefer it without friction. He still felt too tired, in the face of Godfrey's enthusiasm, to be dragged into a quarrel; also too wary, too unconfident, perhaps too envious. Later he might be ready for some cautious revelations.

Every morning Godfrey wrote up his notes: the clack of a typewriter through the house while Isabel cooked and swept, laughed and minded her uncertain kitchen duties. Later he would follow Clive round the plantation with notebook and camera; or spend the day with the copra cutters, the cocoa boys; or go fishing with the saltwater boys; or sit in the village with his tape-recorder, asking for memories, dreams, fears, ambitions, opinions of the white man. Every evening with Clive at dinner, or afterwards on the veranda, he queried and suggested and teased out the material to fit his thesis. The last thing Clive heard before sleep was his guest quietly recording more thoughts for tomorrow's typing.

'Would you say,' Godfrey asked, 'that you appeal to the patriarchal aspect of their society?'

'I'd be amazed to be thought a patriarch by anyone.'

'It could hardly be otherwise, with the characters involved.'

'Long ago,' Clive said, trying not to be immodest, 'I found I had a talent for leading men. Will that do for you?'

Godfrey considered for a moment: 'It's not a fashionable talent these days. For my generation – '

'Leadership's a dirty word?'

'Though yours is an unusual brand, a mixture of the conventional and – '

'Thank you.'

'Don't get me wrong, Clive – I'm full of praise, I just want to get all I can.'

Clive was ambivalent: reluctant to talk about himself as if afraid to give himself away, yet needing to share, to talk and listen. And he had nothing to hide, he told himself.

One evening Godfrey said, 'You think I'm a rabid socialist.'

'Aren't you?'

'Hardly political at all. Just a prying student.'

'That's bad enough.'

'Come off it, Clive – you're not the reactionary you make yourself out to be. I've not been wasting time here. What about the bonuses you started? A pay rise every year, a superannuation scheme, paid holidays – they must have been unthinkable twenty years ago, but now they're government policy, compulsory for everyone.'

'For me it wasn't policy. It just seemed best.'

'Nobody's ever been sacked, I'm told. So what happens if a man doesn't do his job?'

'I find him another – there's always something.'

'The benefits you provide – a hurricane lamp for each house, a bottle of oil a week, free milk – '

'For the piccaninnies – it's important.'

'Who else does that in the Mendanas? The children sent away to secondary school, a canoe to take the pregnant women to hospital.'

'The bubbly Marys.'

'A cow every Christmas for them to roast.'

'They love it, they sing carols round it.'

'What I'm driving at,' Godfrey said, 'is what you get in return.'

'It's give-and-take, it's mutual.'

'They give you hard work?'

Clive smiled: 'Or the nearest thing to it they know. They give me devotion too.'

'Why?'

'Because I care.' Softly, as if wondering if it were true, Clive said, 'I go to their hearts – they're very sentimental. I know all about them – their marriages and love affairs and debts and superstitions and hopes and chronic runs of hopelessness.' Clive resented the way Godfrey drew these things from him, though found it somehow pleasant; and noticed, to his own perplexity, that he took a stance a little to one side of his natural one, or a little above. He exaggerated himself to the point of caricature; adopted words and attitudes that were neither fake nor true, but gave fodder for Godfrey's typewriter and amusement to himself. The suspicion that his guest was making fun of him only tweaked the joke: the last laugh, after Godfrey went away, would be Aurora's.

At the end of the month, on the evening of pay day, all the children came to his house and sang 'London bridge is falling down'. Clive couldn't say who was more ridiculous – Godfrey, too busy with tape-recorder and flashbulbs to enjoy the concert, or himself in tears over twenty children, some of them his grandchildren, singing a song they didn't understand; who didn't know London from Tulagi and had never seen a bridge. 'They give me happiness too,' he said afterwards to Godfrey, who was checking his machines – all Japanese, as Clive saw. He got out the whisky and ice – 'It's the only domestic duty I allow myself, I'm not a kitchen man' – and caught Godfrey repeating it to himself, memorizing it for his thesis. Already Clive knew that the subject was veering closer to himself.

'Did you ever lose your whisky?' Godfrey asked.

'A bottle was stolen once,' Clive told him.

'You knew the thief?'

'There wasn't one. These things are impersonal.

Passive, if you like. Something gets stolen, but not by anyone. Theft is a condition, not a crime.'

'So what happened?'

'Next morning some of the copra boys didn't turn up for work. There was a sultry look among the others.'

'What did you do?'

'What white men are born to do. I raged and shouted.'

'It did no good?'

'Only to myself.'

'Nobody got punished?'

'Someone got knocked to square leg for a boundary.'

'Someone got what?' Godfrey reached for his pencil.

'Knocked to square leg – Christ, didn't you ever play cricket?'

'Only about twice, thank God.'

'I loved cricket,' Clive said, simply. 'I'd be sad to hear that English boys no longer learnt to play.' One afternoon he went with Godfrey to the village football ground for a match against the Mendana police team. 'We're national champions, but I'm sorry it has to be this wretched game.'

'Inferior to cricket?'

'A low class game – I'd prefer rugby. Though they don't do badly.' They beat the police easily, but disgraced themselves on the field, dancing, hugging, even kissing when they scored a goal. 'It's disgusting,' Clive said.

'It's modern,' Godfrey told him.

'It's unmanly.' At the end of the match Clive cornered the young Aurora team by the goalpost: 'You behave like a bunch of schoolgirls.' Certainly, in brief white shorts and vests and still hopping with energy after the game, some of them had a bursting animal allure, sleek and shameless but oddly ambiguous. After his harangue Clive quoted, ' "If you can meet triumph and disaster. . ." ' One of the footballers took up the next line: ' "And treat those two impostors just the same – " '

'Jesus Christ!' Godfrey exclaimed. 'Come to a tropical island and hear Kipling on the football field!'

'Quite gratifying, isn't it?' Clive's annoyance quickly vanished. 'Little things like that – one soon calms down.'

'But where the hell did he get it?'

'Long ago I offered five dollars to any piccaninny who could recite the whole of "If" from memory.'

'Wonderful! – there can't be another island in the world where the only white man among hundreds of blacks. . . .' Godfrey was rehearsing his notes. After a month at Aurora they were more colourful, less drily professional, than when he came.

'Five dollars was a lot,' Clive said, 'and several of them learnt it.'

'The words meant nothing?'

'Something stuck – you heard.'

That night on the veranda, under the myriad stars, Godfrey said, 'I can't get over it – we had porridge and sausages and Oxford marmalade for breakfast, shepherd's pie for lunch, raspberry jam and cake for tea – '

'I'm afraid Isabel's not the cook her uncle was.' A disloyal father, Clive was making excuses.

'There's nothing wrong with Isabel, she's gorgeous.'

'Loloa used to bake scones and gingerbread.'

'I don't complain – we have excellent wine for dinner every night.'

'Champagne once a year.' Clive couldn't help encouraging the picture, false or not.

'On your birthday?' Godfrey's questions showed how his thesis was slipping towards biography.

'On Trafalgar Day – but you won't be here.'

'The navy's still important to you?'

'It was my first job. Twelve years of my life.'

'Your university?'

'I can't rub it out, I wouldn't want to.'

'Aurora depends on it? Naval punctilio, scrupulous routine – the Nelson touch?'

'An eye for detail, a fair deal for all – or we'd be sunk.'

'Isn't it rather sophisticated for them?'

Clive laughed: 'You think they're simple people?'

'With discipline like that, there must be disputes.'

'We sometimes clash. I've learnt not to over-react. They have their primitive instincts rumbling under the skin. So do I. There's a no-man's land between us, I'm glad to say. We watch each other across it, and try to understand –

up to a point. But nobody knows everything, thank God. Or even wants to.'

'Something I'd like to ask,' Godfrey began. 'I don't know how to put it.'

Clive could take it: 'Fire away.'

'You must have been about my age when you came here.'

'Arrived on April Fool's Day,' Clive said proudly.

'It's a lucky man who can see what he'll do with the rest of his life.'

'Lucky? Or d'you mean enviable?'

Godfrey ignored him: 'And sets about it with such energy and success.'

'So what d'you want to ask?'

'You didn't come here to escape. That's too negative for such a – '

'Such a what?'

'Such an assertive man.'

'So?'

'What was the reason?'

'Spondulicks, in a word.'

'That's a new one to me.'

'Money, to spell it out.'

'Don't believe it! You're trying to stay obscure.'

Clive got uneasy. Money and motives weren't his choice to talk about. 'It wasn't all straightforward,' he said. 'Early on, I made mistakes, listened to the wrong people.'

'Who?'

'I planted a thousand cocoa trees – a variety recommended by an expert, a bloody idiot who – '

'Don't tell me, Clive – he had a doctorate.'

'He'd never seen cocoa growing except in a greenhouse, he couldn't tell a frangipani from a beetroot.'

Godfrey gave his snigger, nearer to a real laugh than usual: 'So it failed.'

'Five years wasted. There were other setbacks.'

'What kept you going?'

Clive pondered: 'A feeling for the place. A belief in Aurora.'

'And in yourself?'

'And knowing it was shared by the people I brought here.'

'And it paid off? The spondulicks were a long time coming, but when they did – '

'I'm not a man to boast.'

'You must be very rich.'

Clive dodged: 'My cattle are the best in the country – reserved for sale to the government, to improve the stock.'

Godfrey smiled: 'Your style must be unique.'

To entertain his visitor, or to muffle him, Clive got out Odette's gramophone and at night on the veranda they listened to Gracie Fields sing 'Land of Hope and Glory', then a selection of Churchill's war speeches, with Clive grunting in approval. 'I wasn't there at the time,' he said to Godfrey, 'and you weren't born.' At the full moon he put on a Mozart symphony: 'I find Beethoven too rich for the climate.'

'Doesn't it make you more isolated than ever?' Godfrey asked.

'Listening to music? – it's one way to keep in touch. There aren't many left.' Clive paused. When the music stopped another noise, the throb of an engine, reached them through the moonlight. In a few minutes a Japanese fishing-boat came plugging across the lagoon, lights and radio full on. When it had passed Clive said, 'I don't regret my isolation, I'm thankful for it. From what I see of modern life, I'm missing nothing that I'd like.'

'Next time I open a tin of tuna in my London kitchen – '

'Let it pass me by!'

'You like being an anachronism?'

'Love it.'

'Not for you. . . .' In the dark, half to himself, half to provoke Clive, Godfrey was trying out phrases to be recorded when he went to bed: 'Not for you the uncertainties and apologies of this post-imperial age.'

Cautiously Clive said, 'But I'm sorry Rebecca's stopped writing. I valued her letters.' It was as far as he would go.

'She valued yours, she told me.'

'I can't imagine why.'

'She admires you – is that so wrong?' Godfrey said. 'So

do I. Wishing to be marooned. Deciding to be yourself. Nobody else's man. I'm puzzled, of course, which is what you want, isn't it? You'd hate anyone to get through to the marrow, to extract – '

'There's nothing there – it's a waste of time. You're up the pole.'

'I happen to be interested.'

'For your own purposes, your thesis.'

'I happen to like you, Clive.'

'That puzzles you too, no doubt.'

'I admit, we haven't got the world in common. You don't exactly remind me of my friends.'

'Friends!' Clive said wistfully. 'I've forgotten what they were.'

3

'I was *raped*!' Godfrey sobbed, with appalling evidence: trousers torn, shirt and socks missing, shoes undone. His hands clutched camera, notebook, broken glasses like a victim's last possessions – all he had saved from the assault. An eye was swollen, an ear was bleeding, the beard had bits missing. Weakly he stumbled into Clive's house, late for lunch, smeared with mud, dribbling indignation, fouled, plucked, ripped to the shreds of his academic integrity. '*Raped*, I tell you – it's the only word.'

'Who by?' Clive hadn't waited for him; had eaten an omelette and was enjoying the end of Godfrey's Stilton.

'Six of them, they felt like six hundred, all together, came at me like a tribe of monkeys, smothered me, I couldn't get rid of them, fucking maniacs, then one after another, taking turns on me, every way up, inside out, I couldn't stop them, couldn't stop myself. . . .' A touch of humour, the merest trace, showed through Godfrey's misery.

'In their gardens?'

'I wanted some pictures, they looked so pretty.'

'Working together, were they? Weeding?' Clive could
see it: the clearing at the forest edge with rows of
vegetables in the fertile soil, a welter of leaves, red and
yellow and green, and vines twisting on their stakes, trailing foliage to snatch at brilliant skirts or brush on deep
brown arms and legs – an idyllic pastoral scene. 'A party
of women alone?'

'Not a man in sight – it was a trap, I swear.'

'It's an exclusive job, weeding – for women only. It's
bad enough for a man to come near – '

'And now you tell me!'

'But to stop and watch – '

'Taking pictures of them!'

'Especially a man from another village.'

'From London!'

'A stranger.'

'A white one!'

'He's fair game, they have a right to turn on him.'

'More than rape – it went on and on, for about an hour.'

'It'll go well in your thesis, Godfrey.'

'Before I knew what they were up to – '

'I've heard of it, but never at Aurora.'

'Tossed me on my back, sat on my hands and feet,
pulled my clothes off, pulled their own off, grabbed
me – '

'You were a gift.'

'Tickled, stroked, using everything, fighting for first
go.'

'Pity you couldn't take pictures.'

'A dozen tits all over me, lovely ones.'

'They massage them, they learn quite young.' Clive
helped himself to more Stilton.

'Got what they wanted, I couldn't help it, and one of
them sat down and stuck me – '

'Her first white one – you should be honoured.'

'The rest held me till they thought she'd had enough,
then pushed her off for the next one, squatting on me and
slipping off and another taking over, back to front or
twisting or whatever she felt like, I don't know how I
kept – '

'Lucky they didn't beat your balls with stinging nettles – it's an old tradition.'

'It was funny in a way, to begin with, before it got nasty.'

'Sit down, Godfrey, and Isabel will bring your lunch.'

'One of them was on me, doing her thing, and another caught my foot and stuffed my toes – '

'They've got a lot of imagination.'

'Then the other foot, then my fingers, shrieking like witches, six naked black – '

'You'll get over it, don't worry.'

'But it turned filthy, revolting.' Godfrey retched, wiped his lips, picked something off his tongue. 'One of them came down on my face, I thought she was going to put my nose in it, but she only farted and the others got the idea, they held my hair, ears, anything, and pissed and screamed and shitted, my mouth, my eyes, till I was sick, I just threw up.'

'It's their revenge – you polluted their gardens so they paid you back.'

Godfrey couldn't face the omelette; limped to his room to wash and change, mend his glasses, patch up his confidence, write up his notes and sleep it off.

That afternoon a storm, two hours of wind and rain, swept away, leaving Aurora cooled and dripping, cleansed of any infamy; also leaving a bright white yacht anchored in the lagoon. Spars and fittings sparkled, a spinnaker blew from the masthead to dry, the Australian flag ruffled at the stern, suntanned figures lay naked on deck.

'Stone the crows!' Clive muttered, stumping up and down the veranda. 'I suppose they like that sort of thing.'

'I rather care for it myself,' Godfrey said, coming from his room in swimming trunks. 'Can't imagine a better cure, after this morning.' He dived off the veranda, heading for the yacht.

'Now I suppose,' Clive fumed, 'you'll invite them all ashore.'

At sunset Godfrey came back in a dinghy with two men and two women, replicas of people Clive remembered in

Sydney thirty years ago: handsome faces, bronze limbs, expensive sports clothes, a whiff of skin lotion. At first he was barely polite, but offered drinks and a terse response to their curiosity. They had been cruising for months, had heard about Aurora and its eccentric owner, had watched him through binoculars after the storm today, but wouldn't have dared come ashore – they had meant to dive for the kamikaze plane on the bottom of the lagoon – if Godfrey hadn't swum out. But they were too frank, too uncalculating and friendly for Clive's annoyance, which melted with the second drink.

When they said it was time to get back to their yacht he sent Godfrey into the kitchen to warn Isabel of four more guests tonight. She loved a party, she would have a chicken killed, curry it with rice and mangoes and open a tin of English strawberries. Clive knew it was what the Australians hoped for – dinner with this legendary character, something to embellish their cruise – and was pleased not to let them down. They drank for another hour while Isabel cooked, then she served the meal with a self-possession that stirred her father's blood. The Australians watched her gliding in and out of the kitchen curtain, leaning across the table to pass the dishes, seeming on the brink of laughter without going over; and blushed and winked and wondered, as Clive saw, about his lovely black-brown servant.

Godfrey had recovered and for once wasn't Clive's only visitor. He exploited it to entertain the others: 'Everything you've been told about him merely skims the story. The rest he keeps in a shell and you'll never crack it.'

Clive withdrew into silence, letting himself be teased by this clever man, knowing he would be beaten in an argument unless he resorted to his age or place as host. 'I came halfway round the world,' Godfrey went on, finishing the chicken curry, hungry after missing lunch. 'I gave up my summer vacation.' He was making a speech at the dinner table, getting drunk. 'I've grilled him for his past, his motives, his secrets.' Isabel brought in the strawberries. 'I've tried every trick in the book and angered him to hell in the process, but that's nothing to what he's done to me.' The Australians chuckled, toying with spoons and glasses, partly in embarrassment. 'So we'll drink to the lord of Aurora, white master of a South Sea island, the ineffable, impeccable, inscrutable and maddeningly unfathomable Mr Clive Ackerly!' They stood and drank and clapped and drank more, with Clive somehow holding his temper.

From the head of the table suddenly, to take control, he looked at them all sharply: 'Let me tell you about my devil-devil.'

'Your what?' The Australians shifted in relief.

'Everyone's got one, who's been here long enough.'

'Sorry, Clive, I'm mystified,' Godfrey said, cheated of his speech. 'I don't know what we're talking about.'

'Your devil-devil?' one of them repeated.

'Or rather, my devil-devil's wife. The old man's a friendly fellow, quite harmless. His wife's another story.'

'Have you ever met her?'

'Not yet. But I know what to expect. In the forest, when everything's absolutely still and there's a sudden rustling of wind in the trees with the smell of a bat – if that happens, it'll be her.' Clive's eyes grew with mock horror, or it could have been genuine. 'And something dire will follow.'

'Clive, really!' Godfrey protested. The others waited for more.

'I thought the same once, when I first came here twenty-five, thirty years ago. All that funny stuff about a devil-devil in a tree or calamity in a heap of sticks or the danger of disobeying someone in an epileptic fit – now I don't think it's funny any more.' He stopped abruptly, dismissing it. 'That's all.'

They said nothing. After dinner Godfrey announced, 'Now we'll dance!' and got out the gramophone, sorted through the records, picked some of Odette's from ballet and musicals, films and night clubs and dance halls. Round the room, out on to the veranda by lamplight, they tripped to the old tunes, sentimental, impossible, full of tropical stars and perfumed dreams and infinite love, familiar but obsolete which made the two Australian couples smile. 'Who'll dance with me?' Godfrey cried, and hauled Isabel from the kitchen to purge his ordeal of the

morning. Laughing at last, she stepped barefoot and eager
into his arms, the best dancer of them all, adept at waltz
or foxtrot, tango, rumba, samba – the craving half-caste
music of her body.

Suddenly a purple kingfisher, piping shrilly, flew
through the house as they were dancing. 'Did you see
that?' someone almost screamed.

'Oh yes,' Clive told them coolly, 'we get lots of those.'

They tried to tempt him to join them but he declined,
he hadn't danced since Odette's visit: 'I've forgotten the
steps, I'd only break someone's toes.' Instead he watched
and sometimes changed the record. In another life he
might have played the bagpipes at Strathpolly for his
beautiful daughter to dance reels with her young friends.
Or for Isabel it might be a night of gong-beating thigh-
slapping ecstasy in the forest with her tribe. He knew he
shouldn't be sad or angry but was glad he could still feel
both, without wanting to know why.

When the threadbare tunes came round for the third
time he slipped away to his bedroom; lay listening to five
strangers in his house, with Isabel. He would win in the
end, he knew, and tried to think how: in action, not
argument; in a physical way that he couldn't lose. His
half-black daughter wouldn't be much help: he might
consult his full-black son, Beaconsfield. Dimly through his
sleep, with one more laugh from Isabel, he heard the
visitors get into their dinghy.

He was woken in the dark.

'Mr Clive! Mr Clive!'

It was Laki on the veranda, softly calling him from sleep:
a fisherman drawing an octopus from its hole, whispering
to it through the water. 'Come with me, Mr Clive – quick!'
Straight out of bed, trusting the old saltwater coxswain
without question, Clive was being paddled in a canoe over
the black lagoon, past the anchored yacht, into the fading
night. 'Something you must see, I think.'

In the half-hour before dawn, while Clive wondered
and dreaded and found the only answer, Laki's constel-
lations – a crocodile swallowing a dog, a prisoner being

carried to the feast where he was to be eaten, an eagle
with an almond in its beak, a man teaching a boy to
copulate – were thinning in the sky. Soon the morning
star, the fish-chaser that told a night fisherman it was
useless to stay out any longer, hung alone in the east, the
last to go. Then in a moment, almost with a laugh, the
world was lit. The morning skittered across the lagoon
and the first frigate-bird, long forked tail and enormous
wingspan against the brightening sky, came wheeling
from its remote islet in the ocean: ally of saltwater boys,
they hoped, to be inlaid in mother-of-pearl on a canoe or
tattooed for luck on a man's back.

Long ago, Laki had once told Clive, there was no night
and the world was always day. The ten brothers living in
it, on an island, got tired of the endless light and asked
the eleventh brother, the eldest who had created them
and everything else – pigs, fish, trees, rocks, water – what
he could do about it. So he put a fine pig in a canoe and
sailed away to the foot of the sky, to buy the night from
the infinite darkness that lived beyond the horizon. He
learnt how to make night and sleep in it, and to make
dawn and wake up, and in exchange for the pig he sailed
home with a turtle dove and a piece of red coral. He
taught his brothers to weave beds out of coconut fronds,
and for the first time they saw the sun moving across the
sky, sinking in the west. 'It's crawling away!' they cried
in terror. He warned them it would soon be gone and
they would see a change over the world; and cutting away
the sunset with his piece of red coral, he let go the night.
'What's coming out of the sea and covering the sky?' they
cried. He told them to lie on their beds and be quiet, and
they would feel something heavy in their eyes. They
began to blink, and then it was dark. 'What's this? Are
we dying?' He told them to shut their eyes and sleep, for
this was night. When it had lasted long enough, and the
turtle dove began to sing, he cut through the night with
his red coral, to let the day in. The brothers woke and
saw the sun, and were happy to be free of endless light.
But soon they got bored again, and asked the eldest what
he could do about it. So he created women for them, to
make the nights more fun.

Laki paddled hard, urging the canoe over the lagoon, dipping at each stroke. With bare feet, the twisted toes left by Goldilocks, Clive tried to bale out the slopping water, the first trick learnt by saltwater babies, but only splashed himself. Salt stung in his eyes, he squinted ahead over the prow; searched the islands, rocks, reefs for what he wanted but hated, the thing he had known since Laki called him out. Suspicion or jealousy, it was nothing to admire and showed a degradation that he had thought was buried. He was ashamed of being here. The frigate-bird saw a gull catch a fish far below; dived superbly from the sky, a scarlet patch of feathers gleaming on its throat like a pirate's necktie; forced the gull to sick up the fish in mid-air; snapped the falling food before it reached the lagoon and on huge disdainful wings climbed back into the sun.

'I wish to be that frigate-bird,' Laki said, speeding for a small island that Clive had never been to. They pushed through mangroves and pulled the canoe out of the water. 'Come quick,' Laki whispered. 'And quiet.' He led Clive into the trees. 'I think. . . .'

Clive knew exactly. They came out on the far side of the island, on a low cliff over a tiny moon-shaped beach. A fringe of casuarina trees – weird grey trunks and shadowy foliage, never silent but sighing in a calm or shrieking in a wind, giving an unearthly sanctity to a place – grew like an eyebrow above the crescent sand. In today's soft breeze, an echo of last night's dance records, they crooned with false yearning for the beach. On it, in the morning sun, alone and lost and unaware, Godfrey and Isabel were making love. The dinghy was tied to one of the casuarinas, with their clothes.

'I tell you, Mr Clive,' Laki said, paddling more slowly back to Aurora, 'long long ago there was no death. No man ever died. He grew old and then he changed his skin, like the snake and the big red prawn. But one day a man went fishing and left his child with the grandmother. When the child was asleep she went to the stream to wash, and saw a crab change its skin, so she knew it was time for her to do it. She took off her skin and threw it in the stream, and went home in a new one. But the child was frightened, and cried and cried, 'My grandmother wasn't like that, my grandmother had warts and wrinkles.' She was sorry for the child, and went back to the stream and found her old skin caught in a tree. She put it on again, and since then every man must die, because a child cried and made a woman sad.'

'Laki,' Clive asked later, 'how did you know they were on that island?'

The old coxswain laughed, but didn't answer. The frigate-bird, far up in the brilliant sky, dipped and stalled and plunged into another dive for a lesser bird's fish.

At sunset the yacht weighed anchor and with a cheer, a wave from a naked figure on deck, an uncertain saluting of the flag, it sailed out of the lagoon. 'Stone the crows,' Clive muttered.

'How's the fieldwork going?' he asked Godfrey at dinner, carefully: he mustn't let his secret out. 'Getting all you want?'

'Scraping it up, one way or another.' Godfrey was being careful too.

Isabel brought in the beef for Clive to carve, giving no sign of last night's party or her morning affair across the lagoon. Not looking at her, her latest lover helped himself to cauliflower and potatoes. When she had gone back to the kitchen Clive said, 'What a scene this is! – like something I once saw in an awful film.'

Godfrey seized it for an attack: 'Or out of a novel. One of those female writers, full of innuendoes and little digs at your belief.'

'Female?'

'You know – there are dozens of them.' Godfrey began to eat, enjoying himself, satisfied with what he saw.

'I read *Gone with the Wind*,' Clive said. 'That's by a woman, isn't it? – I've forgotten who.'

'There are more famous ones.'

'Who else is there? I can't remember any.'

'Who wrote *Pride and Prejudice*, for a start?'

'I've never read it. Who's it by?'

'And *Emma*?'

'Who is she?' Clive's patience was slipping. 'The one who wrote *Gone with the Wind*?'

Godfrey almost jeered: 'A hundred years earlier – some people say the greatest.'

'But who is she?' Clive's voice was rising, shaking.

'What about *Jane Eyre*?'

'Is that her name?'

'And *Wuthering Heights*?'

'Who are you talking about?'

'And *Middlemarch*?' Godfrey would get all he could from this.

'But what's her name? I'm too old to be. . . .' And too broken by this morning's insult. 'Just tell me her name.'

'Surely, Clive, you've heard. . . .'

Clive stood up at the table with his knife and fork, carving the air in front of him: 'For God's sake. I won't be treated – '

'What about Virginia Woolf?'

'I don't read books like that, I don't know who it's by.'

Godfrey choked on his food, suppressing laughter: 'Gone with the Woolf. . . .'

Clive was blubbering, almost crying: 'I won't have it, I know I'm not a clever man, but why should I stand for it, why should I let you?' Then he began to rage: 'You're all the same, you, you. . . .' The knife and fork clashed in his hands. 'You – '

'Who, Clive?'

'Who? That's what I mean – who? Who *are* you?' Who was he talking about? He could see them at the table – the glib evasive grey men with cold superior smiles, the faceless officers of their own bleak authority, the bureaucrats, bank managers, mortgage grinders, property mongers, pension biders, arse-lickers, champions of mediocrity, princes of indifference, brokers of real men's lives. But there was nobody there, only Godfrey. 'Who are *you*? You're nothing, I tell you. Nothing, to the . . .' What was he to say? Nothing to the forces of imagination? 'You're nothing, nobody. . . .' Isabel came in with the gravy – half-Mendanan, half-Ackerly, Godfrey's whore, to see this sudden exhibition. 'Nobody – nobody has done this to me before, in my own house. . . .' At the sight of his daughter Clive recovered; dropped back on his chair, limp and tired. He had given away something more precious than this morning's secret. 'What's her name? I only ask you, Godfrey – please tell me who she is.'

On the veranda afterwards, where they had danced last night, Godfrey blew cigar smoke and brandy fumes over the lagoon, flavoured with Isabel's pineapple mousse to sweeten the air: 'I'm sorry, Clive – it was very rude.'

'We'll say no more about it.' Clive poured them each another brandy.

'Do you want me to leave? If you can't stand me here – it's only ten days more, but I'll cut it short.'

'Of course not.' They were polite again: two Englishmen on an island in the tropics.

'I'll go tomorrow if you like.'

'Please don't – I mean. . . .' To Clive it would be the last blow: being left when he was most vulnerable. He must keep this man, who might somehow save him, or they might save each other. He saw a need between them – as he had once with another man, strange and odious and powerful – and drank his brandy: 'I'll tell you something.' He hardly knew he was saying it, or even what it would be: 'The older I get, the more I have a horror of. . . .' He listened for a moment as if the word would drop out of the night: 'Blood.'

Godfrey chuckled slightly: 'I thought you were going to say women.' A new tone had come into his voice, closer to kindness. He may have been moved by Clive at dinner, and now saw more in him than a source of good material.

'I squash a mosquito that's bitten me and get my own blood on my skin.' Clive poured out more brandy. He would go too far tonight, he knew, and didn't mind: the release might soothe today's pains – his glimpse of lovers on a moon-shaped beach this morning, his outburst at the table this evening.

'But you must have seen buckets of it in your life, fighting in your battleship or as a prisoner.'

'At that age I felt nothing. Now it makes me ill. I can't bear it when they kill a bullock for a feast, I keep away.'

'You tucked into your roast beef tonight.' Godfrey would also go too far. 'And you approve of games – they can be violent enough. You must have played when you were young.'

'It's one thing to knock another boy's tooth out in the boxing ring – '

'So long as it's sport?'

'I've been lucky, I've never had an operation, not even my appendix out. Someone cutting into me, opening the flesh – it's not the damage or the pain, it's the blood.'

'I still think,' Godfrey said slowly, sipping his brandy, 'that it's to do with women. It's very primitive. The people here are drenched in horrors, aren't they? – of the monthly flux, the bloody curse, whatever.' He paused for Clive to protest if he wanted. 'I'd say that's why you got so rattled about female novelists. It's your indignation – they're an inferior race. A woman can't do anything original, can't be unique, can't show she's important in herself, let alone lead the pack – that's for a man.'

'It's not her job.'

'Churchill for making speeches, Gracie Fields for singing songs.'

'Not what she's brought up for.'

'Is that why you came here? To get away from women doing all those manly things? If someone like Becky – '

'Becky?'

Godfrey laughed: 'That's another female novel – *Rebecca*.'

'Should I have read it?'

'Stick to your heroes, Clive. But if Becky got the top job in her library, captain of the ship – '

'I couldn't take orders from a woman, or be reprimanded.'

'Reprimanded! Take orders! You live in a system of command – one man above another, all men above women.'

'Not *above* them. A woman's a goddess or a witch.'

'Nothing in between?'

'To be loved or feared.'

'But the most manly thing of all, the ultimate man's function – being a man to a woman – '

'I was a husband once.'

'Becky told me.'

'I still feel . . .' Clive stopped.

'Gallant? But distant? You don't want to get too close? You're frightened?'

Clive stood up to fill their glasses. Suddenly he said, 'There's another woman writer, or so-called woman – the one who wrote those marvellous books about the empire, quite astonishing.'

'Who had a sex change operation – more blood, you see.'

'I saw a picture of him among a lot of Himalayan climbers with a thick brown beard.'

'So he's a traitor? He let us down? He could be trusted when he was a man, but now – ?'

'What I can't take is, he did it for *choice*. He'd rather be a woman.'

'It diminishes the rest of us?'

'It shatters me.' Clive swallowed his brandy in one gulp. It had been a strange, unhappy day. But he would salvage something from it before going to bed. He said, 'There's a pile of old rocks that Beaconsfield keeps worrying me about. I'd like to see them one day. I thought you might like it too. Could be interesting. Far up in the forest, a sort of sacred ring. The Stones of Bau.'

'Native sculpture? The Henry Moore of the jungle?'

'Rather a Stonehenge, from what Beaconsfield says, though he's never seen it.'

'Local colour – just what I'm after.'

'When he was a child he heard about it from his father, who's been dead for years.'

'I can work it into my thesis. Which reminds me . . .' Godfrey stood up, ready to go to his room, yawning. 'I must get my notes on tape, if I can stay awake.'

'Beaconsfield wants to take his own son there.'

'He's got dozens of them.'

'One's enough, for continuity. Passing on the magic, down the generations. Probably I'd do the same if I had a son. In fact. . . .' Clive stared into the night. It would be a test of his own nerve as well as Godfrey's stamina: 'We might borrow one of Isabel's.'

Quickly Godfrey said, 'When do we start?'

'Give it a couple of days.'

'Could Beaconsfield find the way? And back again? I haven't got much time left, I'd rather not spend it hacking about in the – '

'Trust a bush boy. Drop him blindfold in the forest anywhere, give him a leaf or two to feel, give him a moment to take breath, and he'll lead you home.'

'By the sounds? Smells?'

'Something more private. Signals, a sense of waves.'

4

They left Aurora before sunrise. Clive and Godfrey and Beaconsfield with two small boys: one of Beaconsfield's sons, about ten years old, as darkly charred as his father, and one of Isabel's – Clive's eldest grandson, about six, rather paler, as if milk had been poured into him at birth. 'They've got names of some sort,' Clive told Godfrey, 'but we'll call them Black and Tan today.'

First they followed the derelict road built twenty years ago by Dikea and the British engineer – now no more than a thinning of the undergrowth, a vague memorial to futility. 'Pretty solid in there,' Godfrey said, watching the edge of the forest grow darker with the dawn. 'It'll be a tight squeeze.' He wanted to sound confident, feel safe. They mustn't go too fast for him. But he could be reassured: Clive was twice as old, Beaconsfield was small and frail and growing bald, shrivelling still more, and the two boys would soon get tired.

The sun topped the trees, the heat would strike unless they turned into the forest. Beaconsfield was searching for a chink. 'There!' he said suddenly, pointing to a red-leafed tree. 'Not the obvious way in,' Godfrey said. He would try facetiousness, disdain, anything to cover his alarm. Beaconsfield scowled at him without a word; opened a cotton sack, took out a bush knife, slung the sack over his shoulder and looked up at the early morning sun – to tell the time or say goodbye.

It was like going indoors on a hot day, plunging into the darkness, into the dim comfort of an alien religion; up towards the extinct volcano of Bau. It was also a lesson in human decadence. Beaconsfield moved with utmost economy, his energy as spare as his figure. He hardly seemed to breathe, just passed through the forest all day, up and down the foothills at a steady speed. With his knife he snicked and swiped, parted the leaves and sticks and branches, cleared a way for the others, perhaps also for his own future use – he came hunting wild pig up here – or for his descendants. The boys scampered round his legs like puppies. Clive crashed along behind them through sheer force, rejoicing to see how well his grandson moved. Godfrey, panting for his doctorate, struggled to keep in sight. 'I'd no idea,' he gasped when Beaconsfield stopped to let him catch up. 'I've only seen you on a motorbike before, riding down the plantation paths.' The old black man didn't smile.

Sometimes they travelled along a forest ridge between deep valleys that fell on either side. Sometimes they dropped into a gulch, slipped down steep mud flanks, waded up a stream, the cool water a relief on blistered feet and bleeding legs, then climbed out on the far bank, up the valley side, clutching, slithering, grabbing. There were awful spiky things, a rope of needles to hold or a vegetable hedgehog to tread on; and fallen trees to climb over or duck under or balance along – a bridge across the undergrowth; and wild yams with prickles like a shark's jaw; and razors and daggers and sticky pin cushions and sponges that exploded with a stench of evil; and orchids, ferns, mistletoes growing high above the ground; and whistles and cackles, the crash of an animal, the clamour of insects, the ancient noises of fear and protest; and immense trunks rising from the squelch of roots, supported by thin buttresses, their tops out of sight with a ropework of lianas, rattans, vines hanging loose like the rigging of some crazy giant ship, and the men and boys were shrimps or beetles creeping through its wreckage.

'Pig!' Beaconsfield whispered and stopped dead, frozen to his own footprints. Black and Tan turned into bits of tree or plant, motionless and invisible. But there was nothing that Clive or Godfrey saw or heard. They couldn't see far, enclosed in such density, though in the play of shadow and beams of light, among the windless shivers of the leaves and dimly agitated pools and patches, there were visions of unknown life, mirages of something vaguely mobile but too strange to grasp: a ghostly figure, a beckoning hand, a face with staring eyes and a faint smile. Everything had a meaning, though it was contradictory and inconsequent.

Later Clive said, 'Look at him!' and pointed to a ridiculous bird, between parrot and chicken, that couldn't fly. It managed to glide down from a branch on its silly ungrown wings, but had to get back by climbing a vine in pathetic hops and flaps, using beak and claws. It belonged to a different stage of evolution, forgotten in the forest here.

'I've never felt so excluded from the world I belong to,' Godfrey said, helplessly. The sky was as remote as in a dungeon, the ground soggy and matted and rotten with burrowing streams.

About noon the rain began, falling solidly through the foliage, becoming part of it. Leaves were battered, branches tossed, the noise grew to a roar of fury. Godfrey's sodden clothes were an extra weight to carry, but Clive hardly noticed it, driven by defiance and purposefulness. The boys became water puppies, sloshing upwards, always chattering. Beaconsfield cut a bunch of fronds to hold over his head and kept dry. After the storm the forest dripped for hours, with the odour of decay enriched by rain. And there was plenty to drink, cupped in grateful hands from the enormous leaves.

Climbing always higher, by late afternoon they reached a rim in the ground where it fell away in front. 'Must be the edge of the crater,' Clive said. Godfrey stumbled up to join them and flopped on the ground, panting for a rest, though the forest was too dense for any view. Daylight hung somewhere above the trees, a hole opened in the world below.

Beaconsfield wouldn't wait. He slid down into the steep crater where the fire and vapours had been plugged a million years ago. The others followed, crashing and tripping behind the old bush boy to the bottom. 'Bau! Bau!'

he cried with demonic excitement and fell headlong at the
foot of an immense block of granite. There were dozens
more, upright or lying flat among the trees.

'The Stones of Bau!' Clive cried too, and prostrated
himself next to his tribal son, either in prayer or from
fatigue. The Stones were the size of coffins, some
rectangular, some six-sided, irregular but too smooth to
have been cut by nature.

'Bau! Bau!' Black and Tan, the tireless puppies, barked
and tumbled beside the men.

'Jesus Christ, at last!' Godfrey collapsed with them all
on the sopping ground. He hadn't disgraced himself, but
couldn't go a step further. 'I made it. Jesus, Jesus, Jesus
holy bloody Christ, I made it!'

'Careful with your words, Godfrey,' Clive warned him,
catching Beaconsfield's discomfort. 'You never know
who's listening.'

'Who the fuck's going to – ?'

'One of us has a brother, don't forget,' Clive said, 'who
happens to be Bishop of Tulagi.' Uneasiness, more than
exhaustion, settled on the three men and two boys. From
his sack Beaconsfield got out bread and bananas and a tin
of tuna fish, and they picnicked among the Stones. 'I've
never seen rock like this.' Clive's voice was low and
sombre: the place demanded reverence. 'It's not the usual
volcanic stuff. Probably from another island. They must
have built a raft of canoes to carry them.'

'Who are *they*?' Godfrey asked.

'Who indeed? People with more energy than anyone in
the Mendanas now, who wanted a heap of rocks up here.'

'You mean they dragged them through the forest? Up
the way we've come? What the hell for?'

'What for?' Clive repeated to Beaconsfield. 'A sacrifice?
Something nasty going on?'

'Don't go into the woods tonight,' Godfrey sang to the
tune of 'The Teddy Bears' Picnic', and was stopped by the
scorn on Beaconsfield's charcoal face. 'But what are they
for? A pile of rocks as big as refrigerators – it's not a castle.'

'Not a castle,' Beaconsfield said, the charcoal nearly
catching fire. 'And not refrigerators.'

'Come on, Beaconsfield, old man,' Clive said. 'Don't be

frightened, we're on your side – you can trust us to keep it dark.'

'Now who's being careful with his words?' Godfrey protested. 'That's a funny one to choose.'

'You see,' the black man began, then looked round as if for help from somewhere in the forest. 'One time is big-big feast and many-many people coming.'

'Cannibals?' Godfrey suggested brightly.

Beaconsfield ignored him: 'But are having no food.'

'I told you – one man's meat. . . .' Godfrey saw Clive glowering at him and stopped. Black and Tan nudged each other for support or safety.

Beaconsfield went on: 'Because the chief is wanting to marry new beautiful wife, number five or six maybe, and wanting sunshine for his wedding, so is telling the rain man to stop rain with his little red stone, and rain man asking ten pigs for it, and putting his little red stone in a coconut shell and filling with water and putting by the fire and saying magic on it, and the water steaming away into nothing by the fire, and when coconut is empty and stone is dry there is no more rain but sunshine for the wedding, so chief is happy and people also. But is sun-shine-sunshine always sunshine, and chief is telling rain man to stop sunshine and make rain again, and he asking fifty pigs to put little stone in coconut shell and say magic on it for water to come back and then rain also, but chief is saying he pays fifty pigs for new beautiful wife and she worth more than rain, so is no rain for long-long time and people very-very hungry, and going to the forest to find wild fruits and leaves and nuts, but is nothing there, and getting disease on skins and in stomachs, and starting to die like yams in gardens and water in streams, and rain man also dying because no food, and now is nobody who knows magic to make rain. So people very-very angry against chief and wanting to kill him, but he is telling them if he dies it is sunshine without rain for ever and ever, and is taking little red stone of rain man and saying he knows how to make rain, because up here on top of Bau mountain is big hole, very-very big like giant's coconut shell, and is full of pigs and opossums and mangoes and bananas and plenty-plenty water to make rain on stone, and chief coming up here and people following to have feast with him, but is nothing here also, nothing-nothing, so people more angry and chief frightened, and he is taking little red stone and saying he can make rain with areca juice on it, but first telling people. . .' Beaconsfield stopped, afraid that he had gone too far.

Quietly Clive prompted him: 'He told the people what?'

'Is saying they must be quiet, must make no noise while he is making rain, and they must swear it.'

'We'll do the same, old man. It's a promise – don't worry.'

'So people all are quiet, because are swearing it and keeping it, and chief is chewing areca and some leaves and spitting into the sky to make clouds, to north and east and south and west, four magic ways, and is spitting last bit on the little red stone and all the time is saying magic, but not proper magic because is not knowing it, is only saying make-rain-come-back, make-rain-come-back, for-us-to-eat, like singing in church, and still is sunshine. And is one woman who is number one bad woman because is not obeying the promise, is breaking it and laughing, very-very loudly when she is wrong to make a noise, is making a big-big laugh.'

'What happened?' one of the white men, Clive or Godfrey, asked without moving his lips.

'You see, woman is laughing and while is doing it. . . .' Beaconsfield spoke to the two boys, his son and Clive's grandson, saying something very solemn but quite simple, something old and true that he had known all his life and wanted them to keep for the rest of theirs: 'Her ear is dropping on the ground.'

'My God!' Clive uttered in a hollow tone, empty of obvious meaning but oddly convincing. 'Her ear fell off – my God, my God!' His voice went on echoing inside him after the words had come out. He put his fist to his chest as if to stop it, and stared hard at Black and Tan like someone telling a fairy tale, half-believing it himself and challenging their disbelief. But he needn't have worried, they were hushed and waiting for more.

'You see,' Beaconsfield said, 'more people are starting

to laugh when woman's ear falling off and so their ears falling off the same, and then noses, and is a sickness that the people catch, all are laughing and parts are falling off because they must be quiet and are swearing it but not obeying, so arms and legs and heads dropping on the ground, and nothing is left except bodies which turn to stone.' Beaconsfield surveyed the Stones of Bau in triumph and reproof. He knew no more, or wouldn't tell it yet.

There was silence. Godfrey looked sceptical, though trying not to laugh or even smile, and caught another flash of Beaconsfield's contempt. Black and Tan sucked their bananas like lollipops. After some time Clive asked, 'Was the chief turned to stone too?'

'Chief is last,' Beaconsfield said. 'When is seeing people all are stones, is crying very-very loudly and so is also turned, but just before it, when is crying, his tears are dropping on rain man's little red stone and suddenly the sky is full of clouds and now is raining, and rain-rain-rain, so streams are beginning again and gardens growing.' The old bush boy packed up the rest of the food and put it in his sack.

'How long ago was it?' Godfrey asked, sounding as if he might believe it with more evidence, though it was unlikely.

Beaconsfield wouldn't speak to him. He wandered away among the Stones.

Godfrey turned to Clive: 'I mean – it wasn't yesterday, was it?'

Clive answered angrily: 'You give yourself away. You just don't understand him.'

'Understand him?' Godfrey pretended innocence.

'You think of history as a succession of events going back, each age preceded by an earlier one.'

'Is there another way?'

'You push myths and legends even further back, before anything else. To Beaconsfield that's ridiculous.'

'But when he says,' Godfrey imitated the bush boy's voice, 'one time long-long ago is big-big feast – '

'He means as far back as he can remember. Or possibly

in his father's memory. Beyond that is one huge store of living facts, in no special order.'

'Sorry, Clive – it won't stand up.'

Clive went on more calmly, subdued by this sacred place: 'Time has no meaning in your sense of one thing happening before another.'

'You can't get away from it – these Stones must have a date.'

'You want to put them in a museum, labelled and catalogued.'

'They belong to the past – let's agree on that.'

'What you call the past – for Beaconsfield it's ageless. It didn't go on for a million years like yours. It's in the present and will be in the future. It can't be lost.'

'But the ancestors – '

'The ancestors are here and now, or quite close, and the people in the stories too, and they'll stay for ever.'

'Sounds to me as if you and Beaconsfield might see eye to eye.'

'I try to see what he sees.'

'Teach him evolution and he'd laugh?'

'Everything is eternally the same. Eternally new and real. And don't tell me your view is any better.' Clive was troubled and restless. He stumbled with Beaconsfield over the granite blocks, felt their texture, examined the shapes and positions, measured them with his eye; then came back to Godfrey: 'Don't you think you should look at it his way? Try to see his vision of the world?'

'It's just so alien.'

'It might lead you somewhere you never dreamt of.'

'Thanks, but I'll stay with what my eyes and ears tell me.' Godfrey patted his notebook.

'It might show you something of your own world too – from its very strangeness, don't you think? You might be surprised to find what you have in common.'

'You must be joking.'

Clive was going to speak – more with pity than anger, from the look on his face – but returned to the Stones and only muttered, 'My God!' once more and nothing else.

'Well,' Godfrey said after a while, feeling a need to be

practical and lift, or lower, the mood from this uncomfortable state. 'It'll take a long time getting back, won't it?'

'Not a hope,' Clive said, with an effort to recover his
good temper. 'Too late to think of it tonight – we'd never
make it. We'll have to camp up here. Safe enough, as long
as we don't laugh.'

'You're sure?' Godfrey asked.

'Beaconsfield will take care of us, or else his friends.'
Clive tossed a glance round the Stones. 'But show a little
humility if you can. Treat them with respect, that's all –
the way you'd treat the tombstones in a church, only more
so. There's a lot we'll never get to the bottom of – you'd
be amazed.'

Night arrived swiftly in the crater. Flying foxes came
over in the brief dusk, hunting for fruit like squadrons of
owls wheeling between the trees. Before it was quite dark,
with a few swipes of his bush knife and the help of Black
and Tan, Beaconsfield cut some canes from the undergrowth and built a shelter for them all, with plaited vines
and a thatch of leaves. It took ten minutes and looked
absurdly easy.

Clive and Godfrey tried to get a fire going, but nothing
was dry enough to kindle and it only smoked. The boys
made a bed of foliage inside the shelter and fell instantly,
puppyishly asleep. Later, having given up the fire,
Beaconsfield and Clive and Godfrey crept in to join them.

Clive lay awake, waiting not so much for sleep as for the
dawn. There was utter lifelessness. Not a whisper of wind
or the least crackle of twigs. No moon, not even a firefly.
The world might have stopped, or been suspended. The
only disturbance was the breathing of his companions, as
quiet as they could make it.

His body was stiff, full of aches. He longed to ease it
but to move at all, unless for some ritual purpose, was a
sort of profanity. He had never know such a dark, still,
oppressive night. He was choked with airlessness,
clammy with the wish to be anywhere else, with anyone
but these sleeping forms of men and boys beside him.
He would almost rather be back in the camp hut among

prisoners, tracing his fantasies on bamboo slats. When his hip at last found a hole to sink into, something hard stuck up to pierce his kidneys. The damp that penetrated him could be from the ground under him, or his own sweat. Whatever it was that tickled his cheek, before he could scratch it, ran away. In the end, after midnight, he slept in a desultory way, worried by dreams.

Was that a dream? Or a laugh? He woke up. Or was he still asleep? It was the heart of the night. The pit. The deepest black. Though he could make out nothing in the shelter he knew he was alone. His first feeling was anger, then fright. They shouldn't have left him. He would have shouted, 'Bugger you all!' but was stopped. By fear, he thought. Then by something else.

Nothing visible, but a quick rustling in the forest. A squall blowing through the dark. A vortex of air spinning across the crater, picking up no leaves but quivering suddenly in the trees. A tremble in his blood. And an unmistakable smell. He remembered it from somewhere long ago. It was a village temple in Thailand where the prisoners had rested on the march up from the plain into the forest, to work on the railway: a few hot hours in a twilit shrine with shaven, saffron monks dabbing little acts of piety at an image between long pauses of emptiness and sleep. It was also, further back, the roof at Strathpolly where Clive and Victor had played as boys, climbing through a trapdoor, stepping among the beams, squinting between slates at the daylight outside. In both places, in the strange cold mystery that teased his nostrils, there had been a smell of bats. Here it was again, in the middle of a tropical night, in the crater of an old volcano among some queer stones. But this was flying foxes, of course – a giant kind of bat.

The stillness of the night returned and probably he slept again, he couldn't be sure. He was very tired. He believed he had a dream, but couldn't remember it afterwards. Nothing gave warning of the approach of day till suddenly before dawn the faintest waft of breeze, with the sound of a theatre curtain rising, stirred the sleeping trees. When Clive opened his eyes it was already light and he was still alone. Bugger them all, again. Now he would have to find his own way back to Aurora, and the thought defeated him. He was too old, he wasn't a bush boy, he had been deserted by Beaconsfield, his son, who had taken the others with him. He would lie a little longer before making a start, putting it off. The living forest, the countless furtive hints of birth and growth and decay and death, came seeping into the shelter.

But they hadn't left him, as he found when he crawled out. The sun was up, though not high enough to filter through the trees and fall into the crater. The thinnest mist lay on the ground like a cobweb left carelessly by the night, soon to be taken away. There had been cobwebs in the Thai temple and the Strathpolly roof too. Clive saw Black and Tan first, sitting on one of the Stones – two boys of different colours wrapped in the same sullen air of having suffered. This morning the puppies were meek and dispirited. One of them gave a shiver when he saw Clive and the other caught it, but neither spoke.

Beyond them stood Beaconsfield. He was framed between two trees, dwarfed by the trunks, but his slight figure defied their size. It exuded power. He turned stiffly and blinked at Clive. In the burnt black eyes, far inside, an unholy spark glinted, transmitting a message that might be victory or terror.

In a moment Clive knew why.

'My God!' It was his own voice this time.

At the same moment his dream came back. He had heard Godfrey's cry, 'Oh God!' too, and then his laugh. Clive knew it was fatal, and had shouted like a command, 'Godfrey!' It wasn't an appeal, more of a reprimand, and it worked instantly, cutting off Godfrey's laugh at source.

'My God!' The dream had gone again. 'Godfrey! What happened?'

Godfrey was sitting propped against one of the Stones, arms dangling on the ground, head tilted, eyes fixed on nothing. A faint grey colour lay under his cheeks, a trickle of dry saliva issued from his mouth. Clive had seen men killed in battle or sucked from the world by cholera, but never anyone who had died of a heart attack. He thought they might be bruised with purple or horribly contorted.

Perhaps this wasn't a heart attack. He touched Godfrey's shoulder and felt only the sardonic mockery of a corpse.

'My God, what happened?'

Beaconsfield stepped lightly out of his frame of trees into the guilty, inexplicable morning, and came to stand by Clive – returning from the night's event, whatever it was: 'He is dead since long-long time, Mr Clive.' He was the plantation headman, reporting nothing serious.

'But how?'

'Heart is stopping, altogether finished.' The old bush boy might have been speaking of his motorbike. 'Now is with father and father's father and father's father's father.'

'Gone to join his ancestors. But why?'

'Mr Clive, I tell you. . . .' Beaconsfield stopped.

'Tell me what?'

'Is nothing.'

It was useless to get angry. Uselessness filled the morning. Useless to ask questions, to shout or weep, to expect anyone to tell them what to do with a visiting academic, unwelcome when he arrived and now dead. They could make a stretcher – Beaconsfield would knock it up as easily as last night's shelter – and get the body down to Aurora, then away in a boat to Tulagi, to be buried in the cemetery there, blessed by the bishop, Beaconsfield's brother, or sent back to London by air. It would be a daunting job. The two boys wouldn't be much help. Beaconsfield, though supreme at moving in the forest, was hardly muscular. Clive himself was weak with shock, and glad when he saw the bush boy take charge.

Beaconsfield began hacking with his bush knife into the soft, decaying ground. When he was deep enough, he and Clive dragged Godfrey's body to the grave, lowered it in, tipped back the dark mulch of leaves and roots and earth. In that stuff it would quickly moulder. They tore down the shelter and laid the sticks as a covering to keep wild pigs off. Afterwards they all stood there in silence, two men and two boys, praying or cursing or just wondering.

'Godfrey, I'm sorry,' Clive said, but not aloud, remembering the survivors standing in the forest cemetery, their last hot morning on the railway. 'I wish I'd saved you. I truly wish that. Not just saved your life from death – I don't believe anyone could. But saved it from the life it was. I should have tried harder. I didn't hate you, even that morning on the beach with Isabel. Even though you probably knew she was my daughter and were doing it to get at me. I haven't hated anyone for years, I've lost the knack. When I was your age, on the railway, I hoped that one day I'd come to love everyone and I think I've nearly reached it. You made me angry, of course. Made me shout and cry. I expect you meant to. And it was good for me. Nobody has done that to me since I was a prisoner. I should have thanked you, instead of dragging you up here to die. Though I don't know what happened last night. Nothing at all, I expect. It doesn't matter, does it? But before I go, I want to tell you something. God knows why I didn't tell you before. Absurdity feeds on itself. So listen to this. I once let a man called Hutton drown when perhaps I could have helped him. I once listened to a man called Awang bin Daud having his eyes cut out, then his stomach, because he had sheltered me. I once watched a man called Smithy being smashed to death with a hammer for defending me when I was ill. That's all. It's nothing, is it? Hutton, Awang, Smithy – they were men like you and me, Godfrey. They had to die one day, they were just unlucky to do it then. If I'd told you when you were alive, I believe it might somehow have saved you. Saved me, too, possibly, though I'm old now and there's nobody to care. I don't care about myself. But you were young, like the ones we left in the forest, who died on the railway. If you'd got away, I could have tried to show you the choices you had. Which way you could go. How you could avoid the faceless grey men. Because you weren't really one of them. Or not yet. Otherwise Rebecca wouldn't have sent you here, even if she didn't like you. And I did like you, better than you thought. That's another knack I've lost – friendship. We could have made friends, I think, if you hadn't died. I'd like to have a friend again. Now I've missed it. That was my fault – not making it clear. I had a chance. And you had a chance. That's what I should have shouted about. I'll do it now. I'll shout in silence. It'll do me good, Godfrey, though it can't save either of

us. I'll shout inside me all the way back to Aurora today.
And Godfrey, another thing – you got your material,
didn't you? In the field. In a crater. I'm glad about that.
It'll make a wonderful thesis. Good luck, Godfrey.'

Beaconsfield brought out the rest of the food and shared
it with the boys. Clive ate nothing, he was hungry only
for all he had lost. The morning grew warm, the chill
slowly left the crater. The sun dropped pools of light, a
flicker and splash through the trees, on the Stones of Bau.
Soon it would be very hot.

'Come on, let's go,' Clive said. He felt feverish, at the
brink of delirium, impatient to get home.

They followed Beaconsfield back through the forest.
Yesterday's trail seemed to be overgrown already, or else
he led them by another. None of them could have found
the way down to Aurora without him in front. Black and
Tan were very quiet, and Clive didn't care to question
them on the night's happenings. Truly, he didn't want to
find out. Curiosity was irrelevant, overlaid with sorrow,
fury, a mounting rage. He became dizzy with heat and
his emotions, as confused about the events as about the
forest track. He might have been anywhere, at any time.
That little man ahead, he dimly knew, was his son. The
two boys, in different ways, were both his grandsons.
Once, when he stumbled, Beaconsfield looked round and
for an instant, in Clive's stupefied eyes, though the bush
boy's face was as black as ever, it was the face of Clive's
father – the fading army officer's face, which he knew
only from a bedside photograph.

In his house Isabel took away his dirty clothes and
brought him tea. She uttered one sharp gasp on hearing
that Godfrey was dead, then stifled it as if she shouldn't
be surprised. A brief wistfulness passed over her face,
and her hands went down to touch her stomach. Probably
she knew there was to be another child, fathered – on a
crescent beach, in the morning sun – by the man in the
moon, paler than the others.

The next day Clive's fever was better. In two days it
had gone. He went into Godfrey's room to pack up, and
found a file of typewritten pages. He saw it was mostly

about himself, but didn't read it. He didn't want to know, or not from Godfrey.

Part Seven

The Yacht

1

Thirty years after Clive arrived in the Mendana Islands the colony was granted independence. Though he meant to avoid it he saw the Royal Yacht sail past Aurora, touring the islands on its way to the celebrations. In a fleet of canoes old Laki and his saltwater boys paddled over the lagoon to wave. The Prince of Wales had come to give away the bride.

In Tulagi the prince saluted and smiled and sweated; planted a tree, opened a parliament, inspected a fire engine and some boy scouts; and watched his princess being clutched, clawed, almost pleasured on the dance floor of the club by Dikea, once a road contractor, now president of the republic. One of the last scraps of empire, a spattering of red dots far out in the Pacific blue, was wiped away by freedom. To clinch it, the black president cracked his fingers and squeezed the white princess tighter.

Beaconsfield wanted to take the bush boys to hear the bishop, his brother, preach an independence sermon in St George's Cathedral to the prince and princess, the old British administrators and new Mendanan politicians, and any foreign visitors. But Clive had no desire to see the Union Jack pulled down and another flag hoisted – blue and green for sea and forest, with a black frigate-bird on it, the pirate of someone else's booty. At that moment, as he had promised, ownership of Aurora would pass to Beaconsfield. He persuaded his heir to stay for a better ceremony.

Over a fire of driftwood and coconut husks they roasted twenty-six young pigs – twenty-six bladders to make footballs for the piccaninnies – one for each year since Clive had brought his people here. For a table they laid a strip of banana leaves through the village, spread with fruit, puddings, beer. In the roasting pit the new owner of

Aurora, till today its headman, carved slabs of pork with his bush knife for the people who now were his. They squatted in two rows, saltwater and bush boy families facing each other, waiting for meat to be brought by picca-ninnies and tossed over their heads on to the banana leaves between them.

Clive had never been so happy at a feast: eating and drinking, watching and revelling in his own new freedom, his view of the world he had made in this lovely place, his retirement ahead. He caught Beaconsfield's eye and they exchanged a secret laugh, a quick delight in some-thing too private to utter – father and son gnawing at a young pig's flesh: perhaps a vision of their years together since Beaconsfield first worked for Clive as supercargo of the *Catriona;* or a thought of wartime when Beaconsfield was a runner for the coastwatchers while Clive was slaving in another forest; or even a memory from Beaconsfield's childhood which he had shared with Clive – of being given bits of unknown meat, wrapped in leaves, tasting sweet like pork. The bush boy's feelings, Clive believed, must reflect his nostalgia for the dim, heady old days before the white men came and his dubious joy that they were now departing.

With the best plantation in the country, so one of the richest Mendanan islanders, Beaconsfield would be as much a paradox as Clive. He felt no patriotism for the new republic. To a member of the ancient aristocracy who had escaped into the forest to save themselves from white contamination, President Dikea and his colleages were contemptible, worse than their previous colonial masters. Under Beaconsfield for a time, from sentiment as well as habit, Aurora might keep some of Clive's unique style. But nothing would stop the return of the undergrowth one day – the encroaching darkness where a bush boy felt at home.

Two days later a big motor yacht rumbled into the lagoon and anchored in front of Clive's house. Not quite the Royal Yacht; but from its scale and splendour and the crew's uniform these weren't ordinary round-the-world

tourists. The flag was neither the colonial one nor the
frigate-bird and hadn't flown at Aurora since an aircraft
carrier lay there, target for a kamikaze pilot. That vivid
Stars and Stripes took Clive back, the moment he saw it
across the water, to the day he played his bagpipes for
Churchill and Roosevelt in a wooded Newfoundland bay.
He must have seen it again at Rangoon after being set free
from the railway, or on the voyage home by troopship –
he couldn't remember.

Suddenly the moment turned to dread. Clive felt something he had forgotten for more than half his life: the
intuition that had hit him, without being put into words,
on getting Jenny's answer to his telegram after his release.
There had been no need to spell it out, the meaning was
too visible.

A speedboat was lowered and came curving over the
surface to stop precisely alongside the veranda. A
boathook, a rope, a salute from a young American sailor.
A letter handed up to Clive, with an eagle on the
envelope. The handwriting hadn't changed. She had
written the same letter to him thirty years ago in Sydney.
This time he couldn't move on: there was nowhere to go.

'Clive! Don't be angry because we gave you no warning.
We wanted to make sure of you – that's why. No more
chances to escape. In Tulagi we heard such tales! The lord
of Aurora, the most famous man in the islands – we felt
honoured you weren't a stranger to us. Though Max has
never met you. It's his last posting before retirement –
most of the Pacific Ocean, ambassador-at-large. Very large
these days, overweight, the price of lifelong parties. We're
here for the independence circus. Too many poodles, not
enough clowns. Representing our own great republic, the
first to cut loose from your grubby forsaken empire. Lining
up to curtsey at the princess. Rub noses with the prince.
Watch him unveil the president. Lots of jolly British blacks
and timid hungry whites. Hardly surprised not to see you
among them. I know you too well. Or do I? But to be in
the Mendanas without calling on you was just not possible. And Becky sent special love, hoping we'd meet you.
It's our hope too – desperately. So please don't run away
again, Clive dearest. No excuses or apologies or recrimi-

nations, I promise. Or speeches or fireworks – enough of those in Tulagi. Only us. Being us. Can we come ashore?'

She was five years younger than Clive. Nearly sixty now. Not the Jenny he had talked to for so long on the railway. She belonged in a gentleman's occasional double bed or in his own shirt in their Chelsea kitchen or in a lonely Welsh pub for a few days' escape from the blitz or in her ambulance while the bombs dropped, or even in Clive's dreams of Strathpolly while he squeezed out his torment on the bamboo slats of a prison hut. Anywhere but at Aurora. She was at Waterloo station in a belted coat with a cameo, her hair set in ripples down the sides, with tears in her voice, not in her soft grey eyes; with something to tell him. And again in a theatre mirror, pretending to be her daughter Rebecca. He couldn't see her at anchor out there in his lagoon, the American ambassador's wife on board a luxury yacht. As for Max, after the first image of a handsome army officer in London during the war, villain of an old story, Clive had never tried to put him and Jenny together. Now here they both were, coming from a party with a prince and princess; sailing out of nowhere.

'Yes, yes, of course,' he said to the young American in the speedboat. 'Tell them to come ashore at once.'

The man saluted: 'Yes, sir.' The last time a sailor had done that to Clive was on the brilliant morning when the *Prince of Wales* was sunk. The speedboat ripped back to the yacht and was soon returning with two passengers. They had been waiting on deck, to give him no time.

It was ridiculous, the final outrage. The finale too. The farewell scene of their little play, tying up the ends. It couldn't go on for ever. Clive would see it through and then be free; go out into the night and never come again. And there might still be unexpected twists. He could offer one himself. Amazement or exhaustion, or something more gentle and gracious and loving, took the pressure out of his fury. He would put on a gallant performance, even if it was his last: a perfect host, generous and good-humoured, to surprise them.

'Well, Clive, at last!' The veteran diplomat, deft at smoothing, polishing, flattening – Max knew how to begin.

'We've caught up with you! No more dodging over the next horizon. It's been years and years.' A big man with short grey hair, thick flesh like an old bull, affability in his voice. He came forward with both hands out in front to greet Clive. A woman followed slowly, letting Max make the moves. He pumped Clive's hand in his. 'It's been far too long, we've been round the world a dozen times, we never had a chance till now and here it is, we couldn't pass it up.' American ebullience, American magnitude, American vowels. The woman approached behind him, taking cover. 'Clive, I want to tell you, the minute Jennifer suggested it I just knew. . . .'

Jennifer? Of course, it was her proper name, kept in reserve for her second husband. 'Over my dead body,' Clive had said, nearly forty years ago.

'Sweetheart. . .' Max dropped one of Clive's hands, stepped aside and picked up one of Jenny's, linking them. 'Strictly it's for you to make the introductions. You met before – remember?'

The big grey eyes were the same, but softer and this time full of tears. There was nothing in her voice. She couldn't speak though her lips said, 'Clive.'

'Jenny.' She was moist, blurred in his sight. They had had tea in the buffet at Waterloo, hardly speaking, fumbling in the emptiness. There was no emptiness now. The moment was overflowing. Nothing much else had changed. Taller, he thought, and more slender. Grey streaks in her hair. Some pretty wrinkles, a vague refining everywhere. In place of youth a different beauty, another excellence.

Max said, 'Well, I'll let you two. . . .' He put their hands together, a priest uniting them in a ritual of his own, and turned away; walked to the end of the veranda and leant on the rail, staring hard at the lagoon. Discretion, understanding, synthesis were his profession

They kissed. Clive took Jenny's other hand and pressed them both. He felt intensely himself: Clive Ackerly of Aurora, now visited by another self, the one he had lived down, husband of this woman who had come to him with her husband. There was a catch somewhere. Happiness

could turn to pain. Jenny gave half a sob, half a laugh.
They kissed again.

'Sorry,' she said.

'Why?'

'I couldn't help it.' Coming here, she meant. Or crying.
Or laughing. Or being Jenny.

There was no precedent for this. 'Give me time, Jenny.
Wait for me to recover a little.' The words came back from
Waterloo. Then in the confusion Clive caught a memory
of Victor, the first time he went down to Brighton. 'Isabel!'
he called to her in the kitchen. They would have champagne and drink to the buried years, the apocalypse today.
On this impossible occasion, fraught with unlikely
entrances, it almost seemed that Brenda might come
through the door, fresh and wet and plump, clasping a
bottle in her flipper fingers.

Jenny wiped her face, Clive fetched the champagne,
Isabel brought glasses. A party had collected in the
kitchen, drawn by the American visitors. Already, probably through Beaconsfield, everyone in Aurora knew that
this was Mr Clive's wife with her second husband. Max
left the veranda rail at the sound of a cork. 'Clive,' he
said, 'I can guess how you feel, or I like to think so, and
I'm sure it's hard to find words for it, they're darned
elusive things, except the wrong ones.'

'To us!' Jenny held up her glass. She was still girlish –
the Jenny she always had been; tender but unbreakable.

'To us.' Clive was incredulous, not daring to be too
happy.

'To you both,' Max said.

'To you too, Max,' they said in one breath, and laughed.

'To all of us.'

'You must stay for ever,' Clive said. The champagne
eased the awkwardness, helped them enjoy their astonishment. Isabel brought pieces of coconut and fried
potatoes. The day glittered on the lagoon. A big canoe
drifted past the house, full of saltwater boys singing a
version of 'The Bluebells of Scotland'.

'How are the bagpipes?' Jenny asked. She had a trace
of American accent, a hesitant new flavour in her voice.

'Fell to bits years ago.'

'You didn't get new ones?' Max asked, as if disappointed: his picture of Clive was incomplete without them. 'I'm sure the Japanese – '

'Clive,' Jenny said. 'We've got two days free – can we stay in your lagoon?'

'Stay for ever – I told you.'

'Dinner tonight!' Max loved to make arrangements. 'How about that? You come to our place. On deck, under the stars, country cooking – nothing like it. Make Becky jealous when she hears. We'll send the speedboat for you, Clive.'

The yacht had brought a sense of passing. In two days it would sail away, leaving no chance of return. An indefinable need to celebrate its transience settled on Aurora.

'Is that right, Clive – what we heard in Tulagi?' Holding a beer can, glistening in the deck lights over a charcoal grill, Max prodded three steaks with a fork. 'You gave this place away?'

'To Beaconsfield, my headman.'

'He's a millionaire – you realize?'

'He deserves it. If you had a son – '

'You had a freehold?'

'They cancelled it at Independence.' The yacht stirred on the sleeping, breathing lagoon. Clive remembered his nights in harbour on board the schooner, *Catriona*. There would be a smell of fish frying in coconut oil, and someone arguing with Beaconsfield over the price of razor blades or fertility pills.

'They gave you compensation?'

'They offered me a lease.'

'With security?'

'With conditions. I'd be on sufferance. At the people's whim – the people in power.' Stars rocked a little in the dark water, disturbed by canoes: the people of Aurora were coming out into the night for a closer look.

'They'd tell you what to do?'

'Grow cucumbers, plant daffodils, dig for uranium – I'd never tolerate it. Someone in Tulagi, some clerk who doesn't know if it's Christmas or Marble Arch – '

'Clive!' Jenny, content till now to let the men talk, choked on her drink.

'No joke – they could insist on some fancy scheme dreamed up by a pair of international lunatics over lunch, too qualified and dignified and rarefied and . . .' Clive heard Jenny's choke turn to a chuckle. 'Too sozzled to see beyond their lobster thermidors.'

'Make you invest in it?'

'Dismiss me if I didn't. Deport me, even. Confiscate the lot without paying for what I'd done here.'

'Your improvements? Your capital?'

'They'd get it for nothing if they wanted me out. I wouldn't argue. I won't play kiss-me-charlie with politicians.' Clive liked the archaism.

'You mean black ones?' Max turned over the steaks.

'Any colour.'

'That Dikea's a good guy.'

'I wrote letters to him before Independence.'

'You should see some of the other presidents I've had to get drunk with.'

'I suggested a research plantation here, or agriculture college – to benefit everyone.'

'A fine legacy, Clive.'

'Not if it was let go – if it went back to what it was before I came.'

'What's wrong with that Gladstone of yours? Or Palmerston, Disraeli – what's his name?'

'Beaconsfield,' Jenny prompted.

'He'd never work for Dikea,' Clive said, 'any more than you would.'

'Dikea made a great hit at the United Nations.'

'He never answered my letters.'

'He danced nicely with the princess.' Max poked the charcoal; added more from a bag; rubbed garlic, twisted a pepper mill, squeezed a lemon. 'I know how Jennifer likes her steak – OK if I do yours the same, Clive?'

Jenny said, 'It's sad, don't you think, Max? – that the people who got so much from Clive. . . .' She spoke warily, still unable to trust her voice. 'I mean, what irony! No man could have done more for the people he chose to live with.'

Clive protested: 'They chose to live with me.'

'You gave them everything,' Jenny said. 'Your energy, advice, example – but it's not enough, they want the rest.'

'The rest of what?' Sitting with her while her husband cooked, Clive smiled and put out his hand: the woman who had kept him alive. 'There's nothing.'

'The rest of your life, the years more. . . .' She took his hand briefly. Soon she would recover confidence. 'The time you might enjoy here.'

'To them I'm nobody.'

'You're too big for them,' she said. 'They have to cut you down. Steal your future. Your hopes.'

'None to steal.' Hope had once been nourishment, he could have told her. Now he didn't need it.

'Come off it, Clive!' Max said. 'You made a million anyway – don't tell me.'

'Max goes on about the money.' Between the two men their wife – once Clive's, now Max's – was referee. 'Profit equals a rich life, is his idea.'

'Stacked up in the Sydney stock market.'

'Most of it's in the bank at Tulagi,' Clive said. 'Blocked by your friend Dikea.'

'Not allowed to take it out of the country? Jesus, that's tough. So what'll you do?'

'Make sure my people are all right – that's what matters.'

'But yourself?' Jenny asked.

He could only be frivolous. 'I might settle in the Sydney suburbs. Go in for old roses. Keep racing pigeons. Tie salmon flies. What do you think?'

'Seriously – '

'Or retire to a golf club. Among the pines and rhododendrons, comparing niblicks, birdies, stymies – can't you see me?'

'Who are you kidding?' Max asked, busy at the grill.

Jenny said, 'You're teasing yourself, Clive.'

'I couldn't live in England now,' he said flatly. 'I've never swept the floor in my life. Or washed up, cooked the dinner – any of those things. Look what Max can do. I try to be realistic. And not too regretful. Not unaware.

I know what's happened – where I stand. I can hardly put the kettle on for tea.'

'I've seen it everywhere,' Max said, testing his steaks again, grinding more pepper over them, adding butter. 'India, Malaya, Kenya – you loved your empire, I guess.'

'I'm not ashamed of it. It was like a box of chocolates.' Clive enjoyed the picture. 'It was lovely while it lasted.'

'And you're sorry they're all gone.'

'Pity we didn't hang on to the Mendanas, to see me out.'

'But you made your own colony here,' Jenny said. 'A true bit of the Raj. Beaconsfield will preserve it, surely?'

'In his way, for a while.'

Max announced, 'Chuck wagon coming!' He dished the steaks on to a trolley, wheeled it over the deck to Jenny and Clive, handed out sauce, mustard, chilli beans, salad. Voices came quietly out of the night from the canoes. Clive heard the gurgle and slap of swimmers round the yacht. Half the children of Aurora must be in the water. His people weren't indifferent. They were a comfort out there in the dark, showing that he belonged with them, not to these lavish foreigners. He would like to tell them that this meat, butchered in America months ago, was nothing to the pigs they roasted on Independence night.

'I thought of ending up,' he said, 'in a place I read about, up in the mountains of Argentina where the rivers are full of trout.'

'But the British aren't welcome there any more?' Max suggested.

'Maybe I'll settle on another island. How about St Helena?'

Jenny cried, 'Your own Napoleon!'

'That's where Becky said I'd finish,' Max said.

'Only four mail boats a year – I wouldn't be bothered by visitors.'

'OK-OK, just give us tomorrow,' Jenny laughed, 'and next day we'll disappear.' Slowly she was letting herself loose. She might be free before they sailed away.

'I'll do the same when the time comes,' Clive said. 'I won't make a fuss. Simply pack up and go. Take my fishing-rod and vanish off the map.'

'Vanish off the map,' Jenny repeated quietly. 'It's what you once promised we'd do at Strathpolly, after the war.'

'Sweetheart, doesn't it make you thankful,' Max said, padding over the deck in rubber flip-flops to fetch more beer, 'that we secured that Washington apartment to be near Becky when we retire?'

Then Jenny let out a gulp of shock, almost a scream. 'Clive, your toes!' He too was in sandals. 'What's wrong with them? What happened, for God's sake, Clive?'

It was careless, he should have worn socks. He had been going to show them to her when they undressed that night – a present from the railway. He drew his feet under the deck chair. 'Sorry, it's something I don't talk about. I forget the details, I got it in the war – a sort of medal. For keeping out of battle. But Rebecca. . . .' It was too late – about thirty-five years – to bring up Goldilocks' little job with a rifle butt. 'How is she?'

Max said, 'Eat your steak and I'll show you pictures.'

'She met you, those five minutes in a bar,' Jenny said, still shocked, 'and knows you better than I ever did.'

Clive laughed: 'I doubt it. You had me in a nutshell. I haven't changed.'

Max cleared the plates on to the trolley, brought out whisky and a packet of photos: Becky as a bride, the girl in a museum library who had sent Godfrey to Aurora and his death; Becky in a night club with her husband, one of the men in the London theatre though Clive couldn't remember him; Becky with her two children on a beach; Becky glamorous, Becky motherly, innocent, sporting, dreamy, Becky the darling daughter of unfaithfulness, poisoner of a marriage, sickening pride of an ambassador-at-large, tantalizing double of this Jenny, this inimitable wife of a battered prisoner labouring to build a railway and survive to live with her.

'What you miss!' Max was getting sentimental, cordial with drink. 'She's the most wonderful thing. I tell you – I'm sorry for any man who hasn't got Becky for a daughter.'

Clive said, 'Don't apologize, Max,' and passed an uneasy look to Jenny, who returned it. Probably she had guessed about Isabel.

Max burbled on: 'She's posterity for you, the mother earth, sowing the fertile race, handing on the precious empire – you don't need colonies if you have a couple of grandchildren like those.' He slapped a fat hand on the picture of a boy and girl posing in the snow.

Clive knew that several of Isabel's multi-coloured moon-begotten piccaninnies – his own grandchildren who had never made a snowman for the camera but could climb a coconut tree, cut a turtle out of its shell, track a wild pig, make medicine from a kwako tree – had swum out to the yacht, only their glistening eyes and pale palms and soles of their feet showing in the dark water, and were swinging on the anchor chain.

Next day Aurora entertained America. Beaconsfield, master of the place and shrunk like a nocturnal animal – nothing but two bright eyes on a minimal body with something drier than mildew, a faint nap raised by the years, showing on his dark old bush boy's skin – led the ambassador's party round the plantation. The football team were disgusted to find that the crew of the yacht couldn't play the English game. But Laki, white-haired as if crowned with coral and almost blind, called up his saltwater boys and challenged them to a canoe race. The Americans lost badly. At the finish the winners turned round and capsized them, then pulled them deep down into the lagoon, the way their ancestors used to finish off their enemies. Mr Clive's wife, it was agreed, had been a fool to go and live with such men. Mr Clive had come to the right country.

At lunch in Clive's house Max said, 'I've seen Tahiti, Samoa, Fiji, but none of them are so beautiful. Nowhere can touch it – don't you agree, sweetheart?' Jenny only smiled. Her husband kept getting up from the table to look at the view from the veranda, hitching his trousers, drooling over the possibilities. 'What you've thrown away, Clive! What a place for a holiday! Bring in a good developer – imagine!'

'Develop it? More than I've done? You should have seen it before. After it was abandoned in the war.'

'First thing is an airstrip.'

'God help us!'

'That canoe race set me going. I can see water skiers round the lagoon, in and out of the little islands.'

'The Japanese trawlers are enough.' Clive saw that Jenny had caught him shuddering.

'Chalets among the palms.'

'I like it as it is – an occasional yacht for a day or two.'

'Beach trips, fishing trips, diving off the reef, surfing – it's crying out for it. Put a casino on one of the islands out there. Take a boat and gamble – make it adventurous, a bit naughty. Motor gondolas – why not? With gondoliers who used to eat their passengers. The Venice of the South Seas. Romantic, exotic, far away out in the blue – it has everything.' Isabel brough in a sliced pineapple and cream. 'Cheap servants too, I guess. And what I saw of President Dikea, he'd help all he can. Come in on it himself, I'll bet. He's no savage out of the trees like some I've seen. Quite smart. I'd like to write to him. Give him a few names in America, pass it to the right people – no problem, Clive.'

'It's kind of you, but it's out of my hands now. And I can't see Beaconsfield . . .' Isabel brought coffee, cleared away the lunch, went back to the kitchen.

'Isn't she sensational?' Max hadn't seemed to notice her before. Suddenly she was the symbol of Aurora as a tourist haven, the girl in the travel posters of this island paradise: 'Sensational, sensational . . .' The word dribbled from Max's mouth, diminishing each time. 'Have you seen such a beauty anywhere, Jennifer? It's that rare colour – I wonder where she got it. Not pure Mendanan, I'd say.'

'Who wants purity?' Jenny asked. 'Would Rebecca like to be pure American?' She knew for certain, Clive saw, that Isabel was his daughter. 'But Clive, there's something I want to ask. You've given Aurora to Beaconsfield because – '

'He's my son, quite simply.'

Jenny was smiling: 'Say you had a daughter.'

'I know what you mean.' Clive was glad to share it with her. He would make it more oblique, more Mendanan.

'Listen – it's a matter of ancestors. And descendants. And yams.'

Max exploded: 'Yams! Is this your darned English humour?'

'A man plants a yam in his garden. It's a tuber growing underground, spreading into more yams.'

'Like a potato.' Max hated to be mystified.

'It remains there with its new yams, in the garden, and they'll become this year's harvest. But it also sends up a stalk like any plant, with leaves and flowers.'

'Potato flowers – you've seen them, sweetheart.'

'The flowers die and the seed gets carried by birds or blown on the wind into other gardens, into the forest, anywhere.'

'Wild potatoes – we have them in America.'

'Next year, when the man plants his garden again, he takes yams saved from last year's harvest – the ones that came out of the original yam. He'd never go and dig up yams from the seedlings – they've flown away, they're no longer his. All his domestic yams, the food to keep his family for another year, are grown from that first old yam. So there are two kinds of yam descended from a single ancestor – the ones that never leave the garden, breeding generation after generation in the same ground, and the ones that settle somewhere else and give new yams to another man and produce more seed that scatters again, moving further on, year after year.'

'I know, I know!' Jenny understood. She laughed and waved her hand at the kitchen where Isabel and her multiple relations were cooking tonight's dinner behind the curtains. 'Yams that stay in the garden are the men, yams that fly away are women. Sons belong in the soil, daughters are tossed to the winds, thrown to the birds, lost in the forest where anything can happen to them – who knows? Who cares? So Beaconsfield gets the land.'

'It all comes back to purity, I guess,' Max said, with a flicker of comprehension. 'Now it's my turn to ask something, Clive. We're away tomorrow early, we're dining with you tonight, but if the afternoon's free – may I take a couple of those fellows who ducked our crew in the canoes and put them in the speedboat with me? Do some fishing, maybe. Take a look at the beaches. Have a swim. That is – if you think I'm safe with them, they won't get hungry.'

'Max, of course – '

'And if you feel safe with Jennifer.'

'Max – '

'Will you trust me, at large in Aurora? I swear not to develop it. Not this afternoon. Could you fix that?'

2

'I like him.'

'No, you don't.'

'He's totally good.'

'I've been squirming since we came.'

'He decided we should be alone. I'd never have suggested it.'

'I see him as you do. Boring and conventional. I only stand it because I know how it's happened and what he's like behind it.'

'So why can't I see him the way you do?'

'He must look like a living cliché.'

'He knows exactly what he is.'

'And drowns it in government liquor.'

'He knows what you see and probably what I see. That's why I like him.'

'Thanks, Clive. And you're right – you haven't changed.'

'So where do we begin?'

'I'll tell you where. You were always going to take me there but never did. You talked and talked about it till I never wanted to hear the word again. But it was where you came from, I knew it so well and longed to go there. And now I've come. It's here, isn't it? It's Strathpolly.'

Clive laughed. 'I suppose – '

'The fantasy, the semi-mythical family home, the tribal ground.'

'Jenny!'

'Ancestors stretching back, descendants going on – '

'The day I came here I wanted to stay for ever. I felt it strongly – a life ahead. Even if it was imagination it was so real, it didn't matter. I'd never felt it before – my own capacity for creation and sacrifice. For remaking myself.'

'You sound like a monk. This is your monastery. You've vowed obedience and silence. Forget the chastity. Though by the way, she's lovely – your Isabel.'

'I think Rebecca guessed too, from something in a letter.'

'She never told me. She can be discreet when she wants to.'

'Actually,' Clive considered, 'Aurora's better than Strathpolly because it's true. You know, I've been terribly lucky. That day I came back, at Waterloo – '

'Clive darling.'

'If Victor hadn't sold it, if I'd gone straight up there that night, there'd never have been an Aurora. No reality, just the myth.'

'Clive, we've got to go over that, haven't we? There won't be another time. I'll be sorry always, if I sail away tomorrow and we haven't – '

'There was only one thing I wanted to tell you. I remembered it too late. I stopped the taxi and ran back into the station, but you'd gone. I wanted to tell you – '

'That I'd saved your life.'

'You knew?'

'Yes, I knew.'

'How, Jenny?'

'Because I knew you. Knew myself. Knew us both so utterly. It hammered in my head – I saved his life, I saved his life. It was nature's medicine to cure my conscience. Or nature's punishment for my guilt. It ruined Becky's birthday party. It went on for months, years, it still comes back – I saved his life. It's an old friend now. Something I live with, like your broken toes.'

'I suppose you knew about those too.'

'In a way I did. That's why I was so horrified. It wasn't surprise but recognition. Face to face with something I'd known about but never seen. Ever since I got your telegram saying you were alive I've been through every moment of your life a million times. Being sunk and captured and tortured. Every possible event. Everything I heard they'd done to other men, must have happened to you. Every detail of those years when I thought you were dead – I've sifted them like grains of sand, one by one.'

'What did you find?'

'Nothing, till I learnt what I was looking for.'

'It was yourself.'

'Probably you did the same, Clive, didn't you? Went through my life in London. Tried to feel what it was like for me.'

'I'm afraid I didn't. You weren't anywhere when you weren't with me. A blank. I only went through our old life together. Meticulously – Christ, yes! Each minute I could remember, each word we'd ever said.'

'I was a blank all right, after the *Prince of Wales* was sunk and you were missing. Wiped out. Try and imagine – a widow of twenty-two.'

'That's what you said at Waterloo.'

'Thank God I was an ambulance driver. Something hard and physical. I came back to the flat worn out, but I couldn't sleep. The cold empty bed – I couldn't change the sheets in case there was something of you still on them. A hair or a stain or a smell. I wore your pyjamas, to feel you wrapping me. In the kitchen I searched the crockery for anything that hadn't been washed away, that might have been yours. I sat on the lavatory and felt you'd sat there once, and lay in the bath where we sometimes made love. I grubbed in the waste paper basket for scraps of you. Your last letter, you wrote from Singapore, came weeks after the admiralty telegram. I fainted when I saw the writing. Literally fell over. Found myself ripping it apart like an animal. It was all about the voyage out and a cricket match in the naval base. At the end you put PS and nothing else. I never knew what you meant to say and didn't. I wondered if you'd tried to tell me what it was like being dead, but couldn't because it was unspeakable. Death is nothing, so there's nothing to say about it. I'd torn the paper when I opened it, and felt I'd damaged you. An assault on you. This awful violent ungrateful wife. I kept it under the pillow and put my fingers on it. Like touching your body. It got thin and limp. Falling to bits at the bottom of the sea. How wonderful it would be to go to sleep and wake up with you down there. In the morning it was under the pillow again, getting more ragged every day.'

'Just what I was doing – you weren't far wrong.'

'For the first weeks I didn't believe I was alone. Sometimes I wished I was very old and then perhaps it wouldn't hurt, but perhaps I wouldn't mind either and I wanted to mind, it would be treacherous not to. Thank God for the bombs and the ambulance job, to stop me thinking too much. But even the war reminded me of you. The silver barrage balloons over London looked so lovely in the sun, but I couldn't bear them because you were missing them. I didn't want the spring to come that year unless it could come for you also.'

'We had no seasons on the railway – just hot or wet. Nothing new, only the years that never changed.'

'I kept thinking of things I wished I'd said to you.'

'Or wished you hadn't.'

'It sounds trite, but I was young and only half-alive. I loved you to bursting point, and burst. People saw me and said, "Don't you know there's a war on?" to jolly me up. We had to be cheerful or we'd lose. I was expected to be proud of being a war widow, and felt ashamed of being miserable. Cut off from everyone. From myself as well. A great door had clanged shut, blocking my life. I was in prison and terrified. Whatever I did was meaningless, futile – except my job. Other men made me sick. I went to the dentist to have a wisdom tooth out and he gave me gas, and I had a dream about you and me walking naked through the woods, Strathpolly probably, and woke up and saw his obscene face above me, and I wanted to throw up. I fled to the lavatory and cried and cried, but I'd lost my handkerchief and there was no paper, so I pulled off my pants to cry into, which only make it more bitter – helpless tears being soaked up in my pants. If I'd had a baby it would have been different. Something moving on, not stopped dead. I wanted to take root, like a tree. To

give fruit. To be a blessing to someone. Beautiful and
desired and useful. And then the flat was bombed. I came
back after a raid and it had gone. Nothing, nothing. For
a moment I wished I'd been in it. The agony of possessing
life! Death was the answer. Then I saw that this was
better. The prison was knocked down and I was free. All
the futility lay somewhere under the rubble. They
wouldn't let me go on driving an ambulance and anyway
I wasn't needed, the blitz was petering out. Our flat had
caught one of the last bombs. So I got a job in an American
officers' club. A huge mansion in Belgravia that had
belonged to a maharaja – his London palace which he
gave up to help the war. I had a room under the roof
and did reception work, arranged flowers, theatre tickets,
weekends with the English aristocracy in their stately
homes – all that. The future was beginning. I felt like
someone in a cinema when the projector breaks down,
one picture stuck on the screen while they mend it, and
now the film was moving again.'

'And Max walked on to the screen one day.'

'Clive darling.'

'Do you want to tell me?'

'I must. If I go away tomorrow without – '

'We've got hours yet. The saltwater boys are in heaven
in that speedboat. They'll keep him out till sunset.'

'I thought if I ever had another man he'd be the closest
to you I could find. He's the opposite. He wasn't so fat
then, but I could see it coming. Worldly and ambitious.
Immensely kind, though, in a selfish way – d'you understand? He wanted to scoop me up, rescue me, for his own
sake. Perhaps it was what I wanted too, or needed. Or a
kind of revenge. If you could have death, I'd have Max.'

'The next best thing.'

'I tried to tell him about you, but he wouldn't have it.
Or talk about his own wife. They were getting divorced,
it was finished, irrelevant to us. We went to theatres and
restaurants and walking in the park. I was a girl again,
from being a widow. It was grotesque, but London was
so false in the war. Whatever one did was a travesty. I
knew how it would end. I was thrilled and impatient. And
frightened of myself. Of something drastic. Like being a

virgin again. There had been men before you, Clive, so you don't mind – '

'I'm only wondering what I was doing at that moment. Working in the cholera hut, probably.'

'Max had a staff car with a big black driver. I'd never seen a black man close to. And I hadn't been out of London since that pub in Wales with you. It seemed a time for losing chastities. We drove into the country and stopped at Windsor because Max hadn't seen it. It all looked beautiful, and if I felt any guilt it was because it was autumn. We should have waited till spring, it would be more suitable – this was too melancholy for what we were doing. Unless I was another falling leaf. It was terribly predictable. The classic dirty weekend. Max had got me to book a room in one of those riverside hotels by the Thames.'

'Maidenhead, no doubt,' Clive said. 'He was piling it on.'

'Where the Duke of Windsor first slept with Mrs Simpson, he said. The black man delivered us, like dropping two children at a party to be picked up afterwards, and we went straight to bed and almost never got out. I gave him a marvellous time, I know. I hadn't done it for so long, and this mixture of innocence and debauchery – I was good, I really was.'

'I remember.'

'But all the time I thought how much you were missing. What a waste of me, that it wasn't for you. Clive darling – '

'Don't stop. I love it.' He caught his own sarcasm, which he didn't intend.

'You were the breath of life. And this was another mockery. On Monday morning the driver came back for us and said he hoped we'd had a nice time, and I found myself looking down at my skirt like a child who's spilt something.' She turned to Clive on the veranda.

'Max got a flat in Regent's Park, and I gave up the club and moved in. He was obsessed with England, the Tower of London, Cleopatra's Needle, everything I'd never seen. It was a complex he had – the deprivation of America. We

were for ever going round the bombed churches, reading
up their history, tut-tutting over the ruins.'

'Why didn't you get married? – you were a widow.'

'His divorce dragged on. And I'd had one war marriage,
I didn't want another. We'd wait till peace and see what
happened. Meanwhile make the most of it. Max was rich
like all Americans and spoilt me outrageously. Showed
me off to his friends – his English moll. No mention of
you, Clive. I kept you locked inside and sometimes took
you out to give myself a treat when Max wasn't looking.
I didn't cry for you, to be truthful. I felt as dead to you
as you were to me. I remembered that photo of your father
you told me your mother kept by her bed. You'd fade too,
I knew. Or was Max the salmon that had pulled me in,
to finish me off?'

'Did you ever see Victor?'

'Once or twice after you were sunk. But we didn't know
what to say, we'd never got on. And I lost touch when I
was bombed out. Partly on purpose, I suppose. Then Max
said he'd met a man called Ackerly at some conference in
the War Office. I never knew about Max's job. Vaguely in
intelligence. He had to investigate people, though they
weren't American, who might be in sensitive places. But
it was Max who was sensitive. Or jealous. In theory he
loved my Englishness, but it was a threat. He wouldn't
let me near Victor. Later he found that Victor had got into
a mess, living it up in London, putting money in some
mad scheme for a night club in the boilerhouse under the
Albert Hall. Lost the lot. Had to sell Strathpolly and was
eased out of the War Office. I suspect that Max was
gloating. But Victor had picked Brenda out of the night
club wreckage, where she was to have been a hostess,
and took her off to Brighton.'

'You know he died? Ten years ago, fifteen.'

'You told Becky that time you met – you'd gone to
England to tidy up. And Brenda?'

'I still get a Christmas card. I can see her puffing round
and round in that flat, oozing faintly.'

'Two years after you'd gone I had Becky – October 1943.'

'Just when we finished the railway and the first train
came up. We got a tin of tuna fish each.'

'Having a baby was like peace coming. A new life in
that strange little person. A chance. I can't tell you what
she did for me. Max couldn't share it and didn't understand. Becky was everything that I'd lost with you. She
made me feel human again, and that made me love Max
more. After the Normandy invasion he went to France
and across Europe with the American army to the end in
Germany. I hardly saw him except for a few days' leave.
For a year I was alone with Becky, watching her become
a child. 1945 was a lovely summer and she was a lovely
age. We had such fun with the swans in Regent's Park
and boats on the lake and the elephants. Mother and
daughter together, oblivious of everyone else. Feeling
rather superior. Caring for nobody but each other. Already
I thought I saw more of you than Max in her. Or I only
wanted to. Too happy to last. But then the atom bomb
was dropped on Japan and it seemed that the world was
being given one more chance to live at peace, like Becky
and me. If not, up we all go. Max came back and soon
he'd be off again to America, to be demobilized. I'd pack
up the flat and follow with Becky. But next thing, more
devastating than any bomb – '

'Jenny, Jenny, Jenny!'

'They had my address because of the pension. Clive
darling. . . .' She stopped. Dried up. The afternoon was
falling. Aurora stirred from the day's heat; settled towards
the quick evening. Out in the lagoon, pushed by a new
breeze, the American yacht turned slowly on its anchor
to face the west, ready for the sunset. Canoes drifted out
from the village for another look. Isabel brought tea, with
English plum cake, on to the veranda for her father and
his woman.

'Don't go on, Jenny, unless – '

'I rang the admiralty in case there was a mistake, though
I knew there wasn't. I don't believe in miracles. I wanted
you to be alive so much, yet my life had at last turned
happy with you dead. I was two women, but only allowed
to be one of them. What was I to do? Who could tell me?
The voice on the telephone – some faceless welfare officer?
Or Victor, with his tart in Brighton? Least of all Max. He
was stunned, he couldn't take it in. I'd have been sorry

for him if I could cope with any emotions but my own. Only Becky could help. She had the answer, if I could just get it from her, like an oracle. I sent you a telegram back.'

'I saw what it meant, without quite facing it. I was stunned too.'

'Those next weeks waiting for you were the worst of my life. Worse than after you were sunk. This was what I had ached for, with every particle, and now it was pure horror. I tried writing, I started twenty letters to you. Every night I saw the way to do it, and in the morning it looked wrong. Perhaps silence was the only decent thing. But coming home in a troopship, stopping at ports to pick up mail and not a word from me – what would it mean for you? I was a coward.'

'Braver to face me. To tell me when you saw me.'

'I wanted to be dead, Clive. Desperately. To change places with you. To have the death that you'd come out of. Becky kept me alive, though I wished she hadn't. I moved into her room, I couldn't be in bed with Max. My mind twisted into knots all night. I had two men and the child of one of them – it should have been simple. I saw Max's agony too but I want to tell you, Clive – he never tried to persuade me.'

'He's utterly good – I said so.'

'Becky decided, at the last moment. She was having her birthday party and you were due that afternoon. She was only two, but before I took the bus to Waterloo she gave me a wonderful wise look, and laughed. It told me what I knew. I couldn't ask Max to let her come with me, back to you. I couldn't abandon her, for him to take to America without me. That left – '

'Waterloo station.'

'You only know your side. Did you ever wonder about me?'

'At the birthday party?'

'After it, Max got drunk. Violent, brutal – I'd never seen him like that. It's why he's where he is, ambassador-at-large, without much imagination or brains. He threw Becky into her room and locked the door. Ripped off my clothes. It was what he needed and he showed me I did too. No use weeping or praying or harrowing over the ground for ever.'

'It's roughly what I'd planned for myself,' Clive said. 'Perhaps I should have done it anyway.'

'Got drunk?'

'Got a woman. But I couldn't for years. I couldn't forget. . . .' He faltered. 'Jenny, I've had such scorn for my body sometimes. And with you – remember? – it was infinitely more than what was going on in bed. The ideas it led to, of other things – jokes, meals, funny little thoughts. A whole universe, like a colossal aphrodisiac, far beyond anything we were doing. Though we had to be doing it, or craving for it, to open a way for the rest.'

'I know what you mean. Making love, you begin to build something outside it, bigger.'

Clive laughed: 'A vast mental erection.'

'But you've missed the worst. The habitual thing it can become. The endless push-pull business. A function, no more. Banal and dry. Longing to get through and go to sleep.'

'It's true – I didn't often wonder about you.'

'It's not exciting. The regular career. The marriage routine. Automatic, pleasant, comfortable, gross – it suited Max and he carried me along. Squabbling and screwing. The standard middle-aged couple, loveless but too tired to do much about it. The old two-part invention. There were times when I didn't even like him, but he knew it and held his breath, like waiting for you to come home, while I untangled myself. And Becky made it fun. She loved being half-English. I told her everything, except what I knew you'd been through. That was my private penance. Probably she guessed as she grew up. In a way she saw you as her origin. She was mad when we got to Australia and you'd fled. Max was relieved, but slowly he felt less threatened. When Becky met you in London and was so thrilled, he couldn't spoil it. Now he knows he's safe. In Tulagi I said let's visit you and he jumped at it. Perhaps he had something to purge.'

'Did you too, Jenny?'

'I've done it. Tried to show you why it was, when you came back, that I let you go. I wasn't just faithless, but

contemptible.' She put out her hand for his; took his
thumb, the familiar way. 'Now it's your turn.'

'You know it all. Through and through.'

'Come off it, Clive.'

'There's nothing more.'

'Four years in the darkness. I've read every word any
prisoner wrote. Every glimmer, to find out what
happened.'

'Then that's enough.'

'I'm still interested. Because I love you. There are other
scars, aren't there? – besides the toes. You wouldn't be
human if there weren't.'

'There was a friend of Rebecca's who came to stay.'

'Godfrey? Who died here? I never met him.'

'He got it all out of me. It was his profession. All my
secrets.'

'All?'

'The man who was drowned in the *Prince of Wales*. The
man who had his eyes gouged out, then his stomach. The
man who was smashed to death with a hammer.' The sun
was dropping into the lagoon, the sky turning to emerald
and rose: the colours of dawn being repeated at dusk, like
the first notes of music returning at the end.

'You think you could have saved them?' She spoke as
if they weren't news to her, she had heard about them
long ago. 'I'm not surprised. It's the man you are – to
believe that.' Clive said nothing. 'But what about the ones
you did save? In the life raft. In prison. On the railway.
With kindness, when they were dying in the cholera hut.
With vegetables from your garden by the river.'

'How did you discover that?'

'You see, I'm better at it than Godfrey. But there's something deep down in the darkness.' She had his thumb in
her fingers, exploring the joints. The old pleasure still
came.

'What else do you know, Jenny?'

'I feel like a witch, looking into my crystal ball. You're
hiding something and I'll find it if you give me time.
You've given me hints already. Won't you tell me, Clive?
Better if you do.'

'I did once tell it. To a real old witch down by that river. I had a feeling she could pass it on to you.'

'I caught a whiff of it.'

'That was her cheroot.'

'At Waterloo,' Jenny spoke slowly, reaching back nearly forty years for the words, 'you said I'd done nothing wrong. Nothing to what you'd done. If anyone had betrayed anyone – '

'It was for me to be ashamed.' Clive found the words too.

'You couldn't have a woman for years, you said just now.'

'Unless she was you.'

'You couldn't forget.'

'Forget you.'

'Not someone else?'

Clive wouldn't protest: 'Go on. I'm fascinated.' He had been keeping it for her at Waterloo. Aurora was a better place.

'You had such scorn for your body, you said. Not because it was starved or battered.'

'All this was going to come out the night I got back.'

'Like the broken toes. But it never has.'

'Perhaps it never happened. So much was unreal. Unbelievable. It couldn't be true.'

'You lost hope?' She was working on his thumb, persisting.

'Not for ever, but long enough. We heard the shots. Four men who tried to get away. I can't explain it otherwise.'

'You hated him?'

'Not hate. Something extraordinary. A desperate hunger. If you can eat snakes and kittens – '

'Was he the one who broke your toes?'

'No.'

'The one who beat you up?'

'No.'

'Who?'

Clive laughed: 'When I used to go to London I stayed at the Ritz. The manager had a slogan – "Only the very best for the very best, Mr Ackerly." '

'So it was the commandant.'

'He was odious. A demon. An enemy.'

'He was human like you.'

'Why did I let him?'

'You tell me, Clive.'

'There were two things. One was bamboo. Nothing but bamboo. We cut it down and uprooted it and split it and built huts of it and slept on it. Made chairs and tables and mugs and spoons of it, built bridges with it, got music out of it, smoked tobacco in it.'

'You were beaten with it.'

'Cooked over it and burnt our dead and made crosses in the cemetry with it – bamboo, bamboo. But you know all that.'

'What was the other thing?'

'The smell. From the pits, the rice, the men – their breath and bodies and diseases.'

'So, the bamboo and the stink – you had to get away.' Jenny spoke as if in a trance, watching a scene she could see only dimly; guessing, feeling for the truth. 'In his cabin the bamboo walls were hung with paper scrolls? There were mats on the floor? Perhaps there was a faint perfume? Persimmons, was it? Rose water?' She gripped his thumb harder, to keep the vision.

Clive also spoke slowly, with gaps between each sentence: 'We were crowded like rats. Lived and died like rats.'

'You had to reach out.'

'Each in his own condemned cell. Stricken with loneliness. The same for everyone.'

'For him too.'

'He had a singing bird, a present from his grandmother, and when it sang he was carried to his garden in Japan. When it stopped singing he killed it. But I didn't need a bird to sing, I knew my place by heart.'

'Perhaps you sang inside, and couldn't stop.'

'Except that once.'

'It doesn't matter what you did. You see that, Clive, don't you?'

'I insisted on living. I'd do better than Hutton or Awang or Smithy.'

'Defying the insistent death.'

'I'd defy the guilt too. I'd live it down. *Live* it down. It was only a germ, like cholera. I'd inoculate myself with an extra dose, to be immune. Sink to the bottom where I could go no lower.'

'Then start to come up.' She let go his thumb; withdrew her hand. 'You've been climbing ever since.'

For half an hour they watched the emerald change to purple, the rose to crimson, then everything to grey. In the dark Clive said, 'There's something I learnt on the railway.'

'Forgiveness? I know – you taught it to me.'

'It's not just an emotion. Or a good intention. It's a law of nature. Like gravity.'

'And what have you learnt at Aurora?'

'How can I tell you?' He stopped for a while, considering. 'As Max said, words are elusive things.' He paused again, for the right ones. 'But I think I found that the impossible is always just within one's grasp.'

'The impossible?'

'Happiness, justice, love – one only has to reach for the apple, instead of waiting for Eve.' Later he heard a sob: hardly more than the gulp of a fish breaking the surface of the lagoon. 'Jenny,' he said, 'we've reached something we never could before. We've been more married then we ever were.'

'Noble,' she said faintly, through tears, 'is the only word I can think of. Sorry.'

Suddenly the speedboat was roaring towards them from the night. 'Thank you,' Clive said. 'It's the nicest thing anyone has ever done to me.'

With her family and friends behind the kitchen curtain Isabel had worked all day on an elaborate dinner for Clive and his American visitors. She knew she could do better than their barbecue on the yacht last night; and hid a frangipani flower in each of their paper napkins, to drop out when they unfolded them.

'Turtle soup!' Max exclaimed, already full of gin, shining in the light of four candles on the table and a pressure lamp on the bookshelf. 'First time in my life. Trust an Englishman alone on a tropical island.' Clive knew that the soup came from a Fortnum's tin with some clever adjustment in the kitchen. But the skipjack fillets were straight from the lagoon. The pork chops, from one of the pigs that had escaped the Independence feast, were drenched in the mustard-and-ketchup sauce that Isabel had been taught by her uncle Loloa. The beans and potatoes were from her garden. The dessert was her pride, the inevitable pineapple mousse with tinned cherries and dabs of condensed cream. The wine was Clive's best.

'I'd love to stay longer,' Jenny said.

'Sweetheart, maybe we'll be back.'

'You'll be paid off soon and we'll retire.'

'To your Washington apartment, near Rebecca?'

'But Clive,' Max said, 'don't count on being left alone another forty years.'

'I count on nothing. I never do. But I'm glad you came – truly.' Glad too that he and Jenny had touched the deepest, darkest echoes today. He shared her feeling: that it would be always a sorrow otherwise. Tomorrow the yacht would be gone.

'Maybe bump into you in a theatre one day,' Max said.

'I don't think Clive would like Washington,' Jenny said.

'In the end probably I'll hang on here. Never go away. There's nowhere I want to move to. Nowhere better.'

'Don't forget, if you want a developer – '

'I told you – it's up to Beaconsfield. I don't know what he'll do with it. Nothing drastic, I imagine. But I can't see the future as clearly as when I came here.'

'Not so much of it to see,' Max said, 'for any of us.'

'And for what there is, I haven't got the energy. I must be running out of steam.'

'Running out of steam!' Jenny protested. 'Nobody'd notice. But running – yes, running. You've always been running from something. Or someone.'

Victor and Odette had said it, and now Jenny. It must be true: 'Running from myself, that's all. To be myself.'

'But you can never get away. There's always someone following.'

'Only myself. But I won't run much further. Up the hill a short way – that'll do. I could never leave Aurora.'

'Give up this house?' Max was planning it as the reception centre for his tourist paradise, with coffee shop, drugstore, handicrafts. There would be a cage of hornbills and cockatoos, a tank of amazing slothful fish, a nightly show of native dancing. 'You'll let Beaconsfield move in?'

'He'll help me build a little house above the plantation, at the edge of the forest. Like your Washington apartment.'

'Close to your daughter?' Jenny said quietly, smiling.

'Hoist the Union Jack over it.' Max wanted to save the empire. 'Flying over the trees, the last example.'

'Up there I can watch Aurora.'

'And they'll keep an eye on you,' Jenny said. 'That's nice.'

After dinner Clive remembered something. Till the last moment he wasn't sure he would do it. But Jenny had decided to come here and he could return the gesture. From a mould-ridden trunk in his bedroom he brought a small packet. 'I haven't had it out for years,' he told them; and carefully undid the string, unwrapped layers of tissue paper, took out a fine silk tartan sash.

'That's a very pretty piece,' Max said. 'It's not local, I'd say.'

'My mother's.' Folded inside it, in more tissue, was a small box. Clive gave it to Jenny: 'I hope it's not too late.'

'Darling.'

He saw that she guessed; watched her open it, hold it to the candles, slip it on a finger; waited for someone to speak. In the empty moment he said, 'I got it in Rangoon. A quick bargain from a Chinese jeweller, very special cheap price for honourable English liberator from Nippon jackboot, so probably it's a fake.'

'Looks good to me,' Max said, peering across the table. 'Zircon, is it?'

Jenny got up and kissed Clive, holding her mouth long to his cheek, briefly to his lips, saying nothing.

He was holding the tartan sash: 'I thought maybe . . .'

Jenny said, 'Give it to Isabel! Wouldn't she look lovely! Her grandmother's – '

'I thought of that. But honestly it wouldn't last a couple of Saturday nights. The lovers would fight over it or the piccaninnies wipe their noses – '

'Clive.' Jenny turned the ring on her finger. 'Clive, don't be angry. I've had my present. The best in the world. Enough for a lifetime. This visit is all I want. I know you'll understand in the end. It's this.' She took off the ring. 'It'll survive better than a sash.' She went to the kitchen curtain; disappeared through it while they waited; came back with Isabel by the hand; led her to the table; raised her hand to the candlelight, tried the ring on each finger till it fitted; then kissed the lovely woman as she had just kissed Clive, the woman's father. Isabel stared at the ring; at Clive, Max, Jenny; at the ring again. A look of unfathomable joy transfigured her: something from far back in her ancestry, a vision of fire in the forest, a burning infinite magic. It couldn't last, or she couldn't bear it. She tried to speak or laugh or give more than the gentlest gasp that came out of her soul – out of the night – but only turned and fled back into the kitchen.

'Jesus,' Max said, shaking his head. 'That was just a wonderful thing to see. Wonderful, wonderful – '

'Thank you, Jenny,' Clive said. 'I think it's true – it'll last for ever.' He was still holding the sash: 'But this?'

Jenny took it; ran the tartan through her fingers; wound it over her arms, shoulders, waist; held it to her face, breathing the silk worn once by a woman she had never known, drowned long ago in a salmon pool.

'It's no good to me,' Clive said. 'I'd be happy if you had it.'

'Clive, I'll tell you what. I want to give it to Becky. Is that all right? She'd adore it. She'll look terrific.'

Max agreed: 'It's a great idea, Jennifer.'

Clive wrapped it in the tissue paper: 'Give her my love.'

They didn't stay late. Max was sleepy, Jenny exhausted. Clive didn't encourage them to linger: better to get the farewells done quickly. Anything now would be flat and disenchanting. Max, who had saved the awkwardness of their arrival two days ago, knew how to smooth their departure: boisterous and tactful, humoured with drink and pleased to be moving on. Jenny's grey eyes held Clive for uncountable seconds, unknown years. He would keep them, they both knew, as Isabel would keep her zircon ring. From the kitchen, to endorse it, a laugh of unbelieving rapture at last came through the curtain. Not once during the visit, Clive realized, had Jenny given her own marvellous laugh, on the point of mockery. He hadn't heard it since meeting Rebecca, who would give it again when she saw the tartan sash. Instead Jenny uttered another soft gasp like Isabel's, from far inside her. Or else it came from the kitchen.

They stepped off the veranda into the speedboat. The American sailor saluted the ambassador and his wife. Max, in the cockpit, passed on the salute to Clive, turning it into a great two-handed wave. Jenny only smiled: already out of reach, returning to the past. The boat ripped away into the night. Next morning the lagoon was empty.

Part Eight

The Forest

From his small native house on the slopes above Aurora Clive watches the lagoon in front, the old volcano behind. They aren't as sharp as when he first came to live up here at the edge of the forest, some years ago. Often he can see them better if he shuts his eyes.

It is the same with books. Many have rotted with damp or been eaten by insects, and fall to pieces as he opens them. Mercifully he doesn't need to read his favourites. For ten minutes he looks at the title page to catch what he can remember, then flips through the chapter headings, not bothering with the text. He has trouble too when he worries at a chess problem in an old number of *Country Life* or tries to finish a crossword he once began in the *Economist*. The print is too small unless he takes it out into the sun, where the heat is too strong. But he gets pleasure merely staring at the black and white squares; feels excited by the pattern and the thought of what he once could do with it.

His subscription to the papers ran out long ago. About the same time, when he didn't renew the orders, his supply of food, wine and books stopped coming from London. He can't remember when he last had marmalade, tinned strawberries, anchovy sauce, claret. He doesn't miss them, he likes this simplicity, uncluttered with habits, obligations, sentimentality. If it had happened more abruptly he might have been alarmed. But this fining down, reducing of his life, freeing himself from pretensions, came slowly.

He has no pressure lamps left. The mantles were broken and new ones can't be bought. After dark he sits by a hurricane lamp. The oil is poor, the wick burnt, the glass always blackened: Isabel has stopped cleaning it. He would like to play the gramophone sometimes but there are no batteries. He talks aloud to himself, or to Jenny.

He seldom goes down to the plantation, he finds it too sad. Beaconsfield's grip is failing. His motorbike broke down for lack of spare parts and he hasn't got Clive's energy to tour the place on foot. The pruning is neglected, the paths are never brushed. Bags of copra are left out in the rain and get spoilt. Lumps of coral are put in the bags to make up weight. A load of cocoa was dropped off the jetty into the lagoon. The pedigree herd of cattle is dwindling as they are killed for feasts. Not many people can afford beer, so they distil palm wine which makes them drunk more quickly.

Laki, the old coxswain of the schooner *Catriona*, chief of the saltwater boys, is dead. He paddled away on a long voyage in his canoe and was never seen again – the sea god returning to the sea. Without him the saltwater boys have become unruly. They resent Beaconsfield's ownership of Aurora and know that it they chased him over the lagoon again in a fleet of canoes, armed with fishing-knives, Mr Clive would be useless defending him this time and there is no Laki to intervene. The historic feud with bush boys often breaks out in a fight. Even football matches, once played in a spirit of British sportsmanship, can get dangerous.

Last year some saltwater families who had planted coconut trees on one of the small islands across the lagoon went to cut the copra there, and had a party afterwards. They lit a bonfire of dry fronds and husks on the shore, then pushed it out into the water. It floated away with the evening tide, a raft of fire like a funeral launched on the lagoon, trailing a streamer of smoke, and might have burnt itself out. But a squall blew up and the flames leapt from the water, roused by the wind, hissing in the rain. The saltwater boys cheered as the drifting blaze was blown towards Clive's old house, where Beaconsfield now lived. No rain could quench what the wind stoked. Sparks landed on the iron roof like warning shots before the raft reached the wooden veranda. Beaconsfield's family, who long ago had eaten the opossum living above Clive's bedroom, screamed and ran away. In twenty minutes the roof, red hot and buckled, dropped on the burning house. In another twenty, after the wind and rain had gone, there was nothing but a smell of wet cinders and some charred, sodden coconut husks floating among beer bottles on the lagoon. Since then the ruin has been abandoned to crabs and the insidious undergrowth.

Recently the copra drier also went up in a sheet of flame: the work of a devil-devil, Beaconsfield said. Building a new one has been held up for lack of metal straps for the chimney. They have been ordered from Tulagi but nobody believes they will come. Nobody minds. Copra is now dried in the sun, the old way, which needs watching in case of rain and gives inferior quality.

It is twenty years since Clive went to England and nearly ten since he visited Tulagi. He never thought much of it – a toy capital, though unpretentious – and from what he hears it is now full of international advisers, profiteers, politicians, rushing in and out to nobody's benefit but their own. The Chinese pull out their money when they can. Nobody invests. Nothing useful is imported. Nothing is predictable, except the climate and its effect of apathy. Independence means uncertainty. Shops and warehouses are empty. The Frazer shipping line was bought by a Japanese company which stopped regular sailings and threatened to cut out the Mendana Islands altogether, till President Dikea arranged a subsidy from one of his financial interests.

Corruption in the government is hardly denied. Ministers, irrelevant and incompetent, last a few months before being banished to their home islands. After his notorious career as a road contractor Dikea, who owns the club and the biggest whisky agency and the only newspaper and a half-share in the airline and all the land beyond the airport where the runway will have to be lengthened – and has learnt not to crack his fingers – strives for respectability by flying off on a state visit to another independent country or to make a speech at the United Nations. There have been riots in Tulagi which could easily spread through the islands like any other new fashion – cowboy boots or Jamaican music or swastikas tattooed on the forehead.

In his sermons the bishop, once a bush boy, Beaconsfield's brother, tells the congregation that heaven isn't

Tulagi or Tokyo or Moscow or Washington, but a secret glade up in the forest, full of dancing angels and roasting pigs and the sound of eternal gongs and enough drink to keep even a bishop happy. But for many people the bar of the Tulagi hotel is blissful enough; though probably, if anyone there remembers Clive out at Aurora and asks for news, they are told sadly that he has gone native.

As the outer world becomes more distasteful and incongruous, he retreats further into seclusion, an inner citadel of vague but precious hope, entirely real.

Rain comes through the roof. Toads hop in and out of the house. Lizards inhabit cracks in the walls. A rat lives in a hole in the floor. In the kitchen the squalor is supreme: sacks over the door and windows, shelves made from food boxes, everything thick with fat, mould, cockroaches, filth. The few old tins are rusty and without labels: they might be Irish stew or peaches or condensed milk – Isabel doesn't know. Behind a screen where Clive sleeps, a pair of ivory-backed hairbrushes with his initials in gold, a christening present from his parents, mocks the disarray. The remaining bristles are still stiff enough to smooth his thick white hair, but his shirt is tattered, his baggy shorts are split up the seam so that when he stoops – he wears no underpants – his testicles fall out. Sometimes Isabel borrows the hairbrushes, and Clive likes to find dark hairs on them, but she avoids looking into his shaving mirror: her reflection, which is herself, might be stolen by the spirit behind the glass.

The admiralty chart on the wall is going the way of the bagpipes, disintegrating with mildew, but Clive knows the island by heart and has the real lagoon and mountain fading in his eyes as well as on the chart. The shotgun is on the bottom of the lagoon where Laki once hurled it, near the kamikaze plane that sank in the war. The old Strathpolly fishing-rod is still hanging on hooks and Clive often takes it down, carries it out of the house for the feel of it in his hand: the spring and bend and sudden tug of an imaginary fish. Isabel will cook it for him with herbs and wild ginger. He reels it in, a fine big trout, sometimes a salmon, and scoops it from the water to flap around his feet: feet crushed by the butt of Goldilocks' gun, with toes still crooked.

He hasn't eaten fish for a long time. Isabel used to get prawns or pieces of skipjack or shark or turtle from the saltwater boys, but now they are hostile. They give her nothing though many of them were once her lovers, paying her in fish, and she doesn't dare ask even for seaweed to make a salad. Sometimes she begs a piece of pork from Beaconsfield or a chicken from one of the bush boys. Mainly she and her family and Clive live on what she grows in her garden and anything her piccaninnies bring home.

She boils yams and mushrooms in a pot lined with banana leaves. She puts vegetables in a hollow bamboo on the fire to cook. She peels taro with an oyster shell sharpened on a piece of coral – a steel knife would spoil the taste – and pounds it into pulp after boiling; mixes it with coconut milk, rolls it into cakes, wraps them in leaves and bakes them. For an oven she has scraped a hole in the kitchen floor. In the evening she builds a frame of sticks in it, sets it alight, adds yam leaves or taro peelings, watches it flame up; then places a dozen round stones, the size of hens' eggs, in the fire. When the stones are hot she pours water on them to make steam, and lays the food among them – bits of opossum or pigeon or flying fox caught and skinned by her piccaninnies, wrapped in banana leaves. She covers it with more hot stones and earth, to bake all night. She lets a breadfruit smoulder in the fire till it is charred; peels off the black outside and tears the soft flesh apart in her fingers, to be eaten in hunks. The seeds taste of roast chestnuts: Clive loves them.

He loves everything done by Isabel. She is the essence, the heartbeat of his days. He feels his life is fused with hers in a mutual unspoken need, a single pool like the glade between Aurora and the forest where they live together. Beyond it he has his memories, she her piccaninnies.

The biggest piccaninny has a thin moustache and a look, Clive detects, of that dim officer in khaki in a photo by his mother's bed. The smallest is at Isabel's splendid breast.

Probably she doesn't know who their fathers were. Some are dark, others less so. One of them, a pale child of eight or nine, must be Godfrey's. All of them love their grandfather. They knock down a coconut, peel off the husk, cut a hole in the shell and bring it to him for a sundown drink, cool and sweet. In the forest they burrow in the rotten wood of a fallen tree for grubs, yellowish and bigger than their fingers, which they fry for him as a delicacy, turning transparent in the cooking. They skewer grasshoppers on a stick and toast them for his supper – better than prawns. In return he tells them stories about two brothers who once lived in a wild country of mountains and rivers, far to the north, and played magical games that nobody else understood.

He is often close to crying and the smallest sentiment, a tickle of the soft nerves that hold his heart, will start the tears. It puzzles the piccaninnies: a white-haired white-skinned old planter weeping at some secret thought. But he is glad to do it. Age hasn't muted his imagination. He knows he was never the insensitive, boorish man he created, whose mask he wore. Jenny knew it, and left him. Perhaps Isabel knows it, in her silent way. And he hopes that his grandchildren will not forget what they see, even if it bewilders them.

His health is strong, though he can't do anything strenuous. He gets pains in his chest and sometimes passes out. The attacks have been more frequent lately. He should ask the piccaninnies for some medicine from the kwako tree or go down to Beaconsfield for something stronger, but is always putting it off. Instead, like Isabel, he chews areca. He keeps burnt coral lime in a coconut shell, dips a stick into it, wipes it on a vine leaf, adds crushed areca, munches it all day. Isabel can crack the areca in her teeth, but Clive's are weak: he has to grind it with a stone or ask Isabel to crack it for him, and spit it out. His teeth and lips are stained crimson like hers, but he likes the hot taste and it soothes the chest pain, or anyway clouds his mind.

These last days have been very troublesome. The day

before yesterday four men came up to the house – not Aurora men but strangers from another island, all carrying copra knives. They stalked round the house several times as if looking for a way in, then stopped in front of the door, swaying slightly in a bunch, their eyes fixed ahead: four men, a pair of pairs, an omen as good or bad as four frigate-birds wheeling in the sun.

'Good afternoon,' Clive said politely, coming out. 'What do you want?' They ignored him and stared into the house, swinging their knives. 'What have you come for?' They had no leader, there was nobody Clive knew. 'Then please go away and don't disturb us.' He remembered the time he had saved himself and Beaconsfield from the saltwater boys by talking to them. Now he was speechless, with his only weapon a fishing-rod.

One of the men laughed and all four stepped forward; pushed without a word past Clive, through the door into the kitchen; inspected the piccaninnies, settled on a girl of twelve, led her by the hand out of the house.

It was her willingness, a gladness in her trusting child's face at the honour of being chosen, that silenced Clive; stopped him interfering. Though she was his grand-daughter he was helpless. He could only submit like her to something unarguable. She didn't speak or look back, but went with the men down to Aurora. After she had gone a weird noise started out of Isabel, the howl of a wild animal, an inhuman wail that might have been forced from her by some ritual power. It was the only protest at the girl's abduction. Clive wished he had struggled with the men, or could at least howl like Isabel.

Next day, yesterday, Isabel said nothing but gave him a strange, half-terrified, half-triumphant look. Clive had seen it once before, on Beaconsfield that morning in the crater of Bau after Godfrey died. He was sure that some-thing more would happen. Isabel cooked no food all day, but stayed in the kitchen with her piccaninnies. The older ones showed their fear by teasing, smacking, bullying, then over-cuddling the babies. The sound of gongs and singing rose continuously through the trees from the plan-tation. Sometimes a trumpet joined in, or it might have been a saxophone. It might have been Independence again, or a wedding or Clive's birthday. He couldn't think what they were celebrating down there, but knew it would end in an orgy of drink and lust.

In the evening Isabel went to the top of the plantation and listened, as if through the noise she might hear news of her lost daughter. Nothing, nobody, came up. Clive left her alone. For him a day of fasting would do no harm. He had no appetite. The pain in his chest was worse. Isabel never came to pull down the mosquito net before he went to bed.

This morning he lay in bed, wondering if the terrible scream that reached him in the middle of the night was a dream; knowing that it wasn't; knowing too, without precise details, what must have happened. As he expected, when he got up, there was no sign of Isabel or her piccaninnies, and a sinister quiet. No sound rose from the plantation today.

Clive was hungry and looked for food, though he had hardly been in the kitchen before and didn't know his way round. He found only a packet of tea, half a raw yam, a tin of Japanese tuna fish. Isabel had locked the store and taken the key. There were no matches. Clive would like to try and make tea. He couldn't remember ever doing it and wasn't sure how many leaves were needed. But without matches to light a fire – the paraffin stove had had no fuel for months – it was impossible. He picked up the tin of tuna, took it to the door, threw it as far as he could into the forest; then began to nibble the uncooked yam.

The pain shot through his chest, stronger than ever. If it came again he would faint. He dropped the yam and lurched to his bed; lay down, hoping to escape the pain, hunger, silence.

Now he hears something stir. It must be midday or early afternoon. Hot and dead. He has been asleep; woken by the faintest rustle, hardly more than the disturbance of a woman turning over or sighing beside him in the bed. But he is alone; has been alone for years. There is nobody in the house. And the pain has gone. Only the soft throbbing

in his ears, though there isn't a breath of air. It is one of
those still, windless days when a canoe cuts the lagoon
so sharply that it might crack the surface and fall through.

Up here the same metallic feeling hangs among the
trees: not heavy like the hour before a storm, but sharp
and bright and brittle. Soon the gentle pulse increases. If it
gets any louder something will break. Perhaps this fragile,
dangerous day will splinter or explode. Clive lies like King
Gilgamesh at the end – a hooked fish or a wild animal
caught in a trap – knowing he can't escape. But he can
fight. He rolls off the bed, puts his weight cautiously on
his feet, stands up; walks slowly, blinking at the brilliant
day, to the door. Below, the lagoon is a stainless sheet of
silver. Above, over the trees, cupping the Stones of Bau
up there, the crater of the old volcano has never looked
so inflammable. Put a match to it, like a firework, and it
would go off. Dazzled after sleep, Clive can see the bonfire
when his father came back from the war, the rockets
streaming up from the lawn.

There are no matches. Isabel locked them up. And Clive
is parched as well as hungry, thirsting for tea. He had it
with Jenny in the station buffet at Waterloo. She might
share it again. He fumbles round the kitchen, picks up
the piece of uncooked yam for another nibble, spits it out;
staggers out to Isabel's garden and pulls up a radish,
onion, lettuce – vegetables he once grew in a garden by a
river, watched by an old woman with a cheroot. But these
are all useless. The roots are rotten, or a spider runs from
the leaves, or Clive's lips and teeth reject the food, though
he is ravenous and would eat anything. An iguana caught
on the railway, a rotten duck's egg from the river barges,
a frog found under the hut and fried with green chillies,
would do. But those walnut cakes that a prisoner feeds
on, and cherry pies and treacle toffees, are just for
dreaming. No better than this stuff taken from Isabel's
garden. And something tells Clive – perhaps Beaconsfield's voice, years ago – that gardening is unclean, like
copulation. It mustn't be done in times of war, sickness,
catastrophe, when the ancestors are angry and have with-
drawn their power to protect. A devil-devil will swoop in,
to take advantage. This is an easy victim. A mere sketch,

a travesty of himself. An old skeleton with a dim resemblance to a man he once knew and loved. He has been two days without food, he needs a feast.

A feast. The Stones of Bau: there will be food up there. A feast indeed, of wild pig and mangoes and bananas. Or anyway a chief's promise of it. This time it will come true. Saliva floods Clive's mouth, he swallows hard. But he must remember not to laugh. That won't be difficult, there is nothing funny. And he isn't delirious, he knows exactly what he is doing.

He takes down his old fishing-rod from its hooks on the wall. Out of the house. The moment he is outside, the throbbing noise grows stronger. It comes up from Aurora, an affront to the intense stillness of the day. And suddenly the pain cuts like a sword blade through him. Like fighting for life in a wreck. Being gouged with bayonets. Split with a hammer. It has never been so bad. But he can take it. He is reassured by the fishing-rod. The friendly cork handle in his palm. The long golden cane whipping in the sunlight ahead of him. It has a life of its own and will lead him up to Bau.

The road built by Dikea thirty years ago is obliterated by vegetation. Without the fishing-rod to follow, Clive would have to hack a path. Upwards, upwards, he will be absorbed in the forest vastness; will evaporate like a raindrop. Almost at once his foot strikes something hard. Probably a rusty Japanese helmet left there in the war. With his toe, twisted by a Japanese corporal, he turns it over: the tin of tuna fish he threw away this morning. Take a fishing-rod to catch a tin of tuna. A gift from Nippon for finishing the railway. He kicks it further into the leaves.

The pain increases at every step, with the mounting noise. Now it sounds like an engine. Perhaps Beaconsfield has got the motorbike going and is coming up from the plantation, the first time for months. A good son for an old man. He will cut a way up through the forest to the crater as he did before. And Godfrey is up there still, where they left him, waiting for Clive. He will have food and drink ready. A friend at last. Another white man. Isabel's only English lover. Almost a son-in-law.

But it isn't an engine. It isn't another wave of bombers coming in. People are shouting. Aurora is angry, seething, dangerous. They must be fighting down there. Bush boys against saltwater boys. The fools – like shipwrecked sailors crammed on a raft in the South China Sea. Probably Clive always knew it would come to this in the end. There is no help for them now. No destroyers to rescue them. He is glad to have got away, alone. What he did here was fine and worthwhile, he knows. He has no sorrow, except for having shared so little. Slowly he pushes on upwards, clutching the fishing-rod and the pain.

'I'm not afraid,' he hears himself saying through the shouts and throbs. It is what he told Jenny on the other side of the world, in battle before the *Prince of Wales* was sunk. That day he learnt how happiness could lie in danger, when life was heightened by its fragility. 'I'm really not afraid.' It is true again today. He feels no fear. Only stunned by the absurdity. The insolence of such pain. And the certainty that love and magic are the same.

Without warning the air gives a heave. The world stutters in a giant hiccup. It is a squall of wind off the lagoon down there, or the hot breath of the old volcano ahead, blowing away the stillness. Clive suddenly sweats heavily, breaking out all over. There is a rustling in the trees and the unmistakable smell of a bat. It is *her* – the wife, without a doubt. And it is a way to finish off. No worse than Spanish flu, or being drowned in a salmon pool, or falling off a balcony on the Brighton seafront. And what was Isabel's way?

But he will be safe if he can reach the Stones. One more tree. And the one beyond. And the next.

He doesn't get far. When he is struck, felled by the unforgiving pain, he is still at the edge of the forest, hardly out of the glade where he built his house. The fishing-rod is snapped as he falls to the ground.